I0562108

Andrei LIVADNY

The Reapers

Thank you FOR your support
and inspiration!
They mean so much to me,
Andrei Livadny.

The Neuro

BOOK THREE

MAGIC DOME BOOKS

The Reapers
The Neuro, Book # 3
Copyright © Andrei Livadny 2018
Cover Art © Vladimir Manyukhin 2018
English translation copyright © Irene & Neil P. Woodhead 2018
Published by Magic Dome Books, 2018
All Rights Reserved
ISBN: 978-80-88231-55-4

TABLE OF CONTENTS:

CHAPTER ONE

AGRION MARKET SQUARE was uncrowded. Not many players online today. Only the NPCs continued living their own computer-generated lives.

For them it was business as usual: merchants praising their wares, a crooked old lady shuffling her feet past the swordsmiths' row. She leaned heavily on her staff and mumbled something to herself as she cast watchful glances around in search for any newbs whom she might reward with a social quest for their penny's worth of alms.

A gust of wind raised twisters of dust, stripping a lone tree of an armful of yellow autumn leaves which floated swirling onto the cobblestones.

Business as usual indeed, had it not been for the cold in my chest and the group of high level riders who'd just dismounted by the tavern.

The city patrol seemed quite alarmed by their arrival. The guards officer and two lancers hovered nearby, casting sideways glances at the tired warriors and their lathering horses. The tavern keeper hurried to greet them.

I didn't know any of the warriors in the group apart from their leader Friedrich White, Enea's father. Their gear was worthy of note: it lacked the usual abundance of useless elements so typical of fantasy armor. Normally, a group of high-level warriors can be quite a motley bunch as each player strives to stand out in the crowd as much as their wallets and Strength numbers allow them. Especially Strength numbers. If a player's stats permit them to lug around five hundred pounds of fancily decorated metal, that's exactly what he or she will do.

Still, this group's minimalistic and practical brigandine armor and chainmail were also remarkable in their own way. The fabric *cotta* dress which was meant to protect the armor plates from the sun, dirt and rain, hung in tatters. It looked like the group had had to fight their way here.

All these seemingly insignificant details

began to fall into a picture, confirming the truth of what White had just told me. The minimalistic practicality of the group's gear must have had something to do with the neuroimplant's peculiar nature.

So this hadn't been a nightmare, after all. Enea and I had indeed visited the very kernel of the experiment carried out by Infosystems Corporation. Our minds must have collapsed, unable to sustain the information overload.

No. I refused to believe it. Agrion looked the same as normal. And as for Enea's father, he must have hired someone to level up for him. That way he could have made the Top 100 within a mere couple of days.

Why would he lie to me, then, saying that it had been several years since we'd last met? He treasured his daughter and wouldn't have toyed with her respect so stupidly.

The cold in my chest kept growing. I needed a definite answer. I wanted clear-cut evidence.

The guards' captain... I didn't know him. When had they replaced the old one?

The old lady hobbled past the guards. Normally she never pays any attention to NPCs. She's only interested in newbie players. This time, however, she stopped.

The officer seemed to have expected it. He

leaned toward the woman and handed her a small object wrapped in a piece of cloth, then nodded at the alchemists' row.

Without saying a word, she turned round and shuffled off toward it.

There was only one buyer in the alchemists' row, a level-92 rogue. His high-level Veil of Secrecy wouldn't let me read his nickname, but his avatar looked familiar.

Well, well, well. If that's not Heilig! The cheeky PK with whom I'd already crossed swords twice.

Last time we'd met was only a few days ago, or so I remembered. Then he'd been level 35.

I headed toward him, overtaking the old lady on my way.

"Hi. Looking for new potions?" I asked just to attract his attention.

He gave me a lopsided grin. "Alexatis. You owe me, remember?"

Our level gap was enormous now. This may be a safe zone but he was too vindictive to miss his chance.

I highjacked the situation by playing on his greed. "So how about the cargonite? Two hundred pounds, wasn't it? Are you still looking for it?"

He appeared interested enough to suppress his animosity. "We're generous today, aren't we? Where did you disappear to? They closed your castle and shut down the entire sector, why? Yeah, they did open some sort of mirror but it was BS. You weren't there, anyway."

"Why, were you looking for me?"

"What do you think? The Ravens weren't happy with you, were they? Your scuffle cost me very dearly. And the next day the admins changed my login location!"

"You don't mean it! What, just like that?"

"Well, they did send me a letter. Like, *'due to technical difficulties, we were forced to temporarily close the Agrion cluster. We apologize for the inconvenience'*. Yeah right! What happened to your clan, then? And the Ravens? You both disappeared off the radars. I find it weird."

"You could say that. One question: do you log in via your implant?"

He shrugged and spat at his feet. "How else do you want me to log in? You're worse than a noob sometimes. The questions you ask..."

What a relief.

The uncertainty of the last few hours was gone. Enea and I were alive and back in the Crystal Sphere. That was the main thing. The rest we could sort out later.

"So whassup? Are you gonna pay up?" he grew impatient, assuming his invincibility. Even if I didn't give him cargonite, at least he'd get even with me and stealth out like he must have done many times in the past.

Before I could reply, the old lady had finally caught up with us,

"Good sir, spare a trifle for a poor woman," she addressed Heilig.

"Piss off, bitch. Do you think I'm a noob to be interested in social quests?"

The woman looked visibly upset. She stopped and leaned on her staff as if catching her breath. "No one wants to help me," she complained weakly. "What if they're right? Do I really need this kind of life? Do I?"

She whipped out a dagger from her rags and buried it in Heilig's throat in one practiced, powerful thrust.

* * *

What happened next was surreal.

The already-familiar bluish haze comprised of neurograms poured out of Heilig's slit throat, breaking into separate puffs which reached out for the old lady, the alchemist vendor and a few more NPCs who had chanced nearby.

"A Reaper!" one of White's riders thundered in, then flung his heavy pike at her.

The pike pinned the old woman to the vendor's stall. Once again the murky haze poured forth: the bluish cloud of neurograms containing the identity of the disembodied PK player. The cloud fell into separate strata, groping for the nearby NPCs and pouring into their transfixed bodies.

A noisy murder of crows took to the wing from the crenels of the city wall. Was it my imagination or had I noticed the hunched outlines of crossbowmen on the walls?

The spine-chilling glitch in gameplay was rapidly snowballing into an uncontrollable event.

The marketplace dissolved into panic. Vendors, buyers, passersby and idle onlookers — they all scattered in every direction, pushing each other and knocking over the stalls. They separated me from Enea who was still standing next to her father on the steps of the city hall.

Old Friedrich White wasn't a slouch though. He gave his shield to his daughter and bared his sword, pointing it at the guards' captain,

"A Harvester!"

In the meantime, the NPCs unlucky enough to have been infected with Heilig's neurograms began to recover from their stupor. Heilig had never been among the cream of humanity to begin with. No points for guessing what kinds of thoughts had possessed them once the remains of that unrepentant PK's identity had altered their behavioral models.

Agrion was a starting location always swarming with low-level players, even in off-peak times. None of them seemed to be affected by the panic. They looked around curiously, apparently believing the tragic events to be a mere glitch.

An NPC greengrocer's name tag blinked. A new icon appeared in it: a pictogram of a blood-red skull.

"Watch out!" I shouted.

The greengrocer barged into a swordsmith's stall, grabbed a morning star mace and swung it mercilessly at a petite wizard girl who'd chanced to be next to him.

Other players were even less lucky. In several more places, the ominous blue haze rose into the air.

The city guards, however, chose to ignore the unfolding mayhem. With the new Reapers' support, they threw themselves onto the warrior who'd hurled his pike.

In compliance with gameplay, his name tag had turned fiery red. Now it was everyone's duty to kill him, sending him back to his respawn point and stripping him of his levels and expensive gear. The marketplace was a safe zone and the old woman was a quest NPC. Attacking her had been a very unhealthy idea. Her age and appearance didn't matter.

"Alex, go away!" Enea's father shouted,

fighting three guards whose levels were on a par with his own.

Now I could see: he'd leveled up all by himself. The neuroimplant radically changed the entire fight pattern, and I knew this better than anybody else.

He was actually a great fighter. He'd dropped his shield and used a two-handed grip on his sword, increasing both impact and damage. Without parrying the lancers' attacks, he kept dodging their sharp thrusting blows with remarkable cool.

One of the guards had lost his patience and flung himself onto him, commencing a well-practiced combo. Not that it helped him much: Friedrich White sliced through the man's spear in one calculated motion, then shouldered his opponent onto the wide steps. The guard lost his balance and came rolling back down.

The two others stepped back, taking cover behind their shields, but White's sword drew a wide arc through the air, throwing both off balance and forcing them to weaken their defenses.

I froze with bated breath, awaiting a coup de grace, but no: White had second-guessed their counterattack and recoiled just in time, so that their spearheads barely grazed his armor. Then he dealt one last powerful slashing blow.

The guards' bodies rolled down the steps of the city hall.

"The crossbowmen!" Enea shouted.

White reacted instantly. Picking up the shield left behind by one of the lancers, he dropped on one knee. The heavy bolts thudded into the shield's wood right through its thick rough leather.

"Leave!" he said to his daughter in a muffled voice. "Go inside!"

My interface blinked with a new message,

Friedrich White has invited you to join his group.

As soon as I clicked *Accept,* the battle chat came to life,

Crossbowmen on the wall! A Harvester in the square! Finish off the guards and wait for my orders!

Alex, wake up! Get out of there ASAP!

Only now had I noticed the change in the guards' captain. I could barely recognize him. He'd grown considerably taller and broader. His eyes glowed with a dark fire. His tarnished armor was dropping flakes of oxidation as if it had been reborn in some invisible furnace.

Harvester. Level 200

By now, the market square was almost deserted. The crossbowmen continued to shoot, this time targeting those of the NPCs who'd accidentally absorbed some of the killed players' neurograms. They eliminated them mercilessly and efficiently.

But why?

The answer was not long in coming. The familiar bluish haze drifted low over the ground. Confidently the Harvester stepped into it. The murky haze heaved and reached out for him, enveloping his body in its swirls like a slow, unhurried tornado.

You're witnessing neurogram absorption.

Short but pretty clear. The Harvester was ingesting fragments of the dead players' identities.

The horror of it was in the fact that this manner of death had caused his victims to die in both worlds.

There was no way we could stop him. I could only guess at the mechanisms behind this process. By now, the bluish haze had enveloped him completely, permeating his armor. With his level 200, there was precious little we could do to stop this process even if we attacked him all at once.

The rattling of weapons had died away. White's warriors had already disposed of the guards. The local NPCs had made themselves scarce. The tavern keeper alone was still standing by his front door like a pillar of salt, bug-eyed, his white-knuckled fingers locked over the wooden banister.

Just by chance, I happened to be the only one left in the square. I secreted myself behind the upended stalls, watching the Harvester while keeping a cautious eye on the crossbowmen on the city walls.

There were about ten of them. They behaved weird to say the least: now that they'd stopped shooting, they stood up peering at us through the gaps between the crenels with greedy, insane eyes. Their tags contained an icon of some buff unknown to me.

The Harvester exuded a wave of heat. His charred armor began to flicker. His face was distorted, his lips cracked, his burnt hair crumbling to ashes.

The bluish mist had all but disappeared as he'd absorbed most of it by now. Only a few faint wisps of it still swirled around his sinister figure. The vendors' upended wooden crates heaped around him smoldering, about to catch fire.

Suddenly his body arched in a spasm. His skin rippled with interference. His level numbers began to change at random as did his appearance while he was consumed by a chain of metamorphoses.

An old man. A girl wizard. A young warrior. A spice vendor. The Harvester's face now resembled molten wax which some crazy sculptor was molding into grotesque masks, crumpling them and starting anew.

"Now!" White's snapped order singed my nerves.

Was he crazy?

Like an uncoiling spring, his words launched the five dark knights into the Harvester's path.

A *defective mob*. That's how the Corporation workers used to describe them.

But those I'd seen before were known as Reapers. And this one appeared infinitely more powerful than any of them. A *Harvester*? What kind of new sick monster was this?

The knights knew what they were doing. Their expertise wasn't limited to martial arts. They lashed out at the crossbowmen with a Chain of Lightning while showering the Harvester with poisoned arrows, sending his damage-taken counter into a spin. Predatory vines broke through the cobblestones under his feet, entwining them in their grip. The knights changed their weapons on the run as they surrounded him.

In the meantime, the Harvester's random change of stats had logically led to his drop in levels. By absorbing the identities of low-level players, he'd lost his unique abilities, rapidly becoming weaker and slower. The game engine had recalculated his characteristics, replacing the question marks in his tag with the number 98. His Life bar plummeted.

Still, the experienced warriors weren't fooled by their now seemingly easy prey. They hadn't changed their tactics.

Two of them, armed with heavy shields and long steel-shafted pikes, carried out a series of powerful attacks, stripping the Harvester of half his hp, then immediately switched back on the defensive, blocking his response blows.

In the meantime, a knight armed with a two-handed sword attacked him from behind with a well-calculated combo, stunlocking him.

That was it. Now one last coup de grace...

The Harvester roared back to life, shaking himself out of his stupor and busting himself free from the vines' embrace.

His virtually empty Life bar soared back up. The number 200 reappeared in his tag. With a shattering circular blow, he crumpled the knights' steel shields, sweeping the fighters off their feet.

He didn't stop there. Once again he raised his black two-handed sword, lower this time, and drew a humming arc through the air, splitting the upended stalls into cascades of wood chips and slicing clean through the knights' legs as they struggled to get to their feet.

The five knights' avatars rippled and turned dark, then disappeared.

He'd smoked them! Just like that, in two mighty attacks!

What had Enea's father told me? I should have vacated the market square while I still could.

Slowly the Harvester turned round. His avatar had already stabilized. His eyes glowed with an ethereal light.

The air in front of him thickened, forming a translucent arch surging with fiery charges of energy. With a soft popping sound, a cloud of crimson haze filled the arch, swirling.

The Harvester stepped into it and disappeared.

* * *

The smashed crates were still smoldering. The market square resembled a deserted battlefield.

Contrary to the rules, most of the players' avatars hadn't disappeared. Riddled with crossbow bolts, they remained lying on the cobblestones amid the scattered remains of market stalls and the vendors' wares.

Scared horses whinnied softly by the tavern. The breeze had brought a whiff of burned flesh: the Chain of Lightning which had killed the crossbowmen on the wall had also set the roof of the parapet on fire, collapsing it on top of them.

White looked over the disastrous panorama. He picked up his helmet and sat on the city hall steps with his graying head hung low.

"Dad?" Enea came running up to him. "What's going on? What are you doing here?"

"I was looking for you."

"But you saw me only a few days ago!" she said, uncomprehending.

"You're wrong. Not days. Years."

"That's impossible!"

"He's right, Enea," I said.

She cast me a look of reproach, "Alex, please. We were in the library all this time, you and I. It's only been a few days."

"Enea, I can prove it."

"Be my guest."

"Not here. We need to get back to the castle."

"He's right," White said grimly, staring at the humble cloth bundles left where his dark knights had once stood. "This place isn't safe."

"Your knights, will they be all right?"

"I haven't noticed any blue haze. I don't think they've lost any neurograms. Which means they should make it."

"Do you want me to pick up their stuff?" I asked. "Or should we wait for them to respawn? Where's their respawn point, anyway?"

"It's far from here," White leaned heavily on his sword, clambering to his feet. "In a nearby cluster. It'll take them some time to get back. Leave the bundles. There's nothing in them, anyway. Our gear is all no-drop. It's also charmed against theft. We leave nothing behind. We've learned our lesson: you can't imagine how hard it is to get items with these kinds of stats."

The expression on Enea's face was hard to describe. I could almost bet she'd never expected her father to be so well-versed in gaming slang.

"No point staying here, then," I summed up. "Let's port to the castle. Then we can talk."

"Can we port from the tavern?" White asked. "I'd hate to leave the horses. Also, there're some useful things in the saddle bags."

"We can't cast a portal in the square. The guards will be on us straight away."

"Then I suggest we go to Dimian's old

shop," Enea said. "I have the key to his back yard."

* * *

The Resurrection Hall of Rion Castle met us with deep silence.

Holding two of the horses by their reins, I looked around, habitually taking in my surroundings.

Top-level NPC guards stood watch by the portal, impassive and silent.

The torchlight cast uneven shadows on the walls. The cold green glow of the respawn zone reflected in the precious stones decorating the ancient wall carvings.

My heart warmed to the familiar sight.

Sarah, the mountain lynx that Enea and I had brought back from our recent trip to the Azure Mountains, stepped softly out of the dancing shadows. Her green eyes betrayed an intense hope. The masterless pet had taken the habit of waiting by the portal, hoping that one day her beautiful Drow owner would step out of it.

No idea what could have happened to Liori and Kimberly, though. They had disappeared in a most mysterious way, complete with Master Jurg.

The lynx may have found a new home in

our castle but she wasn't in a hurry to show any signs of attachment to anyone. She was her own master walking by herself wherever she wanted. Even Lethmiel, my Blood Elf majordomo, couldn't explain how she managed to cross the numerous magic barriers.

I could see that she'd been leveling up. No wonder: she spent every night prowling the moors, bringing her prey to the castle gate every morning. A couple of times she'd even brought us some very badly shaken goblins, which had complicated our already strained relationship with their local tribes.

"Oh hi, Sarah," Enea stroked her back.

The lynx emitted a nervous growl, sniffed White all over, headbutted my knee by way of greeting, then ran and lay sprawled on the floor.

The protective magic seals flared. The tall doors swung open, flooding us with daylight.

The servants I'd hired took the horses away to the stables. Lethmiel was the next to arrive.

His eyes lit up with reserved curiosity. Lethmiel still remembered White: for him too, only a few days had elapsed since Enea's father had been here.

"Any news?" I asked.

"Not good, I'm afraid. The Elves have returned, the ones you sent home to see their families. Their settlements have been pillaged.

The forests have been stripped of everything that was alive."

"Do you know the reason?"

"No. They've brought back some refugees but I haven't spoken to them yet."

"Make sure they're comfortable. What about the Guards of Gloom?"

"They haven't found a trace of their people, either. Only some long deserted camps."

"I'll speak to them later. Anything else?"

"There's a Raven raid spotted by the approaches to the moors. Two hundred people at least."

"Have they already entered the moors?"

"Not yet. They've set up camp about one day's hike from Chaffinch Creek."

"I want you to double the watch on the walls. Tell Archie to send out some scouts. Get on with it and don't bother us until I call you."

"Very well, Sir."

I turned to White, "Would you like to get some rest?"

He shook his head, apparently not happy with the news. "Let's set the record straight. I'm afraid, time is against us."

***

The future.

I'd never wondered about it. Would it arrive unawares or would it just smolder without crossing the invisible line which separated us from new discoveries capable of changing the lives of billions of people?

And now it *had* arrived.

Who were we now? Digitized phantoms whose immobilized physical bodies were confined to their in-mode capsules, reliant solely on life support systems?

My eyes met Enea's. Words just stuck in my throat. Would I ever be able to tell her?

She glanced at me, then at her father. "Please. Don't try to spare my feelings," she sat down in an easy chair.

Young, beautiful, smart — but pale and tense. I'd never seen her like that before.

"I want to know what's going on. You tell me. Don't keep anything back. I can take it."

"Are you sure?" her father asked.

He meant it, too. He was stubborn enough to dig his heels in and refuse to say anything.

"Dad, look around you. The Crystal Sphere is my dream world. I have only two people whom I love more than anything in the world. It's you and Alex. You're both with me now. The rest we can manage. Don't you think?"

White slumped into a chair. He removed his steel gauntlets and put them away into his inventory, then sat silent for a while with his hands locked.

"So you think you can take it? Very well..." he looked up at her and added in a low voice, "The Crystal Sphere has changed a lot. I'll tell you more. The real world as you knew it is gone too."

"You're kidding?" Enea asked mechanically.

"You and Alex disappeared three years ago. When it happened, the admins sealed the Agrion cluster. No one could gain access to this place."

"Wait," she covered her face with her hands. "Wait a sec. What do you mean, we disappeared?"

"We had an agreement, remember? You were supposed to log out in a week's time and join me for dinner. Remember that?"

"Of course I do! Why?"

"You stopped taking my calls. Your online status was *Unspecified*. The night we were supposed to have dinner I drove to your home. Your door wasn't locked. The status panel next to it said, *For Rent*. I walked in. It was absolutely bare. Your in-mode capsule was gone, mountings and all. Everything was so clean and impersonal as if you'd never existed. Can you imagine what I felt?"

She didn't say anything.

Of course. Desperate to find his daughter, White was quite capable of anything.

"I knew where to go and which door to kick open," he said. "And that's what I did. Only I didn't find a single clue. Infosystems denied everything. The company which had installed your in-mode capsule seemed to have disappeared off the face of the earth. My assistants Ylien and Stephen were gone too. Someone had broken into our country house and taken all the Crystal Sphere equipment we'd used to log in. My neuroimplant had been disconnected. It became a dead trinket taped to my temple. I just couldn't take it any longer. Me too, I had big problems. All of a sudden, my business began to sink. Then one day it started disintegrating under a very focused, well-coordinated attack. Despite our excellent safety margin, the company had to file for insolvency."

"That's impossible!" Enea cried out.

"That's what I thought too. You wanted the truth, didn't you? So there you have it. TransEnergy had three of the biggest buyers: Infosystems Corporation, the World Government and the Military Space Forces. All three of them filed complaints, returning huge shipments of our products. Our reputation was gone, our accounts frozen, our factories stopped. We suffered billions in claims. All this happened within a few days. A month later, I was on my own and penniless."

"How did you manage to survive this?" she asked softly.

"I knew you were alive."

"How?"

"I demanded answers from one of corporate technologists," White replied reluctantly. "He refused to tell me anything at first. Still, I can be very persuasive when I have to be. Finally, he admitted that both you and Alex had experienced some side effects while testing neuroimplants. They said that both of you had suffered significant brain damage. Still, according to him, the data you'd received was extremely valuable for the corporation which was why they were going to do everything possible in order to save you and reclaim the Crystal Sphere."

"Did you believe him?"

"He gave me what I needed: hope and purpose. Which was more than enough for me then."

"But you had nothing left!" Enea exclaimed. "How did you live?"

White's eyes warmed, losing their prickliness. "I don't give up so easily, you know me. I had to spend some time in the gutter, sleeping in those downtrodden capsule shelters. I had to dispose of the implant so they couldn't track me. Luckily, that particular model was easy to remove. All you had to do was pull the nano needles out."

"So you were hiding from your creditors while waiting for the Corporation to unseal Agrion?"

"That would have been a signal that the two of you had been returned to the Crystal Sphere. Still, it didn't quite work out like that. After a year, the cluster was still sealed. While the real world... I'm afraid it had fallen prey to some rapid and irreversible developments."

Enea jumped to her feet, crumpling a fine lace napkin, and walked out onto the balcony. There she leaned over the low parapet and froze, staring in front of her.

I didn't follow her. We all need to be alone sometimes, if only to come to grips with a sudden and terrible blow. We need to take a deep breath and listen to our own uneven heartbeats.

White and I exchanged glances.

"It's all right, Alex," he said. "She can manage."

He didn't shower me with accusations even though he could have.

Was it by accident that Enea and myself had decided to participate in this implant testing program?

I didn't think so. My own fate had long

been sealed. A cripple and a car crash victim, I was meant to die in the name of progress.

I'd never really believed in the corporation's academic altruism. The data which they'd made us process under the guise of some unique quest had proved much more important for them than any amount of human lives.

Enea had fallen in love with me. She'd decided to be with me no matter what — and unwittingly shared my fate in the process. Even White had lost everything he had for the same reason.

"Cheer up, Alex," he raised his wine goblet and took a swig. "We'll make it. I still managed to buy a country estate in a nearby cluster and even hired an alchemist. But... I suppose it's the Reapers who're there now drinking my wine," he fell silent, hearing his daughter's light step.

"Sorry, Dad," she said, sitting back at the table. "I didn't mean to interrupt you. What were you saying?"

* * *

"A year after your disappearance Infosystems made an absolutely inexplicable breakthrough in neural cybernetics," White continued. "The company which traditionally created virtual worlds had now introduced the prototype of the first neural implant featuring an integrated mind expander. It was called Neuron.[1] At the same time, they started building so-called in-mode centers where anyone could hire a new-generation VR capsule complete with life support. Let me tell you that equipment of this caliber had never been used before outside of spaceship technologies."

Enea gasped. "And now they put it on the mass market? By making it affordable?"

I couldn't understand the cold revulsion in her voice. "Why not?" I asked. "If lots of people can experience full immersion VR, what's wrong with that?"

"If life support cartridges are changed regularly, nothing prevents them from spending years in the in-mode without detriment to their health," White replied. "Now try to look at it from a business prospective. All those game consoles, environment generators and high-density holograms have been around for decades. Their user spends a few hours a day online while

---

[1] Neuron was the first model of the neural implant. Synaps (which is mentioned in Phantom Server) was a later model which came in three modifications: Synaps A, Synaps B and the most advanced one Synaps Z which allowed for the possibility of connecting additional cyber modules.

remaining perfectly active in real life. Alex knows what I'm talking about. He used to live this kind of life for years. And in this case they should have left this system well alone. The mass introduction of the new technology has crippled the real-world economy. The game developers have got us hooked on the incredible authenticity of the experience. But what have they achieved?"

"Earth has become deserted?" I offered.

He nodded. "Compared to the Crystal Sphere which is over-populated, yes. This so-called progress benefits no one. All it does is it rapidly brings our civilization to the brink of a complete collapse."

"Then I don't understand anything," I said. "Why did they do it? With whose permission?"

"Nobody confronted them. On the contrary: the World Government actively lobbied Infosystems Corporation. This was all carefully planned with the full consent of the powers that be."

"But why?" Enea demanded, uncomprehending. "I just don't see the point of such rapid changes worldwide! There must be a reason!"

I couldn't quite follow their logic. Unlike myself, neither Enea nor her father had lost their touch with the real world. I would never have paused to consider the consequences of these recent developments... but now White got me thinking.

Still, if we'd indeed become the Crystal Sphere's permanent inhabitants, what was the point in searching for answers?

"Dad? Was there an official explanation? Not everybody likes playing computer games, you know. A lot of people would have required some powerful motivation in order to rent an in-mode and change their lives forever."

"The toxic emissions," White replied. "They were getting out of hand. The in-mode centers are located in secure bunkers deep underground. There were talks of the upcoming remodeling of the cities," White took a large swig of his wine. "I personally think that's BS. They used every trick in the book to coerce people to embrace virtual reality. You couldn't even get a job without having a neural implant installed. The cities became deserted," he paused, thinking. "The fact that the government and the Space Forces were in it together with Infosystems makes me believe there must be a certain threat to our existence. I'm just afraid that their best intentions might lead us directly to hell."

"Wait, what are you talking about?" Enea demanded. "Can't we just live here? I don't mind all the game rules! In fact, I'm quite happy with them!"

"The Reapers."

"Do you mean the defective mobs?" I asked him.

"Yes. That was a side effect that the implant developers hadn't expected."

Enea frowned. "You two seem to know what you're talking about. Would you terribly mind telling me what it is? Please."

White was about to reply but I motioned him to stop. "Infosystems received their new technologies from the Space Forces. They're a product of an alien civilization. Apparently, the military discovered a prototype while doing some space research."

"How do you know?" she demanded.

"Dietrich told me. He was the first Reaper. He started it."

White tensed up, viewing me with cautious suspicion. "Keep talking."

❋ ❋ ❋

I told them everything, starting with my first accidental encounter with the two "defective mobs squad" workers in the underground vault on my second day in the game. Then I described my first meeting with Dietrich (which had happened just before I had to fight Reguar the Arch Demon). Finally, I tried to give my own interpretation of what had happened to us in the library of the Temple of Oblivion.

"I think I remember something too," Enea whispered. "So do you think that when our minds went into overload, they put us into an induced coma?"

"Exactly. Still, Dietrich managed to contact me."

"Why would he?" White asked dryly. "How can you even be sure it was him?"

"He was looking for an ally. I know it was him because I recognized a phrase he'd used before. Back in the Rion dungeons he'd warned me saying, *'The Corporation is using you. They'll drain you dry and leave you to die.'* And those were the exact same words he started our last conversation with. He somehow penetrated the biocybernetic lab network and altered my in-mode's settings to temporarily bring me out of my coma."

"Please don't get me wrong," White said. "Are you sure it's not your imagination playing up? Can you prove it?"

"As a matter of fact, I can. My mind expander made a copy of it," I waved my hand, conjuring up a small crystal screen.

Two sarcophagus-like pieces of equipment were mounted on massive pedestals. They were connected to several transparent pipes and cables which reached out from the wall. Pumps were wheezing, sending fluids up and down the pipes.

The servodrive creaked again. Obeying my surge of emotion, the camera zoomed in. I peered through the tinted plastic at the face inside.

Enea.

She was pale, her eyes closed. But judging by the moving graphs on the medical monitors, she was alive.

The camera turned again, then refocused.

I peered through the lid of the other sarcophagus. That was me inside.

I zoomed in some more to focus on the inscription embossed on the pedestal,

Life support unit. Property of Earth's Military Space Forces.

A door hissed open. Two Infosystems officials walked in, followed by a Space Forces colonel...

Enea and White watched their unfolding conversation in dead silence.

"So that's where they took your in-mode to!" White's cheek twitched. "Mind rewinding it a bit? I'd like to take a better look at that guy over there..."

Did he mean Borisov? Why? True, he'd had a hand in my and Enea's tribulations but still...

"I can't believe it! You bastard!" White gasped, staring at the screen. "I trusted you! I saved your life how many times?"

He turned to me. "Alex? Do you still have that summoning scroll?"

"Yes, why?"

"I want it. Please!"

"Here you are," I pulled the yet-unused scroll out of my inventory and handed it to White.

The seal cracked open. The scroll crumbled to dust.

A flash followed but no one arrived. Instead, the air condensed, forming the quivering, unstable outline of a portal.

White leaped to his feet, very nearly upending his chair. He hurried toward the filmy opening, about to lunge into it. Still, it bounced him back.

"Borisov! D'you hear me?" he shouted, furious.

His face was distorted with rage, his eyes frantic. I wouldn't have wanted to swap places with that Corporate worker whom he'd grilled after Enea's disappearance.

"Calm down," I said. "You can't use it. Trust me, I know enough about portals. The best we can do is take a look inside and try to copy the place's coordinates."

"Do it!" he snapped.

"Dad, please! What's Mr. Borisov done to you?"

"Not to me — to *you*! Is that not enough?"

"But judging by this video, he was on our side! Alex," Enea turned to me, "what if we try to stabilize the portal?"

"Wait a sec. I'm trying to copy the coordinates."

A map materialized over the table, with a bright dot flashing at its center. I uploaded the data from my map-making app and activated Pioneer.

The image of an ancient tower appeared before us, several stories high and surrounded by overgrown ruins.

I reached out and touched the portal.

It bounced under my fingers, giving in to the pressure. My hand began to prickle.

Enea grew worried. "What are you doing?"

"Wait a sec. We'll soon find out where it leads."

White squinted at the image. He didn't seem to recognize it.

Neither did we. Judging by the map, those ruins were located far from Rion Castle, on a continent that lay beyond the ocean.

It worked! I was really grateful to Lethmiel

for the Elven spell he'd shown me. I'd been practicing it a lot just lately. So now I'd managed to use the remaining energy of the not-quite-fully-formed portal to create a Magic Eye.

Another image appeared next to the first one.

It was a room — or rather, a wizard's abode. A candle flickered weakly on the table. A pale morning light seeped through the vaulted window. This looked like early morning.

The bed was unmade. The scorch marks on the walls must have been caused by some fire magic. The chair by the table lay upside down, next to a torn piece of still-smoldering fabric.

"Borisov, where are you?" White thundered. "Come out!"

Pointless. I didn't think he'd reply. Struggling to control the Eye, I made it turn around. Now we could see a broken door hanging on one hinge. And next to it lay a dead body burnt beyond all recognition.

We heard a noise. Someone was climbing the spiral staircase in the hallway behind the splintered door.

"He's gone," a muffled voice said.

"Impossible," someone replied irately. "How could he? The tower's surrounded!"

"He's a powerful wizard. He might have ported out."

Two men climbed up the stairs into the hallway. They appeared to be players even though their name tags weren't visible, which pointed at their high levels and maxed-out stealth.

"We need to search the place. He might be hiding here somewhere."

"Pointless. He ported out, I tell you!"

"He couldn't have. Look what I got from the Reapers," one of the two, a tall warrior, showed some kind of cargonite amulet to the other. "It blocks all portals. We need to search the place. Tell your men to make a ladder and climb the roof. He has to be here somewhere!"

"Wonder if he's stealthed up?"

"Then they'd better search the place with their halberds, every inch of it!"

"Okay. We can do that. Why are the Reapers so mad with him?"

"He used to work for Infosystems. They say he very nearly killed Dietrich. We need to get rid of him. Otherwise, they'll never set us free."

"But," the other one faltered, "what if he's more dangerous than the Reapers?"

"Just find him!" an Orcish growl escaped the other man's closed helmet. "I'll take care of the rest."

He produced a rather unusual-looking dagger. I took a few screenshots just in case,

---

even though the item wasn't easy to forget to say the least. Its short blade was covered in tiny rectangular shapes which looked suspiciously like microchips. Each was marked with a glowing rune of the Founders' language, forming a sequence of symbols yet unfamiliar to me.

"What does this dagger do?"

"It releases one's identity."

"Dammit! Why did we have to make this deal with the Reapers!" the other one wiped away the large beads of perspiration from his forehead.

"Don't you understand? Serving them is much better than receiving the point of a dagger like this one. I saw a couple of Reapers suck neurograms out of people. I don't want them to rip up *my* identity and share it between themselves!"

"We're humans," the other ventured. "They're just freakin' NPCs!"

"Oh, please. They're not NPCs anymore. They're *hybrids*. Enough of your nonsense. Let's find this wizard. He can't have disappeared!"

The image began to fade, then expired. The unstable portal rippled and collapsed.

* * *

I slumped into a chair to restore my strength. "How do you know Borisov?"

I'd failed to keep the portal open. The only reason the scroll had worked at all was probably because of the two men's mysterious portal-blocking amulet whose effect must have resonated with it.

White paused, trying to calm down. "He was in my group for a while. We met over a year ago when the Reapers first came about. Then he disappeared."

"What *are* those Reapers? Can somebody tell me?" Enea demanded. "What are we dealing with? What happened to the Crystal Sphere?"

"Reapers are what used to be NPCs," White replied curtly.

"Very informative!" Enea snapped. "Mind telling us a bit more? Or is it that you don't know anything yourself? Are we supposed to just accept their existence?"

"Please don't. It's not so easy to explain."

"We're not in a hurry, are we?"

"Very well. I'll do my best," he walked around the room, collecting his thoughts. "About two years ago, just as the first mass neuroimplant campaign had begun, we had a series of accidents with players who apparently hadn't survived the effects of full immersion."

"I thought you'd fine-tuned the feedback?" I asked sarcastically.

White shrugged. "People are all different.

We couldn't have foreseen all of the implants' effects."

"So why did you risk it?"

"Enea, I don't work for Infosystems. I'm still trying to figure out why they did it! Now, if we found Borisov and spoke to him..."

"Sorry, Dad," she took a gulp of water.

White reached into his inventory for a small container which he then set on the table. Gingerly he opened it.

A greenish light poured forth from the vessel. I saw a small transparent sphere set in a cargonite frame. It looked rather like a standard magic lamp.

"This is an ancient artifact," White said. "Borisov gave it to me before he disappeared. He asked me to save it for him."

"What does it do?"

"This is a Soul Trap. Touch it. Don't be afraid. It might feel scary at first but you've been through much worse. At least this way you'll understand what the Reapers are and how they came about."

"All right," I offered my hand to the sphere.

The greenish glow enveloped my fingers. They began to prickle. Then a tidal wave of somebody else's memories flooded over me...

ARRUM THE TREE GIANT used to live on the very edge of a thick forest next to the ruins of an Elven temple.

Twice as tall as any human, he had a powerful body and the strength to match. The problem was, his fibrous limbs had become wooden over the years which negatively affected his agility.

His behavioral patterns (like those of all other mobs in the Crystal Sphere) were generated by a neurocomputer. Several neural networks allowed him to use a few combos and even endowed him with a couple of very unpleasant abilities — unpleasant for the players who'd strayed away into his parts of the world, that is — but overall, he wasn't really aware of his own existence.

His main neural networks were still dormant. The game developers wanted Arrum to develop slowly, gradually gaining XP. That way he would need no updates, becoming stronger and smarter with each year.

That unfortunate morning, he was sitting on the hill as was his habit, offering his limbs to the sun. He had no foreboding of the looming tragedy...

Frostil, a level-20 wizard, was going through a bad patch. His longstanding career as a warrior had hit a brick wall in the Crystal Sphere, forcing him to delete his account and create a new char.

The neuroimplant — that wretched piece of new state-of-the-art technology — had completely changed his game experience, highlighting his biggest weakness. As Frostil had recently discovered, he couldn't stand the slightest pain.

He did his best — but it was only getting worse. The mobs whom he'd used to fight with gusto, now evoked a desperate and almost subconscious fear in him, forcing him to cower in the undergrowth waiting for an opportunity to attack them on the sly.

This couldn't go on for much longer. Finally, he'd bitten the bullet and deleted his account, hoping to start from scratch.

He really should have chosen a crafter or some other non-aggressive class. Still, old habits die hard. After a long deliberation, Frostil had chosen combat wizard, reasoning that the use of distance spells might rid him of the necessity of getting too close to the enemy.

Still, it didn't quite work out. His char had turned out to be both weak and lacking. His new cloth robes annoyed him no end. Frostil was ashamed of how he looked. He especially hated his staff, that piece of gnarly wood, but unfortunately, he needed it to cast spells promptly.

His first visit to the city catacombs — the starting location for most newb wizards — was another eye-opener. The narrow, dark maze of tunnels required him to stand motionless while reciting the spells he'd so laboriously memorized. But how are you supposed to stay focused when a horrible monster armed with a rusty scythe lunges at you from the depths of a tunnel? In moments like those, an uncontrollable fear surged over him, forcing him to scramble to safety.

He'd made the first ten levels purely by smoking rats. He'd found a barn where he could climb a ladder up onto the rotting beams and scorch rats to his heart's content from their relative safety. What else could he do? His so inopportunely awakened self-preservation instinct was a power to be reckoned with.

His further development appeared problematic: difficult and way too dangerous. With every new level gained, he received less XP for each rat he'd smoked. Still, his fear prevented him from pushing his limits, becoming his shadowy companion in everything he attempted to achieve.

He spent some time in the city doing petty social quests — but it couldn't go on like this for much longer.

When he finally ventured beyond the city

walls, he stuck to a single simple tactic. Every time he saw a mob, he'd appraise his chances, then attack from the farthest distance possible — and only if his spells could deal enough damage to prevent the enemy from coming any closer than at arm's length.

What do you want me to say? The world of the Crystal Sphere is enormous. There's place for everyone there, heroes as well as cowards.

Gradually Frostil had come to grips with his sorry lot. He'd become ever more fearful, frustrated even. The soul of the ex-warrior had shrunk; the first seeds of treachery had begun to germinate in his heart...

That sunny morning, as Frostil walked along the mud road skirting the woods, he noticed a tree giant napping on a hill.

Frostil froze, prepared to run for his life. Still, he looked the monster up in Wiki just in case.

The information whetted his greed. The tree giant was strong but rather clumsy and vulnerable to fire damage. A few direct fireball hits could fetch Frostil 1,000 XP!

Also, if the comments were to be believed, the giant could drop a couple of gold and even a random precious crystal.

Two gold! Thoughts began flashing through

his mind. He was so fed up with living from hand to mouth. He could use a good meal. And hopefully, some new clothes to replace his old rags.

Overcoming his fear, Frostil approached the giant from behind and launched two fireballs in rapid succession. Then he gulped, trying to catch his breath, and resumed his spell casting.

The first projectile hit the giant directly on the head, setting him on fire. The second one singed his shoulder.

And after that... well, after that things went awry as usual.

With a long cracking sound, the monster activated one of his abilities, transforming into a large ball of intertwined branches. Accelerating, it rolled toward its attacker, stamping out the flames.

It happened way too quickly for Frostil to spring out of its way. The fat gnarly branches pierced his body, pinning him to the ground and forcing a brief shriek of pain out of him. His mind shut down.

He didn't respawn, though. Something irreparable had happened.

His body had collapsed, unable to survive the 100% authenticity of the experience. His brain had failed to tell fiction from reality.

His heart — the heart of a fifty-year-old

man — had stopped. There was nothing the life support systems could do. He died instantly...

Having gotten rid of his attacker, Arrum resumed his usual shape and turned around, about to return to his sunlit hill, when he froze.

Something extraordinary was happening to him.

The squashed remains of the hapless wizard began oozing a faint bluish haze. It reached out to the tree giant and was immediately absorbed by his digital body, awakening the yet-dormant neural networks reserved for his future development.

The last moments of Frostil's agony, his pain and the fear that used to control his mind were added to Arrum's neural matrix. Plus the few words of the spell the wizard had never completed.

A sound came from behind.

Still glitchy and groggy with the experience, Arrum turned round. A warrior was running toward him, impatient to avenge a fellow player's death.

Arrum emitted a muffled creak. Fear overtook him: an acute feeling yet unfamiliar to him, forcing him into action.

In those few split seconds, a whole new world had opened up to the tree giant, crushing him under the weight of human emotions he'd accidentally imbibed. He became aware of his own existence — which was admittedly inadequate and miserable, a sad stretch from one respawn to the next.

The fear made him furious. He was cornered. The warrior was much stronger and more agile than himself. And Arrum couldn't reuse his transformation ability.

His desperate attempts to find a way out forced his updated neural network into overload.

Creaking, Arrum spread his long branchy arms.

The words of the spell unfinished by Frostil fell from his lips.

The warrior didn't expect that. He dodged a few blows of the branches, dealt a couple of slashing blows with his sword aiming at the giant's wooden torso, then rolled over, about to complete his attack with a coup-de-grace combo when a fireball swept him off his feet.

A crit!

A furious bunch of branches pierced his leather armor, sending the player back to his respawn point. The warrior's avatar rippled and began to fade, leaving behind a small bundle of his stuff.

The bluish haze of Frostil's neurograms still hung in the air. Now Arrum had absorbed it

---

all whether he liked it or not — and with it, he'd absorbed a life's worth of his attacker's miserable emotions and experiences.

Arrum's eyes lit up with unquenched fury. His gnarly fingers ripped the warrior's bundle apart, scooping up ten gold coins.

An alien thought flashed through his mind. *I could use a good meal.*

Still, the snippets of weird human desires didn't last, leaving him with a few stronger emotions and bits of knowledge he might use to his advantage.

His name tag blinked and turned red. A new sign added to it, saying, *Defective Mob.*

But that wasn't all. His new fear had subsided, replaced by a spiteful rage which boiled within him, demanding an exit.

Arrum turned his attention to the road where a group of unsuspecting players walked toward him, feeling perfectly safe.

* * *

The prickling sensation in my fingers had stopped. The green glow began to fade. I looked up.

"What was that?" Enea shrieked weakly, freeing herself from the nightmare.

"You've just come into contact with the

neuromatrix of a typical defective mob," White replied. "Now I know where Borisov got these kinds of items. He worked for Infosystems, didn't he?"

"He was better than most of them," I said in all fairness.

"He knew about you but he wouldn't tell me! He used my confidence to collect information."

"It doesn't matter," Enea said, rubbing her temples. "If I understand correctly, the arrival of the Reapers was a sporadic effect caused by the interaction of several revolutionary technologies. On one hand, the neuroimplants, which were built using some alien prototype, were forced onto unsuspecting users without first studying them for any possible side effects. The fate of Frostil speaks for itself. Few of us are capable of surviving 100% authenticity."

"That's right," White agreed. "I had to learn how to bear pain. And on the other hand, the Corporation had also developed neural computers which were first introduced in the Crystal Sphere. They possessed extra capacities meant to accommodate the mobs' future development. That's what allowed them to intercept fragments of players' identities. When a player dies in the real world, his identity matrix disintegrates into separate fragments which Infosystems workers call neurograms."

Enea looked at him. "That's not all, is it?"

He gave a grim nod. "The defective mobs are dangerous but they can be defeated. The Reapers are the real problem."

"Are they not the same?" I asked. "What makes a Reaper different from that tree giant?"

"The first Reapers were based on the more advanced NPC characters, such as quest NPCs. They're capable of absorbing a much bigger number of neurograms which then form a hybrid identity. But as you well understand, such a patchwork mind isn't self-sustainable. Hybrids behave like madmen torn by conflicting urges. Most of them simply disintegrate — but a few manage to survive and become self-aware. They are the problem. They constantly crave new neurograms — and the only way for them to get them is by killing more players. Did you see that Harvester in the market square?"

"Yes, who is he?"

"Harvesters are Reapers' creations. They're basically a temporary storage. Their job is to harvest as many neurograms as they can and deliver them to the Reapers."

"Does that mean they already possess some form of magic enabling them to create creatures like that?"

"And not only that. Reaper worship is

currently spreading among regular NPCs. The Reapers have seized several castles and even cities."

"Why can't Infosystems close the Crystal Sphere?" I exclaimed.

"They don't control the situation anymore," White replied. "Whatever threat had prompted them to force neuroimplants and in-modes upon us, the real danger came from virtual reality. Nobody could have expected that. As you must have seen in Arrum's example, neurograms may contain knowledge as well as emotions. The few Corporation workers killed by the Reapers could have passed on to them the kind of information even you and I don't have. But still I have a question. If Borisov indeed joined the Crystal Sphere over a year ago, who in that case unblocked Agrion Castle?"

Honestly, my head went round with all the news. I couldn't even imagine the scope of the looming catastrophe and its consequences.

"So what can we do?" Enea asked softly.

"We live as we always did," White replied. "The Crystal Sphere survived the first blow. It didn't fall apart under the pressure from defective mobs. The laws of virtual reality still work here. If we keep leveling up faster than our enemies, we will survive. Then we might be able to look into it and hopefully get to the bottom of it. I'm not gonna lie to you, things didn't go well in Agrion. The Harvester managed to collect the neurograms and left unhindered. Now we'll have a few more high-level Reapers. We need to make sure it doesn't happen again."

"We need to find Borisov," I added. "I know you're mad at him for not telling you about us. Still, now he has no reason to be so secretive anymore."

"He's on a completely different continent. This was the only scroll we had. We can't open another portal. We can't call him."

"We have something that allows us to travel long distances," Enea said, apparently meaning the device we'd found in the Temple of Oblivion, together with the Founder's Glove which allowed us to control it. "You can be mad at him all you want, but we still need to find him."

White frowned, then raised his eyebrow in surprise. "I've received a quest!"

"Me too," Enea nodded.

Several system messages appeared in my interface,

New quest alert: Mysterious Wizard!
Quest type: Unique
Find Borisov and ask him what he knows about the Reapers.
Reward: new information and a new ally

Deadline: None

New clan quest alert: Hard Times!
Quest type: Unique
Unite your players under the banner of the Black Mantis Clan. Find a quick way to level up the clan's combat section to levels 100+.
Reward: +50 pt. to Rion Castle's defense and attack potential
Deadline: 30 days

New quest alert: The Enemy of My Enemy!
Quest type: Normal, Diplomatic
Try to come to an agreement with the Black Ravens' raid leader
Reward: a new ally in your fight against the Reapers
Deadline: 48 hours

The Crystal Sphere's engine was still ticking over like clockwork! This virtual world created by Infosystems had survived multiple glitches and had proven to be highly adaptable.

White had been right: we could still turn the situation round.

Dietrich's words echoed in my mind,

"Together we'll kill more researchers, you and I. We'll get their knowledge and their neurograms! We'll change everything here! The

Crystal Sphere will belong to us!"

Unhesitantly I accepted the quests.

You're wrong, I mentally addressed Dietrich. *We won't surrender our world without a fight.*

CHAPTER TWO

THE CRYSTAL SPHERE
RION CASTLE

FOR ME, THE NEXT MORNING began with bad news and urgent household problems.

The Ravens' raid seemed to be stuck. Peasant fugitives from Chaffinch Creek told us about some strange and ominous goings-on there. According to them, the previous night the sky had changed color, resembling green marble. Two tornadoes formed in it for no reason whatsoever. They skirted the Ravens' camp and headed for the swamps, brushing over a goblin settlement.

"The Ravens are surrounded," Archie finished his report. "The Swamp Goblins claim the incident on 'overseas wizards and their wicked tricks'."

"The goblins, do you think they'll attack us?" Enea asked.

"Not during daytime, no," the warrior replied. "They're scared witless too. If they decide to attack, it'll be closer to nightfall."

We heard a knock on the door. Lethmiel walked in.

"Where do you want me to put the fugitives up?" he asked bluntly.

"You can give them tents and tell them to set up camp behind the castle walls," I said. "Make sure they have everything they need. Any news from Agrion?"

"The townsfolk are worried about what happened yesterday. They blame it on White's men."

"It's got nothing to do with them!" Enea protested.

"That's not what the city officials think," Lethmiel replied. "Dimian went to his old shop early this morning and asked around a bit. Everybody seems to think that 'the city was under attack from the Dark Knights'. The guards captain is dead. And a few vendors, too."

"That's not true!" Enea exclaimed indignantly. "I need to speak to my father. If we don't disprove this blatant lie, Rion's reputation will suffer! Alex, can you wait for me, please?"

We'd been thinking of paying the Ravens a diplomatic visit, but it looked like we'd have to put it off until after lunch.

"Don't worry," I said. "I have other things to do."

Enea left. Archie hurried to leave, too. He still had the clan's combat section to train, war or no war.

I dismissed Lethmiel and walked out onto the balcony to take in the surrounding panorama.

The castle was buzzing with life. Its central court was crowded with scaffolding and all sorts of hanging platforms the dwarves used. They worked hard rebuilding the donjon, meticulously restoring every little detail — not just of the fortifications themselves but also all the finishing touches.

A faint haze of stone dust hung in the air. Several restored statues swayed on the cables as the dwarves hoisted them back up.

The outside perimeter of the castle, however, still lay in ruins.

I peered at the crowd of workers, searching for the fabled Master Walmord of the Copperbeards.

He was busy ordering everyone around on one of the *conarps*: the defense platforms encircling the donjon. Strong and secure as the cliff ledges they were cut into, *conarps* added a touch of ancient elegance to the whole structure.

In the light of recent events, I didn't care much about all the fine ornamental carvings and trimmings. I simply teleported Master Walmord to my balcony. We needed to talk.

"You could have warned me," Walmord grumbled: he hated miniports.

"I'm sorry. I have very little time. How's it going?"

"Can't you see?" he puffed out his chest with pride. "Today, the sequence of Air will be complete! Our stone carvers have managed to fully restore seventy runes. This is one of the greatest achievements of my people!"

Great news. Before, Rion was protected solely by the runic sequence of Earth which had survived since time immemorial.

I made a quick mental estimation. It would take our wizards Rodrigo and Iskandar a long time to work out the sequence of Chaos. "Walmord, I'd like your groups to start working on the outer walls."

He didn't like it, I could see that. "There isn't much XP to be gained *there*."

"Don't be too picky," I said. "There's an enemy raid about to besiege the castle. We need to restore all the walls and the towers ASAP."

"Excuse me, Alexatis," Walmord objected hotly. "That wasn't in the agreement! My Copperbeards work in areas which allow them to level up their professional skills. Go hire some peasants, they'll restore the stonework no problem!"

"Have you heard about the Reapers?"

He gave a reluctant nod. "Only rumors. What do I care? Strangers aren't welcome in our underground cities. They'll never be able to invade us."

"Reapers can appear amid any race. They're not outsiders. They act from within. They're neither a race nor an enemy army."

"What are you implying?"

"I'm afraid you might need to consider moving over here. There's a huge underground dungeon under the castle. The imps built it during the centuries of their lording over this place."

In my eyes, this was an interesting and generous offer. Still, Master Walmord didn't appreciate it.

"Are you mad? Why would I want to relocate my clan?" he actually sounded quite angry.

"It's up to you," I said. "But as soon as the first Reapers arrive in your cities, the offer will become null and void because I won't be able to offer my hospitality to those of whom I'm not sure. You're the head of the clan, so you need to find out more about this looming catastrophe. In the meantime, you need to restore the outer walls."

"You can't give me orders!"

"I'm not. I'm asking you. I insist."

"Every single worker in my clan is already a Master!"

Goodness, he was unbearable sometimes. So cocky and pig-headed. He wasn't a Copperbeard: he was a Copperhead!

Thanks to the castle stonework's unique properties, most of his clanmates had already leveled up their professions. They weren't quite the cream of the elite yet but they weren't very far from that, either. According to our agreement, they worked for a symbolic remuneration as long as they could level up their skills.

It looked like our cooperation had hit a brick wall. After all, I *had* indeed promised not to use them on second-rate jobs.

"Very well," I had to agree with his reasoning. "You're right: I did give you my word. It can't be helped."

He immediately cheered up. "In that case, we'll keep working on the central towers," he said as if nothing had happened. "We still have about thirty feet of stonework to restore before we get to the Element of Fire. Plenty of work for the carvers, too."

"Very well. You can go now," I said, trying to keep my cool. Without the dwarves, Rion Castle would have still been in ruins.

"Lethmiel?" I said. "I'd like to see Quieton and Smarty."

He replied almost instantly, "They're on their way."

He seemed to be using his authority to practice ancient Elven magic at every opportunity. Now, too, a very unusual portal opened up before me, disgorging the two scared peasants enveloped in a faint portal haze.

Quieton hiccupped. "Is there a demon in the castle?" Seeing me, he breathed a sigh of relief and made the sign of the Gods of Light.

"Jeez, it's not for the faint-hearted," Smarty admitted. He was a young lad from Chaffinch Creek.

"How are things going?" I asked them. "How are you settling in?"

"We's a-doin' well," Quieton replied. "We's all workin'."

"How many of you are there?"

"All of us!" Quieton replied. "We's all come a-runnin' here from Chaffinch Creek after those fiends started killin' us," he rendered his own unflattering version of the situation.

Smarty tugged at his sleeve, warning him to keep his mouth shut.

"You're right," I said. "I failed to protect your village, I'm sorry. Still, I had my reasons in doing so. I want all the villagers to move to the castle. You'll live here now."

"Stone houses, that'll be great," Quieton cheered up. "But how about all the fields, the hunting grounds and the pastures? Would we give them up to the enemy?"

"No, we wouldn't."

"When do you want us to start building new houses?"

"How about today?" I said. "Do you have stonemasons?"

"If you want all the villages to move in, we might manage about thirty," Quieton replied confidently. "They don't shy away from hard work."

"Where did they learn their masonry?" I asked, sincerely surprised.

"There're so many of them old ruins everywhere here! We bring stone by boats to our village," he admitted reluctantly. "We use them for foundations. We have to build foundations nice and high because of the floods, you know. Without them, we'd lose all our belongings every time the water rose."

"Very well. I'd like you to bring all those who know how to work the stone. They'll be your foremen. I want you to start by restoring these walls."

Quieton perked up. "I's sure we can do that! And then we might build them houses too. One can't have too many skills."

He was quick on the uptake, wasn't he?

* * *

So many other things demanded our immediate attention.

Food deliveries, stocking up on weapons, finding more craftsmen... my to-do list was so long it made my head spin.

Lethmiel had already dispatched messengers to the neighboring villages with orders to urgently relocate to the castle.

While there was even the slightest threat of a Reapers' invasion, I couldn't leave the peasants unprotected. They might need to become townspeople and learn how to restore castle walls, build houses and master new crafts.

I ported to the castle's inner yard and walked through the gate toward Dimian's new shop. It was on the right just within the second ring of the city walls, next to the recently restored wizards' tower: a tall spired building occupied by Iskandar and Rodrigo.

A clashing of swords and the thumping of

arrows hitting targets was coming from the training grounds to my left, just next to the barracks.

Earlier, White had repeatedly warned me by saying, "Whatever you do, don't trust NPCs".

I knew what he meant. Still, I tended to differ. Without NPCs, life in the castle would have ground to a halt. Besides, many of the more complex toons had already become my friends. I saw no reason to demonize them, let alone banish them from the castle.

Thus thinking, I walked into the shop.

"We need bows and arrows!" Arwan's indignant voice demanded inside. "Proper ones! Not these lame imitations! You understand?"

"Yeah but... where do you want me to get them?"

"Are you a merchant or just a pretty face?" the Elf continued to vent his indignation. "I can buy better gear anywhere in Agrion!"

"Okay, okay! Keep your hair on! You'd better tell me who I can get them from. Alexatis told me to only buy the best of everything."

"Yeah right! The best thing you can do is send a caravan to our forest craftsmen."

"You mean, *Elven* craftsmen? How am I supposed to find them? You said the forests were dying everywhere! There's a map over there on the table, show me! Just point! I can work out how to get there myself."

Well done, Dimian. The guy definitely knew what he was doing.

"Hello, Arwan," I stepped into the room. "What's all this about?"

"We don't have proper weapons!"

I could see that Arwan felt out of his comfort zone. He'd accepted a certain informal responsibility for the Elven refugees he'd brought here from the dying forests — but he didn't have enough experience to either control them or provide for their needs.

"Found a place for everyone?" I asked him.

Arwan nodded. "In the tent camp. Many of us can't get used to it. The druids are complaining about the absence of shrines and relics. Hunters can't feed their families as they can't eat monsters' meat and that's the only game available here. They left in a hurry with only the clothes on their backs. Most of them don't even have a decent bow."

"Can't you make them?"

"We can't find suitable materials. Local plants are mainly hollow-limbed. Also, it's not easy to make a good long-range bow! You need to treat the wood first, dry it, then treat it again and again. It's the same with arrows. You don't think, do you, that they're made of ordinary twigs? You aren't going to send me to the hazelnut grove over the wall, are you? That's what some people told me I should do," Arwan added with a nervous smirk.

Honestly, I had no idea what kind of wood they needed to make bows and arrows with. What I did know was that the game devs were bound to have made provision for such an occasion. This was an elaborate virtual reality, after all.

I switched over to the market interface. Unlike NPCs, players had many more options there.

I started by habitually checking the auction, knowing that you could find all sorts there. I ran a quick search until I found some affordable bows.

On second thoughts, I ran another search, this time for wood suitable for making bows and arrows. It would cost less while providing the Elven craftsmen with the practice they so desperately needed. They might even teach their skill to others.

I paid five gold from my account. A large bundle of wood materialized in my bag. It was surprisingly big and heavy.

"How about this?" I placed it on the counter.

To Arwan and Dimian, this must have looked like nothing short of magic. They froze open-mouthed, then began studying my purchase.

"This is perfect!" Arwan announced.

The bundle contained two roughly planed blanks for the bows as well as a hundred thin straight shafts for making arrows. The fact that it had neither bowstrings, fletches nor arrowheads didn't seem to baffle Arwan. Judging by his sincere joy, he loved the materials.

"We have the oil for treating the wood. Hydra tendons will make perfect bowstrings. Our blacksmiths will forge the arrowheads. And there're plenty of birds around whose feathers we can use for fletching."

"How many experienced archers do you think you can muster?" I asked.

"Our hunters will defend the castle gladly, especially if it becomes the seat of an Elven shrine," Arwan replied. "In case of an attack, I can guarantee a hundred and fifty archers to defend these walls," he added, studying the materials with delight.

"Who's in charge of the Elven camp now?"

"No one. Any disputes are brought before the Council of three druids. Apart from that, it's every man for himself."

"I'm putting you in charge of all the Elves."

"Sorry, Alexatis. You can't appoint an Elven leader, let alone a warlord. He's chosen from the best warriors who must compete for the post."

"Do you really think you won't win it? Especially now that your kinsmen are in mortal danger?"

Arwan paused, undecided. "I don't know, really. It never happened before. Not that I remember, anyway."

"Never mind. I'll talk to the druids. Can you tell me who built the Elven shrines?"

"What do you mean, who? The Elves did!"

"Do you have builders?"

"No, we don't! You see, all the stone buildings were erected by our ancestors during the Era of the Founder Gods. And today's shrines are grown, not built. They take decades to grow, centuries even."

Oh. That was a bit of a disappointment.

The clan quest icon blinked in my interface. A new system message popped up,

New Clan Quest Alert: The Spirit of the Woods
Quest type: Unique
Find a way to build a new Elven shrine in Rion Castle.
Any clan member can join you on this quest.
Deadline: 10 days
Reward: Your Relationship with the Forest Elves will improve. You will receive 150 archers at your disposal.
Penalty for failing or declining the quest:
Your Relationship with the Forest Elves will deteriorate until they leave Rion Castle.

I accepted the quest even though I had no idea how to go about it. I might discuss it with Enea later that night. She might think of something.

"Dimian, can I have the keys to the warehouse?" I asked.

"Here you are. Why?"

"You'll soon see. Arwan, stay here for a moment."

I walked into the large half-empty room and shut the door behind me. Then I reopened the market interface and bought a hundred more bundles of wood suitable for making bows and arrows. Removing them from my inventory and stacking them up on the shelves was some work, I tell you!

After about ten minutes, I called Arwan and Dimian.

"This is witchcraft!" the latter announced, staring at the shelves groaning from the weight of the goods.

I didn't want to disappoint him. "We have new arrivals every day. I'd like you to find out what they need. If you don't find the necessary goods in Agrion, feel free to send caravans to other cities as long as you have your warehouse stacked with everything we might possibly require. Do you understand me?"

Dimian scratched the back of his head. "You bet I do."

"Get on with it, then. Forget everything else for the time being. This is a priority. Forget profits: what's truly important now is regular supplies. Arwan," I turned to the Elf, "can you give Dimian an example of the arrowheads you need? We'll buy

---

them in the Azure Mountains. The bows you can make yourselves now. You have plenty of materials. And one more personal task specially for you," I added. "I want you to ask around to see if any of the local peasant craftsmen would like to learn your bow-making skill. You could employ them as apprentices."

"Sorry, Alexatis. I'm afraid it's not gonna work."

"Why not?"

"I don't think other Elves will appreciate it if I start revealing ancient Elven secrets to the local peasants. They won't approve of it. Please allow us to do everything ourselves."

"Very well. On one condition. I'd like you to give every fifth bow you make to the clan's arsenal."

"That's not a problem," he agreed without disputing it.

A noise from the street invaded the little open window. Apparently, the first boatfuls of villagers had begun to arrive.

They all had to be housed, fed and assigned suitable jobs. I could feel I wasn't going to make it on my own. Too many petty mundane tasks to sort out.

"Lethmiel!" I shouted.

He seemed to have expected my call. A portal appeared in a spiral of light, disgorging my Blood Elf majordomo.

"I'd like you to take care of the camp," I told him. "Think you can do it?"

"We have plenty of food and tents," Lethmiel replied. "Can you take a look at the plans, please? I've drafted them for you just in case," he offered me a sheet of parchment.

He definitely knew what he was doing! On the plan, Lethmiel had housed different races apart from each other, and separated blocks of tents with wide streets. At the center, he drew a large round tent and an awning. Judging by the inscriptions, that's where he planned to set up a second temporary inn and a small marketplace. In the future it might expand, becoming a proper market square.

"Yes to everything," I sealed the parchment with my magic seal. "Get on with it. Report to me in the evening."

* * *

I found both Enea and White in the Practice Hall.

"Keep blocking!" her father's voice was followed by a heavy thump. "Excellent. Step back! Watch me when I attack. That's right. Now kick the bottom edge of my shield! Good! You see? Where's your level and where's mine? — and still I lost my balance and opened up for a second! You should be in control. Always ready to attack but don't push your luck! Good. Let's do it again. Block! Veeeery good! Step back, kick the shield, attack!"

"I can't breathe," Enea gasped, heaving. "I'm not a warrior, anyway. Why do you want to train me? My magic works well, doesn't it?"

"The Reapers are multiclass," White snapped back. "You should be as good as they are. In everything!"

"But I'm just not strong enough!"

"You will be, in a moment," he said, removing a rather plain ring from his finger. "Put this on. It'll improve some of your stats."

"Okay..."

"Now let's do it again. How long does it take you to cast Lightning?"

"Two seconds."

"In that case, you need to combine your skills!"

He lunged unexpectedly at her. Enea blocked it, dodged another attack, then whipped back and kicked the lower edge of his shield hard as he'd just taught her, forcing White to both stagger and disrupt his attack while winning herself the two seconds necessary to cast Lightning. It flashed through the room, branching and forking. The charge knocked White off his feet, stripping him of a few Life points.

"Excellent!" he motioned to her, signaling the end of the fight, then scrambled to his feet, wincing and rubbing the shoulder hit by lightning. "You need to remember: the past is over. Our present lies here in the Crystal Sphere which is now chock full of defective mobs!"

I watched them, unwilling to interfere. Alpha — who was now the clan's mascot — had made himself comfortable on the Cargonite Golem's shoulder, twitching his legs as he watched the fight. He was desperate to join in but Enea had forbidden him to attack them.

White saw me. "Hi, Alex. You're big on sleep, aren't you?"

"I wish! I was too busy doing all sorts of things," I shook his hand, then gave a kiss to Enea still panting from the combat.

"We need jewelry," White got down to business. "Loads."

"What kind of jewelry?" I realized of course that he meant *special* items. I'd already noticed last night that he was hung with chains and rings like a Christmas tree. They were all stat-boosting items improving a characteristic or adding a new skill.

"We need stuff which boosts Strength, Agility, Stamina and Intellect. Ideally, we want rare custom-made items boosting several stats at once. Any chance of farming something like that here?"

"What, on the Moors? I don't think so. Still, I know a place which might be interesting."

"You think you could tell me about it?"

"I might. How about tonight?"

White didn't insist. "Okay. What are you going to do about the clan's combat section? At the moment, their leveling is too slow. Anyone below level 100 has no business getting in the Reapers' way."

"What do you suggest?"

"We should find some locations with mobs levels 70+. That'll allow us to power-level the combat wing non-stop. From my experience, you can make four or five levels a day. But let me warn you that not all warriors will be able to sustain such a rush. We'll have to drop a few people."

"You don't want me to kick them out, do you?"

"Of course not. They'll have to be transferred to a non-combatant role. Only the strongest and sturdiest can stay in the combat section. This is a prerequisite. The only people who can fight Reapers are those who can get themselves killed, respawn and step back into the ranks!"

If the truth were known, I wasn't comfortable with what he'd just said. After what had happened in Agrion, our future seemed bleak.

"Very well," I said. "I understand. Now Enea and I need to go and see the Ravens, and in the evening we can talk. We can meet up at our place and discuss all the possible places and leveling scenarios. Just please don't interfere with Archie, okay?"

I liked him now, I had to admit. These days, White was much less stuck up than he used to be. I could sense some sort of unbending inner backbone in him now.

"Alex, there's no way I'm going to usurp posts of power. But I do want to take part in the clan's life. One thing you need to understand is that wherever Reapers appear, the game balance flies out the window. They're good at both magic and weapons. I'd lost many good friends before I learned to stand up to them."

Alpha fluttered onto Enea's shoulder.

"Is it really so bad?" she asked. "Are we supposed to barricade ourselves inside the castle?"

"No. Shutting ourselves up in here isn't even an option. The Reapers are here to stay. They won't go. They force the very world to change."

"So what do we do?"

"We stick together. We bring other players under our banners. We level up fast, so that whenever we meet a Reaper, we tear him apart and hammer him into the ground, both literally and figuratively. Hybrids have no respawn. There's no provision for it. Once they're dead, they're dead for good. The neurograms comprising their identities will simply disintegrate. That's their only weak spot."

"In that case, why haven't they been killed,

all of them?" Enea demanded.

"Because humans aren't organized," White replied. "The majority only care about their own safety. The stronger clans were destroyed first. The safest way to survive is by making small groups of five to seven people, like my own. Also, few people realize the true scale of the disaster. The Crystal Sphere is enormous. It has billions of players. How many of them have died, unable to survive in full immersion and thus giving rise to more Reapers?"

His question hung in the air, unanswered.

"So you're going to see the Ravens, are you?" he changed the subject. "Are you hoping to come to some agreement with them?"

"I can try," I said. "As far as I know, there were about two hundred players in that raid. All of them were frozen at the same time as our cluster. They probably don't even realize that several years have elapsed. Under any other circumstances, I might have left them well alone. Once they'd gotten the taste of what it was like here, they might have realized they couldn't cross the Moors and would have turned back. But as it is, I can't do that."

"Good," White said. "Talk to them. If we don't interfere, a lot of them might die for real."

"Would you like to come with us?"

"No, I wouldn't. With my level, it might actually harm the talks. You might appear to be trying to put pressure on them. Also it might weaken your position as clan leader. Still, I could give you some advice if you don't mind."

Enea tactfully wondered off, leaving us alone.

I listened to what he had to say. Then I nodded, "Thanks. If the talks hit a brick wall, I'll do as you say."

＊ ＊ ＊

THE CRYSTAL SPHERE
THE EDGE OF THE TOXIC MOORS

The Ravens raid had set up camp on an island not far from Chaffinch Creek.

They'd chosen this particular spot for a reason. The island's gently sloping banks were studded with rows of sharpened stakes pointing outward in the direction of the water. These were the remains of the ancient fortifications, an echo of long gone days when every bit of land in the area had been occupied by the coalition that had declared war on the Order of Disciples.

The island had a stationary portal with the other regions and several sheds and outhouses built by the local peasants. The bulk of the island was sparsely overgrown with pine trees. The Ravens set up their tents right under them. The proximity of the village was important too: the peasants had laid log roads across the swamps.

Enea and I ported to the old mud road which started at a dilapidated jetty.

The Ravens exercised caution. They weren't even trying to do any serious farming. Some of them would venture close to the moors alone or in small groups, hoping to see an unheard-of mob or pick up some rare herbs and roots.

They noticed us straight away. Two warriors and a cleric darted off somewhere — apparently to warn the others about our arrival.

"Look at this," I pointed at a trail of uprooted undergrowth skirting the edge of the moors.

"You think it's one of the two tornados the villagers told us about?"

"It looks like it. But what is it? Just a weather anomaly? Or could it be magic?"

She shrugged. "You can't really tell without seeing it."

"Never mind. Let's go. I don't expect Allan to come and greet us in person."

I wasn't far wrong. The Ravens clan leader was waiting for us at the center of the camp surrounded by his retinue of players. One of them was especially picturesque: the orc who had threatened me when we'd rescued White from his PK kidnappers.

I had a bad feeling about the guy. I had to keep an eye on him. He was sure to do the dirty when least expected.

The Ravens' levels were mainly 45 to 47. The orc (whose nickname was Urgorn) was level 50. Allan (nickname Aln2043), level 52.

The crowd parted before us, forming a living heaving corridor. They cast curious glances at us, defiant even, and still their faces were touched with confusion.

No wonder. For me too, the first days after having the implant installed had turned out to be the most impressive and unforgettable experience of my entire life.

"So what do you want?" the clan leader asked unceremoniously.

"Need to talk. In private. Can we do that?"

Urgorn scowled in disdain. The weight of his orcish armor seemed to considerably hinder his movements. Welcome to the club. You can't lug around a tank track all day, can you?

Alan paused, thinking. Then he nodded, much to the others' disgruntlement, and motioned both me and Enea toward the listing lean-to.

"So what do you wanna talk about?" he perched on a wide bench behind the wooden table.

We sat opposite him.

"I know what happened to your raid," I said.

He frowned. Apparently that wasn't the only problem he was trying to solve.

"Why, what happened?" he replied defiantly.

"You don't seem to attack anything, you don't

farm," I replied calmly. "Are you afraid of hydras?"

"That's none of your business."

"Oh yes, it is. This situation is our fault. I'm gonna tell you it as it is," I gave him a quick run-down of the details.

"Infosystems fitted you with neuroimplants," I finally said. "They're totally cool, I agree. Still, they require some getting used to. The first experiences were very strong and complex, weren't they?"

"How do you know?" he protested. "They can't have cryogenized us! That's bullshit! It wasn't in the agreement!"

"Al, listen. I'm offering you a truce. You've got a stationary portal here. Go back to your castle and take a good look around. Note all the changes. You can't get to Rion, anyway. It's gonna be a wipe before you even clear the moors. Even worse, the Reapers might find out you're here."

Unfortunately, White had been right. My words had only provoked him.

"We're not easily scared," Allan snapped. "So you sent a couple of tornados to us, so what?" he pointed at the strip of uprooted undergrowth which lay very close to the camp almost touching the outer tents. "Next time you should aim better!"

"I didn't do it."

"Who did, then? You shouldn't have bothered to come. We won't be challenged by anyone! No amount of high walls and magic can scare us into submission. We're gonna take the castle away from you, mind my words!"

"Did you hear about the recent massacre in Agrion?"

"So what?"

"Reapers did that. They-"

"Oh, do give me a break! That was a glitch! A g-l-i-t-c-h. Local NPCs got out of order, big deal! Worse things happen but no one makes such a song and dance about it! You just don't have enough warriors to keep Rion, let's face it!"

"I have plenty of warriors. That's not the problem."

"Then go back to your castle walls and wait for us! We won't be long!" he flashed me a devil-may-care smile.

So obstinate. Then again, how could I blame him? He was only a player, passionate and confident. He hadn't yet worked out what neuroimplants could really do. He wouldn't listen to anyone at the moment.

Which meant I'd have to follow White's advice, after all. I needed to show him that we were dealing with a much more complex situation, including a totally different gameplay.

"Would you be willing to take me on, one on one?"

"What, a duel? Absolutely," he agreed with

ease, knowing his level was superior to mine. "One-on-one, right? Till the respawn?"

"Sounds good," I said.

"When?"

"How about now?"

"Good," he pointed at an enclosure which must have very recently served as a cattle-pen. "Wait for me over there. I'll go change my gear."

Very well. I didn't mind the audience. The Ravens needed to see what was going to happen. That might get some of them thinking.

* * *

Enea was visibly alarmed by this change of events. "What do you want to achieve?"

"I just want to teach him a lesson."

She didn't seem to like it. "A lesson in pain? Was that my father's idea?"

"Don't worry. There's no other way I can make him see my point. Whatever I say, my words can't penetrate his gamer's shell. Until he knows what having the implant feels like, our talks will go nowhere."

"You don't think it'd be better to wait for someone else to teach him this lesson?"

"What, just to keep my hands clean? But if he does bring his raid to Rion against all the odds and decides to storm the castle, we'll have to fight to the death against fellow players! And that's something I can't afford."

"I understand. I'm sorry," she flung her arms around me and hid her face on my chest. "Of course you're right."

I'd chosen a patch of trampled ground at the center of the camp, fenced-off with some crooked poles.

Allan walked out of his tent. His clanmates cheered their encouragement. He gave me a defiant look and slammed his sword against his shield, winding himself up before the fight.

"Al, do him!"

"Show him what Ravens can do!"

"Teach him a lesson!"

They catcalled and shouted, impatient for the fight to begin. I couldn't blame them.

"Come on now!" they surrounded the enclosure.

Allan didn't need any encouragement. He felt superior, anyway. He must have heard about my multiclass but considered it a weakness, not a forte. An experienced warrior wouldn't invest in Intellect and other characteristics necessary for a wizard. In his opinion, I was very badly leveled, as simple as that. He probably thought I'd been too greedy when creating my char, choosing some abilities I didn't really need, and that now I was

---

paying the price. In his eyes, I was neither a warrior nor a wizard but a weak, average nincompoop.

He raised his shield and advanced on me.

His polished armor glistened predatorily. It must have taken at least a hundred pounds of mithril to make, the fabled "true silver" which, once treated, became harder than steel.

Somehow I didn't think he wore this set of armor on a daily basis. He'd probably last wore it for some special occasion before he'd received the implant.

Otherwise why had he just stumbled, losing the spring in his step?

The crowd's cheering stopped. The Ravens appeared lost with their leader's indecision. Why wasn't he attacking me?

He did lunge at me, apparently intending to perform his signature combo. Unfortunately, the sheer weight of his armor had slowed him down. I easily dodged his attack and sliced through his arm, dealing him a purposefully shallow wound that would seize his muscles with pain and cause blood to gush down his fancily decorated bracers.

The cargonite blade of my sword came as an unpleasant surprise to him. He must have believed mithril armor impenetrable.

Still, the fight was far from over. Wincing, he recoiled, gasping but keeping a watchful eye on me.

He gave me a crooked smile, apparently believing this to be some dirty magic trick. He activated one of his warrior skills, wrapping himself in a wave of golden light which improved his strength and reduced fatigue, then attacked again.

He missed.

His sword sliced through thin air as I somersaulted out of its path. His armor's momentum dragged him forward, forcing him to take two extra steps. Immediately he paid the price as blood from a new wound flooded down his thigh.

His labored wheezy breath was the only sound in the sudden silence.

Then he worked it out. In one smooth motion he removed his gorgeous set of armor and sent it back into his inventory.

I couldn't deny him his spirit or combat skill. Free from his cumbersome dress armor, he grabbed his sword with two hands and attacked me with renewed force.

Our swords met. Still, his two wounds were bleeding profusely, weakening him. His life hadn't dropped that much at all, though. He was still going strong; he had no need to revert to elixirs; he'd rather save them for emergencies.

Familiar tactic. I used to make the same beginner's mistakes, too.

He parried my blow. For a brief second, we stood face to face.

"Drink your elixirs now, or I'll smoke you!"

"Leave me alone!" he croaked.

Our swords met with a long screeching sound. We circled each other again, pinning each other down with our glares. I was calm; he, intense. His hair was damp and disheveled. Sweat dripped from the tip of his nose.

"You can't take our castle," I said. "Do you know now what 100% authenticity feels like? It's gonna take you hundreds of respawns just to get used to it. Not all of your men will survive it. Some will die for real. I offer a truce."

"Fight!" he gasped.

"If you say so," I said in a deliberately loud voice so that the other Ravens could hear me. "Just remember we have a common enemy now!"

He didn't reply. Instead, he attacked me again with a fury multiplied by his desire to shut me up. I had to use a couple of rather painful blows just to stop him. He staggered, barely keeping on his feet. Me, I hadn't even broken a sweat.

The difference between us was so dramatic that some of the crowd booed their indignation,

"That's cheating!"

"He's using illegal tricks!"

It looked like the situation had reached a deadlock. My lesson hadn't worked. Did each of them have to suffer a virtual death just to finally see that the gameplay wasn't what it once had been?

I wouldn't have put it past them to attack Enea and myself all together, thinking I was indeed using some cheat codes.

"He's got damage disabled!"

The flimsy fence creaked, about to give under the crowd's pressure.

"Step back," the orc said, stepping into the enclosure. He staggered under the weight of his massive armor, clenching a battle hammer far too heavy for him to properly wield.

The next instant, Enea ported to my side. "*You* step back, all of you. Or you'll regret it."

"Dream on," the orc croaked, struggling in the immobilizing clutches of the Staff of a Hydra.

"Alex, let's go!" Enea said, ready to port back to Rion. "You can't prove anything to them!"

She was right — but the goblins prowling around the camp wouldn't miss their chance. If we failed to convince the Ravens to break camp and go home now, they were unlikely to live through the night.

I dodged the orc's heavy swing, then used his shaky balance to knock him off his feet.

The crowd heaved. I braced myself, thinking they were about to attack us but -

The crowd dissolved in shouts of surprise. "Over there! Look!"

A swift shadow, definitely stealthed, rushed over the island. This must have been the combat avatar of a demon, no less!

The blurred outline flashed overhead, disappearing from sight. Another one followed in its wake, flapping its leathery wings. This was an Ancient Wyvern whose shadow momentarily eclipsed the sunlight. Luckily for us, the wyvern ignored us entirely, its attention firmly focused on its prey.

* * *

Urgorn was the first to recover from the shock. Awkwardly he scrambled to his feet and threw his hand in the air, pointing at four small dots in the distant sky.

"Mobs!" he growled in a deep guttural voice.

Jesus. Our "normal" diplomatic quest was beginning to take on a life of its own.

A group of wyverns was rapidly approaching the island. Unlike their boss, they'd already noticed us — and they weren't too squeamish about going after this new quarry. They banked into a steep turn and went for us.

As far as I remembered, wyverns were an evolutionary branch of dragons. Normally they weren't very big, but their long serpentine necks made them dangerous opponents. Two strong legs with sharp claws, a pair of membranous leathery wings and a powerful tail completed their look.

They weren't a common sight in our part of the world. Normally, they nested high in the Azure Mountains.

"Run! Take cover!" I shouted.

Naturally, no one listened. The next moment, the wyverns began spitting fire. Their attack was powerful but not too accurate. The jets of flame singed the moors, throwing up hissing fountains of parboiled mud and scorching a couple goblins who were lying in ambush amid the mossy driftwood.

"Alex, look!" Enea exclaimed.

I'd noticed already. Some tall creatures whose race I couldn't recognize were riding the wyverns.

Finally, the players put their brains in gear and scattered in all directions. No one was stupid enough to take a fiery shower.

The Ravens attempted to take cover behind the limestone outcrops quite common on these little islands. Unfortunately, it was a bad choice. Limestone has a tendency to explode when exposed to sources of rapid uneven heat. And that's exactly what it did, showering the area with razor-sharp rock fragments.

Steered by their impassive riders, the wyverns soared back up, banking into a new attack.

Enea cast a Fire Shield. She hadn't lost her cool. She'd even managed to read the creatures' levels. Apparently, this group was quite doable for us.

"Run to the tents!" I shouted.

The next moment a new gust of fire pummeled the island. Players screamed in agony. Some had been burned, others wounded by the rock shrapnel. Fire raged everywhere — but the fabric tents, true to their digital nature, stood unharmed under its scorching breath.

The only way to avoid a respawn would be by shamefully escaping to one's own personal sanctuary. Still, not many approved of this option. About a third of all Ravens had stayed put and faced the enemy, placing their hopes in their numerical advantage.

The fence around me burst into flames. The raging torrent of fire knocked Allan off his feet.

"Heal him!" I shouted.

Enea and I seemed to be the only ones who'd kept their cool in the surrounding chaos.

Alpha the Black Mantis took off from her shoulder and headed for the top of a lone cliff, maneuvering among the dying tongues of flame. Once on the cliff, he emitted a chirruping noise. His hard underwings fluttered as if sending a signal to someone.

In the meantime, the riders had regained

control of the wyverns and forced them to soar back up.

I kept a watchful eye on the enemy. My Observation Skills ability allowed me to read their tags.

A shiver ran down my spine.

Reapers.

Their levels weren't high. The Reapers themselves were the least of our problems at the moment. The fiery breath of their mounts was the main danger as they resumed their attack, nosediving toward the little island jam-packed with people.

Enea met them with two bolts of lightning cast with both hands.

A crit! The wyverns' leader jerked and listed on one wing, then began to drop. Its Reaper rider lost his balance and fell from the saddle, crashing into the quagmire.

Sensing its sudden freedom, the wyvern spread its wings and shot up, barely avoiding a collision with the ground.

The rest of the flock scattered across the sky; even their powerful reins which made up an integral part of their bodies had failed to keep them in check. With a thunderous roar, the wyverns ignored their riders' desperate tugging and darted every which way across the sky, barely missing the treetops.

* * *

Thanks to Enea, we'd managed to repel the first attack.

Many of the Ravens had proven to be fearless warriors ready to fight till the bitter end. Still, at the moment they lacked a united command which meant they were basically doomed.

The Reapers weren't going to leave us alone now. The prey was too sweet.

Allan was squirming on the ground, his clothes smoldering, his skin covered in blisters. Nobody had healed him.

I darted toward him with a vial in my hands.

As I gave it to him, I took a look around. The wyverns had regrouped over the forest and were now heading back toward the island. There were three of them left now. The riderless one was already disappearing beyond the horizon.

Which meant that they weren't mounts at all. They had been captured and enslaved.

"Archers, aim at the riders!" I strained my voice over the crowd. I was forced to shout because I had no access to their battle chat. "Wizards and healers, wake up! What's wrong with you? Cast fire protection and take care of the wounded! Warriors, to me, now!"

They froze in shock and disbelief with my audacity. Reluctantly they obeyed.

The wyverns were almost upon us. They'd learned Enea's lesson and were now flying low in extended line, their wings almost touching, about to scorch the island with one massive fire attack.

"Listen to him!" Allan croaked. Even though in shock and unable to scramble to his feet, he had the wisdom to delegate command to me.

There were about thirty of us left, those who hadn't cowered in tents despite all the pain and fear they'd just sampled. Three wizards and five archers; the rest were warriors.

Not good.

Bowstrings sang. Their archers were slow. No comparison to Arwan with his natural skill. Their bows weren't that special, either. Still, one of the wyverns shrank away to the side, breaking their formation. It also breathed fire too early, evaporating the swamp and forcing local hydras and other moor creatures to scramble to firmer ground.

"Close shields!"

This time they obeyed ungrudgingly. Their ranks bristled with spears. Enea stayed with the wizards in the rear, casting fire and damage resistance buffs while looking around desperately for her pet.

Alpha was gone!

The wyverns were almost upon us. Black smoke trailed over the island. All the grass had been scorched. Ashes swirled in the air.

Finally, I got access to the clan's local network.

"We need to kill the riders," I said, distributing the targets.

Only the bravest and most desperate stood next to me now shoulder to shoulder. These were warriors and wizards with plenty of gaming experience between them.

The air quivered in front of us, marking the boundary of the magic shield. It might protect us from the torrent of flames, even if only momentarily.

The wyverns breathed fire. Their riders reined them in by tugging on the fleshy reins, apparently unwilling to descend onto our ranks that bristled with steel. The wyverns' heavy wingbeats created gusts of scorching hot wind — but we stood unscathed through this first attack.

On my command, we showered the Reapers with spears. One rider was pinned to the ground but the others had reacted fast enough to rear up their monstrous mounts.

Our protection expired. The riderless wyvern ran amok. It stretched out its neck, lunged at our ranks and snatched a warrior up in its predatory jaws. Its powerful tail swept the place clean of any remaining vegetation. Smoldering tree trunks broke like matchsticks, adding the sweet odor of chipped

---

wood to the acrid stench of smoke.

Battle continued on the ground. Two Reapers forced their mounts to assault us while we backed off slowly without breaking ranks, covering up with our shields and only dealing damage when we had the opportunity.

We wouldn't last long this way. We needed to do something radical.

"Wizards, keep overhealing!" I shouted.

Normally, overhealing is considered the sign of a hapless, clumsy healer. But now there was no way we could calculate the incoming damage. Also, I kept worrying about our pain thresholds, knowing that none of the Ravens was used to their implants. The moment a warrior's health dropped below 70%, he or she would go into shock through pain.

At least I had some good skills in my Neuro development branch which allowed me to attack a wyvern and survive.

In the meantime, our containment tactic began to sag. Even though our shields still absorbed a lot of the incoming fire damage, warriors were becoming exhausted while the enemy's psychological pressure kept growing.

Controlled by their riders, the wyverns tirelessly attacked us again and again, their necks outstretched, their powerful talons ploughing up the charred earth.

"Keep your formation! Allan, are you better

now? Take command!"

Time for me to jump into action. We couldn't hold the island on our own — nor could we expect help from anywhere. The only way we could turn the tide in our favor was by killing the Reapers themselves. Once they were out, the wyverns wouldn't be able to maintain coordination.

Our wizards were low on mana. They'd already run out of vials — and the natural regeneration of mental energy took too long.

By now, hydras had climbed out of the boiling quagmire onto the island's shallow shores, furiously attacking everything within sight. The wyverns became distracted by this new threat.

Great timing. This was our chance.

I lunged forward, leaving the ranks. Breathing fire, the nearest wyvern craned its neck toward me, its teeth chattering, as it tried to grab and swallow me.

Its jaws snapped shut around thin air. I was already standing behind its back.

The monster kept swishing its tail, sweeping away the surviving hydras. I knew better than to play that game. Instead, I jumped up and grabbed on to one of the bony spikes lining the wyvern's spine.

I climbed up onto its back and found myself within mere feet from its rider. I struggled to keep my balance as the wyvern's powerful muscles rippled under my feet.

The Reaper noticed me. He used his dagger to slice through the leather straps which kept him in the saddle, then swung round.

That was all he'd had time to do. His severed arm hung listlessly, still grabbing the reins. Sensing its freedom, the wyvern reared up.

I crashed to the ground and rolled aside, having lost 30% life. Immediately I jumped back to my feet and raised my shield as the riderless wyvern flew into a blind rage, aggroing everyone in sight.

A bolt of lightning and a few arrows distracted it somewhat, sobering its fury.

Not that it had helped us a lot. By now, only one of the wyverns still had a rider but the others were just as lethal in their uncontrollable blind rage.

My solo performance had impressed the Ravens but hadn't changed the course of the battle that much. Unlike the wyvern who'd been wounded first, the others showed no intention of fleeing the battlefield and were bent on destroying everything around them.

Our small group held a position between two clusters of cliffs on the edge of the island. Our tents stood unscathed among all the smoke, soot and tongues of fire. Hydras kept climbing out onto the shore *en masse,* driven out by the unbearable heat of the boiling water.

The remaining Reaper must have decided to put an end to us. Raising clouds of ash, his wyvern ploughed its way through the hydras that chanced in its path and came directly for me, growling and stretching out its long neck.

Its broken right wing dragged behind it. Its thick hide was bleeding. The broken shafts of spears peeped from its wounds.

An even more threatening growl came from behind me. With a rustling noise, a swell surged over the shore.

I swung round just in time. An Ancient Wyvern waded its way across the quagmire, wounded and exhausted — a dreadful monster which made all the others pale into insignificance.

Level 190!

Its harness was in tatters. The lower half of its rider's body still hung in the saddle. Someone must have cleft him in two with one clean sweep.

A loud rustling sound added to the surrounding noise.

"Alpha!" Enea exclaimed with relief.

A whole swarm of Black Mantises was approaching us from the opposite side of the island.

The quagmire heaved.

Something indescribable stirred in its depths. This must have been the combat avatar of the unknown top-level demon we'd sighted earlier.

The creature's leathery wings were singed, its body covered in rotting algae. Black blood poured down its armor ripped apart by powerful claws.

A weak protection aura still flickered deep inside the demon's wounds. The monster's eyes glowed.

So that's who the Ancient Wyvern was after!

Finally, the giant demon scrambled to the shore where it collapsed to its knees. Leaning on a heavily indented sword, the creature attempted to struggle back to its feet.

A familiar weak voice touched my mind,

"Alex, help me... I'm dying..."

"Christa?!"

She collapsed to one side in a heap, her fiery eyes fixed on me, begging and hopeful.

* * *

Smoke trailed over the scorched ground.

Raising a powerful wake, the Ancient Wyvern waded knee-high to the shore. Even with the remaining measly 1% health, the wounded monster would make quick work of us the moment it reached the ground.

The Black Mantises descended upon the island in a merciless swarm, stinging the mobs indiscriminately and aiming for their eyes. The hydras hissed their desperation. The wyverns squawked in alarm.

Christa's life had been bled dry. Her hp bar was barely flickering. And we had nothing to heal her with! Regular healing magic and elixirs didn't work on demons, did they?

"Alex, do something!" Enea cried out. "Can't you use Dark Regeneration? That should work!"

She was right. I'd never had the chance to use the uncategorized spell I'd studied while purging Rion's dungeons. Averse as I was to using dark magic, this indeed was Christa's only chance.

I pointed at the last Reaper-controlled wyvern. "Contain it!"

Blinded as the creature was by the Mantises' neurotoxins, its rider held on to the reins, showing no intention of giving up.

By now, the island was sheer Bedlam. The hydras convulsed, throwing long tentacles in all directions. The wyverns breathed tongues of fire and swished their tails, clawing the ground and overturning giant rocks.

The surviving Ravens chose the last-ditch defense without attempting to attack. I understood them. Their wizards had no mana left, their warriors exhausted, scared and demoralized. None of them had expected to end up in a slaughter like this.

They'd heard my order, however, and

immediately jumped into action. Crossbows began snapping without any system, their poisoned bolts piercing the wyvern's thick hide. The Reaper must have gotten his fair share too, judging by his spinning incoming damage counter.

The Ravens had managed to distract the monsters from me. No idea for how long. Not that it mattered, really. Everything was going to happen in the next few seconds before the monstrous Ancient Wyvern reached the shore.

Enea ported to me.

"Come on, Alex!" she gasped impatiently without taking her eyes off the bleeding Christa. "Forget everything, just do it!"

Instinctively my lips went cold. The words of the ancient spell fell from them like clouds of freezing mist. I felt enveloped in subzero cold.

Darkness entered my mind. Every fiber of my soul strained, resisting it, then snapping one by one.

I looked over the area, selecting enemy targets. I then struggled to turn my frozen neck and highlighted Christa as the object in need of healing.

A wall of black flames arose around me.

The earth began to tremor, its rocky surface rippling. The dark runes which sealed the spell materialized momentarily in the air, then crumbled to ashes.

Cold spread over my chest as if I'd been hit with an ice spear.

Enea turned pale. The precious stone topping her Staff of a Hydra pulsated madly, protecting its owner from dark uncategorized magic.

Darkness shot out in all directions in sharp, predatory strokes, hitting the dozen targets I'd selected and turning them into clouds of crimson spray. The red haze reached out for Christa and enveloped her, pouring into her terrible wounds.

Everybody froze as the evil magic flooded over them, drenching their bodies in an otherworldly cold. You know it when you feel it.

Even the Reaper momentarily lost control of his wyvern, releasing the reins and immediately paying the price. Blinded by the neurotoxin, the monster craned its long neck and sank its teeth into his throat, taking its unbridled fury out on its rider.

Christa's body convulsed.

In the meantime, the Ancient Wyvern had scrambled out onto the shore. It couldn't fly anymore. Its wings were broken; a bloodied hole gaped in place of its left eye. Its life was deep in the red. But even in this state the monster was lethal, capable of sending any of us back to our respective respawn points with a single blow.

Groaning, Christa struggled to her feet.

Her hp bar quivered and began to grow. Her

---

wounds were still horrifying even in her current Infernal avatar. Her armor was mangled. Thick black blood trickled down fingers that still clenched the darkness-enveloped sword.

The fiery aura filling her wounds gleamed marginally brighter, its crimson glow seeping through the cracks in her mangled armor.

The Ancient Wyvern hissed its disappointment. It had nowhere to run. It may have expected an easy prey but it now faced an opponent every bit as powerful as itself.

The Wyvern's long neck shot out, its jaws spewing a jet of fire. Christa mini-ported out of its path and materialized by the monster's side, investing all of her remaining strength into a series of merciless blows.

The Wyvern's severed head went flying into the boiling bog. Its enormous bulk convulsed, then stopped moving.

* * *

The incinerated island was strewn with the dead players' avatars. Some had been lucky enough to end up back at their respawn points, leaving behind cloth bundles with their possessions. They'd proven resilient enough to survive the agony of being burned alive.

The bluish haze of loose neurograms still

---

hung over the island. In the absence of Reapers, there was no one here to absorb them. The fine mist of unlived lives was slowly dissipating, disappearing without a trace in the digital space of the Crystal Sphere.

Enea looked around herself in horror. Her father had been right all along. Virtual reality had changed irreversibly, crumbling under the Reapers' attacks.

The skin on the nape of my neck erupted in goosebumps. I was trapped in this 100% authenticity. At least one-third of the Raven raid wasn't going to resurrect, ever.

They'd died for real. Burned alive.

The lump in my throat grew bigger as the fact began to sink in.

What the hell was going on? What on earth had prompted the corporation to introduce neuroimplants if they already knew that inexperienced players couldn't survive their effects?

I felt shell-shocked. My head buzzed. The belated realization of the significance of what had just happened was akin to a crushing blow.

Back at the market square in Agrion I hadn't felt anything like this. That day, my mind had shut down, refusing to accept all the traumatic information. My lack of experience had suggested an unlucky coincidence, a play of chance rather than the advent of a new order.

The surviving Ravens looked around themselves, unable to believe it was over.

Christa staggered away from the water's edge. With a practiced hand, she drew a few symbols on the ground, then watched them explode into tiny tongues of black flames.

A thick haze enveloped her. When it had dispersed, we saw an ordinary girl, dark-skinned and clad in a fine suit of leather armor. She looked nothing like a demon.

The tag over her head wasn't legible. She'd changed a lot since our last meeting. She didn't flash her Dark affiliation around anymore.

Her change of avatar hadn't healed her wounds, though. She took a couple of tentative steps, then slumped onto a hillock, groaning and squirming with pain.

"Here," Enea walked over to her and gave her a hug, whispering in her ear as if the two were the best of friends.

Christa's dull stare warmed. A weak smile fluttered on her lips. She turned to me and mouthed a silent thankyou, reviving my soul and her own as she began to thaw out after the lethal combat.

My own chest too began to thaw as I gradually recovered from using uncategorized magic. The Founders' spells required the supreme effort from my entire body.

The pristine white raid tents stood defiant amid all the desolation. No one was leaving them. Apparently, those who'd found refuge inside had no idea the danger was already over.

Allan froze over Urgorn's charred body. I could understand him. Instead of a cloth bundle containing a fellow player's stuff, he was now faced with his mangled corpse, burned to cinders and trampled into the ground by the wyverns.

"What does that mean?" he asked in a muffled voice without turning his head.

"Your friend is dead. I'm very sorry."

Slowly he turned. His eyes glowed with madness.

"I did try to warn you, man," I said. "You didn't believe me. I'm really sorry. We can't do anything now. If you think you can listen to reason, get your men together and follow us back to Rion. At least they'll be safe there. And then you can decide whether you'd like to stay or go back to your own castle."

The swarm of Black Mantises which had so promptly arrived to our rescue circled a few times over the island. Then it scattered as Alpha's brethren went about their business.

* * *

"The second wave should be coming now," Christa's voice broke the depressing silence.

"We've killed them all!" Enea snapped, shaking. "None of them got away!"

"The Reapers don't attack in small groups anymore. Those on the wyverns were after me," Christa explained. "They saw me and followed. There were more of them on horseback. I saw them as I flew past."

She reminded me of White for some reason. Like him, Christa had managed to survive in this evolving world which had left an indelible stamp on her.

"The duckboards can't support their weight," Enea objected. She seemed so eager to believe that at least today's problems were over.

"They'll walk. Nothing can stop them when they're on the prowl."

"How did *you* get here?" I asked before I could stop myself.

"I was looking for you. All of you. I have a message from Bors — Mr. Borisov."

"You? No way! Do you know him?"

"Yes. He once helped me with a rather sensitive problem. A couple of weeks ago he found me and asked me to return the favor. He wanted me to give you this scroll as soon as the Agrion cluster was unblocked. Here, take it."

She handed me a rolled-up sheet of parchment, sealed and tied with a length of string.

"What is it?" I asked. "A letter? A spell?"

"I've no idea. In any case, whatever you decide to do, you'd better do it quick. The Reapers will be here in a moment."

"I'm not leaving the others behind!"

"Fair enough. I think I'm gonna stay too. You can use my help. Do you mind?"

"Your help will be most appreciated."

"You think you can repeat your Dark Regeneration trick?"

"Unfortunately, no. It has a two-hour cooldown."

"My combat avatar is out of the question, then. Never mind. I've used up all my abilities on that Ancient Wyvern, anyway. I'll stay as I am now. That way at least I can be healed."

I cast another glance over the scorched island. Allan had stopped halfway to the tents and was crouching on the shoreline staring into the dark water, trying to digest everything that had just happened.

His warriors and wizards didn't look much better. We would have to send them to the castle. They wouldn't survive a second combat.

"Enea, I'd like you to cast a Magic Eye and keep the area under its surveillance," I put Christa's scroll away into my bag and contacted the castle. "Lethmiel? I want you to cast a cargo portal to the Ravens' camp. Archie, sound the call to action stations!"

The cargo portal burst forth in bright circles of fiery magic symbols, blowing away the ash.

Archie, Arwan and White were the first to arrive. Enea's father took in the blackened panorama and looked around, searching for his daughter. Having seen her, he strode toward us. "What the hell happened here?"

"Reapers," I said. "On wyverns' backs."

"Any get away?"

"No. But another group on horseback has been sighted approaching the moors."

"Who saw them?"

"This is Christa," I said. "She can tell you about it."

I turned to the other two, "Arch, I need you to take care of the perimeter. Post your warriors so that all the duckboards are covered. Arwan, get your hunters to skin all the dead hydras. There're at least thirty of them lying on the beach."

Another portal flashed open in surges of golden light. This time it was Platinus, followed by a group of peasants with large wicker baskets on their backs.

Ignoring the blood-curdling scene, Platinus beelined for the Ancient Wyvern, fully intending to check it for any rare ingredients.

Having finished dishing out the most pressing orders, I walked over to the surviving Ravens.

"You put up an excellent fight," I told them. "It's enough for today. I want you to port out to Rion. A Blood Elf will receive you and issue you some tents. His name is Lethmiel. He'll show you where to set up camp."

"How about the others?"

"I'm taking care of them."

"No, you aren't. You're collecting our loot."

I gave the warrior a long look. "Each hydra skin we're farming now might save someone's life tomorrow. Take my advice and go to Rion. Get some rest. If someone's worried about their share of the loot, we can always discuss it when I'm back."

"Are we your prisoners?"

"Please. What's wrong with you, guys? We've got another group of defective mobs coming this way. Anyone willing to stay and help us defend the island?"

The Ravens grew quiet. They'd have enough traumatic experiences for one day.

"Very well," they mumbled. "We're leaving."

Their disorderly ranks shuffled toward the portal.

White was busy discussing something with Christa. Enea was helping Iskandar. Our warriors had split into groups guarding parts of the shore where the duckboards were relatively intact.

Allan was sitting apathetically on the hillock. He hadn't put his armor back on.

I walked over to him. "Any ideas how we might lure the others out of the tents?"

A player's personal tent is their safe zone which guarantees their immunity for twenty-four hours. The Reapers were bound to know this, so they would simply stay put and wait till it expired. Which meant we would have to defend the island all along. And we couldn't afford to keep fighting for twenty-four hours.

"Allan? Wake up!" I gave him a light shake. "You think you can close the camp via the clan interface?"

"Probably. I've never done it before."

"Well, do it, then! Get everybody out of the tents! Tell them to pick up the respawned players' stuff and port to Rion. The rest we can discuss later once the danger's gone."

CHAPTER THREE

THE CRYSTAL SPHERE
RION CASTLE

FTER THE TURBULENT EVENTS of the last few days, we'd entered a period of relative quiet. Even the goblins had decided to give it a break. Once we'd moved the local villagers to the castle, the cheeky little mobs had nobody to pester anymore. Before, they used to rip the peasants' fishing nets and steal the fish or bring a train of hydras to a village — but now the moors around Rion were completely deserted apart from an occasional Elven hunters' raid — and goblins knew better than to mess with them.

The Battle of Chaffinch Creek had quickly become a breeding ground of the most incredible rumors. Already the following day, local taverns had filled with stories of my supposed duel with Allan, followed by the Ravens' defeat and the invasion of wyvern-riding demons who were then completely eradicated by a small group of Rion warriors.

Dimian puffed his chest out with pride. He was now the most desired guest in the whole of the city, enjoying dinner invitations from high-standing NPCs who couldn't wait to hear every detail of the recent events.

I read him the riot act, telling him to keep his lips sealed. As if! He stood his ground, referring to all the good deals he'd struck with Agrion's officials thanks to a few largely exaggerated tales of Enea's and my adventures. Indeed, our warehouses were rapidly filling with everything we might need for a siege.

Finally, I gave up. Let them gossip. Especially because some devil-may-care players had found their way to Chaffinch Creek and uploaded a video of the incinerated island complete with vultures feasting on the wyverns' rotting carcasses.

Our clan's ranking had grown a bit. New applicants had begun to trickle in again, thoroughly vetted by Archie, Iskandar and Rodrigo.

Today, our main cadre had sworn the Blood Oath.

Enea and I had meticulously reconstructed

every detail of this ancient ritual. The pressing threat of the Reapers' advance had accelerated our research. As a result, we'd lost 6% of our clan members who'd openly chickened out, unwilling to take the oath even though it didn't bind anyone to Rion in the slightest. No one was obliged to live here or restrict his or her travels.

Still, the prospects of lifelong debuffs in case of treason had resulted in this unavoidable 6% dropout rate. Which, if the truth were known, did us a lot of good.

The Raven clan had 153 survivors. We'd buried the avatars of the 24 dead players on a small island not far from the castle.

The next morning after the battle, Allan wanted to talk to me.

"I think we're deep in it," he said. "You know anyone we can turn to?"

"What do you mean?"

"I sent a message to the admins. No one replied. We want to quit the experiment, all of us. I know you have friends among Infosystems workers. I'd like you to help us cancel our contracts."

"I'm afraid I can't do that."

He cast me a frowned look. "Are you with them?"

"No, I'm not. My Logout button is blocked, too. There's no special treatment for me, if that's what you mean. That's not the problem. I think the corporation has lost control over the Crystal Sphere. We're on our own now."

"Impossible!" he said. "That's not what we were told! They said that the real world was becoming unfit for human habitation. They were moving us here while they were demolishing the old cities and building new ones!"

"Nonsense. Ask White if you don't believe me. Or find someone with a working Logout button. No one's building new cities, let alone demolishing the old ones. They're falling into decay even as we speak."

He stared blankly at me. "What's the point?"

How could I explain? I had no real evidence. And I couldn't very well show my mind expander video footage to all and sundry, either. I'd seen the truth twice in its most painful and agonizing form — plus I knew the bits of intel that White had shared with me — and still I couldn't quite wrap my head around it.

All I knew was that something disastrous had happened on planet Earth. But still I had no idea what that had got to do with luring the entire population into the mushrooming in-mode centers.

I offered Allan a rolled-up sheet of parchment.

"What's that?"

"This is a mass teleport scroll with Rion's coordinates already entered. A guest portal, naturally. It's set up on the small island by the barbican."

"Why are you giving me this?"

"Just in case. You never know."

"Bullshit. Two clans sharing one castle? Don't be ridiculous."

That morning, neither of us had understood the other.

I couldn't blame Allan, really. His neuroimplant had drastically changed his outlook.

"The offer still stands," I said. "Whenever you change your minds, there's plenty of space in Rion. Are were friends now?" I proffered my hand.

He returned my handshake. "Sure. Thanks for coming to our rescue," he turned round and headed for the Ravens' tents.

A new system message appeared in my interface,

Quest alert: The Enemy of my Enemy. Quest modified!

Quest type: Normal, Diplomatic

Don't engage in any hostile acts against the clan of Ravens.

Reward: a potential ally who might still take your side in need and battle the Reapers with you.

Deadline: none

* * *

I found Enea poring over ancient manuscripts.

"I woke up but you weren't there," she said.

"I spoke to Allan."

"And?"

"He plays his cards close, that one. He wants to get rid of the implant and go back to the real world. He didn't even listen to me. When I offered them to stay in Rion as an independent clan, he refused point blank. They're breaking camp now."

"Shame," Enea sighed. "Still, we can't force them to stay. Don't worry about them. They can get back home safely and quickly by using stationary portals. In any case, the feud between our two clans is over, and that's already a lot. Would you like some breakfast? Did you get the chance to take a look at Christa's scroll?"

"Not yet. We can do it together now."

"You're not even asking me about her."

"If she wants to stay in Rion, I don't mind. But that's her decision. A demon of her caliber is a great addition to our garrison."

"Alex, please. She's not a demon anymore, can't you see? She may have kept her combat avatar, but that's the extent of it. She's changed a lot."

I sat down at the table. "How do you know?"

She smiled. "We spent some time in chat this morning. Come on now, show me the scroll," she hurried to change the subject.

Admittedly, my heart missed a beat when I broke the seal.

The dry sealing wax snapped, crumbling in my fingers. No magic visual effects followed. I unfolded the scroll.

Enea leaned over my shoulder. A loose lock of her hair tickled my cheek.

"That's weird," she sounded disappointed.

Indeed, Borisov's last message hadn't lived up to our expectations. The parchment was filled with hurriedly scribbled, uneven columns of numbers which appeared to be some kind of coordinates, followed by a long list of codes and the hasty postscript below,

Alex,

You can only use this in the direst emergency. Hold on. I'm trying to fix things.

I opened my map-making app and entered the coordinates.

My mind expander zoned out, going through its map database of the Crystal Sphere, then reported the search result,

No matches found
The coordinates you provided do not exist

I sighed. "This makes no sense."

"I don't think he would've sent you something if it made no sense," Enea said. "Mind if I make a copy? I'll think about it when I have a moment. You don't think it could be some new location which isn't marked on the maps yet?"

"Even so, the marker itself should show on the map, even if it's covered in the 'mist of war'. But it says that the coordinates themselves don't exist!"

"Could it be a typo? What if Borisov misspelled the numbers?"

"I'll try," I started a partial match search. Its progress bar didn't even budge although I could sense the growing pressure on my mind from the map-making app processing data.

Someone delicately knocked on the door.

"Come in," Enea switched off the shield.

"A very good morning to you," Dimian faltered in the doorway, realizing we were having breakfast.

"Come and sit down with us," I said. "Would you like some coffee?"

"I'd rather have some water," Dimian replied cautiously. He wasn't really used to all these new exotic drinks from overseas. He probably wondered how we managed to get them by bypassing the trade agency.

"So, what brings you here?" I asked, pouring

some water for him. I wasn't in the mood to explain that it was Platinus who'd developed the coffee formula. That would scare the hell out of him. Dimian never trusted alchemy, only using a few tried and tested old elixirs.

"The shops are running out of stock," he complained. "New people keep arriving, and it takes ages for supply caravans to get here."

"So how can we help you?" Enea asked. "The nearest sea port is five days away. We can't change that."

"Oh yes we can!"

I already knew what he was driving at. "Come on, spit it out. Just don't expect us to use teleport scrolls. They're only for emergencies. It's up to you to handle regular deliveries."

"I understand that. They probably cost a fortune. I have another idea. There's an old road, the Ogres Road. It's two days shorter. It fell out of use, though."

"Why?"

"Because of the ogres. It was a long time ago. My grandfather was still young. They killed travelers and robbed caravans. Nobody could do anything about it. That area is very rocky with plenty of cliffs and caves."

"Has anything changed now?" Enea asked.

"My father used to tell me that all the monsters were dead. Some wizard had sent a plague upon them. I was still a little boy when it happened. But the road fell out of use."

"Why?"

"Why do you think? It's scary!" he fumbled with his beard. "Some are afraid of the ogres, others of the plague. Still, those who occasionally use it come back in one piece. So I thought, what if we check it out?"

"Good idea. Now tell me, what's the catch? Couldn't you just ask the travelers themselves?"

"I did. They say the ogres are gone. Some old bones lying around, that's all. There's another problem. The road goes past Warblerford. There used to be a bridge there, but not anymore. It was swept away during the last spring flood. Whenever the villagers need to cross to the other side, they use the ford but it's too narrow and the current is strong. A loaded cart won't get across there. And if we cross by boat, we'll lose a whole day just by loading and unloading. We need to restore the bridge."

"And what do the Agrion authorities think about it?" I asked.

"They don't care, do they? If the road is restored, they'll have to ensure the caravans' safety. Too much extra work for the city."

I glanced at the map. A chain of relatively safe low-level locations lay between the Toxic Moors and Warblerford. There was indeed an old road there which went past the moors and led directly to Agrion.

"You can restore it, I know!" Dimian continued, hinting heavily at my uncategorized magic. "It'll only take you an hour. And it would mean the world to us. All the profits we lose!"

"He's right," Enea agreed. "The two days saved on each trip would pay for the works. If Agrion's not interested, it's their problem. We, however, could gain a lot."

"Okay," I agreed. "Let's go there and see for ourselves. The Warbler is a wide river, as far as I remember. We could check out the work and see if we're up to it."

* * *

The stationary teleport brought us to the outskirts of Warblerford, not far from the ford itself. This was near the local inn where I'd met up with Enea once.

That's right. Here was the small impromptu market — and next to it, a guards' post alongside some stacks of logs. It looked like they were indeed going to build a bridge here.

"It's so quiet," Dimian looked anxiously around.

"Where is everybody?" Enea echoed.

The market was deserted, and so was the river bank. No guards had been posted. The place looked dead.

Our bank of the River Warbler was high and steep; the opposite, flat, with forest encroaching on the waterline. I could make out a few logged clearings in the distance.

The road in question cut through the forest, disappearing by some cliffs which marked the beginning of the bordering location.

And the sky... I didn't like it at all. Cloudless on our side, it was gloomy and overcast with thunderclouds on the other. Gusts of strong cold wind rippled the water on the opposite bank.

"Go back," I told Dimian.

He looked around him uncomfortably. "How about you?"

"We'll check the area. Come on, quick, go back to the portal!"

"Do you want me to send someone to help you?"

I gave it some thought. Enea's father had left the castle early that morning in search of his group, having promised to be back before nightfall. Archie had taken the clan's combat section to the moors for a bit of leveling. There were no players left in the castle, only NPCs.

"It's all right," I said. "We'll manage."

"I'll be off, then," Dimian warily hurried over to the portal.

The only street of the village was equally

deserted. A biting wind was raising dust, rustling the leaves and swinging the creaky sign saying *The Ford Inn*.

Enea let Alpha out. The Black Mantis had no problem in finding a crack in one of the inn's still-locked doors and shutters. He crawled inside and began streaming us his vision of the place. The weird-colored mosaic picture wasn't easy to work out but the main thing was clear: the inn was empty and in perfect order.

We found the same scenario in the other houses. No trace of fighting, furniture undisturbed — but all the village NPCs had vanished without a trace.

In the meantime, the weather on the other bank had grown worse. The heavy thunderclouds flashed with unusual discharges which didn't resemble lightning. Could it be magic?

Enea and I exchanged glances. There was no cheerful curiosity in her eyes this time, only a fleeting trace of fear.

"We need to take a closer look," she said.

I remembered my Blood Ties ability which allowed me to instantly transport to Rion once every seven days. "If the going gets tough, grab my hand and hold it tight. Whatever you do, don't let it go," I told her.

"Very well. Let's just wait till Alpha comes back."

Unlike ordinary pets, Alpha the Black Mantis couldn't be summoned or unsummoned. He was always by his mistress' side.

This time we called him twice — but to no avail. Alpha hovered around the village's well, stubbornly refusing to come. We had to go and get him.

"What do you think you're doing?" Enea began.

Alpha didn't even turn his head. He kept peeking into the well, scratching his legs nervously against the stonework.

"Alex, look! This is players' stuff!"

The grass around the well was wilted and trampled down by constant use. Several identical pieces of white cloth lay trodden into it.

Those were players' bundles, empty.

Normally when a player is killed, he or she goes back to their respawn point leaving a bundle with their possessions behind. The player then has twelve hours to return to the scene and pick up the bundle before it disappears. The only exception is during PvP fights when the winner gets access to the loser's possessions straight away.

Whatever had happened here? I counted seven empty bundles.

Enea looked into the well and turned pale. "Alex!"

I was next to her in a flash. "What is it?"

"Help..." a weak voice echoed inside the well.

I looked down but couldn't see anything at first. The taut rope of the well disappeared into the clouds of thick swirling fog.

The rope jolted. The faint sound of metal hitting stone came from below.

"Pull!" Enea grabbed the broken handle of the withered old crank.

"No! Wait! Can't you see the rope is almost worn through? We'd better cast Levitation!"

The spell didn't work, though. It shattered against the swirling haze, exploding in cascades of special effects.

I lay on my stomach on the edge of the well and tried to reach out for the part of the rope which hadn't rubbed against the stone. I grabbed it with both my hands and pulled hard.

It was heavy. The sounds of metal screeching against stone grew closer. Finally, a disheveled head appeared from the mist, followed by its shoulders.

The player's deformed steel suit of armor was rather plain — the kind preferred by newb warriors — and already touched by rust. How long had he spent there — two days, three? Or was the mist so corrosive?

All these thoughts flashed through my mind as I tugged at the rope praying it wouldn't break.

Enea did well. She kept her cool. The

moment the torso of the newb knight peeked through the mist, she cast another Levitation. This time it sort of worked, taking some of the weight off the rope. The kid, too, cheered up and tried to help us, fending himself off the walls of the well with his steel greaves.

We pulled him out.

The player rolled over the well's edge and collapsed heavily onto the wilted grass. He lay there groaning, unable to move with fatigue.

Lloyd. Level 10. Warrior

We turned him over on his back. The kid's face was pale, his eyes hollow, his lips chapped. The Exhaustion icon flashed red in his name tag.

"I'm cold," he wheezed.

Enea moistened his lips with a healing elixir. The kid gulped. Color began to return to his cheeks.

"That's better," Enea supported his head. "Drink it slowly... that's good."

I perched myself on the edge of the well. "Who did this to you?"

"You'd better get down, man..."

"Don't worry. I'm not gonna fall in."

"It's the mist... it syphons your strength..."

"Okay, okay," I rose, tied some string around the neck of an empty vial and lowered it into the mist, then pulled it out and put the stopper in. Platinus would know what to do with it.

"You didn't answer my question," I said. "What happened here?"

"The villagers..." Lloyd said thickly. "They seized all the players who were in the inn and threw them down the well. I grabbed at the rope... No idea how long I spent there. I tried to climb out bracing my legs against the walls but I couldn't."

"How about the others?"

"They're all down there. The fog has bled them dry."

"Why did the NPCs attack you?"

"No idea! They wanted to sacrifice us to some Reapers, whatever that's supposed to mean. That's all I understood from it. This is one hell of a glitch. They seemed completely deranged. They said, *'Let's throw them in the well and head over to the Ogres Road. If the Reapers accept the sacrifice, they'll meet us in the forest and escort us.'*"

"Escort them where?"

"No idea. The location ends there by the cliffs, doesn't it? Also, they mentioned some guy called Dietrich. Apparently, whoever wants to join his army has to offer a sacrifice first."

* * *

"Do you have a place to stay?" Enea asked.

"No idea. The inn is closed. The Logout button is blocked, just as the in-mode rental contract says," he cast a look around. "I'm not in the mood to seek new adventures, to tell you the truth. Could I stay with you for a while?" he asked, apparently impressed by our levels.

"You think we could take him to Rion?" Enea whispered in my ear.

"I don't know. What if he's a Reaper agent? Or, God forbid, a Harvester?"

"I don't think so. He's only level 10. He seems okay."

"How lucky does one need to be to grab at a conveniently hanging rope to stop one's fall?"

"Please don't be so... so uncharitable. The kid is what, fifteen years old? Not even."

"Very well. Let's go back to the castle and bring reinforcements. It's too dangerous to continue on our own."

"Do you want to call up a raid?"

"Oh, no. Raids are too loud. A small group will be enough."

"Are you talking about me?" Lloyd asked bluntly.

He was standing aside, crestfallen. Even Alpha seemed to cast sympathetic glances at him. The kid had had it tough. I wouldn't have survived one hour down that well.

"Have you ever heard of Rion Castle?" I asked him.

He perked up. "Sure!"

"You can come with us. We have strict discipline, though. You'll have to spend some time in a tent by the castle wall. No one can get inside without a thorough vetting."

"I don't mind. I've got nowhere to go, anyway. All I need is grab a bite to eat, get warm and get some sleep."

How quickly things had changed in the virtual world! Before, no one used to give a damn about neither food nor sleep.

Enea smiled. "This I can promise. Let's go to the portal now. Don't be afraid."

"You're talking to me as if I'm a little kid," he said.

"Sorry. How old are you, fifteen?"

"I'm twelve. So what?"

Enea frowned like a schoolteacher. "And where are your parents?"

The preteen warrior sniffled. "They're on an expedition studying Jupiter's moons. They rented this in-mode for me. Tell me, is it true that Rion Castle is ruled by an uncategorized wizard? Do you know him?"

Enea gave me a wink. "Yeah, sort of. We met him a few times."

"Aren't you afraid of him? They say his girlfriend is a shapeshifter!"

She frowned. "Who told you that?"

"A cleric told us in the inn. This Rion wizard, he fought the Ravens' clan leader. And when he was cornered, she turned into a demon and healed him with Dark Regeneration. There was a battle on the moors like you can't imagine! Demons, goblins, humans... they were all fighting each other."

Enea sniffed. "They don't know what they're talking about! Wretched gossips. Alex is okay, I assure you. He fought an honest fight."

"How do you know?"

"Because I'm that demon they're talking about!"

"No way!" Lloyd slowed down.

"Joke. But you, my friend, are a bit too gullible. Do you really believe everything you hear?"

"Are you kidding me?"

"No, I'm not. There *was* a demon fighting there. Only it was a different girl entirely."

"Wow. Does he have two girlfriends?"

"You talk too much," I took him down a peg.

I still couldn't bring myself to think of that battle. My use of Dark Regeneration had cost me dearly. A sliver of darkness had stuck in my chest like a block of ice, and nothing I could do could melt it. As for the arrival of Christa, that was a different subject entirely.

"Oh, come on," the kid said. "Everybody's talking about them. Lots of people say Alexatis is an NPC. He doesn't belong to any known class!"

Enea frowned. "You meet him first before you speak."

"If you say so. Thanks for saving me."

We stopped a few paces away from the village portal.

The weird weather on the other bank had grown worse. Greenish bolts of lightning forked through the darkness overhanging the old Ogres Road. Snowflakes danced in the unrelenting wind.

"Come on, then, let's go before we freeze to death."

The flash of the portal swallowed us.

* * *

Two hours later, we returned to Warblerford.

This time we'd come prepared. The danger here was much more serious than a couple of stone giants or a gang of highwaymen.

This time we'd taken along only those we could trust.

That meant we couldn't take Arwan with us, unfortunately. He was an NPC himself. As it was, he'd already received a couple of neurograms during my battle with Reguar the Arch Demon. Too risky.

Iskandar caught up with me. "How do we cross the river?"

"We could use the ford, I suppose. But I'd rather take a boat."

"Are there any boats there?"

"There must be. There's a jetty just next to it. You think you could help me? Do you know how to row?"

"Sure."

The village was still deserted, all the NPCs gone without a trace. Three boats rocked on the waves by the jetty.

Rodrigo eyed them with suspicion. "They're falling apart!"

He picked the strongest one and cast a durability spell on it. Lately, we'd been constantly forced to adlib, seeking ways out of a multitude of petty but annoying household problems.

"It doesn't work," he said. "It's still leaking."

"Let me try," Platinus said, climbing into the boat. "We need to bail the water out first."

Archie and I removed our helmets and began helping him scoop out the murky sludge covering the bottom.

"I can see it!" Platinus peered at the bottom, then poured one of his vials onto the damaged place. "Now it'll work!"

While we were fixing the boat, Raoul and Iskandar had fetched some oars and a long pole.

"What's wrong with porting over there?" Togien grumbled. "It's not as if we don't have any scrolls!"

"They'll notice it," Enea replied. "Quite a few wizards can sense the disturbances in the air."

"There's nobody there!" Togien muttered. Grumbling for a dwarf is his life's bread. "I know the Ogres Road. It runs parallel to the river bank. Where the forest ends, there are some cliffs that mark the end of the location. There're a couple of caves there but they're tiny. You can't hide an army in them."

"We'll see," I sat down on the wide bench and inserted the oar into the rowlock.

Iskandar picked up the other oar. Raoul stood on the stern holding the pole. Enea and Rodrigo sat on the bow behind a wicker shield which could serve to protect us from arrows in case of any emergency. Togien and Archie looked watchfully around, crossbows at the ready.

Platinus pushed the boat away from the bank, then jumped in.

We began to row. The current was fast and strong here, so it was quite a challenge. The bank slipped by slowly.

"So what's there?" Iskandar asked nervously when we were halfway through. He didn't feel comfortable sitting with his back to a potential danger.

"Seems okay," Enea replied, peering at the riverside vegetation. "Keep slightly to the left."

Finally, the boat's stern lodged softly in the sand.

Trying to move noiselessly, we climbed out. A nut grove ran along the narrow bank.

Everything was drowned in a thick gray fog. The rubbery silence was unsettling. No birds singing, no leaves rustling. The light breeze seemed unable to shift the heavy, unyielding layers of fog.

The sky shimmered with acid green sheets of dubious light.

"Gosh it's spooky," Enea said, releasing Alpha into the air.

The Black Mantis dashed for the trees but was back almost straight away. He flitted out onto the sandy bank and ran along the water's edge, shaking the droplets of fog off his wings.

"Let's find the road," I peered at the location map. "We've been drifting downstream. We need to walk another couple hundred feet or so."

* * *

The old Ogres Road started right there by the ford. It crossed the little wood, then turned off toward the first banks of cliffs.

The visibility was better here. The fog was gradually thinning out, separating into layers.

Togien, Archie and myself walked in front.

Aha. A signpost!

Two signs were nailed to an old stake cracked with age and overgrown with moss.

—> *To the Ford*

<— *Port, 15 miles*

Someone had scribbled a handwritten note below,

Roadway checked. No ogres. The caves are farm-worthy, lvl 20-25.

Archie stopped. "Let's take the road?"

"I suggest we check the caves first," I said, consulting the map. "We'll see a tall cliff in a minute. The entrance to the caves is just behind it."

That's exactly what we did. A barely visible trail took us in the right direction.

"Look," Iskandar pointed at some tree stumps by the roadside. "They've been cut recently. Look at the moss, how it's stripped off the wood. I think they dragged the trees over there," he pointed to the cliffs.

Rare snowflakes fell from the sky. This was weird. It had never snowed in our region before.

"What's going on?" Togien stopped. "The cliff

is gone! But I remember it very well! Gwain and I were here together looking for some ore deposits! You just can't miss it!"

"The trail goes that way," Archie said in surprise. "This is also a road! It's been used recently!"

Platinus sniffed in the cold air. "Can you smell the smoke?"

"Someone's got a fire going?" Raoul suggested. "Alex, can't you launch a Magic Eye?"

"I don't think it's a good idea," I said. "We shouldn't attract attention to ourselves. We can't see anything in the fog, anyway. And if I try to fly the Eye higher, they might see it."

"Who *they*?" Togien snickered.

"This is what we're going to find out," I stepped forward.

Nothing happened. Even though, according to my map, I'd just crossed into the neighboring location.

The others seemed to understand this too.

"Could it be an update?" Enea tentatively offered.

About thirty feet further on, the fog began to thicken, then dissipated completely. It felt as if we'd walked through a thick wall of cotton wool out into a boundless distorted space.

This was a different reality altogether. There was no sun here. A diffused light seemed to be seeping from everywhere at once.

Cracked barren ground lay underfoot. No sight of vegetation anywhere, but plenty of fire and ice.

Icy banks lined the deep fissures in the earth which breathed underground fire, their edges overgrown with permafrost. The cold transparent air would occasionally thicken, forming the spirals of Mortal Cold as if a powerful invisible wizard was attempting to freeze the remaining life out of the place.

The fissures exuded a crimson glow. They spat occasional clouds of ash which trailed along the ground.

Not a very cheerful setting, if you ask me. A dark strip of unknown origin stretched along the horizon at least several hours' hike away.

Right. I'd had enough. Time to use some magic.

I formed three Magic Eyes and motioned them into the air.

We awaited the first results with bated breath. The three cameras streamed pictures without a glitch. The maps kept updating to include this new region of the Crystal Sphere which hadn't been marked on them before.

Gradually, the mist of war was disappearing, replaced by the terrain's outlines.

And what the hell was that?

A fortress?!

Oh, no. It was a modern multi-level highway lying in ruins. Several junctions, spiraling up and down. Their surfaces had collapsed in places, their support pillars corroded as if they'd been drenched in concentrated acid, exposing their skeletons of rusty construction steel.

But that wasn't the biggest shock by far.

This technogenic monstrosity was enmeshed in a web of freshly-laid dirt roads. They were packed with NPCs, both mounted and on foot, their carts groaning under the weight of their meager possessions.

Further on, I saw some kind of building site illuminated by bonfires. There, creatures of various races were busy working stone, gradually filling in the gaps in the corroded steel structures.

A motley makeshift army had set up camp slightly further up. Each and every one of the Crystal Sphere's many races was present there. Contrary to their custom, they showed no antagonism toward each other.

These were Reapers.

Or at least those who'd been infected with neurograms accidentally. Several Harvesters walked among them, keeping a watchful eye on the crowd.

Finally, one of the Eyes chanced upon a mounted group of high-level Reapers.

They rode unhurriedly, feeling quite at home. They had excellent weapons and gear. We watched them with some trepidation as they stopped by one of the bonfires and called a priest.

He listened to their orders and nodded. Whipping out his sword, he swung round and slew a dozen unsuspecting peasants sitting around the fire.

The cauldron with their humble stew went flying into the fire, hissing and extinguishing it.

Bluish whiffs of the peasants' neurograms trailed over the ground. The mounted Reapers imbibed them greedily.

Then they noticed our Eye.

A priest shot his hand up in the air, pointing. One of the high-level Reapers thrust his lance upward, its tip enveloped in a ghostly light. The picture disappeared.

"We need to go," I croaked. My throat was so dry as if I'd spent several days without water.

I couldn't quite grasp what I'd just seen. What had happened to the location's borders? Where were we?

"These are the Corporation's testing grounds," Enea said softly.

"How do you know?"

"The two other Eyes managed to fly on a bit further," she forwarded the picture to the group chat. "This is what they'd filmed before they were detected and shot down."

We saw a different area of the same location. This too was a camp, only a well-appointed one, not like the chaotic mess we'd just seen. It was equipped with the kinds of tents and marquees used by players. A little further lay the collapsed edge of a ravine, with a dark mouth of a car tunnel gaping in the middle of it.

Next to it were several holographic signs,

Infosystems Corporation Training Grounds

Recreation Zone

Advanced Research Sector

Neurocybernetics Sector

Phantom Server Project Sector

A red sign flashed below,

Warning! The training grounds have been compromised! The defective mobs automatic elimination protocol has been initiated. All virtual staff are advised to log out ASAP.

The Reapers were bound to work out our position pretty soon.

"Let's get out of here," I said.

* * *

White returned about midnight, tired, hungry and quite annoyed. He wasn't happy when the two Guards of Gloom controlling the portal informed him of my request to meet me at the Conference Hall.

Stephen, Iskandar and Rodrigo had built a 3D map of the area which was now hovering over the ancient round table which still remembered the meetings of the Cohort of the Chosen.

"I haven't found them. My group seems to have vanished from the face of the earth," White collapsed into a chair, locked his fingers as was his habit and began studying the map.

He noticed the destroyed highway straight away. "What's the Corporation technopark got to do with it? Did any of you log out into the real world? Wait a sec... What the hell are NPCs doing there?"

"These are the Corporation's virtual testing grounds," I replied.

"You don't mean it! It's an exact copy of the real thing! I've been there. It's their Mont Blanc technopark," he explained. "Now tell me what happened here."

"Our locations have merged," Enea explained. "We wanted to check the old Ogres Road. According to Dimian, it could save us two days' journey to the port city. Instead, we found this," she pointed at the map.

The 3D model made by our wizards resembled an enormous screenshot of one of those ancient strategic games with the camera pointing down at a slight angle. We could clearly see the terrain's relief as well as thousands of NPCs. Some still had name tags hovering above their heads, others' were hatched in with gray.

Before going back, we'd used up all our mana supplies to launch about a hundred more Eyes. Even though the Reapers had eventually discovered and destroyed them all, the total amount of the information they'd sent us was huge. Stephen — the clan analyst — was now busy processing it. As he worked, more and more little symbolic NPC figures appeared on the map.

As White studied the map, I told him about the empty village and the young warrior Enea and I had rescued from the well.

"I heard about it before," White replied. "These things began to happen about two months ago. NPCs would attack players and throw them into wells, caves or mountain gorges, apparently sacrificing them to the Reapers. We thought that any such glitchy NPCs had been removed from the game. Apparently, they haven't. It's much worse than I thought. Could you upload our side of the location, please?"

Iskandar nodded. Together with Rodrigo, he began to conjure up a new image. We saw the edge of the moors, the village of Warblerford and the river. The old Ogres Road snaked around the cliffs.

Then the invisible boundary disappeared, connecting the Crystal Sphere to the Infosystems training grounds. We could clearly see the breach where the two virtual worlds merged together: a small area which abounded with caves and cliffs.

White frowned. "I see now. Those caves must have been the transition point between the training grounds and the Crystal Sphere. Putting it plainly, they are basically high-capacity data exchange channels. Other objects can play the same role, such as wells, caves and gorges. Very clever of the Reapers!"

"But why would Infosystems want to connect the two virtual worlds?" Archie objected. "Their staff could log in whenever they wanted, anyway. Receiving the information from the Crystal Sphere was never a problem! Why did they have to over-complicate things?"

"What if they didn't?" Christa offered. "Could it be Dietrich who created all this?"

A cold shiver ran down my spine.

"But that would mean he did get hold of the corporate workers' neurograms. Which gave him access to the game's control interface," Enea said.

"In that case, why does he need all this? An NPC army, what's that for?"

"Oh, do me a favor!" White snapped. "You make him look like some kind of super hacker. Well, he isn't. He's a criminal sentenced to death. He agreed to become a test subject for a neuroimplant prototype. Apparently, something went wrong. He lost his identity. His physical body died. That's how he became the first Reaper. Their forefather, if you wish."

"How do you know?" Christa asked.

"Ask Alex. He met him."

"Alex? Is that true?"

I nodded. "He may have died but his phantom imprint has survived somehow. It began prowling the test grounds looking for neurograms to piece a new identity together for himself. Then he discovered the passage to the Crystal Sphere."

"He can only exist in VR," White added. "So he's obliged to follow this world's rules. That's why he needs the NPC army. He wants it to manipulate the security systems. He's a defective mob, don't forget. Hacking is the only weapon available to him."

"Let's not underestimate what we're dealing with," Christa said. "The facts speak for themselves. The two virtual worlds have merged. Also, Dietrich somehow managed to build Harvesters."

Heavy silence hung in the air. We just stood there not knowing what to think. Rumors of the Reapers' occasional forays into the Crystal Sphere were one thing. Seeing the two worlds actually merged was quite another.

The true horror lay in seeing the desolation at the testing grounds with our own eyes. Now we knew that most Infosystems researchers had died — while the results of their revolutionary experiments had fallen into Dietrich's hands. That was truly horrible.

Raoul who'd been silent until now looked up sharply at us. "So what's the number one thing we should be doing?"

"No idea," Enea replied. "Personally, I think we're stuffed. A lot of people whose Logout button was still active tried to get out. They all say the same thing. The real world is deserted. There's no one left to maintain the planet's technosphere. It's about to collapse. Which might lead to a number of sporadic natural disasters."

"But Dietrich has survived," Raoul insisted. "Okay, maybe not as a human being but as a virtual imprint. Can't you see?"

"Which means we can do it too," Christa agreed. "As long as we can preserve the Crystal Sphere and save it from all those defective toons!"

White's eyes lit up. "Can we see the footage you took, please?"

"In a moment," Stephen's voice replied from the Hall of the Elements. "We released a hundred and four Eyes in total, didn't we? I'll just finish processing all the data."

The map came to life. The static Reaper figures began moving about.

For our convenience, Stephen added a fine grid to the image. "Tell me if you want to take a closer look at a particular section."

As we didn't have computers, we were forced to process all the data using our mind expanders which demanded a lot of energy, both physical and mental. Back in the Hall of the Elements, the clan's healers and elemental wizards surrounded Stephen, pumping him up with the energy they syphoned from the castle's runic sequences.

The animated picture offered us a new source of information. Now we were watching the events from a bird's eye view, noticing the details we couldn't have seen before.

The glowing skies above the training grounds parted, releasing a falling human figure.

The picture zoomed in on him.

A player. A warrior. His name tag was already dimming but still legible. His face was distorted with fear. The thickening air flickered around him.

He fell to his death, releasing a cascade of neurograms. Their faint glowing haze surged in all directions, forming fading images and snippets of memories.

Harvesters were already heading to the scene. They absorbed his neurograms instantly.

What followed next made our blood freeze. Several NPCs saw what was going on and walked over to the Harvesters. They were peasants who'd been sitting by the fire next to a lopsided makeshift cabin covered with frost.

An old man with a scraggly beard stepped forward. "We too have made a sacrifice," he said.

"I know," one of the Harvesters turned to him and swept his arm out. Wisps of bluish haze fell from his fingers. They reached out toward the NPC and filtered through his clothes into his body.

"It's so warm," the old man whispered, his lips blue with cold. "So good... Why didn't I ever feel it before?"

The others muttered something unintelligible, apparently in shock as they tried to absorb the yet-unknown experiences.

An orc who had somehow ended up among the peasants growled his fury, "They killed us for fun! They killed us over and over again!"

This was yet another NPC who'd just become aware of the sad role he'd played in the game, thanks to the memories he'd just received. The dead player must have been a frequent visitor to the orcs' lands.

The Harvesters knew very well what they were doing. They knew exactly which memories to give to whom.

This was disturbing. Sick. The infected NPCs were about to start their own sporadic development. Now that they'd gotten a taste of human emotions, they craved more of them. They'd become Reapers. But how were they supposed to quench this craving?

"If you follow Dietrich, he'll give you more," the Harvester said, then walked away in the direction of the collapsed highway.

"Jesus holy Christ," Enea whispered.

* * *

"Hey, look what I've found," Stephen's voice disrupted the silence.

The picture changed. Stephen zoomed in on the Ogres Road where it led down to the ford across the River Warbler.

A group on horseback was moving toward the river, closely followed by the spirals of Mortal Cold.

"The training grounds' defenses are still active," Stephen commented. "They're trying to destroy Reapers."

"They're not very good at it," Rodrigo said grimly.

"Are you familiar with this spell?" White

asked. "What does it do?"

"It syphons Life and brings both Strength and Stamina down to zero," Rodrigo replied. "It does it gradually, depending on the target's resistance, of course."

"Let's see if it can do it, then."

Large snowflakes floated in the air. The horses were enveloped in clouds of mist. The Reapers' armor was covered in the fancy patterns of ice flowers.

Where the road turned toward the ford, the frosty haze thickened, blocking their path.

Two of the Reapers dismounted. Both had staffs in their hands. Their name tags showed levels 150.

Judging by their hesitation, the haze was an impassable barrier to them. Unwilling to take risks, the two wizards sent a warrior forward. He took a few steps. Once the haze reached his knees, he froze, turning into an ice statue.

The wizards didn't look too discouraged. The remaining warriors formed a cordon around them. Using the sharp tips of their staffs, the two wizards began scratching runes of Fire into the frozen ground.

Tiny flames arose into the air but expired almost straight away. Still, the wizards were patient. They proceeded to work in silence with machine-like precision.

Unable to trigger the testing grounds' defense mechanisms, our Magic Eye floated low enough for us to survey the scene in every detail. The Reapers kept shuffling the runes around, creating their own sequences out of the available symbols and trying them out.

After yet another failure, they spent a long time discussing something. They must have decided to change their tactics as they produced a few scrolls and began reading them, mouthing the spells.

It didn't work. I lip-read the spells anyway, just in case. Not that I needed to memorize a failed practice, but still.

A new gust of cold wind brought a flurry of prickly snowflakes, reducing visibility over our part of the bank.

The Reapers hadn't left.

A sphere of transparent blue flame formed around them, shutting the snowstorm out.

The frozen warrior stirred, shaking the crust of ice off his body. He could barely move. His hp was deep in the red. Still, he took a few steps back proving that Reapers could override security programs.

The fiery blue sphere looked familiar. This was one of the numerous variations of a high-level Air spell which briefly boosted one's strength and stamina.

Even though such a limited-effect spell couldn't possibly allow the Reapers to leave the confines of the testing grounds, this was a worrying sign. The enemy wizards had displayed remarkable perseverance. They were both methodical and ingenious. They didn't hesitate to ignore the standard routine by shuffling the runes — which could result in either a lethal outcome or a success.

White must have come to his own conclusions. "They're weaker now than the levels displayed on their tags. But once they shake off the debuffs, we'll have a problem. That's why we need to face them and kill them where the locations meet: on the river bank."

"Stephen, how long do you think it might take them to completely disable the security programs?" Enea asked.

Our analyst gave it some thought. "A couple of weeks at least."

"Then we need to use these two weeks to speed-level the clan," White said. "As I already said, we'll need good gear and lots of stat-boosting rings. I hope you all understand that the Reapers will invade the Crystal Sphere. In which case, Rion will be the first hurdle on their way."

"We need to find Borisov," I said. "That way we might solve several problems at once."

"Did you manage to locate the scroll's portal exit?"

"I did. It's on one of the Yonder Isles."

"The Yonder Isles are a myth," Archie said. "There're no known routes there."

"They're not a myth," I said. "The Yonder Isles are a series of locations meant to be activated during a future update."

"So how on earth can we get there?" Archie asked.

"You'll know in the morning. I want you to throw a raid together and choose some scouts who could stay in Warblerford and keep an eye on the Reapers.

* * *

The Clan's senior officers parted ways: some to prepare the raid, others to arrange surveillance of the River Warbler, and some just to grab a couple hours of sleep.

Christa rose, too. "It's getting late. I should be going. Alex," she turned to me from the doorway, "I know for a fact that no updates have been installed in the last year. Borisov was the only person who could have brought you and Enea back and activated the Yonder Isles region. If you're going to look for him, I'd like to be part of it. I owe him a lot."

"She's right," White agreed. "We could use some help. Especially because this concerns everybody."

Enea nodded a silent agreement.

"You don't trust me, do you?" Christa said. "I can swear the Blood Oath if you wish. I'm not going to hurt the Oathing Stone, I promise. I'm just fed up with all this constant traveling."

We needed to forget the past. We had to stop thinking in terms of demons and good guys. The world wasn't black and white anymore. What we had now was humans against Reapers and their henchmen. New times were upon us.

"Please stay," I asked Christa. "You're right, we were about to talk about Borisov."

Was it my imagination or did I glimpse a flicker of respect in White's gaze?

Enea breathed a sigh of relief. She definitely liked Christa. Human feelings can sometimes be difficult to explain by logic alone.

"So how do we get to the Yonder Isles?" White asked.

"We have the Founder's Glove. It's one of a kind. It can open long-distance portals amongst other things, can't it?"

"Yes, but you still need the coordinates! Did you copy them?"

"I tried to. It didn't work."

"Why?"

"Because whatever they used to block Borisov out is still active. We'll do it in a different way. Lethmiel once visited the Yonder Isles. A visual will be enough to open a portal."

"He can't have! It's only been activated very recently!"

"Yes, but all of the Crystal Sphere's future events and locations were set up by its script writers well in advance," I said. "Lethmiel believes his memories of visiting the Isles to be true. According to him, he went there when he was still young, two hundred and fifty years ago. And this looks like our only chance of getting there."

"Would you entrust the Glove to him?"

"I can't see any other way."

"Can't you tweak the coordinates ever so slightly? Just to make sure that the portal doesn't open too close to whatever device they used to block Borisov?"

"Not a good idea. It'll require some trial and error, otherwise the portal might open over the sea or above some cliffs. It's too time-consuming. I should trust Lethmiel. I don't think we'll be so lucky as to locate the tower straight away, but the Isles answer our other objectives. We can use this opportunity to level up the raid. In the past, the Isles were famous for their Master Jewelers so we might see some very interesting loot there."

"Excellent. When do we start?"

"I've already asked Lethmiel to come. He'll be here any moment. We'll run a quick test first

— then if everything works well, we'll set off for the Isles tomorrow morning."

CHAPTER FOUR

THE CRYSTAL SPHERE
THE YONDER ISLES
WESTERN ISLAND

THE PORTAL'S ALMOND-SHAPED EYE emitted a low humming noise. White and Archie went in first, followed by Enea and myself. Christa and Platinus were in the rear with the others. Platinus insisted on joining the raid point blank, hoping to find some rare potion ingredients.

The midday sun shone bright in the clear sky. The air was hot. The portal's humming died away, replaced by the buzzing of insects and the long cries of unknown animals.

Stepping noiselessly, Arwan ran up onto a

small hillock and drew his bow. Raoul took up a position next to him, ready to heal whoever might need it from the convenience of his vantage point.

The portal turned out fine. It took us past the barrier of shoreline cliffs. To our left lay a crystal clear lagoon.

Two shipwrecks lay in its center, their wood dark with time, their masts listing, the gold coating of their figureheads flaking. Their storm-worn sails and rigging hung in long tatters from the yardarms. The sharp ribs of the ships' frames were visible through holes in their sides.

The lagoon was quite deep. It must have been an excellent safe haven for ships wishing to sit out a storm. Provided you had an experienced pilot, of course, who knew how to steer a ship safely through the narrow channel amid the treacherous reefs.

White cast watchful looks around himself. Even though there was no apparent danger, he kept his shield ready, tense as a taut spring. Archie was slightly more relaxed, looking curiously around. Future adventures seemed to be calling his name. I could say the same about all of us, I suppose.

Iskandar controlled the combat section wizards with Rodrigo by his side. Archie had the clan's best warriors under his command. Stephen and Ylien were in the rear. White had insisted we took both of them along: Ylien for a bit of speed-leveling and Stephen, in his capacity as the clan's analyst. He'd never been on a raid as analyst before.

The strip of cliffs was still visible at a distance. A flat rocky slope led down into a large savannah area studded with occasional groups of wide-canopied trees. The slope itself was overgrown with prickly bushes covered in large, meaty crimson leaves.

The place seemed to be rife with adventure. I counted five groups of ancient ruins. Their roofs had long collapsed but the columns and archways were mainly intact. Their moss-covered walls resembled delicate Elven buildings quite a lot, even though here they were also overgrown with vines.

While Enea and I were taking all this in, our support team had begun to set up the large raid tent complete with a mobile respawn point.

In the meantime, the raid had regrouped. The warriors fell in in single file behind White and Archie's backs. The wizards stayed by the portal higher up the hill: their long-distance spells required a good field of vision.

I was in charge of the raid. Stephen was busy receiving and processing the logs. His calm confident voice sounded in the battle chat,

"Mobs level 70+ at twelve o'clock, range three hundred feet."

We'd agreed to use a simplified form of o'clock directions, with White and Archie's position being twelve o'clock.

I glimpsed a movement in the cliffs to my left.

"Two mobs, level 80, at nine o'clock!" Stephen promptly informed us. "Aggro radius, sixty feet. Susceptible to cold. Natural armor absorbing 50% of physical damage."

Giant pythons had been basking in the sun when we'd scared them off. Their muscular spotted bodies slithered noiselessly away, threading their way amid the rocks.

"Archie, off we go," I said. "Wizards, control them! Cast distance damage!"

A raid's strength is in its choreographed coordination. Each member should know their part. Still, at first I repeated all my commands in the battle chat for everyone to see. The first minutes of any combat are the most intense and dangerous.

White stood unwavering, prepared to back up Archie. His level 132 gave him a serious advantage but the objective I'd set was challenging even for him. We didn't want our Dark Knight to act solo, making mincemeat out of mobs and spreading the resulting XP thin over the other raid members. What we needed was to practice teamwork and test our fighting efficiency, allowing each raid member to show what they could do.

Archie stepped forward, crossing the invisible aggro radius.

Immediately the two pythons shot bolt upright. Both their bodies were the size of a good log and extremely agile.

They attacked us with lightning precision. Their hissing jaws, big enough to swallow any of us whole, exuded an unbearable stench.

The wizards cast cold spells, slowing them down. A wave of frost ran across the ground toward the pythons, climbing up their spotted bodies and bringing their strength and agility into the red.

This helped Archie (who was already level 75) to withstand the pythons' double attack. The warriors immediately joined the fight. Enveloped in frosty auras, their sword blades took seconds to strip the monsters of their hp. With a loud hissing sound, the pythons' bodies slumped to the ground.

White breathed a sigh of relief. "We did it."

We had no time to celebrate. A raid is a mob-killing, loot-picking machine.

"Keep going! Not too fast, not too slow!"

Both our tanks proceeded down the slope, covering themselves with their shields. The warriors followed closely behind. Enea, Christa and myself remained as strategic reserve.

Old habits die hard: I struggled to stay in the rear, desperate to join them in search of adventure. Still, today we had to work as a group.

We walked past the python's bodies sprawled over the rocks. Platinus was already busy there.

The wizards kept up with us. Raoul was walking parallel to us while Arwan had moved to the right flank, seeing as we were now protected on the left by a precipitous range of cliffs.

The mobs Stephen had warned us about were packs of level-70 gorilla-like creatures. I could clearly see at least three groups of twenty animals each: one skulking in the ruins, another lurking in the treetops of a nearby copse and a third one having a party in the purple undergrowth eating berries and hunting some little critters — lizards, most likely.

This was our first serious fight. The pythons had had no chance, really. They might have been dangerous for a lone traveler but not for a raid. Now the "gorillas" were quite numerous. The problem was, we had to handle them in packs. The mobs' social nature didn't allow us to aggro them one by one.

With every step, the tension continued to grow.

I could already see the tags hovering above their heads. Those were truly dangerous monsters: eight foot tall with long claws and sharp yellow fangs. Their muscles rippled under their short black fur, betraying remarkable strength.

"Stone-Skinned Gorillas," Stephen read their

tags out loud. "Highly aggressive. Their natural Skin of Stone buff is a sign of their high resistance to both cold and fire. They also possess a 10-second Berserk ability which gives them explosive bursts of strength and agility allowing them to ignore initial blows."

Oh well. Despite their cute apish appearance, they were extremely dangerous.

"My advice would be to first deplete this ability with a long-distance attack," Stephen continued, perfectly calm.

"Raid, halt!" I commanded. "Hold your positions. Wizards, control the area!"

My PM box blinked. It was White contacting me,

"Alex, I think you're making a mistake. Twenty mobs will make mincemeat out of Archie and myself. We can't use the standard tanking tactic here. You need to think some more."

"Wizards, belay that!" I said. "Change of scheme. First a distance attack, then you control them, but only when they reach this mark," I highlighted a large boulder on the ground. "Second line of warriors, step forward! Once the wizzies control the mobs, you smoke them in short bursts. Raoul, you heal the warriors. Enea will help you. Arwan, you keep an eye on the area. Platinus stays in the rear. Let's do it!"

Fireballs streaked through the air, leaving a

smoky trail in their wake. They weren't supposed to deal much damage: their job was to aggro the pack.

Immediately the gorillas went for us in long low leaps. Rocks, clumps of earth and sods of turf flew from under their paws.

Iskandar attacked them with an Inferno, dealing blanket fire damage which wasn't meant to harm them, either. Its job was to trigger their Berserk ability, forcing the creatures to use it.

For a split second, I froze in place with shock. Still, our wizzies knew what they were doing. Once the mobs reached the boulder, a wall of barbed brambles rose into the air. Their long shoots entangled the mobs' legs, their venomous thorns piercing their stone skin. The harder the gorillas tried to struggle free, the deeper the thorns sank into their bodies.

Our warriors promptly joined in. Each of them hurried toward the targets they'd already selected. They'd deal a couple of blows, then recoil. Rinse and repeat.

The gorillas' incredible strength combined with their impressive survivability (700 hp each) and their ability to absorb 30% of the incoming damage made them extremely dangerous opponents. Our warriors gave it their all but that wasn't enough to deplete the mobs' lives.

Eric, one of the clan's best warriors, lingered a moment too long. He tried to roll out of their reach but was still caught. He lost 50% life in one clean sweep as one of the gorillas sent him flying through the air. He dropped to the ground about ten feet away, struggling fruitlessly to get back to his feet.

Immediately two gorillas managed to wrestle themselves free from the vines and threw themselves onto Eric, their claws ripping through his body.

Enea and I dashed to his help.

Eric looked lost. He screamed with pain, trying to protect his head. Blood spurted everywhere. He'd forgotten all about his weapons. Raoul's healing wasn't helping much: he kept restoring Eric's life which was in fact only prolonging his agony.

The top of Enea's Staff of a Hydra erupted in a blinding light, slowing the animals down. I ducked under a gorilla's swinging arm and sliced through its rock-hard skin twice with my sword.

The monster bellowed in fury — but I'd already rolled away from under its crashing response blow.

Enea mini-ported out of the other gorillas' path. Alpha the Black Mantis took off from her shoulder. His hard upper wings gleamed in the midday sun. Spewing venom, he sank his mandibles into the gorilla. The monster dropped to the ground and rolled over, blindly lashing out with its great paws trying to shrug off the debuff.

In the meantime, the other warriors had smoked their selected mobs and launched another attack without as much as a breather.

The wall of thorny vines began to buckle. Some of its branches had already lost their magic properties and were about to disappear. The control spells would expire any moment.

Rodrigo and Iskandar reacted just in time. They promptly cast another wall of thorns, providing a brief break for the warriors and giving Enea and myself a chance to finish off the two gorillas and drag Eric into the rear.

His life was already back to full. Thanks to Raoul's efforts, his wounds had already healed, too. He'd stopped bleeding.

Still, he didn't look good. He appeared broken. He was sitting on the ground shaking his head and mouthing something with his pale lips.

"New abilities detected," Stephen's voice echoed in the chat, "Long Leap and Leaping Blow."

Good work! Our analyst had somehow managed to keep an eye on the other two packs, marking down the abilities they'd used while fighting between themselves.

Now that a new wall of poisonous vines stood in the furious gorillas' way, their next step was easy to predict.

"New ability detected: a Hurled Rock Stun."

"First line of warriors, step back! Arwan, try to finish off whoever you can! Wizards, keep building new walls of thorns until you run out of mana!"

Not a moment too soon.

The warriors stepped back, leaving the wounded gorillas to the mercy of Arwan's lethal bow.

The surviving part of the pack used the abilities deduced by Stephen. They cleared the first wall of thorns in long high leaps (which must have required incredible strength and agility) only to get stuck in the next one.

Only two of the monsters had been lucky enough to land in the small gap between the two rows of magic vines. Immediately they began picking up the boulders that lay around and hurling them at us.

Two more warriors were stunned, losing 30% life each. They dropped to the ground, unable to get up. Another boulder made a gap in our brambly defenses, allowing three more gorillas to wrestle their way through the vines toward the raid.

White and Archie saved the day. Enea's father slung his shield behind his back and took a double-handed grip of his sword. He met the gorillas with a long rotating combo, wounding both and giving them a Bleed debuff, forcing them to recoil in an instinctive fear of the lethal strokes of his sword's merciless blade.

Archie promptly joined in. He attacked the mob nearest to him, then performed a dispassionate crit.

His example empowered whatever warriors were still standing.

The gorillas lasted another ten or fifteen seconds thanks to their incredible aggression and survivability. Finally, their mangled bodies sank to the ground and rolled down the slope, their ungainly fall halted by the first wall of thorns.

Raoul and Enea got busy restoring the warriors' shrinking lives. White gave Archie a friendly slap on the shoulder, then walked over to me.

"Excellent location," he said. "Perfect choice for us. Tough but efficient."

In the meantime, the walls of thorns expired and crumbled to the ground.

"Did you say perfect? I don't think we'll make it much further the way we are now."

"True," he nodded. "What tactic do you suggest?"

Was he trying to test me? Not that I minded. This was a serious question — and we still had a lot to do.

"Seeing as gorillas work in packs, it's pointless using tanks against them," I said. "They'll just kill them."

"They will," White agreed. "Even if I was there."

"Which is why I want to bring more warriors and divide them into groups. Each group will have its own backup of healers and combat wizards. The warriors will select one gorilla each and then fight it."

"Good. I can see you're smart. As soon as we know their respawn times, we can level up non-stop. We'll rotate the groups: some will do the farming while the others rest up. That way it might take us a week to study these ruins and bring the combat section's level to 100. By the way," White added, "your sword isn't up to much, is it? It's too short and too light. All it does is chip away at your opponent's life and mana. I suggest you change it for a regular longsword."

"I need to think about it," I said.

"Please do. And please change it soon. I understand you're used to it. A mysterious cargonite sword, what's there not to like? Still, each weapon has also a damage stat, and that's what you should be looking at. It should correspond to your strength and agility. Leave pretty artifact thingies till better times."

* * *

In the meantime, the battle was over. We'd got rid of the first pack, but at what price?

The warriors' eyes betrayed unreserved disbelief. When fear creeps into your very heart, that's the worst thing of all.

Eric was still sitting on a sunlit hillock, shaking his head. He was as white as a sheet. Raoul was still fussing around him. Still, there was little a healer could do there. The guy needed a shrink.

I was about to approach him but White beat me to it. He crouched next to Eric and motioned Raoul out of sight.

Eric was shuddering. This was not a game anymore. The 100% authenticity of the experience had brought back what man of today had long forgotten: his survival instinct.

"I know how it feels," White said. "It won't last. You'll get used to it."

"I don't think I can stand the pain," Eric replied in a muffled voice. "Why did I have to have this implant installed! Everything was so good without it."

"You can't change it now."

Eric breathed in fast, shallow bursts. "And how do you want me to go on? Those mobs were ripping me apart!"

"The only thing you can do is level up and

prove to yourself that you can do it. It'll be getting better. When you reach level 90 or so, your pain threshold will rise. You should invest as much XP as you can in stamina. That helps, trust me."

"And what am I supposed to do with this?"

Eric stretched out his hand. His fingers were shaking.

"I don't think I'll ever be able to face a mob again," he said. "I'm scared I might turn my back on the enemy and run. I'd rather go back to the castle. I could help them restore the wall."

"That's not an option," White said. "You can't sit it out behind castle walls. You'll lose all your self-respect. I don't think peasants are good company for you. You're either a warrior or you're a shriveled body stuck in an in-mode capsule! If you start shrinking from every NPC-"

"Piss off!" Eric snarled. "What do *you* know? You're level one hundred freakin' thirty! Just leave me alone. I don't need anyone preaching to me."

I though White was going to yell at him but he didn't. The warm breeze ruffled his silver-gray crew cut. His armor glinted in the sun. Without saying a word, he looked around, saw Raoul and motioned him to approach, then asked him about something.

Raoul's face changed. Still, he nodded and offered White a couple of vials of healing potions.

"Alex, Enea, Christa, I want you to stay out

of it," White said.

He removed his laminated armor and replaced it with a light and supple Elven chainmail shirt. Then he headed down the slope toward the ruins lying to the right of our route.

Enea looked worried. "Where is he going?"

"I don't know, do I?"

"Alex, we need to go with him," Christa said.

Her incredibly high level had prevented her from participating in the fight. She'd joined the raid as emergency backup in case things went fatally wrong.

"No we don't," I snapped. "You heard him. We should stay out of it."

Eric sat up, watching White. We too followed his progress with bated breath. Enea squeezed my hand, restless.

The vegetation stirred. White slowed down and took a double-handed grip on his sword.

Something flashed brightly amid the greenery. We all heard the sound of splintering wood on the ruins' second floor. Four burly warriors in crystal armor dropped to the ground.

Level 135! Higher than White's!

Their charmed quartz shields reflected the sunlight. The blades of their weirdly curved swords were serrated which meant they were specially designed to deal Bleed.

A shiver ran down my spine. Enea clutched

my hand so hard that her nails dug into my skin.

"Arwan, keep an eye on them but stay out of it for the time being," I said.

The Elf drew his bow and froze, ready to loose off an arrow at a moment's notice.

My mind expander ran an automated search and offered up a meager result,

Guardians of the Ruins. The descendants of Ferrigan's Guards.

Ferrigan: the old Lord of the Hundred Isles.

They attacked simultaneously. The curved crystal blades of their swords glistened in the sun, tracing blurred combos through the air.

With an enviable cool, White rolled out of their deadly circle and dealt a powerful blow to one of the Guards' back, stripping him of 30% Life.

Cascades of crimson crystal flew everywhere. By then, White was already out of their reach and restoring in a defensive stance.

Why hadn't he taken the shield? This was something I couldn't understand.

Three of the Guards resumed their attack. The fourth was lagging behind now, limping. A slow trickle of viscous blood ran down his sliced flank, dripping onto his greave. The wound system was quite realistic in the Crystal Sphcrc.

White's lips moved. He shifted his sword to

his right hand. A spell aura enveloped his left one, covering his fingers in a glistening mass of snowflakes bound together with streaks of darkness.

In a precise, well-practiced motion White smeared the glistening magic substance onto his sword blade. He then lunged unexpectedly at an attacking guard.

A crust of frost covered the guard's shield. It exploded.

The two others dropped to the ground, trying to get to White from below. The Dark Knight rolled out of their reach, sprang to his feet and swung round, once again changing the grip on his sword to both hands. He then stopped his opponents with a series of powerful slashing blows, forcing them to back off.

In the meantime, the wounded guard had changed his weapon. He was now holding a long crystal spear with a glittering tip. He attacked White unexpectedly, piercing his left shoulder.

Enea cried out.

Archie dashed to his rescue but stopped as White had already hacked the shaft through, sprang backwards toward the vine-covered wall and gulped a quick healing elixir. The spear tip slid out of his wound which healed straight away, the hole in his chainmail shirt the only reminder of his injury.

The Guardians of the Ruins lost their patience and went for White, attempting to corner him. He grabbed at the thick woody vines, climbed to the second floor, whipped out his bow and loosed off several arrows, aiming at the guardians' heads.

This sudden demonstration of his cool, strength and agility left a deep impression on everyone. My back was bathed in cold sweat.

Having exhausted and seriously wounded the four guardians, White was now nowhere to be seen.

"Did he get cold feet?" one of the warriors murmured.

"Shut up," another one snapped. "What a dumb question. You've no idea what it's like when you're attacked by fours enemies at once."

He was right. I could never understand those who plunged headlong into combat. On the few occasions that I'd been attacked by two or three opponents at once, they didn't give me the chance to parry their blows, let alone fight back. In a situation like that, a tactical retreat wasn't shameful. It's way better than getting yourself killed just because you thought too much of yourself.

The vines stirred ever so slightly in a couple of places as White slid along the upper floor toward a collapsed window.

The guardians crowded below, peering at a

hole in the vine cover. Their lives were at 50%. Finally, two of them separated from the rest and went on a flanking maneuver.

As they walked under the collapsed window, White jumped onto them from above, performing a classic Falling Blow and removing what was left of their hp in one merciless swing of his sword.

Immediately he attacked the remaining two, barreling in between them in a long spiraling motion.

One of the two guards slumped to the ground. The other managed to shield himself but lost his balance and received a crashing coup de grace combo.

A golden aura enveloped White. He'd received a new level!

* * *

White returned to us exhausted.

He perched on a small grassy ledge in the shade of the cliffs. "Everyone can stand pain for a minute or two," he said without addressing anyone in particular. "As long as you can avoid respawning, that's fine. You should always keep some healing potions on you."

"That's cheating," Eric grumbled.

He wasn't a newb, either. He must have realized that White couldn't have achieved such exorbitant strength and agility without sacrificing some of his other characteristics.

"It's not cheating. That's called smart leveling," White replied calmly. "Plus some unique items. Jewelry mainly. This," he twirled a cargonite ring round his finger, "gives you +10% to both Strength and Agility. Which make my blows stronger and faster and my rolls longer. And thanks to this," he touched a signet ring on his index finger, "I can cast spells without disrupting my attacks. It can be very handy in battle when you can heal yourself or cast Frost on your sword."

"How much did you pay for them?" Archie asked.

"I won them in battle. Which is why we are here now," White withdrew a water flask from his belt and took a sip.

"Why did you change your armor for the chainmail?" Eric rejoined the conversation.

"Don't you understand?"

"Not really."

"It's the weight. The lighter your gear, the better your agility, the longer your rolls. I always have two gear sets on me. In my opinion, when you have to fight four opponents at once, mobility is more important than protection. Still, it's something everyone has to decide for themselves. I probably could have done it in full armor, I suppose."

I didn't interfere. Firstly, because White knew what he was talking about. We all could learn a lot from him. And secondly, because he needed to establish authority quickly. I could see he was with us to stay. Still, his short temper might prevent him from endearing himself to people.

Enea calmed down and began casting glances at the lagoon. "Would be so nice to get there," she said wistfully. "I've never seen such ships in my life. I'd love to take a closer look."

She just couldn't live without new adventures, could she?

"We will," I said, "but probably not straight away."

"Can't we get to it from here?"

"I don't think so. Normally, cliffs mark locations' borders. If we don't come across a ravine, it might take us a long time to get there."

"You know how to raise a girl's hopes," she smiled despite her disappointment. Her lust for life filled us with optimism, too.

"I could try and fly over there," Christa offered, admiring the lagoon. "I'll need to change back into the demon, though."

"I suggest you wait. It's too risky," I said. "You might not be able to cross by air, anyway. I already tried to cast a teleport within direct line of sight and it didn't work. Let's not tempt Providence. It's better we try and find a road that can take us there."

In the meantime, White had changed back into his armor.

I looked over my raid members. They'd cheered up a little. Many of them seemed to like what White had just said.

"Archie," I turned to him, "I want you to go back to Rion and form three more groups. We'll be farming this place 24/7 while advancing bit by bit. You should also pick a few peasants and Elven hunters. Let them come here and start settling in."

He nodded and headed for the portal while we walked toward the freshly-purged ruins. We needed to collect the loot and take a good look around.

* * *

The two-story structure had once been built with some sort of brown-tinged stone which hadn't aged well. Judging by the sheer number of archways, it must have once been surrounded by shady terraces. Their tiled roofs had long since gone, replaced by a canopy of prickly vines. The paving stones of the inner yards had caved in, with tufts of grass growing between them.

Platinus was highly interested in the vines. A lot of them had suffered during White's fight with the Guardians. Platinus got busy collecting the sap that dripped from the plants' deep wounds.

The four Guardians had dropped a full set of crystal armor, two of their strange curved swords and a quartz shield.

"Would you like it?" White asked. "I don't need any of this. I'm too used to my current gear."

Formally he wasn't a clan member yet. He'd defeated the guardians in solo combat — which meant all of the loot belonged to him.

"If you don't mind, I'd like to send the armor back to the Clan's treasury," I said. "I'd like to study it."

Our acquisitions were undoubtedly useful but they required level 100+. The crystal swords were even worse: they needed one hell of agility.

Enea looked around. "So what were they guarding here?"

Obeying her command, Alpha flitted off her shoulder and disappeared into the thick vegetation.

"At the time, the Yonder Isles were famous for their crystal mines, jewelry shops and rare plants," Lethmiel's voice said.

Even though Lethmiel hadn't come with us, he still advised us via the clan chat. "Ferrigan's Guards were considered unbeatable," he continued. "Their descendants probably weren't as strong but still no one would have posted guards to a ruin if there was nothing to guard there."

"In this case, I suggest we stay here for a

---

while and check it properly."

We posted a few sentries outside and began inspecting the ruin.

Nothing. No ancient items nor secret stashes with treasure boxes inside.

"That's impossible! You must be missing something," Lethmiel's voice sounded in the chat. The game developers had made his character so adaptable that no amount of new technical gizmos could throw him. All of the high-tech novelties such as long-distance communications, the castle control interface or market transactions that could move your stock from one warehouse to the next in the blink of an eye — he simply explained all of it away with magic.

"Alexatis," he said, "may I leave my duties for a couple of hours and join you?"

"Why, are you so curious?"

"I can be useful. I need to take a look at those ruins. I'm pretty sure there must be some mystery surrounding them."

"Very well, then," I said.

While we waited for Lethmiel, the first groups formed by Archie walked through the portal and joined us. Iskandar hurried toward them: all of the combat section wizards were under his direct command.

My first impressions from our 'unsealing' of the Yonder Isles were admittedly exciting. Still, the question that worried me most was the location of the tower where Borisov had been hiding. The map-making app continued to point at a certain point nearby which was completely covered with the Mist of War.

Enea, Christa, White and myself walked out of the ruins and climbed higher up the hill.

Unfortunately, there were no high cliffs around, otherwise I'd have already been taking pictures of the area from one of them. Shame.

"Rodrigo, why didn't you launch a single Magic Eye?" I asked.

"We tried but it didn't work. They disintegrate a couple seconds after launch. No idea what's causing it. I'm working on it."

"Alexatis, would you like me to check out the area?" Christa offered, understanding the reason behind my nervousness.

"As a demon?" I asked. "Why not? I think it's a very good idea. Here are the coordinates. Try to climb as high as you can and follow the marker. Okay?"

"Not a problem. Mind stepping back for a sec, all of you? My transformation is a weapon in itself."

Good job she'd warned us.

Christa didn't look that different from any other girl. I still couldn't understand how she'd managed to change her character class, preserving the possibility of transforming back into her

Infernal shape while getting rid of every demonic trait in her everyday appearance.

Clouds of gray haze swirled around her. Three circles of black flames rose into the air, weaving and overlapping each other. The grass surrounding them wilted.

Runes glowed brightly.

Christa's form blurred, momentarily dissipating into an ashen mist. Then it reappeared, towering menacingly a good head above all of us.

Her infernal combat avatar spread its webbed wings, releasing a powerful wave of dark energy which ran all along the slope until it hit our raid shield and dissipated into thin air. I managed to glean the wave's stats. The power of it! To an unprepared onlooker, this discharge could have become lethal.

In the meantime, Christa's metamorphosis was complete.

Her awesome new form was enveloped in gloom. In one effortless wingbeat, the girl rose into the air. She must have been using Levitation, that's for sure. At these authenticity levels, you had to possess one hell of a strength and agility to be able to hover in the air. Christa did it with a surprising ease, betraying no effort whatsoever.

She banked in a wide circle, spiraling into the sky while streaming us the picture.

From above, the portal looked like a tiny spot

surrounded by insect-like raid members.

The archipelago was huge. It wasn't for nothing Ferrigan had been known as the Lord of a Thousand Isles.

Narrow channels separated terra firma into tiny islets. I couldn't even see where the archipelago ended, its outer isles disappearing in a misty haze.

The frothy surf rolled over the narrow strips of pebble beaches, then cascaded fuming against the precipitous cliffs. I could still make out the thin ribbons of ancient roads and collapsed bridges that used to connect the isles once.

Finally, Christa reached the desired height and soared upon the air currents, slowly approaching the area that interested us.

The copses of trees scattered over the savannah framed the ruins of dilapidated farmhouses. This must have once been an agricultural paradise.

Closer to the channel separating us from the neighboring island, the terrain rose sharply forming a rocky shore dissected by dark canyons.

"I can see the ruins of a big city," Christa reported. "And the tower. I'll see if I can get closer."

She headed toward the channel.

Dark dots rose from the canyons and made a beeline toward her, blocking her way.

"Christa, watch out!" White and Enea

shouted in synch. "There're some mobs about to attack you!"

"Gargoyles," Christa's breathing hastened. "I thought they were just statues cut into the rock!"

She banked into a sharp turn. The veil of gloom that surrounded her transformed into arrows of dark energy which shot out in every direction.

The gargoyles dodged them with ease. Their levels were lower than Christa's but only just.

This was a serious problem. According to my estimations, this whole island stretched for less than fifteen miles from east to west. Still, although the mobs were quite doable here by the portal, closer to the channel they were twice as strong.

The developers must have saved this region for when the Crystal Sphere finally had players above level 150.

In the meantime, the air above the cliffs seethed with dogfight.

"Are they stone gargoyles?" Lethmiel butted in. "You can't use regular weapons against them," he added, offering us a glimpse into his massive wealth of information. "If Christa will consider my humble advice, tell her to nosedive."

"Why, what will it give her?"

"Stone gargoyles are quite bulky and not very agile. They live in narrow canyons where they can only fly short distances, flitting from one rock ledge to the next."

"Christa, did you hear that?" Enea asked.

"Yeah," Christa replied.

The demonic arrows had failed to deal the gargoyles much damage. Both belonged to the powers of the Dark which made the gargoyles immune to certain types of magic.

Following Lethmiel's advice, Christa took a sharp nosedive, dropping to the ground.

The gargoyles missed her and struggled to get out of each other's way. They promptly started a short-lived squabble, then darted down after her.

They weren't particularly smart, were they? Either that, or they hadn't met a seasoned opponent for quite a while.

Christa had managed to pull off the risky maneuver. Just as her shadow was already trailing on the ground, she changed her course with an effortless grace. Three of the mobs chasing after her had failed to stop their deadly drop and fell to their deaths. The others slowed down just in time, crowing hoarsely in alarm. Clumsily flapping their unyielding wings, they returned to the cliffs.

Soon Christa was back. She landed, then quickly drew a few symbols on the ground.

Once again the little tongues of black flames rose around her, transforming her back into an ordinary girl.

"Could you forward the logs and the footage

to Stephen, please?" I asked her.

"Yeah," she nodded, catching her breath. "Lethmiel, thanks for the tip, man. I'll keep that one on the back burner. Those gargoyles are resistant to my skills. And fighting them in the air isn't worth it. All you'll do is blunt your swords on those slabs of rock."

"I'm glad to have been of help," Lethmiel replied modestly.

* * *

While my map-making app processed the data, Lethmiel began exploring the ruins one by one.

I used my mind expander to create a 3D model of the two islands. The tower was on the other one. It must have once been part of a majestic architectural ensemble — a palace, most likely. Still, by now most of the buildings on the other side of the channel had crumbled into ruins and been reclaimed by the jungle.

Getting there was going to be a problem. The islands' shores were unassailable. The only road on our side led through a dark canyon toward a decrepit air bridge which connected the two islands.

To get there, we had to deal with several groups of high-level mobs. Christa had reported more of Ferrigan's warriors guarding the entrance to the canyon, all levels 130. The gargoyles which had attacked her had been level 170.

And that was just here. What awaited us on the other side?

In any case, today we weren't going to find that out. The raid needed at least another couple of days just to get to the canyon. By then, our combat section would have leveled up enough to successfully handle the cliffs.

I updated the maps, then climbed onto a nearby hill to check on the others.

Supported by wizards, several details of warriors were advancing slowly but surely. They'd already smoked three packs of stone-skinned gorillas. Our casualties: four respawns, none of them fatal. All of the warriors had made two levels each.

That was good. We were leveling up faster than White had anticipated.

Enea and I had received our fair share of XP too.

Still, the master looter's report wasn't particularly brilliant. We hadn't yet received any unique items or ingredients. Just some gorillas' claws and pelts, a dozen gold coins and a few old swords, rusty and useless, which we'd discovered under the trees. That was the extent of it.

Still, it wasn't over yet. Soon our warriors would get to the second ruin, the one guarded by

Ferrigan's warriors.

"Alexatis! I found it! I found it!" Lethmiel's excited voice echoed in the voice chat.

Judging by the local map, our Blood Elf was now inside one of the larger rooms, the one with the collapsed roof. We'd already checked it but failed to find anything of any value.

"So what did we miss?" I asked.

"Come and take a look!"

We hurried to join him. The only conspicuous detail in the gloomy room was a large tree which had grown up through the broken stone floor and was reaching out for the light.

How strange.

"So what did you find?" I asked Lethmiel in a stern voice.

To my surprise, he avoided answering and even averted his gaze, as if saving his clan leader the embarrassment.

The others understood it too. Enea took a screenshot of the room and started a database search.

"Alex, you won't believe it!" she soon explained. "This is a Khmor tree!"

"What, the goblins' tree?" White sounded sincerely surprised.

"What've goblins got to do with it?" Christa asked, studying the room with curiosity.

The moment she stepped toward the tree, its

branches shifted. Its canopy rose up, as if avoiding contact with her. A few seemingly dry branches bent threateningly.

"Don't you remember the totem our goblins are looking for? It was made of Khmor wood, wasn't it? We still haven't found it."

"Let's make them a new one!" White suggested. "Do you have a picture of it?"

"No, we don't."

"Never mind," he said, unfazed. "I'll see if I can find it online."

"They'll see it's a fake straight away," Christa said.

"I don't think so," Enea said. "How long ago was it? Several hundred years at least. I don't think this generation even knows what it looks like, let alone how to use it. If we find a picture of it, I think it's worth trying. Only I suggest we cast some spell on it."

"What do you mean?" Christa asked.

"Well, we could make it attract fish for the goblins or frighten off hydras. And — as a nice little bonus — prevent them from messing with us."

"That's wise," White said. "By the way, I've found a picture."

"So what do you think?" Rodrigo asked. "Should we cut it down? It's a good idea. Even if we do find the original totem, we can't give it back to them. It will only make them stronger which is

---

something we don't need at all. Actually... can't we use your Object Replication? Then we won't even need to find a wood carver."

"Wait... what are you talking about?" Lethmiel stepped in our way, white as a sheet, as if trying to shield the tree from us. "You can't cut it down! It might be the last Khmor tree in the world!"

"Why, are they so rare?"

"They're alive! They're sentient! They were all wiped out hundreds of years ago to make magic staffs and Elven bows! You could only make them out of Khmor wood!"

I paused, pondering over his words.

The tree was still swaying its boughs threateningly.

A thumping sound came from the ruin's second floor, followed by a subdued flash of golden light. Apparently, Alpha the Black Mantis had just made a new level.

"Okay," I said. "Let it stay where it is. Especially if, as you say, it's sentient."

Lethmiel breathed a noisy sigh of relief.

"Never mind. Let's go," White motioned us out.

The earth under the tree roots shifted, disgorging a square object covered in clay.

"Oh wow! That's a treasure box!" Rodrigo bent down to pick it up.

The tree rustled menacingly. Its lower

branches curved back, then lashed out at our wizard, knocking him down.

"Hey, whassup?" Rodrigo asked in indignation. "We didn't mean you any harm!"

"This must be for Alex," Enea said. "He's the only one who can pick it up. The tree won't let anybody else near it."

She was right. I had no problem picking up the box.

I opened it.

Platinus craned his neck. "What is it?"

The First Ring of Ferrigan's Guard.

Made by ancient master jewelers of the Yonder Isles who produced them for the personal guards of the Lord of a Thousand Isles.

Normally, Ferrigan's Guards used to wear five different rings. Few of the guards' descendants can boast owning one of the ancient relics.

Effect: +10% to physical and magic protection.

"Excellent ring!" White exclaimed once I'd made its stats public. "This is exactly what I meant. We really should send one of the groups to find access to the lagoon. I'm pretty sure we might find lots of similar stuff in the holds of those ships."

"You think they traded them overseas? Doubtful," I said.

"What, in Ferrigan's times? Easy! If indeed they had an intensive jewelry trade here, they were bound to export them. They might not be as impressive as this one, but still, how cool is that?

CHAPTER FIVE

THE CRYSTAL SPHERE
RION CASTLE

WE RETURNED TO THE CASTLE in the evening, together with one of the groups who'd just finished their leveling stint.

The day had proved hot and busy. We'd advanced about fifteen hundred feet. The gorillas' respawn times were only two hours. Also, in one of the ruins our warriors had walked right into another group of crystal-clad Guardians.

As a result, the whole combat section had made 5 levels in total. We'd farmed two more sets of crystal armor and three more Rings of Ferrigan's Guard albeit not as awesome as the one gifted to me by the Khmor tree.

Overall, I was quite pleased with the developments. Back in Rion, the restoration of the outer walls was in full swing. The scouts we'd left in Warblerford reported that everything was quiet.

Allan had sent me a brief polite message informing me that the Ravens had safely made it back to their castle.

Enea, however, seemed to be a bit under the weather. After dinner, she'd climbed into a large soft chair and just sat there with her legs tucked up under her, melancholically leafing through an old manuscript.

Alpha was sitting on her shoulder, curiously studying the pictures.

We hadn't noticed the twilight falling. I lit up some candles. "What are you thinking about?"

"I'm looking at these ancient Elven temples," she said. "Don't you remember we still have a clan quest to do?"

I pulled up a chair. "Okay, let's think about it."

The task was anything but easy. We didn't possess the most important element, one which was supposed to breathe life and meaning into whatever architectural design we might choose. We needed a proper Elven shrine.

I looked at the pictures of delicate white edifices. "We could use Object Replication, I suppose. Alternatively, we could ask the dwarves-"

"Won't work," she snapped. Then she added in a conciliatory tone, apparently embarrassed, "Sorry, Alex. Please don't worry about me."

"Are you all right?"

"I don't know. I can sense some kind of force inside me but I can't work it out. I just don't understand it."

"How long has it been going on?"

"Ever since we were in the library on the Island of Oblivion. I didn't sleep at all for the last few days. Every evening, I'm buzzing. I try to pace myself because God knows what I might do. Sorry, I can see you're tired. Go to bed. I'll stay here for a bit, okay?"

"I'd rather stay with you."

"Do you think it might be my mind still processing the data? If they did indeed use alien technologies to build the Crystal Sphere, does that mean that this data could actually control the world?"

"I think you need some sleep. Would you like me to go to Platinus for some sleeping potion?"

She stood up abruptly. "That's not a solution. Why is it I keep thinking about this quest?"

Once again she leaned over the book. The candles' diffused glow struggled to disperse the soft evening twilight.

A bright throbbing light cast sharp shadows

across the room, illuminating our faces.

The Staff of a Hydra — which had been sitting quietly in its custom-made stand across the room — turned translucent. The precious stone topping it had changed its color to an emerald green.

Enea turned to it in surprise. The autumnal aura of the Forest Nymph buff enveloped her.

I turned too. Could it be Lethmiel taking liberties? But no, there was no one else in these vaulted rooms. The doors were closed.

"Alex, what's going on?"

"I've no idea. But... you're so incredibly beautiful!"

"Wait," embarrassed, she glanced in the mirror. "Who cast Forest Nymph on me?"

"Could it be the staff? It's a natural artifact, after all."

"Do you want to say it reacted to the quest we'd received?" Enea cast a meaningful glance at the picture we'd just been studying.

Lush greenery formed the building's walls. A few moss-covered stone columns peeked through the paraphernalia of plants and gnarly branches.

"Don't you think we've seen this picture before?" she asked.

"I haven't. First time I see this."

"Come on, use your imagination. Think of the inner courts here in Rion before we cleared them of all the greenery."

"Yeah, sort of," I agreed. "Only you can't just grow some vines over castle ruins and call it a shrine!"

"That depends!" her eyes glinted. She appeared intoxicated on her own enthusiasm. "Wait... I know! I must be off now!"

"No, wait! I'm coming with you!"

"Please don't! I must do it myself! I need to find some outlet for this weird force within me! See you in the morning!"

A teleport whirled up, extinguishing the candles.

Both Enea and the Staff of a Hydra were gone.

Alpha — who still couldn't get used to her constant mini-porting — fluttered out of the open window, flapping his wings angrily.

I walked out onto the balcony and looked down.

A weak green light flashed in one of the castle's far-off inner courts.

We all harbor the need for self-fulfillment. Enea wasn't an exception. I was the last person to stand in her way, even if just by over-protecting her.

If indeed her mind expander continued to process the data we'd received in the Temple of Oblivion, she might have come into possession of some new abilities she'd been subconsciously trying to achieve.

The flashes of green light became more frequent.

Suppressing my growing anxiety, I forced myself not to interfere. I walked back into the room and lay on the unmade bed, listening in to the crickets' incessant chirping.

I was asleep before I knew it.

* * *

I awoke in the morning to the sentries' screaming,

"Hydras! Goblins! Sound the alarm!"

The clan chat was about to explode with their hollering. It felt as if they were shouting right over my ear.

I sprang from the bed.

Enea hadn't been back yet. I could sense the turmoil enveloping the castle with every fiber of my body. I'd never witnessed such a desperate unanimous panic before.

Mechanically I used my preferred spell which allowed me to port within direct line of sight. That was the quickest way to get to the balcony and take in the whole panorama of the castle premises.

I immediately saw the reason for all the commotion. A huge, absolutely enormous Ancient Hydra had just surfaced midstream and was now wading toward the castle surrounded by others not much smaller, raising giant waves in their wake.

I paused, peering at them.

The creatures' tags were green. They were friends.

A raft appeared behind them. I activated my Observation Skills and focused for a better look.

Well, well, well. If it wasn't the goblins' chief shaman!

He looked so old and fragile that he resembled a crooked piece of driftwood overgrown with moss. Elite level-100 warriors surrounded him. I'd never seen anything like them before.

Their tags were green too.

Now why would they deem us worthy of all this theater? What kind of friendly visit was this?

"Don't aggro anything!" I shouted into the combat chat. Attacking the Hydra could prove to be fatal in this situation. "Arwan, White, Lethmiel, I need you now! Meet me at the level-zero teleport!"

I focused on a spot of the cobblestone square below and ported there.

The peasants' camps surrounding it were in turmoil. Armed with pitchforks, men hurried to line up to block off the attackers. Women and children sought refuge in the ruins of the outer walls.

My warriors came running from the barracks and hurried to serry their ranks, barring the enemy's way to the donjon. Bristling with weapons, another line of soldiers stood in front of the breaches in the outer wall.

The cargo portal disgorged the Cargonite Golem. Emitting a mechanical humming noise, the creature stood up to his full height clenching his halberd and casting fiery glances around, searching for the enemy.

The archers on the walls drew their bows and waited for my command. The Elven refugees crowded nearby, presided over by three druids. I could see they didn't know what to think about it all.

Off-duty dwarves poured out of the tavern while all the others stopped working and trickled toward the square, adding to the crowd.

To add to the commotion, tongues of black flames rose into the sky, announcing the arrival of Christa.

On top of the nearest towers, the catapults' mechanisms creaked into action. I heard Platinus' voice,

"That's not ammo! Those barrels over there, the ones with the green markings, can you see them? Bring them over here! Put the torches away! This stuff doesn't need igniting! It'll go off all on its own!"

"Enea, where are you?" I shouted.

I ran toward the jetty followed by the clomping of the golem, with the two Guards of

Gloom covering my back.

Finally, I saw White — pale, tense and ready to fight.

"Alex, please don't hurt them," Enea's voice sounded weak and tired as if she hadn't slept all night. "I'm coming now."

"Can you explain what's going on?"

"You'll see in a minute. I didn't expect it myself."

"Expect what?"

The crowd was about to freak out and lose control.

I stopped opposite a breach in the wall which offered a direct view of the jetty and part of the shore. "Step back, everyone!"

The clan's combat units continued to line up behind my back. The raid's night shift hadn't been relieved yet which was why most senior officers were still here in Rion: Iskandar in charge of the wizards and Archie controlling the warriors. Rodrigo, however, was still in the Yonder Isles.

Arwan, White and the two Guards of Gloom made up my personal retinue. But where was Enea? What the hell was going on?

Christa kept a low profile in the crowd, apparently not in a hurry to transform into her Infernal guise. Wise decision. The arrival of a demon could only make the situation worse.

In the meantime, events had taken an

irreversible turn.

The Ancient Hydra climbed out onto the shore: a level-230 mob from some top moor location as yet inaccessible to us. Water ran down its lustrous black scaly skin.

The hydra's twelve jaws exhaled clouds of toxins. Strangely enough, the deadly mist dissipated almost straight away, leaving behind a faint aroma of herbs and flowers.

The crude raft hit the jetty. The elite goblin warriors expertly moored it, then reverently helped the ancient shaman to alight onto the pier.

The sky darkened. The crowd dissolved in fearful murmurs and shrieks of panic. A humongous Black Mantis the size of a dragon dove down onto the shore and landed not very far from me, very nearly knocking me over with the downdraft.

The golem's level counter span. He raised a menacing halberd. I stopped him just in time via the clan interface.

This wasn't normal. Between the two of them, the Hydra and the Black Mantis could single-handedly wipe our army out. But it didn't look as if they were going to. The two location bosses were friendly.

Leaning on his gnarly staff, the shaman walked through the breach in the wall and stopped. Both the Ancient Hydra and the Mantis King did the same.

The Elven druids, too, stepped forward and froze with their hands raised above their heads.

The air seemed to be ringing with tension. None of us had any idea what was going to happen next.

A soft melodious chiming rang through the air.

The morning sunrays reached through the breaches in the wall and dissolved into cascades of warm light.

A flickering blue beam dashed over the overgrown paving stones, drawing three circles which flashed brightly, revealing the symbols of the Founders' language.

A portal?

It dissolved in a flash of golden light, leaving Enea standing at its center.

Silence fell.

Magic auras expired all around us as our wizards aborted their spells.

The peasants lowered their pitchforks. The warriors sheathed their swords.

No orders sounded. The sunlit stillness embraced us.

Enea looked unbelievably beautiful. Which had nothing to do with the Forest Nymph buff still flashing in her tag.

She was enveloped in light and clad in

flowing white garments. Her hair was braided with flowers.

But where was her Staff of a Hydra?

It was gone.

Enea's gaze sought me out in the crowd. She gave me an encouraging smile, then walked toward the two location bosses.

The Ancient Hydra bent its tentacles in a clumsy bow and lowered its twelve necks bulging with muscles.

The Mantis King dropped to the ground too, greeting the Forest Nymph. To my surprise, I noticed Alpha standing next to him.

Grunting with the effort, the Goblin shaman sank to his knees without taking his eyes from Enea's face.

The Elven druids began to sing in a rustling ancient tongue, a soft sound reminiscent of the whisper of the wind and the murmur of tree tops.

Enea walked over to the ancient shaman and helped him back to his feet. She ran her hand over the Mantis King's impregnable scaly armor, encouraging him to raise his proud head, then touched the Hydra.

"Follow me!" her clear voice rang over the square.

The crowd obediently parted.

In the meantime the sun rose higher, reaching over the merlons and pointing clearly at the western towers.

We hadn't yet started the works there. The walls there were still overgrown with vines, their canopies forming green roofs over the terraced cascades of the inner courts.

Enea stepped onto the path of warm sunlight and followed it, enveloped in the constant glow of new levels being received.

A giant crystal screen materialized in the sky,

The ancient magic has returned to the world!

A new Shrine of Nature has been built overnight with the power of selfless desire, becoming a new center of life and embodying all the skill and knowledge which was lost to obscurity!

The ancient beings, the rulers of the kingdom of nature, have sensed and acknowledged the new power which has transformed the castle's ruins.

From now on, whenever Rion Castle is in trouble they will come to its rescue!

Each visitor to the Shrine will receive a one-off Regeneration ability granting recovery from the most mortal of wounds.

Enea continued to walk toward the Temple, still enveloped in the constant shimmer of new levels being received. The Mantis King, the Ancient Hydra, the three Elven druids and the age-bent Goblin shaman followed her.

A new system message appeared in my interface,

Quest alert: Spirit of the Woods. Quest completed!
The Elves have received a shrine. From now on, they will remain in Rion Castle as your faithful allies.

* * *

Later, I remembered this morning — which was destined to become the new legend of the VR world — with its incredible abundance of light, intoxicating air and the stunning beauty of what was unfolding around us.

The sunray-woven path directed us to the magically restored part of the castle.

Only yesterday, its crumbling towers had lain in heaps of rubble. Now my eyes rejoiced looking at the delicate archways which rose over its three inner courts.

The magic stone of Rion's walls had changed its properties and color. Now, an intricate floral pattern covered the snow-white columns. Repeating the complex design, thick vines climbed up the stone, vaulting overhead to form a high, elaborate ceiling.

The vines began to release young green shoots which opened one by one, revealing their first sticky leaves. Clusters of blossoms in every possible shape and color filled the air with their delicate scent. Water warbled in lacy cascades amongst them.

The whole scene was permeated by sunrays seeping through the foliage and casting fancy patterns of light across the shady rooms.

The central hall of this new section was large enough to house all of the castle's inhabitants as well as the visitors.

I stepped in and froze in disbelief, recognizing the Staff of a Hydra in an incredible translucent plant veined with a web of finest capillaries.

The ruby which had once topped it was now encased within the staff's crystal body which resembled a tree trunk. Awoken by the drop of Enea's blood she's once shared with it, the stone now pulsated like a giant heart, coming back to life and accumulating the power of nature which surrounded it.

Mechanically I focused on it. A prompt popped up straight away,

The Heart of Rion Castle
Permanent effect: Regeneration Aura. Restores 10 hp per sec within the Shrine's grounds and 1 hp per sec within the confines of Rion Castle.

All pilgrims to the Shrine receive a one-off Regeneration ability which they can then use at their own discretion.

Restrictions: only one pilgrimage per month is allowed to any friendly or neutral character.

Enemies of Rion Castle cannot benefit from the Regeneration Aura. If they attempt to attack the Castle, they will be subjected to the Aura of a Predator which will slow down their reaction times and cause the enemy's stamina to drop 10%.

Enea had transformed, too. She'd finally found her ideal digital incarnation which perfectly reflected her identity.

The words *Combat Wizard* had disappeared from her name tag.

Enea. A Forest Nymph. Level 71

The Druids' song expired on a single quivering note.

Silence fell. Not one voice was heard in the crowd packed into the Shrine of Nature.

The Mantis King touched the Heart of Rion Castle. He froze momentarily, then turned toward Enea and spoke clearly in human tongue,

"O Nymph, You who has brought the ancient magic back into this world, allow me to offer you a gift. Please receive this Summoning ability. From now on, once a month you can appeal to my people for help, and my subjects will answer your call."

Upon saying this, he disappeared into the flurry of a portal as if he'd never been there.

The Ancient Hydra craned her long necks and touched the Heart of Rion. "O Nymph, from now on you'll be able to draw strength from the nature around you. Please receive this Mass Regeneration spell. Use it wisely. Remember: for you to heal someone, thousands of little creatures must share a fraction of their own strength with you."

Another portal popped open, enveloping the Hydra in its whirls and whisking her back to her secret location.

Now, the Goblin shaman.

Leaning heavily on his staff, he hobbled toward the pulsating Heart of Rion. As he walked past me, he mouthed under his breath,

"Don't even think things are different between us now. Until you find the totem, nothing has changed."

He then touched the Heart of Rion and said to Enea out loud,

"O Nymph, please receive this Understanding ability. From now on, you'll be able to speak to any living being, whether a plant or an animal."

Unlike the others, he didn't teleport back. Grunting with the effort, he turned back to me and repeated, burning a hole in me with his glare,

"Remember, Alexatis. We're waiting for our totem back. Now let me through."

The crowd parted. The chief shaman sashayed awkwardly out of the Shrine and headed toward the jetty where the raft was waiting.

* * *

The activation of the crystal celestial screen which informs players of the game's breaking news doesn't happen often. It appears everywhere at once, even in the farthest corners of the Crystal Sphere.

That's why the news of the new Shrine of Nature and the unique properties of the Heart of Rion spread like wildfire, triggering a tidal wave of pilgrims to the castle.

Pilgrimage applications began flooding in. Thousands of players and NPCs visited Rion on the very first day. Our clan ranking soared. We also heard loads of news, both good and bad.

The impromptu celebration lasted well into the night.

Enea was the center of everyone's attention. She didn't have one moment for herself. The curious crowds were a perfect source of information, inconspicuously collected and forwarded to our analyst Stephen who'd been urgently recalled from the Yonder Isles in order to process all this precious data.

The resulting picture was as follows. Many of the game's regions had suffered from the Reapers' attacks. Entire towns and villages were deserted in the areas where the new Reaper cult had taken hold.

"This is definitely caused by the defense mechanisms' activity," Stephen summed up. "Lots of natural disasters have been registered in the places where defective mobs have declared themselves. Droughts, torrential rains, subzero temperatures... There's news of inexplicable livestock devastation and several cases of epidemics amongst NPCs. By cross-checking this information on the map, it's quite easy to see that the arrival of Reapers results in the death of wildlife and the collapse of the local economy. I'd venture a guess that the Crystal Sphere's AIs have proven to be too inefficient against this new threat. Our defense mechanisms aren't effective enough against the Reapers."

"Are you implying that these mechanisms have shifted their focus to target the new cult's potential followers? By destroying their crops and livestock and flooding their villages?"

Stephen nodded. "Exactly. It's not the best delay tactic if you ask me but these programs make their own decisions. They've no idea that by wiping out whole regions they in fact destroy this world's integrity. The Crystal Sphere is crumbling. If we fail to stop the Reapers, few will survive. And even those will be forced to languish in a warped world — a miserable excuse for virtual reality. The Corporation's testing grounds are a prime example. The defense mechanisms won't stop until they chase all of the defective mobs out of there, stripping them of any means of survival."

His forecast was sad to say the least. I hated to believe it but all the facts seemed to point at that particular scenario. Now that most of the Corporation workers were dead, it was the game's emergency protocols making the decisions — and they weren't exactly known for their mental flexibility. They performed the tasks they'd been programed to initiate without giving any thought to their eventual consequences.

The game's NPCs with their neurocomp-based minds weren't much smarter, either. Even the dumbest of peasants amongst them had already put two and two together, believing that the arrival of the Reapers was bound to bring some sort of divine punishment upon them.

So they didn't have much choice really: all they could do was abandon their homes and join Dietrich's banners. Because he was the only one who held a glimpse of hope for them.

The party was in full swing but I wasn't in

the mood to celebrate. I spoke to White, then supervised the raid groups' rotation. Once that was out of the way, I sat down and got thinking.

If we failed to stop the Reapers — which meant the loss of Rion Castle — then we had only one solution left. We'd have to activate the only super long distance portal we had and use it to retreat to the Yonder Isles.

* * *

When the party had finally begun to abate, White and I salvaged Enea from the center of a thick circle of pilgrims.

The three druids took over from her. They were quite used to performing marathon rituals which could last for days on end.

"I'm so tired you can't even imagine," Enea laughed happily as we whisked her away from all the bustle. "And happy! I'm too happy for words!"

"But how did you manage to build the Shrine?"

"I can't even tell you! I was looking through the book until I saw this picture. And I thought I could reconstruct it. And then it all started happening. You should have seen it! Moonlight began to transform the vines and build them into roofs! The magic stones in the walls changed their properties! Alex, I *willed* new plants to grow! Moss climbed over the stairways before my very eyes! Water springs forced their way from underground. This is what I love, building something new which is so perfect and so beautiful. I could do it all day long."

She could hardly keep her eyes open as she said it.

I helped her into bed and tucked her in. "You need to get some rest now."

She gave me a warm happy smile. "Okay."

Then she fell fast asleep without a care in the world while I sat next to her for a long time, thinking about everything which had just happened.

Normally, all game events are predetermined and included in the script — whether they affect the whole game world or just a singular location. The way I understood it, you could always get an inkling of an upcoming event if you looked deep enough into the developments that preceded it.

I opened the castle's 3D model, highlighted the ruins which had served as the base for Enea's shrine and began studying them.

There wasn't a single hint at the possibility of building a temple in that particular area. No matter how hard I looked or how many times I rotated the model, the ruins looked pretty mundane. They didn't harbor any sources of magic power or secret stashes containing powerful artifacts. There were no ancient murals or stone carvings that might suggest the place's connection with the powers of Nature.

I stared at the weathered gray stone of the towers, the tall narrow arrowslits and the collapsed heaps of rotten beams entangled in the maze of omnipresent vines.

Apparently, location didn't matter. In which case, could Enea in her wholehearted enthusiasm have indeed *willed* the ruins to transform, breathing a new form and a new meaning into them?

Also, it wasn't just the ruins which had transformed. Enea had changed class too, receiving new levels and new abilities. It was as if virtual reality itself had faithfully responded to her earnest impulse, demonstrating remarkable compliance and adaptivity. Which, in my opinion, was in contradiction with the very nature of virtual reality.

I pondered over it some more, following this new train of thought.

No matter how much I loved Enea, no matter how happy or concerned about her successes I was, I had to look at the facts objectively. In terms of gaming logic, if what had happened today wasn't a predetermined event (and I'd found no evidence of that whatsoever), then it could seriously disturb the world's inner balance.

Why would the game engine allow Enea to do

something so drastic?

To locate the answer, I might need to go back to the Founders' library. All the knowledge I'd received there was still buzzing in my mind, disturbing and demanding further processing.

If the truth were known, my own class didn't really comply with the gameplay, either. Thanks to all the intense leveling of the last two weeks and last night's clan quest completion, I was already level 70. Two more abilities had opened in my Neuro development branch even though I hadn't yet had the time to check them out.

A new line — Artifact Building — had added to the Secret Knowledge column while a certain Shield of Reason had added to Evolution. Both abilities sounded interesting. Let's take a look...

Now,

Artifact Building

You've acquired Secret Knowledge, mastered Elemental Control, grasped Synergy and found the long-lost Object Replication spell. From now on, you can replicate artifacts. Replication type: simple (halves the artifact's properties). Each XP point invested into the ability will improve the replicated object's properties by 10%. That is to say, once you reach level 5 of the ability, the replicated artifacts won't suffer any loss in their properties. Further leveling can even improve their properties but no more than +130% of the original object's bonuses.

Restriction: The only items you can copy for the time being are those built by the ancient masters. You cannot create your own artifacts yet.

Shield of Reason

By having mastered Evolution, Power of Reason and Secret Knowledge, you've come to realize that each of us grows to become a unique universe best described as Ego.

The death of a human body isn't fatal. The disintegration of one's identity is.

You've spent a lot of time studying ancient scrolls which describe various methods of mind protection from any destructive external influences.

By repeatedly experimenting with the Elements within your control, you've managed to retrieve an ancient protection spell which prevents the enemy from controlling your mind. The protection spell has become your unique ability granting +70% to your immunity to all kinds of mind control. Each XP point invested into the ability adds +3% to the said immunity.

Once you reach level 10 of the ability, you'll be able to cast the spell on any one chosen item of your gear.

That was impressive. These new abilities were well and truly unique. Now that our confrontation with the Reapers was about to grow into a full-blown war, they were especially handy.

This was how my development branch looked now. Once I reached level 150, I would receive three more abilities; the rest were still blocked, unfortunately, until level 200.

THE NEURO DEVELOPMENT BRANCH:

Secret Knowledge, 1:
Observational Skills, 1
Spell Interception, 1
Unity of Schools, 1
Acquisition of Blows and Combos, 1
Reflex Optimization, 1
Unity of Origin, 1
Legacy, 1
Artifact Building, 1

Evolution, 1:
Intense Training, 3
Pain Threshold, 5
Synergy, 5
Crit, 3
Shield of Reason, 1

Power of Reason, 1:
Insight, 1
Self-Control, 4

Enhanced Perception, 5
Energy Transfer, 1
Elemental Control, 1 (activated ahead of schedule)

That night, I sat down and took stock of everything that had happened.

The world which I already considered my home — the world where I'd finally found my true love — was about to collapse. When I'd discussed it with White earlier that day, he'd once again warned me against putting my trust in NPCs,

"Not a good idea," he'd said. "If I were you, I should limit the number of castle staff and stop offering shelter to village refugees. You risk harboring more than you bargained for."

You couldn't very well argue with him. Still, I'd already formed my own opinion.

Human nature was a complex thing. Somehow I didn't think the Reapers would exploit its brighter sides such as friendship, love or fidelity. Could they become the extra push we needed? No amount of blood oaths could compare to the noble impulses of human heart.

Some might laugh and say there are no such things left in our world. Sorry, but I beg to differ. White was a shining example. Even his uncharitable nature of a corporate shark had harbored a sliver of paternal love which had pushed him out of his comfort zone toward misery and deprivation, dooming him to a life of desperate adventure.

Still, the question of putting my trust in NPCs which made up two-thirds of the castle's population remained open.

I looked at Enea. She was fast asleep. I tucked her in properly and gave her a kiss. Then I walked out onto the balcony and ported over to the top of the second wall ring.

As soon as the portal's flash expired, I sensed the sharp touch of cold Elven steel at my throat.

"Arwan, relax," I wheezed. "It's only me."

"Alexatis? You should have told me you were coming. I could have hurt you."

"Yeah, right," I chuckled. "We need to talk. Got someone to relieve you?"

He made a twittering bird call and waited. Soon two Elven figures emerged from the surrounding darkness.

Arwan and I stepped aside.

"Did you like the party?" I asked.

"Oh!" he exclaimed wholeheartedly. "What Enea did was a miracle! The Shrine of Nature has breathed life and hope back into our hearts! No one has done anything like this for millennia," he paused and glanced at me. "But that's not what you've come here for, is it?"

"Do you remember how we first met?"

I didn't need to ask. Being enslaved in the castle dungeons isn't something you'd forget in a hurry. Nor is your consequent liberation.

"What kind of question is that? Of course I do. Why?"

His reaction was too emotional for an NPC. Very humanlike, in fact. Any other Elf would have reacted differently to the same question.

"Ever since we fought that dungeon monster — Reguar the Arch Demon, remember? — you seem to have changed. Wanna talk about it?"

His face turned pale in the weak moonlight. "How do you know? That... that's personal. I never told anyone about it."

"I know. This is strictly between us."

For a while, he preserved a moody silence. Then he shrugged,

"When you pierced Reguar's heart with your sword, a poisonous bluish haze escaped his body. It touched me — and then it just seeped under my skin. It must have been some death curse. My mind went blank for a moment. Then I felt better. For a few days, everything went fine. Then one night I had a nightmare."

"Tell me about it."

"Are you gonna expel me from the castle?"

I gave him a searching look. "Should I?"

He paused, working up enough courage. "I don't know. My loyalty to Rion Castle is absolute but... I have these memories of living in another world. It's strange and very dark. Can you imagine a city with buildings so high they pierce the sky? Its streets are like mountain canyons flooded with moving lights. Crowds of people everywhere, and they're all in a hurry..." he fell silent, crestfallen.

"Is that all?"

"Then I started having these visions during daytime."

"Do they urge you to do something?"

"No. They scare me. They make me cling to this world even stronger."

"Do you feel the desire to go back to that other world?"

"Oh no! Everything I cherish is here! Tell me, is this some demonic curse? I noticed that every time the nightmare releases me, my vision and all my senses become stronger and more acute. I see ordinary things in a different light. Like a dewdrop on a blade of grass. Or forest scents. Strange thoughts come to my head. It's as if I already lost it once — and now I've found it again."

"And?"

"And it feels as if it's my duty to preserve it. I must protect and defend it. Whatever it costs!"

I could see he was perfectly sincere. He had no idea he'd occasionally harvested several neurogram fragments that used to belong to one of the corporation workers — most likely, one of the defective mobs squad members originally killed by Dietrich. At the time, Dietrich had only craved knowledge, hoping it could give him control over cyberspace. All the snippets of memories, disturbing feelings or unpredictable urges which could affect his own actions — he fed them all to the Reguar, then closely watched him for any changes the neurograms could have had on his behavior. Basically, he experimented on him.

"So you think you've overcome it?" I asked Arwan. "You think you're stronger now?"

He noticeably cheered up with my interpretation of his story. "I swore an oath — to you, Enea and Rion! And I will never betray it!"

Now I really should speak to Davre and the two Guards of Gloom. They'd been there too, as well as several other Elves.

"What about your kinsmen?" I asked.

"You mean the archers that were there with me?" Arwan asked. "One was gone the next day. We never saw him again. The others are fine. I can vouch for their loyalty."

"Very good. That's what I wanted to hear."

"Do you think those nightmares will go?"

"They will. They'll fade over time. As long as you stick to your convictions, you'll be fine."

"Thank you!"

"What for?"

"I had no one to talk to. I feel much better

---

now."

* * *

Our conversation made me realize one very important thing. Not every neurogram-infected NPC could become a Reaper. All those snippets of human identities acted as some kind of virus which could affect primitive mobs and NPCs while presenting the more complex ones with a challenging moral choice.

Still, White had been right in his assumptions. I needed to find Davre and all the other NPC team members who'd been with me during my fight with the Reguar.

As night fell, the party subsided a little, then resumed with a new force.

On the little island next to the freshly-restored barbican, the castle's guest portal kept flashing non-stop, disgorging more pilgrims.

I found Davre in the central square in the company of some seedy rogue types. Not a good combination at the best of times, especially as he was already quite drunk. Talking to him now was probably not a good idea.

At least so I thought. Apparently, life had other ideas.

Before I could move, our freshly-baked assassin Ylien slipped out of the shadows and joined them by the fire.

I never liked rogues very much. Of course I knew this was only a game class but I just couldn't help myself. I simply didn't like thieves, period.

They greeted Ylien as one of their own — and thanks to the clan chat, I could now follow every word of their conversation.

"Alexatis doesn't give a damn about you," one of the thieves winced, sipping his wine. "You're a powerful warrior, Davre. You can swat an Elf like a fly. And do they appreciate it?"

Davre preserved a sullen silence.

"No, they don't," another rogue joined in. "They gave the Elves a shrine — and they can't even let you dig a small cave for yourself! They make you serve peasants!"

"That's not true!" the orc growled.

"Isn't it? So you don't carry stones for them at the building site? To help them build their own houses? While you live in some hovel on the outskirts?"

"Don't start! I swore my oath to them!"

"Exactly. That was clever of them, wasn't it? This way you'll have to lug around stones for them for the rest of your life. You used to slave for the imps — and now you're slaving for them. I just can't see the difference!"

Davre looked lost. He didn't say anything — but I could see it had got him thinking.

"And even if you wanted to leave, you can't," the rogue insisted. "They'll cast a disease or a spell on you to make sure you crawl down some hole and die there all alone."

Ylien grinned, playing along. "So what should he do?" he asked the rogue.

"Anything's better than being a servant to peasants! He can always join Dietrich. He has huge respect for great warriors. He can remove his oath no problem."

"Bullshit," Ylien snapped before Davre could reply. "I don't think you've ever robbed anyone outside your own village, dude. Pull the other one."

The thieves exchanged glances. I didn't interfere. Ylien seemed to have the situation under control.

Highr the Kobold walked over to the group and sat by the fire.

Aha. This was another witness to the Reguar's death.

The thieves hurried to pour him some of their own wine. They hadn't touched the pitcher served to them by the Elves.

The Kobold, however, was known for his remarkable resistance to toxins. You had to go some to make him drunk.

By then, I had no doubt that these were Reapers disguised as rogues.

"White, Christa, I need your help," I

forwarded them the footage of what I'd just seen.

Both happened to be nearby. I didn't want to take risks. We had to crush the intruders with stats. I didn't want to risk lives. There were plenty of players and innocent NPCs around.

"Back me up," I said, then headed for the fire.

On seeing me, Davre turned dark as a thundercloud. The Kobold, however, waved a greeting, inviting me to join.

Ylien cringed as if the arrival of the clan leader had ruined his game. He played his role well. The rogues would count on him, thinking he'd take their side.

"Enjoying the party?"

The rogues acted as if nothing had been said. "Aha! Here comes our great uncategorized wizard!" they sat closer, making room for me by the fire.

"What are you doing here?" I asked them sternly just to take them down a peg.

"We're pilgrims," one of them hunched up, faking infirmity and revealing several debuffs next to his name. "We heard about the Shrine. We need Regeneration."

"Fair enough. Why aren't you in the Shrine, then?"

"We were just about to go there," the rogues replied.

Gnarly staffs materialized in their hands.

Leaning heavily on them, the two thieves scrambled to their feet and hobbled toward the Shrine of Nature.

"Liars!" Davre roared, indignant with their brazen transformation. "Alexatis, they're turncoats! They tried to recruit me into Dietrich's army! They pitted me against you!"

The rogues' level counters began to spin uncontrollably as the two realized they'd been found out.

"Harvesters!" the orc and the Kobold assaulted them at once.

The gnarly staffs in the rogues' hands transformed into lethal swords. The orc and the Kobold were killed almost instantly.

Christa joined in. No idea what spell she used. All I saw was some sort of energy sphere entrapping the two villains.

"Alex, Ylien, get the hell out of there!" White snapped.

In moments like these, your body acts on its own. Ylien and I rolled back, away from the dying fire.

Once again the festive sounds reached my ear. Christa's sphere began shrinking until it reached the size of a soccer ball.

"Got you, you bastards!" she gasped. "They ain't going anywhere now!"

"Are you sure?" White asked. "Is it safe

enough?"

"I got this scroll from Borisov. He gave it to me in case I came across any Harvesters."

We'd just avoided a mass slaughter. Had those two neurogram hunters managed to attain their full strength, we might have had a hard time trying to stop them.

I contacted the two Guards of Gloom. Both were posted in the Resurrection Hall.

"Have Davre and Highr respawned already?" I asked them.

"No."

I swung to face Christa. "What happened to them?"

"No idea!" she said. "I haven't got a clue how this spell works. Borisov gave it to me, I tell you. He told me to activate it if I came across any Harvesters that I couldn't handle on my own. And I think this was just the case. It's not as if we had much choice!"

"Why didn't you show it to me earlier?"

"Why should I?"

"Well, I could have studied and copied it."

"Sorry. I didn't think about it," she replied, holding the energy sphere in her palms. I could make out some murky images forming inside.

White cast a hostile look at the transformations unfolding within the sphere. "We need to put it into some secure storage. Or even better, pulverize it. Better safe than sorry."

"Go and port to the Hall of the Elements," I told Christa. "We'll see what we can do about it."

She nodded and disappeared in the swirling haze of the portal.

"Phew, that was close," Ylien said, brushing a layer of fine dust off his pants.

The fire had completely gone out. A dark circle about ten feet in diameter was all that was left of it.

"Hey, I know what this is!" White bent down and picked up a murky crystal ball lying on the ground. "This is a Soul Trap!"

"Is it empty?"

He clenched it in his hand, then winced. "I wish! It's chock full of fragments of memories. Filthy ones, too. A foul cocktail of blood, unquenched desires and other nasties."

"Can you read its stats?"

"Sure. You can, too."

Heart of Evil. Made by Dietrich, the First Reaper.

"This is basically a bomb filled with fragments of neurograms," White concluded. "Had they managed to explode it in the midst of all the pilgrims, there would have been a shitload of trouble."

"We need to move the guest portal further into the moors, away from the castle," Ylien said. "And keep an eye on all the pilgrims on their way to Rion."

"Yes, but how do you want us to tell Harvesters from all the others?" White cussed. "We're no mind readers. And I don't think the goblins will agree to help us. The idea is good, I agree. We can't restrict access to the Shrine of Nature. But we can't let in all and sundry, either."

"I'll speak to the goblins," I said.

"How? Did you see their shaman? He's one nasty sonovabitch. He won't even speak to you without the totem."

"That's my problem. Ylien, continue to keep an eye out. If there's a problem, let us know. We'll be in the Hall of the Elements."

In the meantime, the party picked up with a vengeance.

* * *

Christa's sphere with the two Reapers incarcerated in it was a terrible sight. Dreadful images formed inside, each one worse than the one before it.

White watched the metamorphing neurograms closely. "What are we going to do with them?"

"I don't think the players' thoughts are all

ghastly like this," Christa replied. "Which can only mean that Harvesters are much more dangerous than we thought. Apparently, they're immune to all emotions which allows them to sort neurograms into good and bad."

"In which case, what do they do with all the positive ones?"

"They either keep them in these Soul Traps," White pointed a disgusted finger at the crystal ball made by Dietrich, "or they just destroy them there and then."

"I don't think pulverizing the sphere is such a good idea," I said.

I cast an additional protection barrier around the artifacts. In order to do that, I'd had to sacrifice some of the energy generated by the castle's runic sequences.

"Just nuke it!" White snapped.

"Really? What if the neurograms escape in the process? Christa, are you sure Davre and Highr aren't inside it?"

"Yes, I'm sure. They were smoked just before I broke the seal. They should have returned to their respawn point."

"Only they didn't."

"I've no idea what happened to them!" Christa said. "Alex, do you really think that keeping Harvesters' identities in the castle is a good idea?"

"I have no experience in neurogram

disposal," I replied. "I've switched some of the Elemental energy to the protection barrier. Let's just hope it's enough."

I watched the silent scenes erupting inside the sphere. The fiery glares of ghostly faces were ablaze with hatred and agony. Looking at them sent an uneasy chill down one's spine.

"The Reapers won't stop now. We need to think how to safeguard the castle against them!"

"I know," I said. "I need to go visit the Khmor tree."

"For what purpose?" White asked.

"It's empathic, isn't it? It reacts to emotions and thoughts. I'll see if I can make a deal with it."

"What kind of deal?" Christa was visibly restless. "Are you gonna ask its permission to dig it out and replant it here?"

"Enea can speak the tongue of Nature now. According to Lethmiel, the Khmor tree is sentient. In the meantime, we'll have to close the guest portal and set up an autoreply to all new applications saying something like, *We're sorry! The portal is under reconstruction. We'll notify you about any upcoming possibility to visit the Shrine of Nature in the coming days.* This way we won't upset anyone. At least the castle will be safe for the time being."

"And what do you want me to do?" White asked, anxious.

I could understand him. "You will take command of the castle defenses. Everyone who swore the Blood Oath must patrol the castle grounds to keep an eye on the pilgrims."

"Will do. How about the raid? Shouldn't we stop the units' rotation?"

"Oh no. In fact, I should make new groups and send them there too. We need to reach level 150 as soon as we can. Once we do that, I'll have new abilities open in my Neuro development branch."

* * *

The rest of the night was uneventful.

I let Enea sleep in. At breakfast, I explained the situation to her. Then we set off for the Yonder Isles.

Archie met us by the portal. "We've run out of mobs," he reported sadly. "We'd just got the hang of it when they all stopped respawning! I don't understand. The location must be glitchy."

"Not necessarily," Enea replied.

"What is it, then? Mobs always respawn after a certain time!"

"That's what you think. The game creators did promise 'alternative development scenarios'. Not everyone likes smoking mobs non-stop. Some people prefer exploring stuff, or solving riddles, or even just having a peaceful leveling experience."

"I still don't understand it."

"And what if these isles are supposed to be colonized?" Enea suggested. "Then it makes perfect sense, don't you think? The first groups are supposed to conquer the isles ridding them of monsters and clearing the way for peaceful settlers. I'm pretty sure this place has lots of resources waiting to be farmed. And these old ruins must be packed with mysteries."

"I never looked at it that way," Archie admitted. "I'm a warrior, don't forget."

"You might be right. We need to investigate," I said.

Enea's suggestion indeed made sense. In which case, it was good news. That could open up a whole lot of new avenues for us.

"Colonization..." Archie ran a quick Wiki search. "Oh yes, the game does have this option! It's very vague though. It says nothing about the Yonder Isles. Just a bunch of general statements which don't mention any specific regions or colonization rules. All it says is that players can acquire city houses starting at level 20 and found their own settlements at level 75."

"Very well," I said. "We'll see in the next few days whether we're right or not. If the mobs don't respawn, then this area is indeed meant for colonization. Let's leave a few scouts here and continue to advance. How's our combat section doing?"

"It's level 82."

"Excellent. I want you to send out some scouts to check the nearest locations. Tell them to focus on the old roads leading both to the lagoon and the canyon marked on the map."

"Same farming scheme?"

"Yes. We'll keep the continuous rotation of combat units. How long did the mobs last?"

"Forty-eight hours."

"Okay, then that's the guideline we'll use. If we completely purge the next location within forty-eight hours, it means we can set up an outstation here and start exploring the ruins. We can bring in more people to hunt and work the land. Can you imagine the possibilities? A whole region free of Reapers, available for colonization!"

Archie cheered up a bit. "Good. I was getting a bit worried. Thought it was glitchy and all that. Okay, I'll go see the other guys. Are you coming with me?"

"Not at the moment, no. We need to visit the Khmor tree. The goblin shaman is a tough bastard. He wants his totem, and that's the end of it."

"Can you believe it! Never mind. I'll give the others the good news. I'll tell them we can keep going."

* * *

Archie took the path uphill while Enea and I continued toward the ruins.

My raiders kept smoking Ferrigan's Guards virtually non-stop. They had even developed some sort of unspoken competition for the right to fight them. White's example had proved contagious: lots of other wizards and warriors couldn't wait to test themselves in combat with this high-level enemy. We were not talking solo combat, of course — but groups of seven or eight players were quite successful against the Guards. Winners received various fragments of rare crystal armor. Light and sturdy with a bonus to magic protection, it had already become the most sough-after trophy.

"This land is bountiful and fertile," Enea stopped to admire the view. "Look at all this! I just hope our idea proves correct."

"You really think we can't hold Rion?"

"Oh yes, we can. I'm thinking about the future. It would be so cool to come and visit this place. We could go to the sea. I've already seen some dolphins there!"

Ever since the creation of the Shrine of Nature, she'd been beaming with joy. A child, really. I didn't want to ruin her good mood discussing our current problems.

We walked through a stone archway and found ourselves under the shady canopy of vines.

The Khmor tree sensed our presence. Its knotty trunk bent with an agility remarkable in a tree. Avoiding me, its branches reached for Enea.

She pressed her hands to its wrinkled bark and froze.

"It wants to talk to you," she suddenly said.

"How? I don't understand the tongue of Nature, do I?"

"*You don't have to,*" a rustling whisper reached my ear. "*You're a Neuro. That's well enough.*"

The tree's trunk bent again. This time its branches reached out to me. Its leaves, sharp and covered in tiny thorns, touched my hand without hurting it.

Barely audible, its voice touched my mind,

"*I'm the last one. I'm afraid I can't offer you a branch. I understand your predicament but unfortunately, this is something I can't do.*"

I had no prior experience talking to trees. I'm not one of those types who keeps a pot plant at home and talks to it. Still, I liked this one. Its self-awareness had justly warned it against us, making it realize it shouldn't give us an inch unless it wanted us to waste it completely just to make more totems and magic staffs.

I didn't try to argue with it. Instead, I replayed in my mind the recent scenes of desolation.

Dying forests. Earth parting, breathing fire. Glaciers consuming this world's entire regions.

"Our world is about to collapse," I sent it a mental message. *"We're fighting the evil which is about to destroy everything that lives."*

I tried to invoke simple, clear images as I said this. *"Your branch might help us defeat this evil."*

Once again the tree grew restless. A shiver ran over its trembling leaves. My thoughts must have scared it a lot.

"We need your help, Tree. If we don't stop the Reapers, sooner or later their hordes will come here."

"One branch can't change anything," the leaves rustled anxiously.

"Enea is a Nymph," I replied. *"Even a wilted twig comes back to life in her hands. Please help us. Do spare us a branch to make a new totem. On top of this, I'd like to ask you to give us some of your seeds. We'll grow a Khmor grove next to the portal so that you're not alone anymore."*

The tree grew restless. *"Why do you need a whole grove?"* it asked with some suspicion.

"You can feel other creatures' emotions, can't you?"

"Yes. This is a gift I have. It's for my own protection."

"We need your young to stop the Reapers from getting to Rion Castle. To ensure that the Shrine of

---

Nature is safe. I implore you to stand up for this world together with us!"

A long anxious silence hung in the air. Finally, the rustling of leaves brought the following words to my ear,

"I will believe you. I will give you a branch full of seeds so that the Forest Nymph can grow a new Khmor grove!"

Its branches lowered toward me. *"Chop it off."*

With a clean blow, I swiftly cut off one of the branches.

The tree shuddered. Pink sap poured out of the wound.

"Collect it," it rustled.

I nodded my gratitude and hurried to remove the water flask from my belt. I poured the water out and filled it with the sap.

Enea touched the tree's wound, healing it.

"Remember our agreement, O Neuro. Now go."

CHAPTER SIX

THE CRYSTAL SPHERE
THE YONDER ISLES

ONCE BACK IN RION CASTLE, I decided to check on Platinus in his lab.

He didn't even notice me. Hunched up over test tubes filled with bubbling liquids, he was muttering something unintelligible. A side table was covered in small colorful heaps of glowing magic powders. My interface failed to identify them. All I could see were question marks next to each.

"Plats? Can I distract you for one moment?"

"Eh?" he startled. "Who's there?"

"It's only me. Keep your hair on. I've got a new ingredient for you. Where can I put it?"

"What kind of ingredient?" blinking, he wiped

his eyes. "Sorry. I was a bit busy."

"The Sap of a Khmor Tree. It should be a couple of pints."

"Where did you get it from?" he asked curiously.

"I can't get any more, if that's what you mean. So please go easy on it. Is it valuable?"

"Never used it before. Didn't get the chance. But I'll study it for you. I promise."

"When did you sleep last?"

"No idea. I've got all these ancient recipes, a whole book of them!"

His eyes glinted with the enthusiasm of a scientist who'd finally laid his hands on some forbidden knowledge.

"Okay, okay," I said. "Enjoy."

Pointless trying to talk him into getting some rest. I could always order him to go to bed, I suppose, but what good would it do? He'd just sulk and pretend to obey me, then sneak out back into his lab.

"Have you made the explosives?" I asked him.

"Elementary," he fiddled with one of the burners, turning the fire up. "As long as you have Spectral Dust, you can make as many vials of explosives as you want."

"You think you could apply the mix to arrowheads?"

"Oh, no. You can't just dip an arrowhead in

the mix. It won't work. I'm still thinking about how to do it. I'll work it out sooner or later. Thanks for the sap. I think I saw it mentioned somewhere in those ancient recipes. I'll look it up."

"I thought Raoul was helping you?"

'Sure," Platinus pointed at the glowing powders on the side table. "I gave him a few of the stamina, mana and life recipes. Now he's working with them trying to improve them."

"And? Do they work?"

"Yeah. The Stamina powder is ready. I tested it myself."

"Why? You're not a warrior, are you?"

"It still helps reduce fatigue," he rubbed his eyes again, yawning. "I'm a bit afraid of OD'ing on it. I don't want to get addicted to it. But overall, it works just fine. Sorry, Alex, this stuff is about to boil."

"Okay. I won't bother you. Please look the sap up when you have the chance. It's not just rare: it's unique."

"Sure," he mumbled unenthusiastically.

* * *

The next morning, Platinus awoke me before dawn, knocking unceremoniously on our bedroom door.

"I need a mob. A high-level one. To test the arrowheads," he announced the moment I opened the door.

"Keep your voice down, will you? Enea's still asleep."

He switched to a whisper, "I mixed some Spectral Dust with a bit of that sap! You can't imagine! Get dressed, quick, I'll show you!"

"Wait for me outside. I'm coming."

I hurried to equip my gear. Should I call Arwan? Probably not. I knew how to use a bow, too.

Some inventions were better kept under wraps for the time being.

"Where do you want us to go?" Platinus asked, shifting his feet impatiently. In his arms he was holding three quiverfuls of arrows.

"To the portal."

"What, to the Yonder Isles?"

"Where else do you want me to get a high-level mob for you? All the nearest hydras are under level 30. We could get better ones in some far-off locations, I suppose, but it would take ages."

"Well, whatever. Come on, then."

We walked through the gate into the second ring of walls, then turned off to the barracks. The portal had been set up between two squat buildings standing close to each other, for security purposes as well as convenience.

Today it was Ishtar, one of the two Guards of Gloom, who guarded the portal. I'd managed to instill the importance of the task into their heads.

They relieved each other, protecting the only access to the Yonder Isles. If we failed to keep Rion, that's where our future lay.

Platinus was quiet and visibly nervous.

"You all right?" I asked him.

"It's been a while since I left the lab. Just feel a bit funny."

"Don't be so scared. You do receive your share of the raid's XP, don't you?"

"I do indeed. I invest it all in my profession though. I have no combat skills at all."

"Don't worry. I'll sort the mobs out myself. You'd better tell me how you discovered the formula. Did you find it in one of those ancient books? How does it work?"

"I invented it myself. Spectral Dust turned out to be a universal ingredient. It changes any substance's properties depending on the quantity added. The Sap of a Khmor Tree was traditionally used in medicine. But by adding some Dust to it, I got a lethal toxin! I even thought the admins might strip me of my levels again or block my account for doing it."

"Why should they? Poisons have their rightful place in Sword and Sorcery, don't they?"

"I wish," he chuckled. "When they downleveled me for that explosion, I sat down and read the rules nice and hard. There *are* some restrictions on poison use. Why do you think I woke you up in the middle of the night? In theory, this new formula disrupts the game's balance."

"It can't. The damage dealt by an arrow depends on the bow's properties and the player's stats. If he or she doesn't have enough strength or agility, they'll either miss or deal insignificant damage."

"That's right," Platinus agrees. "If the weapon is poisoned, it works the same way. The poison's effect can be calculated using special formulas. But when I read the arrows' stats after I'd applied the stuff to them, I realized they were imba. You'll see in a minute."

Talking this way, we walked through the portal.

The sun already stood high over the Isles. Three trails led from the portal: one which turned left along the sea shore, another that headed straight toward the savannah (where our raid was still toiling away purging the place from mobs) and a third one which turned right, past the temple ruins and toward the cliff ridge. We hadn't used it much yet. The scouts we'd sent that way had come across some high-level gorillas and got smoked without getting very far.

"Gosh it's beautiful," Platinus said without taking his eyes from the sun climbing the sky. "If only we could get rid of the Reapers and bring normal gameplay back! With safe zones and clear-cut locations, you know. We could use this place as a sea resort."

"Do you miss real life?"

"Nah. I miss the old Crystal Sphere."

I proffered my hand, helping him to climb a rocky ledge.

"I don't miss real life at all," Platinus grunted. In order to climb the low ledge, he'd had to pull himself up until he plopped onto his belly on the rock. His own strength and agility could use some improvement, that's for sure. I doubted he could shoot a bow further than ten yards.

The ledge offered a decent view of the location. The Mountain Gorillas, all of them level 120+, must have thought they owned the place. It was them who'd smoked our scouts and sent them back to their respawn points.

The terrain wasn't easy here. Mountain trails lain by the gorillas threaded the cliff slopes. Deep canyons cut through them in many places, forcing a walker to leap over to the other side. Gorillas could do it standing on their heads, I suppose, but it was quite a challenge for a human player trying to leap across a ten-foot crevice in full gear.

Platinus produced a jury-rigged telescope out of his inventory. Two complex little instruments followed which definitely looked like Dwarven work.

As Platinus had no Observation Skills, it took him some time to inspect the location and notice the mobs.

"Perfect! Alex, I count on you. They're huge. If you miss, they'll wipe these cliffs with me."

"You'd better tell me about the arrows. Why do you think they're imba?"

"Once the poison is applied, their stats disappear, replaced by question marks. Which means they become uncategorized. And whether they work... we'll see in a moment."

He threw a switch on one of the contraptions. A brass clock hand started moving, measuring seconds. The other device turned out to be a primitive range finder.

"We'll start by testing arrows from the first quiver," Platinus said. "They're covered in the following formula: 75% Sap and 25% Spectral Dust."

I strung the bow, notched an arrow and took aim.

"The nearest gorilla is at one hundred twenty feet as the crow flies. I can see its stats clearly. Let's see how much damage the poison can deal it."

"Provided it works," I said.

"True. Still, we're only testing it, right?"

I loosed off the first arrow.

The gorilla stopped basking in the sun and shuddered, then froze on the spot.

"Wow!" Platinus opened his eyes wide. "It's Paralysis! This stuff must be working as a neurotoxin. The debuff icon is clearly visible. Does it say how long will it last? Yes! Thirty seconds!"

The gorilla awoke from its stupor and looked around itself without noticing us.

"Now the second quiver. The formula's ratio is fifty-fifty."

I notched another arrow, took aim and fired.

The gorilla growled, then headed for us in huge leaps, zigzagging from ledge to ledge.

"Back off!" I shouted, raising my shield and baring my sword.

Platinus was ecstatic. I wish I could say the same about myself. The gorilla was thirty levels above me. The level gap would have been fatal had the monster made it to us.

Luckily for us, the beast's repeated damage counter was spinning like hell. By the time he got to us, he only had 10% life left. I killed him with a single blow.

"Super," Platinus offered me the third quiver. "This is 75% Spectral Dust by 25% Sap."

This time I played it safe. I chose the gorilla farthest from us at almost 150 feet. Predictably, the arrow glanced off, causing minimum damage.

Still, the poison's effect proved incredible. The mob tried to go for us but collapsed halfway.

"170 hp per sec!"

I double-checked the arrows. The question marks were gone now.

A Poisoned Arrow. A unique item made by a Master Craftsman. Poisonous damage, 200 hp. The duration and value of repeated damage may vary depending on the target's resistance.

"How many arrows do you think you can make?"

"Maybe a hundred," Platinus replied.

"Why so few? I thought I gave you a couple of pints?"

"Well, some of it I used in my experiments. Besides, this formula is funny. You can't just smear it over arrowheads. It seeps right in. We might reuse the arrows, I suppose, if we collect them up."

Now I understood why our little experiment hadn't run into any problems. Indeed, the game balance had remained unchanged — globally at least. There was no sap left. And while the existence of a hundred lethal arrows could put a certain particular player at a considerable advantage, that was the extent of it.

Out of the corner of my eye, I noticed a movement in the cliffs.

It was a wyvern nesting on a rocky ledge about a hundred and fifty feet away from us.

"Do you have any fire protection potions?" I asked.

"Sure."

"I want you to drink one and go hide over there," I pointed at a deep crevice nearby.

"Okay. What're you up to?"

"I'll try and shoot that wyvern over there."

"Got it! I'm off!"

Platinus gulped a potion and disappeared from sight.

I took careful aim, loosed off an arrow and began to watch.

The arrow pierced the wyvern's neck. The creature showed no reaction, though. An icon depicting some sort of shield flashed momentarily over its head.

What a shame. Apparently, it was immune to Platinus' toxin. A poisoned arrow at close range, and the wyvern didn't even flinch as if it was a mosquito bite! It hadn't even aggroed us!

"And? Have you killed her? Can I come out now?"

"Nope," I said. "It's got some sort of resistance. I suppose if I shot it in the eye it might work. After all, it's not much different from the Mantis' toxin. You've done a great job, anyway. Keep making those arrows. Try to make as many as you can."

"Can't you get some more sap?"

"Not at the moment. I might get some in the future. We'll have to talk to Enea about it."

"So what do we do now? Are we going back? Won't we pick up the arrows first?"

"Yeah right! I don't think so. I like those arrowheads but not enough to risk being ripped apart for them."

"Imagine if someone finds them there one day! They won't know what to think!"

"True. They'll think it's some kind of artifact," I said.

This was a great invention, anyway. Finally we had something to meet the Harvesters with. A hundred arrows were enough to kill them in battle without letting them absorb more neurograms. All other poisons known to me offered 20 to 25 pt. damage max, and this was 200 — and they were reusable!

* * *

We came back feeling quite pleased with ourselves.

The mountain trail offered a gorgeous view of the lagoon. The sight of the foundered ships was still calling my name. I'd love to go there, if only to check out all the mysteries concealed within their hulls.

A barely discernible black line hovered on the horizon. It was the tower where the Reapers' henchmen had captured Borisov. The raid was now very close to the canyon after which lay the shore. I hoped to be able to cross to the other island today and finally get to the mysterious tower.

"Alex? What are you thinking of?"

"Just trying to work out something," I offered Platinus the scroll Christa had given me. A fresh eye can sometimes spot the solution to a problem.

"Why, what's wrong here?" he asked.

"The numbers. They don't seem to mean anything."

"Oh yes, they do. They're coordinates. As simple as that."

"You would think so, wouldn't you? Only the map won't accept them. I've tried several times. The map-making app doesn't seem to recognize them, either. I even tried my Pioneer ability. Nope."

He laughed. "Are you freakin' serious?"

"Nothing to laugh at, man. This is an important message."

"You seem to be forgetting the world isn't limited to the Crystal Sphere. How about planet Earth, for crissakes?"

"Pardon me?"

"These are satnav coordinates. Latitude and longitude. You're supposed to use a map of planet Earth, not flippin' Crystal Sphere!"

Holy Jesus. Why hadn't I thought about that myself? "Thanks, man. You're a legend."

He smiled. "You're welcome. And the columns of numbers that follow the coordinates look like some sort of command sequence. It might contain an access code to be automatically recognized by some device. Hard to tell which one, though. Did that help?"

"Absolutely! By the way, is your Logout button active?"

"Of course."

"Do you use it?"

"Nah. What am I supposed to do in the real world? I'm quite happy here. I have my own lab and my freedom. Once we get rid of the Reapers, I'd like to do some traveling. White shared a secret with me. According to him, death isn't that bad even at 100% authenticity. The trick is, you need to believe you can survive it. You need to remember your name and focus on your loved ones. Or if you don't have any, as in my case, you need to focus on your dreams. Keep thinking about your main goal. He's died many times and he's still around."

I pricked up my ears. White had never told me any of that. I'd love to know why. "What else did he tell you?"

"Nothing really. He popped by once to pick up some elixirs. So we got talking. He's great."

"He is indeed. Should we be going back now? Fancy having breakfast with us?"

"No, thanks. I'm gonna get some sleep," he yawned. "I've made Grand Master in one night! Now I can use most of the ancient recipes. I don't even know what I'm gonna do once I make the Unrivaled Master."

"You can always level up Sorcerer," I said in all seriousness.

We returned to the trail and headed for the portal.

❋ ❋ ❋

Enea wasn't at home. She'd had breakfast without me and left me a brief message,

I'm working on the Khmor grove and moving the guest portal. See you in the evening.

Strangely enough, White contacted me. "Where have you been?"

"Back on the Isles."

"I'm afraid I've got some bad news," he sounded uncharacteristically anxious. "The Reapers are on the move. Last night they attacked Agrion again."

"How about Warblerford?" I asked.

"Dietrich's NPC army keeps pushing their way through the defense mechanisms. They're getting closer to the river. They've managed to move their main camp out of the testing grounds. It might take them a few days to reach the river, if that."

"You still think we should fight them there?"

"I do."

"Very well. I'll tell Archie and Iskandar to come back. I'll also contact Allan and set up a meeting."

"Okay. I'll be waiting for you by the village ford."

In less than an hour, I met them by the inn in the deserted village.

The Ravens' clan leader looked confused. It had only been a week since our duel but he'd already changed a lot. He was wearing a set of light but sturdy armor. He'd made ten levels in the meantime — a very impressive result. As soon as I'd returned home from the battle of Chaffinch Creek, I'd sent him a full report on the Reapers, stressing my need for allies in the looming battle.

"Alex," Allan asked me straight up, "what's with all the RVs in the field? Couldn't you have invited us to your castle?"

"This is where we're going to fight the Reapers," White said matter-of-factly.

"Why?" Allan demanded. "I think it's bullshit. To leave the safety of a fortress to fight an enemy in an open field? How stupid is that?"

"That isn't bullshit," White said calmly. "It's cold calculation. For several reasons. The Reapers' numbers grow with each passing day. If we retreat to Rion, they'll attack us using their so-called

'Dietrich's army' first, all those peasants and low-level mobs. They'll exhaust our warriors and wizards, burn out the castle's runic sequences and bring our defenses down to zero. Only then will they engage their main forces, nice and fresh. That's exactly how the Disciples lost their battle in the past: by locking themselves in the castle. We can't allow the Reapers to cross the river. We shouldn't surrender a single inch of the moors without a fight. They must arrive at the castle completely exhausted!"

"That's nonsense!" Allan snapped. "If they have magic, the river won't stop them! And how do you want us to exhaust them? They'll keep respawning, as simple as that!"

"Exactly," White said calmly. He must have realized that this conversation was way too important to start venting our differences. "This is the only weak spot the Reapers have. Once killed, they don't respawn. Their hybrid identities disintegrate, releasing the neurograms they were comprised of. Those neurograms either find a new NPC host or, if there's no one suitable nearby, simply disperse and vanish forever."

"But Alex," Allan turned to me, "didn't you say that Harvesters collect neurograms? Surely there won't be a shortage of them on the battlefield!"

"I'm sure there won't," I said. "Still, what

White says makes sense. A hybrid identity takes time to grow. Once it falls apart, no amount of Harvesters can put it back together again. To all intents and purposes, once slain, Reapers will be as good as dead."

"As will be many of our own who won't survive the sensations of virtual death," Alan grumbled. The memory of Chaffinch Creek must have still smarted.

"That's why we'll only pick the warriors who've already gone through it," I replied. "Today we're going to go online and make public all the information we have on the Reapers. I'm more than sure that other players will want to join us."

That seemed to have cheered him up. "Do you mean those who'd already died and respawned at 100% authenticity? How about all the others? Craftsmen and such?"

"We'll offer them protection in Rion."

"From what we've heard, Dietrich has some supporters among players now. Aren't you afraid of letting some turncoats into the castle?"

"Enea's working on it now. We might actually avoid all this backstabbing. That's all I can tell you, sorry."

"So that's where we're going to fight them, then?" Allan looked around. "It makes sense, I agree. This way we can collect some logs and test our capacity."

A new system message appeared in my interface,

Quest alert: The Enemy of My Enemy. Quest completed!

The Raven clan will join you in battle against the Reapers.

The Warbler's other bank was consumed by subzero cold. Further up and down the current, the testing grounds defense programs kept incessantly modifying the terrain, attempting to close the breach between the two worlds' adjacent locations.

"This position is excellent," White pointed at the river's steep bank on our side. "We'll plant sharpened stakes all along the water's edge. That way even if the Reapers freeze the river over, they'll have a hard time trying to land. We too can use magic, can't we, Alex?"

He was dead right there. The Reapers weren't going to have it easy, that's for sure.

"They can still port within direct line of sight," Iskandar pointed out. "Or even teleport whole groups provided they know the coordinates."

"We can handle that," Archie said. "I thought that Rion was safe from those kinds of teleports?"

"It is. There's a device there deflecting all incoming teleports. But we've no idea where it is and how it does it."

"Then we need to find it and study it, don't we?" White said.

Easier said than done. I'd already tried to work it out, with negligible results. Having said that... I did have an idea.

"Alex, I'm afraid time isn't on our side," White said, impatient for me to come to some decision. "We need to start preparing our positions now. You've seen how many Reapers have already arrived at the testing grounds. At the moment, they're still affected by the defense debuffs which gives us a decent fighting chance."

"Very well. I'm gonna look into this teleport deflecting device. In the meantime, you can start preparing our positions and accepting new fighters. We'll post any Reaper information online in a moment. Iskandar, we need to deepen the ford. Please don't forget."

* * *

I spent the afternoon doing some in-depth research, experimenting with the castle's main portal and copying the resulting runic sequences from the obelisks.

I'd managed to work out a couple of interesting things regarding the castle defenses, but not the spell itself (the world of the Crystal Sphere was entirely based on magic). Its mechanism just kept escaping me.

Finally, I was too tired to work and ported to the Hall of the Elements to restore my energy levels.

It was a mixed blessing. True, this place allowed you to recover quickly. By the same token, it now housed Christa's sphere containing the captured Harvesters, and that was quite a downer. A bit further away, the Khmor branch hovered in the air. Enea had already collected all the seeds from it.

I needed to get my mind off it all so I summoned Lethmiel.

He appeared instantly. "Alex?"

"Have you worked out what kind of spell you're going to use?"

"You mean, to charm the totem?"

"Exactly."

He nodded. "I've looked into it. Still, I don't think that using a spell restricting the goblins' freedom is a good idea."

"Why not?"

"Their shaman is wise and powerful. He'll smell the rat straight away."

"And you think he won't suspect this isn't the real thing?"

Lethmiel shrugged. "We can always try."

"Very well. In that case, get on with it. I'm afraid, in the next couple of days I won't have the time to study goblin artifacts."

I opened a picture of a goblin totem in my interface and checked its stats.

It was all pretty straightforward. All I needed was a Khmor branch (which in itself possessed some powerful magical properties). Then all I had to do was activate Object Replication which was going to shape it into the desired object.

Pointless dragging it out. I focused on the branch.

Slowly it began rotating in the air, spreading light clouds of sparkling wood dust which disappeared within the energy currents that permeated the Hall of the Elements.

"Lethmiel? Your turn."

"That's excellent," he openly admired my handiwork, comparing it to the picture he was holding in his hands.

"How difficult is it to charm it?"

"I'll manage," Lethmiel replied. "A totem can only have four magical properties. It can attract fish, repel any enemies, endow its owner with longevity and cast a Virility buff on all its worshippers."

"Virility sounds a bit ambiguous, don't you think?"

"I think that's the idea," he replied. "It might turn some worshippers into great warriors and others, into prolific family men. Depends on what kinds of thoughts you approach it with," he cut himself short and concentrated on casting the charm.

A glowing rainbow swirled around the totem, hugging it tight and breathing life into it.

The branch wended its way like a living thing.

"Are you finished?" I asked.

Lethmiel breathed a noisy sigh. "I think so," he said with a touch of pride in his voice.

"In that case, we need to send word to the goblins. You think you could hand the totem over to them? I have too many things to do."

"I can send a messenger to them with the news, yes. But I really don't feel like handing it over to them."

"Never mind. Let me know when they arrive."

"Will do-" he stopped mid-word.

The air thickened. A bright flash shattered the Hall of the Elements, disgorging the goblin's chief shaman, as large as life and twice as ugly.

How on earth? He'd just breached all of the castle's defenses! This wasn't normal! This place was off limits!

His old eyes glinted defiantly. He stood up tall and proud, leaning on his fancy carved staff.

I stared at it in disbelief.

The penny had finally dropped.

The goblins had never lost their totem to

begin with. The shaman's staff was a carbon copy of the artifact I'd just built.

The shaman gave me a gap-toothed grin. "I can see you've worked it out."

"Why did you lie to me?" I asked.

"And you thought we'd just welcome Rion's new lord and master to our lands without testing him first?"

"Oh really? So what do you think? Am I good enough or not?"

"Please, Alexatis. Don't get mad with us. My people had always lived here. You were a newcomer. How were we supposed to know you? Did you mean good or bad? Were you as powerful as people said you were? Would you try and enslave us? Would you start a war against us or greet us as these moors' rightful dwellers?"

"In that case, why did you attack the castle?" I asked, remembering their sudden visit when I'd been forced to use the runic sequence of the Earth against them.

"We were testing you. You didn't repay us with violence, even though you could have."

"Okay," I forced myself to keep my emotions in check even though I didn't find him particularly endearing. "How did you get in here?"

"I'll tell you. Give me the totem first."

"You have one already."

"Mine is almost dead. Yours is young and full

of energy. I can see that you've overcome the temptation to add, should I say, a *personal touch* to its properties. I appreciate that."

"Very well. Take it," I offered him the staff. Not that I needed it, anyway. It wasn't as if I was going to do any fishing anytime soon. And as for repelling any enemies, I was quite capable of doing that myself.

"In which case, here's my return gift," the shaman offered me a scroll so ancient it was crumbling. It was bound with strips of dry algae. "Open it."

I removed the wilted green twine and gingerly unraveled the parchment.

My heart jumped with joy when I saw the faded, barely legible symbols of the long-lost spell recorded in the Founders' language.

I struggled to make out the words. "Where did you get it?" I looked up at him sharply.

The shaman chuckled. "Do you really think that goblins are dumb creatures who only know how to fish and play tricks on humans? Our ancestors used to serve the Founders. They helped build this fortress. Some of its defense mechanisms require ancient magic to work. And I'm the only person who still remembers it."

"Thank you."

"Each gets what he deserves. That's how it works, Alexatis."

"Thank you," I repeated. The scroll I'd just read contained a teleport-deflecting spell.

"If I may be entirely honest with you, I also have an ulterior motive," the old goblin uttered. "We don't like Reapers. If you stand up against them by the River Warbler, us goblins will be only too happy. Don't be afraid of my knowledge. I'll never use it to hurt you or the Forest Nymph. Nor the castle. I swear."

With that, he disappeared.

Quest alert: Troublesome Neighbors. Quest renewed and completed!

Your feud with the goblins is over!

From now on, whenever Rion Castle is besieged by an enemy, they will become your trusty allies.

"Lethmiel," I gingerly handed him the crumbling scroll, "take it directly to the calligraphers. Tell them to get to work immediately. We need at least a hundred copies. I want you to take all the copies to the Hall of the Elements and charge them up. I'll check and seal them all tomorrow."

"I'm on my way, Sir," he replied respectfully as usual, then added, "You've earned the greatest respect, Alexatis. '*Each gets what he deserves!*' I must remember that. These are words of wisdom and justice."

* * *

The world of the Crystal Sphere froze in an uneasy equilibrium right on the brink of looming changes, whatever they might be.

Later after dinner, Enea and I walked out onto the balcony to see the sun set. On my orders, this part of the donjon fortifications adjacent to our rooms had no guards posted. I fully relied on Alpha the Black Mantis to do the job.

Alpha had taken a liking to the statue of an ancient wizard pointing his outstretched hand at the castle's main gate. Now he was sitting comfortably in the figure's cupped stone hand, watchfully guarding our peace.

The sun had just disappeared under the horizon. The first stars twinkled in the darkening sky.

A miniature fountain warbled gently. The castle's architecture skillfully combined the massive security of its defenses with the daintiest of finishes. Hundreds of craftsmen were now toiling day and night, restoring our new home to its old glory.

Suddenly the stone floor tiles dissolved in circular waves of black light interspersed with fiery layers of pictograms. The portal hovered unopened as if unwilling to intrude upon us.

"You can come in," I addressed the empty space. "We haven't gone to bed yet."

Obeying my invitation, the circle of black flames parted, disgorging Christa with White following in her wake.

A demon and a Dark Knight. They made a fine couple. It's a good job there's no such thing as age difference in cyberspace.

Then again, I shouldn't be jumping to conclusions. White might have simply hitched a ride, too lazy to climb all the stairs.

"Hi," he smiled to his daughter, then shook my hand.

Christa cast watchful glances around her. There was something predatory about her. This wasn't the girl I'd known in the days of our joint Middle Earth adventures.

Middle Earth! It must have already died a natural death like all the other game worlds, unable to compete with the Crystal Sphere.

"It's good you haven't gone to bed yet," White said. "I want to talk to you about Borisov. We really need to get to that tower and find out what happened to him. We need to do it before the Reapers cross the river."

"What's the point?" I replied. "It's been a week already. He can't have lasted that long."

"Oh yes, he could. Bors is a powerful wizard,"

Christa said.

"*Bors?* You mean Borisov? Do you know him well?"

"Sort of. I came across him a few times not so long ago."

"Oh did you? How did you know Bors and Borisov were the same person?"

"I found that out. Not straight away, though."

"Christa, please tell us," Enea piped up. "How did you two meet?"

"It happened when I had a falling out with the demons. I can't say I regret my character choice but over time, I realized it wasn't really my thing. It was more for a show, sort of. It cost me an arm and a leg to update my avatar. I tried to use my combat avatar as little as possible. It took me some time to learn how to make do without constantly switching to it. I even bought myself a house in a village. For a while, everything went just fine. But then a werewolf came to live in the local woods, fierce and clever like you can't imagine. That's when Bors arrived on the scene. He posed as a traveling wizard."

"When did that happen?" White asked.

"About a year ago. He couldn't handle the werewolf on his own. So he came to me. Some local 'well-wishers' must have seen me transforming in the woods so they sent word to him. I occasionally practiced in the woods just not to become rusty,

---

you know."

"Did you two kill the werewolf?"

"Sure. Then Bors told me what made it so smart and cruel."

"Was it one of the defective mobs?" I asked.

"Exactly," she cast a quick glance at White and immediately averted her gaze. There was definitely something going on between those two.

Enea seemed to have noticed it too. Unlike myself, she didn't seem to be alarmed by it. A warm, friendly smile played on her lips.

"Bors is a powerful wizard," Christa repeated. "Those mercenaries have their jobs cut out for them. He's either lying low somewhere in the vicinity of the tower or he's still holding the fort. I really should try and rescue him. He's a corporate worker, after all. He might know something we need."

"Sounds logical," I said. "Still, our levels don't yet allow us to battle through to him. And the teleport still doesn't work. I checked it this morning."

"The raid has almost reached the canyon," White said. "You can see the tower clearly from the sea shore. If we act in a small group, we just might do it. Is it true that the goblin shaman has been here? What did he want? Did he try to threaten you again?"

"Oh no," I said. "He left us as our friend."

I told them all about the totem and the teleport-deflecting scroll.

"Excellent," White cheered up. "We've already selected our main positions on the river."

He opened the map. "This is where we need to set up our trebuchet batteries. We'll also need some wicker shields for protection against arrows."

"I'll send some peasants and Elves there in the morning," I promised. "What about players? Anyone joining us?"

"They keep coming, either alone or in small groups. But nothing like the influx we expected."

"Why do you think that is?"

"I'm afraid, there aren't so many human players left," White replied. "This is scary. I've never been afraid of anything in my whole life. And now I am. When I first joined the Crystal Sphere, it had billions of users."

"There must some other explanation. They can't have all died because of their implants. What do you think?"

"That's what we're going to ask Bors about... provided we can find him."

"So it's settled, then?" I asked him. "We're going to storm the tower, right?"

"That's up to you," White replied. "This is your clan and your castle."

"In that case, see you tomorrow morning by the portal. I need to decide who else to take with us."

As we spoke, the air had grown noticeably cooler. Enea and Christa had retired to the fireplace, leaving us alone. The unusually cold nights had forced us to start the fire in our rooms every night.

I could hear them laughing. The faint aroma of chocolate hung in the air.

"Yeah, right," I could hear Christa's voice. "How could I ever forget! What was it you said? *'Leave my guy alone, you bitch!'* You shot two ice arrows at me!"

"Well, it all happened so fast. I just acted on impulse. You looked so... so menacing."

Christa grinned. "Just a demon. Nothing really special."

"Yes, but those were my first days in the Crystal Sphere," Enea replied. "Down in that dungeon surrounded by all the skeletons, you know. At first I didn't even realize you were a player like myself. Alex told me about you later. And when you challenged me here by the castle gates — I very nearly swallowed my heart whole!"

"Sorry," Christa's smile faded. "When you live in hell you tend to lose some perspective."

"Okay. So let's not-"

"Why not? That's how I used to see the world then. It was all about pain and betrayal. Or indifference, if I was lucky. When I spoke to Bors after I'd seen Alex, I thought he was taking the piss. There's no known remedy for the ANM virus. So at the time I thought that the implant and all the game-playing would only prolong the agony. I was freaking out not knowing when and how my life would finally end."

"But everything's fine now, isn't it?"

Artisanal chocolate was heaped on the table next to a fruit bowl. Raoul had developed the chocolate formula. The fruit had come from the magic garden which had grown overnight around Enea's Shrine of Nature.

The deep red of Platinus' wine sparkled in the glasses, reflecting the light of the melting candles.

"Yes... I suppose so," she replied evasively. "I've been okay just lately."

"Right," White raked over the embers, "let's not get on a downer."

I poured out the wine.

The fire rose higher in the fireplace, erasing our sudden awkwardness.

* * *

THE YONDER ISLES

Early next dawn we headed for the Isles, adamant to get to the tower and find out what had happened to Borisov.

"It looks like our raid is seriously stuck," White said, peering into the depths of the canyon where our combat groups had been taking turns to fight their way through for the last twenty-four hours.

The thin ragged strip of the sky zigzagged overhead. The canyon's rocky walls rose up hundreds of feet, their eroded ledges almost closing overhead. I glimpsed a few cave mouths, dark and gaping. They must have been the entrances to some unique virgin dungeons.

The raid was busy fighting Rock Golems. This place was situated between two locations: apart from those stone giants built by some unknown but undoubtedly powerful wizard, the raiders also had the gargoyles to tackle. At first, we'd thought they were statues cut into the rock but the moment the raid entered the canyon, the gargoyles' figures came to life, creating lots of problems for our warriors.

It's not easy fighting creatures of Earth at the best of times – but when they're brought to life by some powerful Dark magic with some truly medieval Gothic spells, you've got your work cut out for you. You blunt your swords on their stone wings which they use as shields while the Golems shower you with lumps of cliff. Had it not been for the game engine which regularly cleaned the area of all obstacles, the canyon would have already been completely filled with chunks of rock.

"Watch out!"

We stopped, studying our warriors.

They'd just attacked the golems and promptly retreated to a safe distance, dodging their blows which stripped you of stamina. This way they cleared the field for the wizards and allowed our battery of three glaive throwers to do their job. Whenever the Golems bent down to punch the ground with their fists, they exposed the tops of their heads which was the most vulnerable spot of every mob.

"Should we help them?" Enea asked, watching two gargoyles dive from the upper cliffs onto our orderly formations.

"You'd do them a disservice," White replied. "They need to level up and get some tactical experience."

"What a bunch of idiots!" Iskandar snapped, watching the wizards. He switched to the command chat, "Whose bright idea was it to use fireballs?"

"Mine," replied Forlight, a level-70 Arch Mage.

"So you think rock can burn, do you?"

"Why not? Everything can burn if the fire's hot enough."

"Have you ever been to school? The Crystal Sphere is based on real-world physics! All that magic does, it allows you to use the laws of physics more efficiently!"

"Why, what have I done? When those wyverns were fighting the Ravens, the cliffs exploded with their breath!"

"That was water-logged lime over there! This is granite!"

"Okay, if you're so smart you tell me!"

"Don't you talk back!" Archie interfered. "You've got sixty seconds to get your brain in gear!"

Of course they were tired. The 100% authenticity had turned certain gaming experiences into hard going. Still, I had to agree with Iskandar. Forlight wasn't the sharpest knife in the drawer, that's for sure.

"I'm not Platinus, am I?" he protested. "He's the egghead!"

"You'll be too if I make you learn your science!" Iskandar snapped, then switched his attention to the warriors, "Keep aggroing the golems so they stay in my line of sight! Don't blunt your weapons for nothing!"

A glaive thrower went off, dispersing the canyon's gloom. Five fiery glaives hit a gargoyle, stripping it of 50 hp.

Jesus. This was no way to fight.

I peered at the warriors and called up one of them, an Elf.

He came running.

"Why do you think I gave all of you

Disintegration Potions?" I demanded.

"They don't work! The moment we smear arrowheads with them, they start to bubble and lose all durability! This potion is worse than useless!"

"You have sixty seconds to think of a better way to use it."

The Elf's face fell. He stood sulking for a while. Then he perked up and said with a mischievous glint in his eye,

"I know!"

He rushed toward the raid's master looter. "Gyll, do you remember we found that chest with all the glass stuff in it?"

"And?" the stingy dwarf frowned.

"There were those tiny scent bottles there, remember? With glass stoppers that are really hard to pull out!"

"Of course I remember. Absolute and utter trash. Why?"

"Can I have them, please?"

The dwarf cast a glance in our direction, then chose to accept the responsibility. "Very well. You can have them. But if you waste them for nothing, I'll deduct them from your loot share."

The Elf scooped the delicate little bottles up and hurried toward the glaive thrower. Clever boy! He poured some Disintegration Potion into each bottle and replaced the glaives' tips with them.

A new gargoyle had just nose-dived off a cliff ledge. The creature spread its heavy stone wings. How did they manage to keep in the air at all? They must have had some Levitation added to their nature.

"One round!" he shouted.

The weapon's torsion bar rebounded, loosing off the large spear-like glaive.

It hit the gargoyle in the wing. A recognizable glow spread around its stone surface as the bottle broke, releasing the Disintegration Potion.

The creature's wing turned porous. A fine web of cracks ran across it. Then it broke off, crumbling to rubble.

The gargoyle went into a tailspin, then hit the ground, raising clouds of dust.

In the meantime, the sky had grown dark. Strange-shaped thunderclouds had gathered all along the canyon walls. A deluge flooded everything.

Still sulking, Forlight watched the unfolding show. I could tell by the sideways glances he cast at our great and terrible Arch Mage that he wished him to publicly fail in whatever he was up to.

No such luck. Soon the weird downpour stopped.

"Warriors step back!"

The golems growled their displeasure, unable to cross the invisible aggro line.

The rainwater had soaked their rock bodies. Quite ancient to begin with, they were now also covered with numerous micro cracks from all the fireball attacks.

The whirling spirals of Mortal Cold formed above each golem's head.

The effect was impressive. The rainwater which filled the cracks in their bodies froze, tearing the rock apart. With a thunderous crash, these colossuses of old crumbled to the ground.

"Is that clear?" Iskandar asked, unwilling to reprimand the hapless wizard in front of everyone.

"Yeah. Sorry I snapped at you. You were right."

"Forget it. What are their respawn times?"

"Thirty minutes."

"Any risk of disturbing their boss?"

"Nah. We only need to walk another hundred and fifty feet. The canyon takes a turn there. That's where this location ends."

❈ ❈ ❈

Soon we walked out to the isle's precipitous shore.

Deep below raged the waters of the channel separating us from the neighboring island. A decrepit suspension bridge hung across the abyss, creaking and rocking in the wind.

"I'm gonna take a look," Christa said.

She changed into her Infernal form and kicked off the edge of the precipice, spreading her leathery wings in the air. Having found an upward air current, she circled the narrow channel a couple of times, then landed on a narrow ledge on the other side and began studying the area.

"This side is packed with Ferrigan's Guards," she reported. "Both warriors and wizards."

"Can you see their camp?" I asked.

"No. They're just ambling about the bridge, either singly or in small groups."

"What else can you see?"

"In the direction of the tower, it's only the jungle and some overgrown ruins. All the mobs are undead," she forwarded us the logs.

"Level 140," White shook his head. "It's not going to be easy."

"The bridge is too narrow and unreliable," Raoul touched the bridge's time-worn cables made of plant fiber. "I just hope it doesn't fall apart while we're on it."

"I could use Object Replication to strengthen it," I offered.

"Can I try?" Enea asked.

"Very well. Go ahead. I didn't know you knew the spell."

She smiled. "I don't. You shouldn't forget I'm one with Nature now."

Beautiful as life itself and mysterious as the

forests' subdued gloom, she still didn't know the extent of her new powers. She'd been spending all her days experimenting, studying the resulting logs in the evenings.

I'd love to know how she was going to strengthen this bridge. There was no vegetation on our side at all, nothing but bare rock. The cables were fixed to the cliffs with crude rusty hooks.

Enea looked around until she noticed a spring. Its water trickled down the ledges, dripping down in resonant miniature waterfalls which ran toward the edge of the precipice.

Enea offered her cupped hands to the dripping water. Whispering something, she splashed it over the dry vines which formed the bridge cables.

The long-dead plants exploded in a mass of new shoots. Before we knew what was happening, tenacious new tendrils clung tightly to the rusty hooks. The entire length of the bridge turned green, covered in new growth which ran toward its other end, covering the cliff opposite with a web of air roots.

The rotten footboards grew a layer of sturdy bark on top.

"All done," Enea gasped.

White bared his sword and stepped fearlessly onto the bridge.

* * *

It didn't take us long to cross. By the time we'd stepped onto the other side, two Guards in crystal armor were already waiting for us. Still, they couldn't do much because of the vines which had wound tightly around them, immobilizing both.

We were entering a true kingdom of nature. A rather narrow trail led us into a shady jungle of exotic plants. A soft, springy layer of moss concealed a cobblestone road below. It was lined with milestones that used to support long-disintegrated road signs.

"Give me one moment," Enea perched on a moss-covered rock. She appeared pale and ill at ease.

"Everything all right?"

"I feel sort of drained."

"Is it because of the bridge?"

"Yes. My mana is down to zero."

"You didn't give the plants all of your energy, did you?"

"I had to. I didn't have enough magic. It's okay back in Rion where things just happen. I miscalculated it. I'll be all right in a moment."

"Why won't you draw some energy from nature? It's everywhere! You can do it, can't you?"

"Don't you remember what the Ancient Hydra said? By borrowing thoughtlessly from nature, I might cause the death of thousands of little creatures. This is a very fine line and I'm not good at it yet. I'd hate to work miracles by having to kill living things."

"In that case, all you need to do is borrow small amounts of energy from strong creatures who have plenty to share with you."

"True," she cheered up a little. "If only I could use your Synergy ability!"

I gave it some thought. "We could try, I suppose."

"Are you serious?" she looked up sharply at me. "How do you want us to do it? I'm not a Neuro, am I?"

"These days, we've all become Neuros to a degree. Why would Reapers possess ability-intercepting skills and not us? Surely we can teach each other how to do it!"

"Don't know. I'm not sure the game engine will allow us to do it. Don't you remember how it downleveled Platinus for testing those explosives?"

"I think it's different now," I said. "The Crystal Sphere has changed a lot since then. I'm pretty sure the game engine is desperately looking for something to counterbalance the Reapers with in order to restore the status quo. I suggest you sit on your available stat points for a while. Don't rush to invest them into anything. Once we're back in Rion, we'll think of how best to do it. I'm pretty sure I can teach others. After all, any wizard or warrior can become a mentor and train others, passing his or her skills on to them."

"Now that would be fantastic!"

"You should listen to him," said White who'd been following our exchange all along. "Before, if you wanted to change class or acquire certain unique abilities, you could only do it through a limited number of quest NPCs, by paying them. But if you think about it, if the Neuro development branch exists, it means it makes an integral part of this world. In which case you should be able to pass your abilities on to other players. How you do it is a different question entirely."

"A 'limited number of NPCs', yeah right!" Iskandar laughed. "Where do you want us to look for them? I bet they've joined Dietrich a long time ago! I went to Agrion's Wizard Guild the other day. The place was absolutely dead."

Still, you couldn't put White off so easily.

"Exactly," he said. "Quest NPCs are becoming scarce but that doesn't mean life is about to stop. Their functions have to be transferred automatically to someone else. Iskandar, I thought you were training new wizards?"

"I am."

"And who entitled you to do that?"

Iskandar shrugged. "It just happened. As soon as the Wizards' Tower was restored, I discovered several new options in my interface.

Spell Training, Promote a Wizard, Bestow an Ability..."

"So that's the answer to your question, then. The game's engine detects all the failures, then tries to restore the original balance. Quest NPCs are vital to gameplay. And as they defect to Dietrich, their privileges are passed on to eligible players."

"Do you mean to say that Alexatis could pass his Neuro abilities on to the rest of us?"

"I think so. We need to try and see. But not now, of course."

Christa glided down from the top of the cliff.

"There used to be a big city just here," she said once she'd returned to her human form. "It's not even that damaged. No idea what happened to its inhabitants. It looks sort of fishy."

I contacted Lethmiel back in the castle and forwarded him the images.

He paused, then shook his head. "It's probably better you turn back now," he heaved a sigh.

"Why?"

"You've reached the outskirts of Oechis, the city which became the undoing of the Empire of a Thousand Isles."

"Which means-?" White asked.

"Oechis is the ancient capital of jewelry and gold work," Lethmiel replied. "When King Ferrigan decided to conquer the world, he gathered the most powerful wizards and jewelers and ordered them to create some incredibly powerful artifacts. Not many of them agreed but among those who did were a few Unrivaled Masters who couldn't level up their craft normally anymore. They made amazing new armor and jewelry for the king, using materials such as life and death or light and darkness. Gradually, they fell victim to false pride. Each of them strove to create something truly unique without giving much thought to the consequences."

"So what happened?" Christa asked.

"The city was plunged into madness."

"What, as punishment from the gods of both Light and Dark?" Iskandar asked.

"Oh no," Lethmiel replied. "The divine pantheons didn't even have to interfere. The arrogant wearers of the new artifacts brought about their own undoing. The items were so powerful that they took over their owners' minds. So if you still want to proceed, do be careful, I beg you. If I were you, I should turn back now."

"Thanks for the tip," I said. "Unfortunately, it doesn't look as if we have a choice. I might contact you later if we need more info."

White chuckled and gave me an encouraging slap on the shoulder.

* * *

As soon as we delved deeper along the jungle trail, the ancient digital legend bared its teeth at us.

These NPCs weren't the descendants of Ferrigan's Guards but their ancient forefathers themselves. Victims of the long-forgotten curse, the undead warriors of crystal stepped out of the jungle.

Their movements were devoid of any system. Neither my map-making app nor even my Observation Skills ability could help me predict their next move. Christa had been perfectly right: they *ambled* vacantly around.

As for Ferrigan's wizards, they didn't use staffs or any other spell amplifiers. This in itself held a serious warning for an observant player and possible death for a reckless one.

The warriors' armor glistened darkly in the shady gloom.

Archie watched one of the undead closely. Weak, listless and stooping, the creature didn't look like much of a fighter. His weapon – a long sword made of quartz – trailed behind him on the grass.

"I'm gonna smoke him," Archie said.

White chuckled. "You can try."

I noticed him cast Stamina on himself in preparation for combat.

Despite his enthusiasm, Archie did

everything by the book. He kept out of the guard's field of sight, apparently planning to first crit him, then promptly perform a coup de grace combo.

White looked expectantly at me. I nodded. He followed Archie softly like a cat, inconspicuously covering him.

The guard hadn't noticed anything. He walked around a large fallen tree and stopped.

The incessant chirruping of exotic birds drowned out the sound of Archie's footsteps. He was just about to perform the crit when the guard, seemingly so listless, swung round.

The long curved blade of his scimitar drew a blurred arc in the air. Archie recoiled just in time, barely escaping with his life.

White reacted promptly. Good job he'd followed him! Just as the guard shifted his body off balance, White sank the whole length of his sword into him, producing a glittering cascade of burst crystal armor.

The guard staggered. His life bar shrank – but only halfway.

In the meantime, Archie focused and attacked the guard in a complex well-practiced combo.

I waved to Arwan.

Three arrows pierced the guard's helmet. Enea and Christa joined in, too. Prickly vines shot up from under the ground, entwining the mob's legs; then a bolt of dark lightning put an end to this brief but desperate combat.

A golden shimmer enveloped all of us (with the exception of Christa). The guard smoked by our joint efforts had offered plenty of XP to go around.

"Now this is interesting," White crouched and parted the tall grass with his hands. I saw a set of familiar-looking armor glistening with burn marks.

It was a Harvester's body mangled beyond all recognition.

"Reapers aren't welcome here, are they?" Archie exclaimed. "I just wonder why he died without bringing all these NPCs under his control?"

"Because he had no leverage against them," Enea replied. "Didn't you hear what Lethmiel said? Ferrigan's wizards had been blinded by false pride when they created their artifacts. Because of that, their creations had awoken all the basest urges in them. The Harvester simply had nothing which was bad or nasty enough to offer them!"

"Which also explains why Bors decided to escape to this particular island," Christa said.

"In that case, how did the mercenaries manage to battle their way through?" Iskandar asked.

I chuckled. "Reapers can't compete with human nature. We're much more stubborn and inventive. A group of well-trained players who weren't too squeamish about back-stabbing or distance attacks could have fought their way to the tower, I suppose. Iskandar, I want you to send a Magic Eye to the tower. Archie, frisk the bodies. You might find something, you never know. Enea, I'd like you to stock up on Nature's energy for your abilities. We just don't know what lies ahead."

My map-making app promptly used the data received from the Eye to create a local map.

The shortest possible route was completely blocked with high-level NPCs. But if we took to the right, we would only have to tackle six of them whom we could aggro one by one.

I laid an optimal route and forwarded the updated maps to the others.

"Alex, take a look," Archie offered me two items: a small cracked ball made of some sort of crystal and a cargonite ruby ring darkened with time.

Heart of Evil. Made by Dietrich, the First Reaper.
Durability: 0

Aha. So Dietrich hadn't in fact made it. This was another Soul Trap, a Corporate artifact which Dietrich must have adapted for Harvesters in order to transport neurograms.

This one, however, was damaged and absolutely useless.

I focused on the ring.

A Bloody Eye. A unique item made by Yite, a Master Jeweler.
Absorbs the opponent's health by detracting from the wearer's physical defense.

Not a good item at all. We could use it, I suppose, but we would have to handle it with ultimate care. It didn't specify how much physical defense it detracted from its wearer nor how much of their opponent's health it thus absorbed. We could only find that out by trial and error – and now definitely wasn't the right moment for dangerous experiments like these.

I showed the items' properties to all the others.

"Bastard," White said, disappointed. "These rings come with strings attached. We need to study them in a quiet moment."

"We're now going to fight our way through to the tower," I said. "We'll be smoking the mobs one by one as a group. No solo artists, please."

* * *

Half an hour later, we'd finally killed the last guard and walked out of the jungle.

We'd made two more levels and farmed three

more unique rings. All of them had some positive properties even though they all harbored an element of the ancient curse inside. We hadn't received any armor this time: the undead had been wearing it for so long that it had long fused with their shriveled flesh.

A monumental structure built with slabs of granite towered over the ancient ruins long consumed by the jungle. *Oechis*, once a prosperous trading city, had fallen victim to its denizens' insatiable pride.

The wall around it had mostly crumbled away. The small marble square beyond it was deserted. A fountain at its center depicted four mythical creatures cut from large chunks of obsidian.

A wide staircase took us to the terraced layers of the Governor's palace, their tiled terracotta roofs gaping with holes.

The tower lay to the right of the castle. Apparently, it used to make up part of the palace's fortifications.

The marble square was perfectly quiet. I'd been worried we might encounter a large number of warriors here but that didn't seem to be the case. We could walk about freely. Some of the marble tiles were marred with round burn marks, still fresh — most likely, left by the recent combat between Bors and his pursuers.

Wary of archer snipers' attack, we hurried to cross the open space. Still, the surrounding buildings too seemed to be deserted.

The dark entrance to the tower gaped open. Its doors had been smashed from their hinges, the masonry around them damaged. A wide spiral staircase led upwards.

White raised a warning hand.

Now I could see why the square was deserted. The tower's ground floor was littered with bodies clad in crystal armor. I noticed three more avatars of mercenaries among them. They must have put up one hell of a desperate fight. Still, the battle had been too unequal.

"What are their respawn times, do you know?" Iskandar nodded at the undead.

A barely visible aura surrounded their bodies. I used my Neuro ability to read its stats. "I don't think they're going to respawn any time soon."

"Are they dead for good?" White asked.

"No, but they're in suspended animation caused by an uncategorized respawn-blocking aura."

"Do you think Bors did it?"

"I'm sure. I can't read all of the spell's properties. It's restricted-use. I've already had to deal with similar ones. This is the kind of spell used by the defective mobs squad."

White perked up. "In that case, we're on the right track. I'll go first."

He stepped onto the spiral staircase.

* * *

Contrary to our heart-chilling expectations, we discovered no enemy on the second floor. Unfortunately, Bors wasn't there, either.

We immediately came across the room we'd seen when we'd tried to activate that portal scroll. It was in fact the only room on the entire floor.

Someone must have put up a desperate fight here. The floor was covered in caked blood. More blood was splattered on the room's walls. The dead orc's avatar lay on the floor amid splintered pieces of furniture.

The bodies of three more mercenaries lay in the corridor outside. One of them was completely charred, the other two must have been slain by the crystal warriors. We'd found nine of those, all immobilized by the same uncategorized respawn-blocking spell.

"Bors must be here somewhere," White said.

"What makes you think so?" Enea asked.

"Why would you block their respawns if you're planning to leave soon? It makes no sense. He could have used the respawned guards to divert the mercenaries. You know what I think? Bors must have realized he was fighting an unequal battle. He must have pitted the guards and the mercs against each other, then taken cover somewhere in the tower, planning to come out once they'd smoked each other."

"In which case, where is he?"

"We need to find him. If he made this place his hideout, he must have prepared some getaway route as well as a safe place to lie low for a while if necessary."

"Okay," I agreed. "Let's take a look around. Arwan, I want you to stay here and keep an eye on the stairs. Let us know if somebody arrives."

It took us about ten minutes to search the floor. Pointless. No sign of Bors anywhere.

I was toying with the idea of climbing up onto the roof to see if Bors could have gotten across to the nearby building when Iskandar's voice called out,

"Over here! I've found a secret passage!"

He seemed to be right. A section of the wall where he was standing looked slightly different from the rest. Still, how were we supposed to get inside this secret room?

Archie tried what looked like the most straightforward method. He pulled a battle hammer out of his inventory and tried to break through the brickwork.

As if!

"We should be looking for some prompts," I said. "Let's check the floor again."

After some time, we came back to the secret door. None of us had managed to find a hidden lever or any other mechanism that might open it. We'd tried all the torch holders but they were all bolted tight to the walls. The masonry didn't contain any conspicuous stonework. In other words, we hadn't found any of the usual gaming prompts.

"Could it be opened with a special word?" Christa suggested.

"Or a skill?" Enea added.

I mentally rummaged through all the available options. I had that particular spell... what was it called, Illusion Breaker? I hadn't used it for ages. Ever since my arrival in the Crystal Sphere, I'd never had the chance to come across any phantom opponents summoned by dangerous warlocks.

"Why not?" I said. "I'm gonna try it."

It worked!

Part of the wall turned out to be an illusion.

A short vaulted corridor opened up before us.

White lit up a torch and stepped into the dark.

* * *

A steel door opened with a creak.

Torchlight cast long shadows across a small room.

Bare stone walls. No furniture. A heap of rotting straw on the floor.

"Mr. Borisov! Bors!" I hurried toward a human body crouched in a corner.

He was covering his head with his hands, muttering unintelligibly. His clothes were soaked in blood. The air was rancid with the stench of his festering wounds.

I'd never experienced anything so graphic before.

White crouched next to him and brought the torch closer for me to see.

Bors' life bar was barely glowing. An amulet on a delicate chain hung from his clenched fingers.

"Raoul, help him!"

As Raoul tried to heal Bors and bring him round, I took a better look at the amulet.

Respawn Blocking Amulet. Property of the Defective Mob Squad. Uncategorized.

Permanent effect: blocks respawns of all players and NPCs within 300 ft.

Restriction: Only for Corporation workers.

"I've healed him but it doesn't look good,"

Raoul said.

"What's up?"

"He's lost his mind," White said, watching drool trickle from the corner of Bors' mouth. "They must have damaged his neural matrix. Do you remember the microchipped dagger the orc had? I hadn't believed it then but he must have been right. His dagger could release the victim's identity."

"Iskandar, I want you to go back and search all the bodies," I said, then leaned over Bors.

We'd invested too much hope into finding him. We had too many questions that needed answers. Besides, I was just plain sorry for him.

"Bors, can you hear me?"

Slowly he raised his head. His vacant gaze slid listlessly across the room. "I haven't... given them anything they could use... The human race is in danger... Contact... Phantom Server... They can help... provided they're still alive..."

His gaze faded. His head hung to one side.

Phantom Server. No idea what it could be. I'd only heard the word a couple of times. Some sort of project. Nothing I could use.

That was it, then. We had no answers. No help coming from anywhere. The last sinew still connecting us to the real world had been severed.

Quest alert: Mysterious Wizard. Quest

---

modified!

Think of a way to help Bors restore the abilities he lost in his fight against the Reapers' mercenaries.

New quest alert: Phantom Server!

Find out more about this mysterious project and its participants.

Deadline: None

Reward: a new survival resource in the dying world.

As I read the messages, Iskandar returned.

"I haven't found the microchipped dagger," he said. "I've been looking everywhere."

By now, Bors' wounds had already healed. His physical health was fine. He stared fixedly past us, irresponsive.

"Very well. Take him and let's go back to Rion."

CHAPTER SEVEN

THE CRYSTAL SPHERE
THE VILLAGE OF WARBLERFORD

IT HAD BEEN A WEEK since our Oechis trip. All that time, I'd been starting every morning with a visit to Warblerford to check on the rapid construction of our defensive positions.

The weather had been fair all week. Still, the river's flat opposite bank was enveloped in mist and overhung with dark low clouds which brought occasional gusts of freezing wind to our side.

A low rumbling noise came from the other bank as the digital catastrophe kept gaining momentum. I could barely make out a few abandoned log cabins through the frosty haze generated by the testing grounds' defense mechanisms in their futile attempts to stop the defective mobs.

The bank on our side was steep and riddled with ravines, with streams running along their clay beds.

We'd been working 24/7. We'd quickly used up all the logs stacked up by the future bridge. Axes kept hacking in a large mixed forest which lay between the fields and the moors' edge. Peasants worked hard felling trees and cleaning them of branches. They then fashioned the trunks into sharp stakes which they dragged or carted off to the bank.

The current here was strong enough to carry our enemy further downstream. That considered, we had to build almost a mile's worth of fortifications.

We dug the stakes in along the water's edge, pointing them out toward the flow of the river. Overhead on the clifftop, wicker shields were being set up with a layer of earth piled up between them as a defense against arrows.

We'd engaged the Elements of Earth and Water to deepen the river bed. They'd done an excellent job even though this was belt-and-braces, really. I doubted very much the Reapers would use the old ford which was too narrow for a comfortable crossing.

Day after day, we continued to strengthen our positions. The support wizards worked hard memorizing the spells I'd found in the ancient manuscripts. Calligraphers were busy copying scrolls which Lethmiel then charged in the Hall of the Elements and sealed with a special seal I'd given him.

Platinus had come up with a whole arsenal of combat potions. His vials were delivered to the bank by the crateful and distributed to the warriors in wide multi-pocketed belts that our leather workers had fashioned for the occasion.

We'd soaked the wooden stakes in fortifying formulas. Magic was everywhere; the air itself seemed to be pregnant with it.

Back in the castle, restoration works were in full swing. We'd already rebuilt the outer perimeter and were now deepening the many channels surrounding the island. We'd closed the guest portal for the time being.

Enea had planted the seeds of the Khmor tree within the castle walls. They had sprouted the very next day. Now a whole alley of young trees lined the alley from the main gates to the Shrine of Nature.

We'd posted all the information we had on the Reapers at every forum, constantly reminding the other players of the looming invasion.

Quite a few of them had responded. The popularity of the Agrion cluster had peaked when hundreds of users from all over the Crystal Sphere had logged in to Warblerford to witness the preparations for the upcoming global event.

Most of them had chosen to stay with us. We didn't have a single empty house left; the village inn and the market by the ford were busy again. Small impromptu camps were mushrooming everywhere. Quite a few players must have considered the "Reapers' phenomena" as a new update courtesy of the devs.

It was getting hot here.

❋ ❋ ❋

THE CRYSTAL SPHERE
THE LOST ISLAND

"Alex, they're coming! Reaper groups are on the move! Harvesters sighted on the river bank!"

I was in the library of the Temple of Oblivion when this alarming report had come in. For the last few days, I'd been researching the ancient manuscripts looking for any spells that might help us stop the Reapers.

"Full clan alert! Bring the raid back! Contact the Ravens and tell them to march out to join us!"

While I was scooping up the scrolls and sealing some of them with magic seals (so that they could go off automatically), heavy footsteps resounded overhead.

"Greetings, O Nymph!" Yorm's voice echoed through the temple.

"Hi, Yorm!"

"Why did you bring a demon?"

"Yorm, I want you to meet Christa. She's very nice."

"You should be ashamed of yourself! Telling lies to old Yorm! A demon can't be nice!"

"This one can. Trust me. You're a cannibal yourself, aren't you? Admit it," Enea sometimes reminded the troll of his old food preferences if he refused to listen.

Yorm sighed. "Well, only occasionally..."

"But you *are* nice, aren't you?" she continued. "Otherwise you wouldn't have been my friend. Is there such a thing as a nice cannibal?"

"Oh yes there is!" Yorm stomped his foot, completely confused. The temple shuddered.

"Don't be so angry. You promised to go fighting with us, remember?"

"Fighting? Oh yes! With pleasure!"

"But you can't go out into the sunlight, can you?"

"No, I can't! Yorm can't do that! He will turn to stone!"

"Well, that's why Christa is here. She will cast a Veil of Gloom on you so that sunlight can't harm you anymore. Do you agree to that?"

The troll grew restless. "Will I still be able to

see? Gloom is when it's dark, isn't it?"

"Don't worry. Just trust me. Okay?"

"Very well. Will you please come and hold my hand?"

"Oh, no. Sorry but I can't. If I do, the dark magic won't work. Just close your eyes if you're scared."

The troll heaved a sigh which made the library door creak on its hinges.

I packed the scrolls into my inventory and walked upstairs.

Christa's demonic combat avatar was the same height as the troll: slimmer and not so broad-shouldered but probably just as strong. A smoky veil of protection spells clung to her new custom-made cargonite armor. The weak glow of her signature Fire Shield was barely visible through the murky gloom.

Enea was still wearing her Forest Nymph robes. Still, today there was something imperceptibly predatory in her looks.

In other words, the girls had come prepared.

Yorm squeezed his eyes shut and froze, clutching a huge club in one hand and a stone shield held together with rusty old anchor chains in the other.

Confidently Christa cast the spell which enveloped the troll in a thick dark haze.

"That's it. You can open your eyes now," she

said in a husky voice.

Enea chimed in, her own voice sweet and flowing despite her combat avatar. "It's all right. Don't be scared. Just do it. We'll be late."

Yorm shifted his feet, undecided. I couldn't see his face behind the magic veil. On top of sunlight protection, the spell had some other very useful stats, like partial water, air and fire damage absorption.

"This is good!" Yorm said in surprise. "I can see everything!"

He swung round and unhesitantly walked out of the cave into the sunlight. Here on the ice-locked Lost Isle, the sun always hung in its zenith overhead.

"How interesting!" the troll's voice came from outside. "I've never been here before!"

Seeing me, Enea and Christa exclaimed simultaneously, "They're coming!"

"I know," I said. "We need to get Yorm back. We don't have the time."

Just as I was saying it, the troll walked back into the cave. "I'm ready! Let's go! You're nice!" he slapped Christa's shoulder.

The portal to Warblerford was already open. We hurried back to the river.

* * *

The village of Warblerford was unusually crowded. While our two clans were busy posting our warriors and wizards to their previously assigned positions, solo players walked around wherever they pleased, climbing the precipitous bank and peering into the impenetrable mist.

The arrival of Yorm caused quite a commotion. A troll enveloped in a veil of dark magic can be a scary sight, I tell you. His name tag was crowded with buff icons which both Christa and Enea had generously showered on him.

Christa's Infernal avatar created quite a stir too. Most players gave her a wide berth, unwilling to stand in the way of a high-level demon.

Our bank was enveloped in what appeared to be a heat haze even though it was a cool chilly morning. The great many spells we kept casting had caused the air to quiver, dissolving in flashes of light as groups of clerics hurried to cast more auras and blessings while support wizards continued to activate passive shields.

A few last-moment portals popped open. The place went quiet.

Deep silence hung over the village. Dogs choked on their own barking. The intense anticipation of the past few weeks had now reached its climax.

The frosty haze on the opposite bank began

to swirl.

"They're setting up portals targeting our rear!" Stephen's voice resounded in the battle chat. "Time until opening: 5 sec."

"To all wizards: let them get on with it," I promptly replied. "Archers, keep your heads down and wait for them to arrive."

The opposite bank erupted in flashes of light.

Over fifty portals! Very well. We'd expected something like this to happen, hadn't we? We had a plan to counter it.

The portals opened behind our lines, disgorging crowds of badly equipped, poorly armed NPCs.

"Harvesters sighted," Stephen reported. "Five of them. Levels 100+."

"We'll take care of them," White instantly replied.

This wasn't the attack yet, rather a recon under fire. The Reapers had engaged the dregs of their army in order to test us, collect some logs and expose our defenses. Also, they probably wanted to see if we had anything to counter their portal tactic with.

The dirt road which ran along the bank became the arena of some desperate combat. The archers stayed out of it. I wasn't going to reveal our potential to the enemy quite yet. The solo players who hadn't bothered to join either of our clans now found themselves in the thick of it.

They were actually rather good. They invested all their enthusiasm in the combat, seeing as the enemy was quite doable. White, Allan, Archie and their groups got busy tackling the Harvesters. Three of them they'd smoked on the spot. The remaining two were about to absorb the dead ones' neurograms when the warriors came down on them like a ton of bricks.

"Harvesters eliminated," Stephen reported.

The short-lived scuffle was already dying away, falling apart into separate skirmishes.

A faint bluish haze trailed over the ground. Luckily, all those neurograms belonged to the slain NPCs. We hadn't lost a single player yet.

The grass was smoldering in places from all the fire spells. The road was littered with NPCs' avatars. Darkness hovered over the Harvesters' bodies.

"Well done!"

Once again the air on the opposite bank began to swirl into portals, more powerful this time. The Reapers must have believed that we couldn't disrupt their portals' work. Now they were going to use them to send some serious forces our way.

"Support wizards, get ready!"

The portal deflection spell which I'd received from the goblin shaman worked similar to the castle's defenses. Iskandar, Rodrigo and myself had taken some time improving it though. After a number of quite risky experiments we'd managed to work out that you could actually enter any coordinates you wanted into the deflection scrolls, choosing an exact spot where the spell would then redirect the portal.

It meant a lot to us. Our front line was overstretched to say the least. One deflection spell wasn't going to cut it. We had a good hundred portals to deflect, otherwise the battle might come to a bitter end pretty soon.

Support wizards stood posted all along the defense lines. Each one of them had three deflection scrolls with sets of coordinates already entered into each.

"Open the portals!"

The simultaneous activation of so many scrolls caused the air above our positions to thicken into a murky haze, dissolving into muffled claps of thunder. The sound crescendoed into non-stop rattle. Gusts of wind swept over us as the fiery circles of the Reapers' portals flashed and immediately expired.

Deep in our rear, fountains of bog water, mud and silt shot up into the sky in the Toxic Moors' worst impassable locations. You could probably see the explosions from Agrion city walls.

Even if any of the Reapers had survived this

magic cataclysm, they weren't in a position to fight now. This was our friendly offering to the hydras and other constantly-hungry bog critters as a small compensation for the inconvenience caused.

"Ninety percent portals declined," Stephen reported calmly.

Some of our wizards must have been too quick on the draw, allowing a few smaller enemy groups to avoid their peers' fate. Now they materialized just behind our positions.

A brief scuffle ensued. Seemingly fast and effortless, it was the result of all the daily training and the sleepless nights I'd spent in the Lost Isle's library, nights followed by some dangerous experiments which had caused both Iskandar and Rodrigo to respawn several times.

Then it went quiet.

The bank behind our positions was lined with deep craters where the earth under the enemy's feet had been ported to the moors with them.

The Reapers had suffered some impressive losses. We had no dead, twelve players respawned. I could see them hurry back from their tents to pick up the bundles with their stuff.

My heart pounded in my chest.

We did it! It had worked! We'd managed to trap and destroy about a thousand of the enemy. Even if they weren't the Reapers' elite, this was a serious loss for them.

Our fighting chances had improved manifold. Now Dietrich wouldn't risk porting again. He'd have to cross the river.

* * *

The players who'd joined us looked visibly disappointed.

In their eyes, this was way too easy. They'd come here looking forward to the mother of all battles — but so far, our first victories hadn't impressed them that much.

They had no idea the worst was yet to come. So far, these had only been the enemy's first and quite predictable steps.

The opposite bank froze in heavy silence. The mist flowed freely now without forming any more portal vortexes. Our scouts reported thousands of enemy soldiers lurking under its cover.

"Wyverns!" someone cried out in fear.

A smattering of black dots appeared in the sky from the direction of the testing grounds, rapidly growing.

"Fifty mobs with riders," Stephen reported. "The riders are wizards levels 90 to 160."

This was a serious threat which called for unorthodox measures. "Enea, you think you can intercept them?"

She turned slightly pale. "I suppose so."

She began casting the Summoning spell she'd received from the Mantis King.

A cloud of Black Mantises appeared above the moors. As they approached, the rustling of their wings drowned out all other sounds. They shot over the river and soared upward toward the wyverns.

The skies above dissolved in flashes of fire as a desperate battle unfolded over the enemy lines. The enemy wizard riders had come prepared. Gripping the wyverns' fleshy reins with one hand, they used the other to cast lightning bolts and fireballs, launching ice arrows and conjuring up toxic clouds.

"Ogres!"

The thick mist parted, releasing the figures of giants. I'd had no idea ogres could be that huge. Each of them was carrying a large chunk of cliff.

Blinded by the mantises' neurotoxins, several of the wyverns dropped down from the sky, breathing fire. The mist below dissipated from the flame; its licking tongues singed the ranks of the Reapers preparing to attack. The wyverns' massive bodies collapsed on top of them, disrupting enemy formations.

In the meantime, a desperate dogfight unfolded in the air. The mantises were in their hundreds — but they were vulnerable to fire damage.

The flashing of flames eclipsed the sun. The losses on both sides were dreadful. The fearless insects aimed for the wyverns' eyes, hacking through the reins and sinking their mandibles into the wizards. Still, their ranks dwindled rapidly.

The clouds overhead were boiling, dropping large flakes of soot.

In the meantime, the ogres began hurling their cliff chunks into the river. I'd expected this to happen and had already ordered our warriors to step back.

Still, the giants weren't aiming at us at all. Not a single chunk of rock had reached our positions: they all dropped short into the water below.

The ogres were trying to block the river!

The water current frothed around the half-submerged rocks. No idea what purpose that might serve.

We engaged glaive throwers. Two of the ogres were pinned to the walls of the log cabins; the others made a hasty retreat.

The sky above showered us with fire and the sounds of furious chattering. The mantises had smoked thirty of the wyverns. The remaining twenty, wounded and desperate, had made it through to our positions. Their mass attack had failed — but even though their riders had lost control of their mounts, even these chaotic assaults could be lethal.

The glaive throwers' positions had turned into a sea of fire. Toxic fumes flooded our bank. The swirling gloom of thousands of mass curses cast by Reaper wizards were halted by our raid buffs. We struck back with Ice Spears, ripping the darkness apart with bolts of lightning.

Once again our bank dissolved into a brief chaos of disorganized fighting.

One by one, the wyverns plopped to the ground and attacked our warriors. I watched the monsters thrash around in agony as their life bars faded.

"Log rafts sighted upstream!" Stephen reported.

So that's what the Reapers' plan was. They'd blocked the river with the chunks of cliffs so that the floating rafts would get caught on them and form a makeshift pontoon bridge.

"White!" I shouted. "Smoke the remaining wyverns and come here, quick! The Reapers are crossing over!"

* * *

Soon the rafts reached the blocked part of the river and slowed to a stop, forming a natural bridge. On the opposite bank, the ogres reappeared with another helping of rock chunks and began hurling them in the water a few hundred feet further upstream. While they were thus busy, the first squadrons of Dietrich's army descended upon us.

We still had a couple of wyverns raging in our rear. Still, several XP-hungry solo players were already taking care of them.

White hurried to deploy the two clans to their predetermined positions. Arwan's archers met the Reapers with a volley of arrows. Those Elves didn't miss!

Our trebuchets fired from afar. We'd already ranged in certain areas. Unfortunately, the Reapers had chosen to cross slightly away from our marks. We watched helplessly as the trebuchets' projectiles splashed into the river to the left of the makeshift pontoon while the enemy pressed on. The river downstream was littered with arrow-pierced bodies — but the enemy didn't seem to care about their losses. They were literally in their thousands, throwing fresh forces into battle non-stop.

Their avant-garde had already reached the middle of the bridge. Some of them hurried to build a shield wall; some of the others peppered the Elves' positions with crossbow fire while yet others were busy bringing up wicker shields to create a small foothold for the approaching main forces.

"Right ten degrees!" the spotter shouted instructions in the battle chat.

The trebuchets fired again. More boulders

tumbled through the air and crashed down on the rafts. Broken logs flew everywhere.

"Wyverns!"

The enemy's pressure kept growing with every minute. The opposite bank was consumed in swirls of frosty haze.

"Multiple teleports," Stephen reported.

"Deflect," I replied.

The earth shuddered as our wizards broke the seals of their scrolls. Still, the enemy portals were empty. They'd tricked us, forcing us to waste our precious scrolls!

Twenty more wyverns were rapidly approaching, aiming for the groups White was now trying to draw to the bridge.

I stood up to my full height. "Enea, back me up!"

A spherical magic shield formed around me, powered by the forces of Nature.

My heartbeat slowed down. I grew calm and focused. The only thing that existed for me now was the group of approaching wyverns. They must not reach the bridge.

The enemy noticed me. Dozens of crossbow bolts, ice arrows and surges of lightning assaulted my magic sphere, reducing it to zero.

The air above the river began to rotate and swirl, forming a vortex in the water below. The words of the ancient spell fell from my lips, summoning the great primal force.

The wyvern riders hadn't noticed the danger until it was too late. The rapidly growing waterspout swirled faster until it turned into a tornado which consumed both river banks, joining heaven and earth, uprooting trees and sucking the river dry.

Like giant fallen leaves, the wyverns got caught up in the twister. They couldn't escape it now no matter how hard they tried. The riverbed had almost dried up.

Finally, I'd used up all of my mana and lost control of the summoned element.

The tornado slowed down. Whatever it had had in its grip, now crashed back to earth: rocks, the wyverns' mangled bodies, lumps of earth, uprooted trees and tons of water.

The river banks quaked, sending most people on both banks flying to the ground. A frothing torrent of murky water rolled past, washing away the makeshift bridge but not the cliff fragments.

A brief pause fell. Then wizards on both sides joined the combat.

I hurried to gulp down some vials, restoring life and mana. We were still going strong, and that was the main thing. The Reapers had sustained substantial losses. Until now, not a single one of them had managed to cross to our side.

The trebuchets' positions, however, had

suffered a lot from my magic tornado. You can't avoid collateral damage when dealing with something on this scale. Had the wyvern group made it to the bridge, they would have made mincemeat out of our positions. This was the price I had to pay for using an uncategorized spell.

We'd leveled up way too fast. We had neither the training nor experience to control powers this huge.

Reports kept flooding in. We'd been suffering losses too. The enemy had deployed groups of high-level wizards whose spells could reach our side.

They seemed to be readying for a new attack. Dietrich was too mad about his losses to retreat now.

＊ ＊ ＊

The wizards' duel had soon stopped as I'd told my casters to quit wasting their powers and retreat to safer positions.

The opposite side was now consumed by the murky haze which was thickening and trailing low above the bank.

"Riders sighted," Stephen reported unexpectedly. "Approaching in an extended combat formation. Levels 100 to 120."

As if in confirmation, a ragged line consisting of a plethora of red dots formed on the map.

How many of them were there? Three hundred? Four?

"Riders at a thousand feet... seven-fifty... five hundred..."

They were galloping on at break-neck speed. What were they thinking of? They were about to plunge into the river rapids!

Seconds flew past, scorching my nerves. White's cheek was twitching. Enea was pale. Christa's eyes glowed with an inner fire.

The murky haze concealing the opposite bank eddied, then reared up.

This magic blow must have cost them kilotons of mana. How else do you want me to describe the sheer power of the spell they'd cast just before the riders' arrival?

The river froze solid from one bank to the other. A bitter cold descended onto our positions. A white layer of frost enshrouded the log stakes.

The icy air singed my lungs. A mass debuff made a hole in our magic auras, halving our stamina and planting the icons of Deadly Fatigue in the warriors' stats.

Our clerics reacted promptly, casting Cleansing and Endurance on the warriors albeit without much success. Our men staggered under the combined weight of their weapons and ice-bound armor. I also noticed a small repeated damage caused by the frozen cargonite of their breastplates. Our gear's durability had dropped dramatically.

The battle chat filled with alarming reports.

The wizards' intellect had dropped; their mana stocks had shrunk 30%.

Our warriors didn't know what to do. The clerics' efforts were little less than useless.

The mysterious spell had neutralized the stakes' magic coating, rendering them very fragile.

The thudding of hooves crescendoed to a rumble.

"Three hundred feet!" Stephen wheezed.

A piercing wind hit us, bringing a wave of freezing cold and blowing the life out of us.

Some of the players wavered and ran, trying to escape the effects of the uncategorized spell.

A surge of paralyzing fear rolled in front of the riders. For each of us, these were the worst moments of our lives. This was the end of it. We had nothing to counter the Reapers with. Any resistance would only prolong our agony.

I gathered whatever was left of my strength and activated the snow obsidian crystals. While they shared their energy with me, I cast Exorcism.

A warm wave of shimmering golden light washed over our bank, sweeping away all the debuffs. Our physical, vital and mental energy counters soared back up.

Within a few seconds, the tables had turned.

The spell's psychological effect turned out to be even stronger. Our warriors stood tall and proud as the ice binding their armor melted away in rivulets of water.

The wind died down. Snowflakes floated on the air. I could hear the neighing of horses and the clanging of steel.

Enea's lips parted, breathing out a short spell. The rejuvenating aura of Natural Vigor enveloped our warriors.

Yes, we were using up our unique abilities but we'd absolutely had to do it. The Reapers had proven much stronger and craftier than we'd originally thought. This wasn't a bunch of loonies: the main body of their army was anything but a brainless mob.

Finally, the several-hundred-foot long line of riders in their frosted armor emerged from the haze: an avalanche of steel bristling with spears, about to descend on our positions.

Our archers were the first to meet them. The poisoned cargonite tips of their arrows thudded against the Reapers' armor, piercing it and knocking the enemy out of their saddles. Their lathering horses ran amok on the ice, dragging their riders behind them.

A wall of fire knitted from hundreds of spells rose across the frozen river, followed by the crackling of lightning. With a low droning noise, fireballs streaked towards the opposite bank, leaving smoky trails in the air. Vials of Disintegration Potion followed in their wakes, hitting the ice under the horses' hooves and melting it into pools of acid-green liquid.

The avalanche of riders didn't stop. The Reapers didn't give a damn about casualties. They employed their elite wizards who cast Meteorite Showers on our bank, followed by another uncategorized spell which dissolved the remaining ice, clumps of frozen clay and broken logs in powerful fire flares.

By now, the several lines of sharpened stakes that had made our first line of defense were well and truly destroyed. Still, they'd served their purpose: the enemy cavalry had been bogged down and lost its momentum. Most of the riders had been unhorsed and had had to fight us on foot.

"More riders," Stephen reported. "A second wave."

Engulfed in flames, the river was boiling. With a thunderous noise, the ice began to crack. Both our archers and wizards continued to fire non-stop, sparing neither arrows nor vials. The Reapers took cover under the rows of stakes, waiting for more reinforcements to come before climbing the steep bank.

The second cavalry wave appeared on the opposite side, advancing in an orderly line.

Level 150. This was basically our limit.

"Archers and wizards, retreat!" I shouted.

The Elves hurried back to their predetermined positions: the banks of earth fortified with wicker shields. These offered the archers good cover while providing an excellent field of fire.

The wizards needed a mana break. Now everything depended on White, Allan, Archie and their groups.

Our warriors locked their shields and stepped in the enemy's path: a thin line trailing along the steep drop of the river bank.

The Reapers' numbers were three times those of ours. Still, they had to climb the bank first. They couldn't attack us *en masse* here so their numerical advantage didn't amount to much yet.

The numerous ravines were the weak spot in our defenses. Even though we'd barricaded them with stakes treated against fire damage, the enemy casters had made them their prime target. Currently, the gorges were consumed by fire. Very soon the cavalry would be able to cross there, especially if Dietrich's wizards cast Mortal Cold again.

And so they did.

The enemy riders split into groups. The whirling spirals of Mortal Cold rose over the flames, extinguishing them and turning the charred stakes into a crumbling mess of ice.

"Platinus, get ready!"

The riders headed for the breached ravines, about to sweep the remaining defenses away. Soon they would have free reign over the area, allowing them to turn round and descend upon us from the rear, crumbling our flanks.

We had nothing to lose. I didn't give a damn if the admins downleveled us for using illegal tactics. We needed to stop them.

Their cavalry squads headed for the ravines and entered them, crumpling our defenses.

Our bank replied by hurling Platinus' "bombs" under the horses' hooves.

Roaring columns of fire rose to the sky.

Their horses bolted. Blinded by the flames, they rushed around the shore, impaling themselves on the sharp stakes. Half of their riders were already dead; those who'd survived were desperately scrambling up the slippery slopes trying to escape the flames.

More enemy groups appeared on the opposite side.

The Reapers tried to overrun the whole length of the river bank. New fresh forces kept joining them, crossing the frozen river which was still engulfed in flames. Foot soldiers carried siege ladders; the enemy archers and artillery doubled their efforts, showering our ranks with arrows and rocks.

White bared his sword. "Rion!"

A shiver ran down my spine.

"Rion!" Christa wheezed.

Enea's lips moved as she cast a short spell: the Headbutt of a Hydra which doubled our attack strength.

The blade of my own sword glinted, reflecting the flames that consumed our bank.

Enea touched her Bracelet of a Metamorph.

"Rion!" Yorm growled, jumping from the tall bank onto the enemy.

* * *

Our daring and unexpected counter attack — plus the experience of all the solo players who'd joined our colors — came as a total surprise to the enemy still busy drawing their forces to our side. If they'd planned on defeating us by storming the steep bank, they now found themselves in a very precarious position.

The flames of Inferno split the still-frozen river in two, cutting off their reinforcements. With a thunderous noise, the ice began to break. Blocks of ice crashed against each other, rearing up and barring the enemy's way.

We came down on them in full force: seven hundred players backed up by Elven archers. It took us less than sixty seconds to crush their defenses, after which the battle broke into hundreds of small skirmishes.

We fought with ruthlessness born of desperation. There was no stopping us. The moral tension of the last several hours had finally found a vent.

The enemy wavered and stepped back.

The earth underfoot was slippery with blood. Yorm had fought his way far ahead. Brandishing his club, he lay his course through the enemy crowds, simultaneously using his stone shield to stave off a few Harvesters who were trying to stop him.

Our combat sections battled doggedly through, leaving the scattered avatars of dead Reapers in their wake. They'd made it to the middle of the river when the ice began to crack underfoot.

I had to think quickly. "Back off! Retreat! Don't stick your necks out!"

Few heard me in the heat of the fight. All of us could already feel the victory. Still, storming the enemy bank enveloped in debuff auras was sheer madness. The moment we stepped on it, the testing grounds' defense mechanisms would strip us of every point of protection we had.

"Retreat!" I repeated the order, ignoring the warriors' grumpy reaction.

The heavy clouds parted under the enemy's

new volley of meteorite shower. Still, this time it worked to our advantage: the fiery white-hot chunks of rock crashing through the ice had sobered many a hot head.

"Allan, White, Arch, take your men back, quick!"

Thousands more Reapers found their death in the seething waters. It looked like we'd broken the spine of Dietrich's army.

Brief melees still erupted everywhere I looked, but most of our warriors had obeyed my orders, retreating singly and in groups.

Christa struck like lightning, killing two Harvesters and forcing Yorm to retreat too. Patches of water had already formed all around him. The deafening cracking of the breaking ice hung over the river.

Once again the opposite bank began to breath cold. Dietrich could be desperate but he wasn't going to give up so easily.

"Stephen, report!"

Yorm had already caught up with me. Enea had ported back to our bank. White was busy coordinating our retreat, mercilessly pulling everyone — his own clanmates as well as lone players — into a controlled formation.

"We've lost two hundred and three respawned," Stephen replied, "plus eighteen more dead. This is only an estimate, eh? The Reapers have lost twenty-five hundred. Dietrich will never recover from this defeat!"

"Get some scouts, buff them to their teeth and send them over to the other bank!"

"I already have. They're stealthed up and on their way."

I breathed a sigh of relief and looked around. The river had begun to freeze over again, barricaded by the rampant ice plates.

I doubted Dietrich had enough wind to launch another mass attack.

* * *

My cheek twitched nervously. More Reapers appeared on the opposite bank: a group of about three hundred warriors, one in ten of them a Harvester.

"Where do they all come from?" Enea exclaimed.

This was the Reapers' fifth attack already. Indeed, where had Dietrich amassed so many well-trained warriors?

The long and eventful day was on the decline. We hadn't surrendered one inch of our turf to the enemy. Still, we too were at breaking point.

The enemy seemed to ignore their losses, throwing more and more fresh forces into battle.

"What's with the scouts? Do we have

anything from them?"

"We do. They've just sent us some footage. I'm forwarding it to you."

Why had Stephen's voice quivered? He'd demonstrated a remarkable sangfroid throughout the day.

A small screen formed in front of us, showing the scene filmed by our scouts.

The Reapers were forcing crowds of peasants into a nearby wood. Literally mountains of heaped-up weapons and gear rose over the frozen treetops.

What was their plan? Peasants don't make good warriors.

Still, the Reapers were worse than a plague. The few surviving Harvesters walked over to a group of timid villagers, then disembodied themselves in front of them, dissolving into clouds of the familiar bluish haze.

The released neurograms immediately dispersed within the crowd, entering their new hosts.

This was a terrible sight, I tell you. The peaceful villagers changed right in front of our eyes. Their name tags turned gray. Their bodies convulsed as they absorbed human thoughts, memories and experiences.

Some of the NPCs hadn't survived the strain and slumped onto the snow, slowly freezing to death. Most of them, however, hurried to equip themselves, picking up weapons and rummaging through the mountains of armor to find something their size.

Their levels began to grow as the game engine recalculated the XP received. This was a well-rehearsed routine. A humble peasant would enter the wood — and two minutes later, he was already a level-92 swordsman whose body language betrayed an experienced warrior.

The neurograms of stressful memories were especially stable. The newly-baked Reapers experienced the traumatic moments of human lives which had been forced upon them. Desperate to avenge the painful wrongs, they were impatient to go into battle without realizing that those damaging memories didn't even belong to them.

Nothing could help them now. This spiteful, vindictive soil would choke any attempt to plant a peaceful experience in it. All these poor souls now possessed was one dark moment of hatred born of a vicious circle of respawns.

They were the cannon fodder for the cleverer ones — who, like Dietrich, cowered behind their backs.

This latter kind was smart. They took their time rummaging through the harvested neurograms, looking for gems to add to their new hybrid identities and choosing the feelings and experiences they'd prefer to absorb.

They weren't living creatures. Not even sentient. They were the fruit of alien technologies which had broken free of the Corporation's control.

My mind blanked.

They launched a new attack. The swordsmen poured out onto the ice, climbing over the ice ridges. A new duel of wizards ensued. Our two surviving trebuchets launched heavy bails of burning hay soaked in oil which flew overhead and descended onto the enemy ranks, splashing liquid fire around.

A dry thunderstorm raged over the river. Numerous bolts of lightning forked and hit each other, flaring up, then expiring, echoed by the constant booming of thunder.

Acrid clouds of acid mist spread over the ice, melting it. The frozen river spewed out geysers of fire. The enemy's magic spears and arrows showered us, leaving deep dents in our armor, then dissolving into a quivering haze.

Our archers were doing their best to smoke the Harvesters. Still, you had to give the Reapers their due: their wizards kept a watchful eye on the Harvesters, making sure they had plenty of additional protection and promptly porting them back to the shore in the case of any emergency.

We had to stop this. Each Harvester was taking back more neurograms which would turn even more peasants into blood-drunk swordsmen!

"Stephen, I want you to calculate the enemy casters' positions."

Once again the battle was gaining momentum. The Reapers' avant-garde had already cleared the ice ridges and were now running toward our bank, followed by more fresh forces. It looked like Dietrich had finally lost his cool and had thrown all of his reserves into the battle.

Crowds of peasants poured out onto the ice carrying long siege ladders and crude wooden gang planks. Unexpectedly for us, catapults fired out of the frosty haze, showering us with boulders which flattened our defenses and collapsed whatever was left of our stockade, crumbling parts of the clay bank.

My map exploded in a maze of red markers. It was Stephen who'd detected the positions of the enemy wizards responsible for porting Harvesters out.

Now they had problems.

We still had two reserve trebuchet batteries left. We hadn't engaged them yet. The enemy didn't know about them. And they were much more powerful than the enemy catapults!

We showered the enemy casters with rocks, bales of burning hay and barrels of oil, turning their positions into a blazing trap.

Finally, their swordsmen had reached our side. They filled the ravines, leaned their ladders against the clay banks and began scaling them. The place turned into a melee of hand-to-hand as we too had thrown all of our reserves into battle.

Waves of icy cold washed over the shore. The frosty air stripped us of our strength, constricting our chests. Still, we had the forces of Nature on our side.

Enveloped in a golden whirl of autumnal leaves, Enea kept casting buffs. She stood like an island of quiet amid the raging battle. Our best warriors led by White, her father, defended her against the waves of Reapers who were desperate to get to her. Christa and Yorm stood by her side, defending her flanks.

The symbols of Mass Regeneration kept flashing through the hazy wintry air as the magic of Nature revitalized our warriors. The icons of Endurance and Tenacity flowed over our formations, re-energizing our fighters and allowing them to ignore the bitter cold.

The opposite bank was consumed by flames. Our trebuchets kept firing. Oil barrels rocketed over the river and smashed onto the opposite bank, spilling burning oil everywhere.

We'd bogged the Reapers down. The entire river bank was consumed by desperate fighting.

Despite the freezing cold, the ice underfoot had turned into bloody slush.

The bluish haze of neurograms trailed along

the shore, condensing.

Now.

"Arwan, tell your men to aim for the Harvesters! Use the arrows with Khmor poison!"

The Elven snipers entered the battle.

Having lost their casters' support, the Harvesters had put up a good fight. Their levels were higher than ours but the Elven arrows treated with Platinus' poison didn't leave them a chance.

All along the extended river bank, high-level Reapers began dropping. The Elves knew no mercy, aiming for their heads, one arrow per target.

At first, the Harvesters didn't know what hit them. The stronger ones even continued to fight despite the spinning frenzy of their repeated damage counters. No one was immune to Platinus' poison made from Spectral Dust and the sap of the Khmor tree.

"We've run out of arrows!" Arwan reported, his voice ringing with the excitement of battle.

True, we hadn't had that many. Still, they seemed to have done their job. The tables had turned again.

The Harvesters' job had been to control groups of swordsmen, imbuing them with strength and confidence. Now that they were dead, common Reapers had lost their cool and relaxed their efforts. We could sense the difference in their let-up straight away.

They were on the brink of fleeing the battlefield.

* * *

The frozen river bristled with rampant ice ridges. Pools of burning oil filled the air with thick clouds of acrid black smoke. Our trebuchet batteries had fallen silent, unable to sustain the pressure of rapid fire.

With the death of most of the Harvesters, the battle which stretched along a thousand-foot length of the bank on both sides of the old ford had gradually begun to subside.

I hadn't enjoyed being the one in control. Still, today the fate of the whole world had been at stake. Desperate as I'd been to join the battle, I couldn't have afforded to bare my sword and throw myself into the thick of it. I had to restrain my impulses.

Once again the enemy wavered. We were forcing them back!

A snowstorm began to rage behind the river bend. How strange. Here, the setting sun hung in the clear skies while there, everything was consumed by a thickening snowy haze.

What was this, the enemy's attempt to outflank us?

"Stephen, I want you to find out what's going

on over there. Send the scouts in to investigate."

I checked the two clan's stats. About 30% of all warriors and wizards had respawned at least once. KIA, 6%.

At this moment, all the solo players had finally lost their patience and chased after the routed enemy. They got so carried away they followed them across the frozen river, unwittingly triggering a new attack.

From the opposite bank, the enemy archers showered them with arrows. Two big groups of foot soldiers appeared from the snowy haze around the river bend.

"Turn back! Return to your positions!"

As if! Solo players were too independent to obey orders — and too excited to notice the new threat in the heat of the battle.

A few of them stopped and took cover behind their shields, only to gulp a quick elixir and resume their chase.

"Large high-level cavalry group approaching from around the river bend," Stephen reported.

This last turn of events could have proven fatal for us. Although I fully appreciated the players' personal courage, they were too uncoordinated — and once they'd crossed the river, they'd be attacked by the testing grounds' defense mechanisms which would strip them of every stamina point they had.

"Clans, regroup! Prepare to engage with the cavalry! Advance to the middle of the river! White, we expect another strike from the right flank! Wizards, block out the opposite bank!"

A wall of fire rose to the sky. The ice began to melt. The resulting mist had sobered the over-enthusiastic players who'd stopped in front of the magic wall in despair, voicing their indignation of the "clumsy wizards".

Glory be to the Founder Gods! The players stopped, recovering from their rage, then began to retreat in small groups.

Enea continued casting mass healing buffs on all the wounded.

Once again the tables had turned. Fickle Lady Luck froze, undecided.

The silence was such that we could already hear the clatter of the approaching cavalry.

Our combat sections had already lined up across the river. Their ranks bristled with spears. On my command, the Ravens blocked the left flank to curb any potential attacks from the opposite bank.

The unhappy solo players had already returned to the shore but weren't in a hurry to climb the steep bank. They waited below, falling into groups.

"Reapers!"

No idea what Dietrich was playing at. We'd

smoked his Harvesters before they could deliver more neurograms to the troops — which meant that the enemy couldn't expect reinforcements any time soon. Their cavalry — about a hundred top-level NPCs — appeared to be more of a last-resort gesture.

Enveloped in his dark aura, Yorm leapt down from the bank.

Arwan's archers and a dedicated group of swordsmen surrounded Enea. Her father had already returned to the frozen river.

Christa followed in Yorm's wake, ready to stand against this new threat.

I began to shudder uncontrollably.

A wave of spine-chilling fear rolled down the river bed in front of the Reapers' cavalry. This was a very nagging feeling which broke through our magic defenses. A freezing, debilitating fear ripped our protection auras apart and sank its claws into our minds.

Our formations wavered and fell apart as some of the warriors broke under this unexpected mental attack, lowering their spears and opening up gaps in our ranks.

Yorm took the brunt of the cavalry's attack. Brandishing his club, he managed to unhorse a few riders before he was knocked off his feet.

They were about to trample him to death.

White didn't hesitate. He showered the ranks

with furious orders, forcing them to close again.

Then the darkening skies parted, disgorging Christa who'd dropped onto the Reapers like an angel of wrath. She'd stolen up on them from the rear, darted into the sky on her powerful leathery wings, then banked into a steep turn, scattering the cavalry's rearguard.

Then everything went awry.

A new wave of fear clenched our warriors' minds. The cavalry struck.

They broke our ranks, slicing through them like a knife through exposed flesh. The second mental attack had rendered most of our warriors too helpless to put up any resistance.

A thick bluish cloud of leaking neurograms rose over the scene.

Realizing the danger, I microported out to the center of the river — but not far enough to escape the treacherous haze.

The whinnying of lathering horses, the rattling of steel and screams of agony hung over the melting ice.

A player next to me was trying to scramble to his feet. His shoulder sported a spear wound, his life was at 50%, his face pallid with pain.

Still, not a single drop of blood had left his tormented flesh. The terrible spear wound was heaving with neurograms pouring out of his body, their veil forming vague images in the air.

A Reaper galloped out of the mist. Without slowing down, he leaned in the saddle, about to finish off the disoriented, helpless man.

In moments like these, time flows differently. The rider seemed to approach in slow motion. The horse's hooves kicked up glittering cascades of slush.

The Reaper raised his short sword. The dull metal of its blade was covered in microchips marked with symbols in the Founders' language.

I'd seen one of those swords before — back on Agrion market square.

This was a very special weapon. Not only did it strip you of your hp, but it also disintegrated your identity matrix. No idea where the Reapers had gotten this technology from.

"Come here, you piece of shit!" I wheezed, trying to distract him from his victim.

The horse shied away from me, scared of the bluish fog that had consumed everything around. I recognized familiar images formed by its swirls.

We were surrounded by the dead players' memories. The thick fog consisted of their neurograms, wrestled from their wounds by the strokes of the microchipped blades. Once the players lost their identities, they had no chance of staying sane.

Or at least that's what I thought in that heart-rendering moment.

The Reaper's horse reared up.

His name tag was gray which meant he wasn't a Harvester. Dietrich must have sent the last hundred of his army into battle. This was his elite retinue consisting of hybrid beings who were fully aware of both their actions and their consequences.

His sword came down on me.

My mind exploded in agony.

I recoiled just in time. Still, the tip of the sword had sliced through my shoulder.

Mind expander failure
Critical error
Your identity matrix is destabilized

The fiery letters of system messages ripped through my mind. Reality had distanced itself. Then a scene — a memory — surfaced from out of the gloom.

A car tumbling down a precipitous foundation pit.

A mangled mess of crumpled metal with me inside.

The ghostly scene lost its shape, swirling, until it turned into a whiff of bluish mist. It reached for the Reaper rider, about to become part of his own identity.

And I couldn't stop it.

Fuck you, mister. You can have it. Why would I need this recurring nightmare? My life would only be better without it.

Your identity matrix is critically destabilized
You're about to be disembodied

We never forget anything. Every moment of our lives gets stored in our memories, becoming the breeding ground for our character and identity. They make up our experience, every crumb of which is precious.

Even if I survived this battle, it wouldn't be me anymore. It would be somebody else. Not the car crash victim I'd once been, the one who'd consented to having the neuroimplant installed.

Painful and traumatic as it may have been, this was *my* memory.

You're not having it.

It's mine.

Mine! the word tolled in my head.

Overcoming weakness, I staggered to my feet. My body went into overload as I invested all of my remaining strength into the blow, sinking my sword into the Reaper's face distorted by ecstasy.

My mind collapsed.

A cloud of swirling discharge enveloped the Reaper's body. His microchipped sword burst into flame, then crumbled to rust.

My orphaned memory clung to me, trying to climb back deep into the wound. The world swam before my eyes, shrinking rapidly. I couldn't see anything.

My name is Alexatis.
I have a girlfriend.
I'm a Neuro.
I'm a clan leader.
I can remember everything.

The dark haze dissipated. The golden spiral of Regeneration rotated over my head.

Congratulations! You've successfully stabilized your identity matrix!

You've received a new level!

You've successfully unblocked the further development of your Neuro branch ahead of schedule!

You've received a new ability: the Founders' Successor!

All around us, dozens of players squirmed on the ground in agony. Reapers circled among them like vultures.

"Enea, cast Mass Regeneration," I croaked. I knew she would hear me.

Emerald aurorae consumed the sky above us, effacing the murky dark haze.

Surrounded by Elves, Enea stood on the steep bank. Her very body seemed to exude a vivifying light. Dozens — no, hundreds of golden spirals wheeled around the players, healing their wounds and filling them with life.

Still, not everybody had come round after the Reapers' attack. Many of our fighters still lay sprawled on the ice, their bodies mutilated by microchipped swords. Stripped of too many memories, their identities had collapsed, leaving a thick bluish haze trailing along the frozen riverbed.

"Clerics, heal the wounded! Wizards, wake up already!" I picked up a spear lying on the ice and hurled it into the nearest Reaper.

The spear pierced his leg. The Reaper swung round and began walking toward me, limping heavily. His unusual curved sword was flaking with rust — but the symbols of the Founders' language glowed defiantly on its blade.

The Shield of Reason opened around me, blocking the sword's disastrous effects. All I'd received was standard damage. Blood gushed out of a deep cut in my arm.

"Keep hp above 90%!" I shouted as I successfully parried his next blow.

The Reaper backed off in bemusement. Why hadn't his microchipped sword worked?

The other riders must have sensed it. Three of them left their victims alone and rode toward me.

"Alex, hold on!" White shouted, battling through to my rescue.

The sunset was glowing red in the darkening sky.

Like a scarlet drop of mercury, the sun rolled toward the horizon. Enea stood tall against its backdrop, exuding waves of Mass Regeneration. Her majestic figure drew all eyes to her.

Most of the Reapers saw her, too. They went after her.

The Elves stepped in their way. They spent their last arrows trying to stop them — but the defective hybrids scaled the steep bank and squashed their defenses.

Enea touched the Bracelet of a Metamorph. A flash ripped through the air, disgorging Christa. The two girls stood back to back and put up a desperate fight.

My perception was crumbling. The world had disintegrated, falling into separate fragments before my eyes. Time moved in fits and starts.

A flurry of system messages flickered before my eyes. My mind expander had gone into overload, just like it had done back in the Temple of Oblivion.

The symbols of the ancient language were burning a hole in my mind. I ran as hard as I could, drawing the surviving clanmates along. Our miniporting ability had been blocked. Our mental energy was at zero and taking way too long to restore.

Fire... Sacrifice by fire... No. That's not what the symbols meant.

I kept shifting the icons in my mental view but none of the resulting sequences seemed to work.

Light... Protection...
Life...
Retribution...
Enea staggered.

A Reaper hurled the dead body of an Elf out of his way and took a swing with his sword, aiming for my beloved. Her shield was broken. Christa was fighting three Reapers at once, covering Enea's back.

A blinding flash of piercing white light exploded in the sky.

The Reaper's sword bounced off an invisible wall. A new debuff icon appeared in his tag. I'd never seen that one before. He'd been stripped of 65% life.

You've cast Retribution!
You've received a new ability: Spell Building

The siege ladders still stood against the precipitous bank.

I couldn't think straight. My head was a mess. My body acted mechanically as we fought our way toward Enea and Christa.

The Reapers crumbled under our pressure. There weren't many of them left, anyway. White and I fought in serried ranks with about a dozen other top-level clanmates who were every bit as good as he was.

Our clerics and wizards had regained their composure. They kept a safe distance healing us non-stop, making sure our health didn't drop below 80%.

When later we analyzed the logs, we saw that this had been the best formula against microchipped swords. That way, our wounds healed instantly without losing any neurograms. All the wounded warrior could feel in this case was a faint confusion which allowed him to continue fighting.

My sword pierced the Reaper's chest. I pulled it out, shouldered his slackened body off the cliff and swung round to take on more enemies.

"Alex!" White grabbed my arm. "Enough! That was the last one! We're finished! Can you hear me?"

His voice barely reached me.

A crimson haze floated before my eyes.

We've kept this side of the river... but at what

price?

* * *

The fading sunset glowed crimson in the sky.

Dead bodies heaped up on the bloodied shore, trampled into the sand, silt and riverside mud.

The breeze brought the stench of fire; it dispersed the remaining whiffs of the bluish haze and tugged at the smoldering tatters of our clan's banner.

I slumped on the ground next to Enea and took her in my arms.

"Alex, please tell me their death wasn't in vain!" her voice rang with bitterness. "How could it happen? We only chose the strongest ones!"

"The Reapers must have hacked the codes and tweaked them. They must have introduced the microchipped weapons. I know it's not what you'd like to hear..."

She sniffled. "No, it's not."

"More Reapers are building up on the opposite bank," Stephen's voice disrupted my thoughts. "They've just got more reinforcements."

Enea wiped her tears. "Do you remember how we met here in the village?"

"Sure. In the inn."

"I want that time back," she mouthed. "In

those days, feelings were real. But death was just for fun."

White and Christa walked over to us.

"We haven't seized a single microchipped sword," White said. "The moment we touch them, they crumble to dust. Alex, we've kept the village and destroyed all the Harvesters and hybrids but... I'm afraid we have to retreat to Rion. We won't survive another attack."

CHAPTER EIGHT

THE CRYSTAL SPHERE
RION CASTLE
TWO WEEKS LATER

THE WORLD AROUND us was changing irreversibly.

It had taken Dietrich a week to cross the moors and besiege Rion Castle.

The video of the Battle of Warblerford had gone viral — but unexpectedly for us, the numbers of new clan applications had dropped dramatically. It was as if there were no human players left in the Crystal Sphere.

I refused to believe it. It's not so easy to kill billions of people.

Those who'd suffered from the touch of the

Reapers' microchipped swords were now kept safe in the Shrine of Nature, supported by its power and the magic of the Khmor Alley. There, the wounded warriors and wizards slowly overcame the consequences of their mental injuries. Quite a few of them had come round; some had to begin life anew, depending on the amount of memory they'd lost.

Borisov wasn't showing any progress. Physically he was perfectly fine. Still, he would neither talk to us nor answer any questions. He ambled about the castle like a ghost.

The testing grounds' defense mechanisms continued to chase after the Reapers. In doing so, they destroyed everything in their path, even changing the terrain itself. Entire regions had fallen into desolation. The only place which still preserved some vegetation was Rion Castle, and then only thanks to our Shrine of Nature and the Elemental protection supported by the energy of the runes. A strip of greenery about a mile wide encircled the castle.

The surviving patches of the moors were now covered in a great variety of magic vines which stood in the Reapers' way, blocking their advance.

At night, thousands of fires glowed around the castle. Anywhere you turned, you could see Dietrich's army camps.

To him, our citadel was both a coveted prize

and a reminder of his defeat. A few times we'd glimpsed him from afar: the First Reaper, surrounded by his retinue of top-level riders about a third of whom were Harvesters and all the others, hybrids.

Slowly but mercilessly, the ring around Rion kept tightening.

We received bad news from other places. The situation was changing rapidly — and unfortunately, not in our favor. Reapers were everywhere now.

All the trade routes had been discontinued. Even the auction had stopped working, not to mention other in-game services.

The game's economy had collapsed. The NPCs' behavior had become unpredictable. The epic "conflicts of old" invented by the game's script writers as part of the world's history had all of a sudden come to the forefront as NPCs had begun to believe them, considering them part of their own past. The rest you can imagine.

The dwarves had left Rion and returned to their underground cities as their old feud with the Dark Elves had suddenly escalated, threatening to grow into a fully-blown war.

We — and by this I mean all human beings, whether players or game developers — we'd created an entire universe populated by multiple races. Then we'd introduced neural technologies. We were way too naïve in our assumptions that a system like that wasn't going to trigger a wave of sporadic self-evolution.

Now the thousands of little things we'd either overlooked or disregarded as irrelevant had finally fallen into a single pattern, creating the kind of developments whose consequences we could never have conceived in our worst nightmares.

Very soon the Crystal Sphere might metamorph into something entirely different: a brave new world which would start again from scratch. There was no one left to forecast the upcoming events; no script writers to invent new plot lines. If we failed to defeat the enemy, we too would vanish into history. In which case, the next history book would be written by self-evolving NPCs while human beings would become part of the local folklore.

At the moment, the Reapers were stubbornly trying to battle through the moors toward the castle. Luckily, we kept repelling their attacks.

Dietrich was probably furious right now. Our defenses were way out of his league. His groups were busy trying to feel us out, looking for our weak spots. They engaged in petty scuffles with the goblins who'd taken cover in the "green strip", all the while waiting for our stocks to deplete.

They wanted to starve us out.

They didn't know about the portal connecting

the castle with the Yonder Isles. Every morning, groups of peasants and Elven hunters walked through it to return in the evening with generous game and basketfuls of fruit.

Currently, our confrontations were limited to the moors. We used every opportunity to raid the enemy's camps. The hard times and especially the return of their totem had reconciled the goblin tribes with us. Although they kept a low profile, they never missed a chance to play nasty tricks on the Reapers or lend a helping hand to our raiders.

* * *

Today I lingered at the castle's outer defense lines longer than usual. First, I'd supervised the trebuchet teams which were busy range-finding. By the time they were finished, it was already dusk: time for me to work on my Observation Skills. I tried to practice a little every day, honing my Twilight Vision and learning to expertly control Magic Eyes, using this practice time to inconspicuously read the enemy's data and forward it to Stephen for analysis.

I'd made level 124 during the Battle of Warblerford.

I also had three new abilities in the Neuro development branch which had opened "ahead of schedule" due to the emergency.

The Founders' Successor

You've perfected the control of your mind to the point where you've successfully managed to keep it together, saving your identity from disintegration.

This ability will allow you to train others in the basics of the Neuro development branch. It will also enable you to stabilize your allies' identity matrices in case of emergency. Cooldown: 1 hr.

Every new ability level you receive will shorten the cooldown time by 5 minutes. Once you reach level 5, you'll be able to create a Shield of Reason spell and copy it to a scroll.

Spell Building

You've used your Spell Interception ability to study various schools of magic and their practices. Your knowledge of Synergy as well as your mastery of Elemental Control will now allow you to combine the elements of various spells in order to build your own. You can, for instance, create an illusion capable of dealing Elemental damage.

Every new ability level you receive will increase both the duration and the effects of the spells you build.

Steel Mist

You've mastered the long-lost magic practice of substance manipulation.

Whenever mortal danger threatens you, select a gear item of your choice which will disintegrate, its particles forming a damage-absorbing spherical shield around you.

Cooldown: 1 hr.

Every new ability level you receive will improve the damage-absorbing properties of the Steel Mist while also increasing its duration.

I'd been practicing these new abilities for a while. I used every opportunity to copy ancient artifacts (rings mainly) and had leveled up Shield of Reason, bringing it up to 10. I'd also learned to build my own spells and practiced the Steel Mist ability which was so admittedly unusual for a fantasy world.

Life in Rion didn't stop at sunset. The townsfolk (because you couldn't call them peasants anymore, really) continued building their houses by torchlight, using the slabs of magic stone left over after the restoration of the castle walls.

I found White in the assault course set up within the second ring of walls where he was busy drilling our freshly-formed rapid response groups.

I switched the Magic Eye to autonomous mode and watched the guys training. They worked hard. You could actually see them joining the clan's elite. The dropout rate in their groups was high, with a discipline to match. Still, White wasn't forcing anyone to join his group or become multiclass.

Most experienced gamers had already adapted to their implants. They'd received our best cargonite gear and bespoke rings crafted by yours truly which allowed them to use non-combat skills and abilities.

Each of them had customized their standard gear as best they could with different paints and colors. Every one of them had his or her own unique combat style — but the moment they had to work as a team, they became a fine-tuned single mechanism.

A signal sent by the Magic Eye distracted me from the scene. Apparently, the device had been circling a particular spot for a while.

Beyond the sparsely wooded area surrounding the castle lay a patch of rough wasteland riddled with ravines. This was how most of the Crystal Sphere looked these days. Wastelands like this were all that Reapers left in their wake.

I noticed a crooked, gnarly figure cowering in one of the ravines. I took a better look.

A forest sprite. And not just any old forest sprite but an old friend of mine. This was Forrest, of all creatures! I'd met him a couple of times but never accepted any of his quests. I'd been too busy at the time.

Forrest was a popular figure in these parts of the world. He lived on the edge of the moors next to Warblerford. His main task was issuing simple quests to newbs — but that wasn't what he was famous for. It was his remarkable vulnerability to fire damage that made him fair game for novice wizards — as well as the inordinate amount of XP you could get for smoking him.

A swordsman could try and fight him in vain until he was blue in the face — but even the weakest of wizards could finish Forrest off in under two minutes with just a handful of fireballs.

Had he become a Reaper too? Had he jumped at his chance to wreak revenge on all the players who'd used to kill him dozens of times a day?

In that case, why was he cowering in the ravine, playing dead and pretending he was just a dried-up piece of driftwood every time the Reapers' patrols walked past?

Something wasn't right there.

I maneuvered the Eye lower. Although it was already dark, my Twilight Vision ability allowed me to make out the outlines of two players skulking in the shadows next to him.

Their avatars were weird. One of the two resembled a cyborg, of all things. The other was a petite girl clad in light Kevlar armor, the kind normally worn by Corporation security staff.

I had a funny feeling I'd seen her before. Still,

I couldn't be too sure in the dark.

The players definitely seemed to be trying to get to the castle but couldn't get past the Reapers' camp.

We had to help them. They couldn't lie in hiding forever. If a Harvester chanced anywhere near, they were toast. Those monsters could sniff out a player from a mile away.

"White, I think you should call it a day, man," I said. "We need a combat group ready for a sortie."

"Coming," he replied.

Almost instantly, a portal flashed open next to me.

"What's up?" White asked.

"Take a look," I granted him access to the video.

"Two players," he said. "They seem to be hiding from the Reapers. I don't think they can get past their camp. We'll need two groups: one as a diversion and the other to pull them out."

"You think we can do that?"

"Oh, absolutely. I've been thinking of testing the guys in the field. Too many people are still pretty depressed after what happened in Warblerford. We need a clean victory."

"We're not ready to face their army yet," I said.

"I know. Still, we need to teach them a

lesson. Put the fear of God into them. And now we have a perfectly good excuse. Can you see those marquees to the left of the ravine?"

"Yeah. I've been wondering about them."

"These are probably some of their command staff," White said. "You think we could cast a portal over there?"

"There're at least five Harvesters nearby."

"Yes, I can see them. But if we buff our guys properly, we can do it. Do you have any Shield of Reason scrolls?"

"I'd rather come with you," I said.

"Don't be stupid. You should keep out of it."

"That's out of the question. Our guys should see that their clan leader doesn't hide behind the castle walls."

"Are you sure? You haven't done much training just lately."

"You think I can't do it?"

"Oh no, I don't. Just worried. Where's Enea?"

"She's at the shrine. No good dragging her into this. She has enough on her plate as it is."

"Very well. Let's do it. My group of ten swordsmen will take care of the Harvesters. If you cast a neuromatrix-stabilizing buff on us, we'll do it just fine. You take five more warriors and pull the players out. Make it quick. We shouldn't get involved in any drawn-out engagement."

* * *

The moon peeked out from the gaps in the clouds, flooding the location with its greenish glow.

No matter how hard we'd tried to keep the sortie under wraps, Enea and Christa had somehow found out about it. Two portals — one of Light, the other of Dark — flashed open almost simultaneously, releasing the two indignant girls.

"Oh, no," I replied adamantly. "You're not going anywhere tonight. This is a quick sortie, not a battle."

"Don't tell me we can't help you!" Enea exclaimed.

I smiled. "That's the problem. If you start helping us, we might end up with an epic battle on our hands. You'll attract every Harvester in the area!"

Grudgingly they had to agree. After the Battle of Warblerford, every Reaper could recognize the two girls' powerful auras.

"How about you?" Enea asked.

"I have my Shield of Reason, don't I?" I reminded her. "Just cool it, girls. It's a five-minute job."

"Okay. We could back you up from here, I suppose," Enea bent down and began drawing a long-distance portal on the stone floor tiles.

Christa didn't say anything. She cast a quick glance at White, then walked over to the crenelated parapet. A faint murky haze formed around her hands: the sign of extreme distress.

The warriors fell in, ready to port. The cargonite alloy of their armor glinted purple, their faces tense behind raised visors.

"Ready for duty," White reported.

"Likewise."

"Let's be off, then!" he broke the seal on a mass teleport scroll.

As we ported, I glimpsed Christa make a quick hand movement, enveloping White in the faint aura of additional protection.

For a brief moment, I lost my bearings.

We stood deep in mud. The dry blackened branches of some brambles scratched against our armor.

We were a dozen feet away from the entrance to the ravine.

My group took up their positions in the shadows, leaving me a clean field of action. A few hundred feet further on, flames arose in the air, followed by yelling and screaming as White's swordsmen attacked the enemy.

The rich fabric of a marquee billowed, then fell. A howl echoed through the night.

The ravine was pitch black. I couldn't see a thing. Even my Twilight Vision didn't help me much as if blocked by some local monster.

A tangled web of dead tree roots lined the

ravine's crumbling walls. They tugged at my feet, hindering my progress.

The darkness grew ever deeper.

I could hear some creaking noises, followed by unintelligible muttering.

"Forrest, you can come out now," I called out. "It's okay. I'm your friend."

A wave of fire singed the ravine bed. It washed over me — but my resistance to elements was too high for it to do me any harm. All I felt was a pleasant warmth. You had to go some to hurt me in this way.

A crooked outline flashed past in the fire's dying light. It was a young lad no more than eighteen years old, his body all lopsided, deformed and partially cyborgized.

Armed with a flimsy wooden shield and an unusual-looking sword, he came for me, a blood-curdling grin frozen upon his face. His upper lip was raised in a snarl.

Still, he was strong as hell. I staggered and barely managed to parry his blow. He promptly shrank back. His face betrayed fearful surprise.

The icon of the Shield of Reason appeared in my stats.

What kind of blow was that?!

"Hey you!" I shouted. "Stop it now! I'm a friend!"

With a creaking noise, something gnarly and

heavy dropped on me from above.

Its roots attempted to entwine my arms, immobilizing me. No such luck: Enea had cast a couple of very peculiar buffs on me just before we'd left.

The sprite's grip slackened. "He fights back!" he made another attempt to immobilize me, this time clasping my legs.

A fiery aura enveloped my left hand. "You'd better leave me alone before I scorch you to death," I said. Like all players who'd started their Crystal Sphere career in Agrion, I knew all his strategies.

The sprite promptly recoiled. "Please don't!"

In the meantime, the lad attacked me again. He moved sideways like a crab, keeping a confident grip on his shield and raising his sword for a slashing blow.

"Wait, I tell you! I'm from the castle!"

"You're lying!"

"Look at my name tag!" I stepped back, readying a fire blow just in case. In its unsteady light, I could see the lad was really scared.

"Kyle, will you stop it?" a soft but firm voice said. A girl walked out of the shadows.

This wasn't happening!

"Kimberly?" I struggled to recognize the young Drow huntress I'd met during my first trip to the Azure Mountains.

"Do I know you?" she stared closely at me,

mistrust in her gaze.

She must have had it tough. I could still remember her cheerful smile. The girl in front of me was a shadow of her old self. Same face, different soul, dark and traumatized.

Her name tag was gray as if she didn't belong in the Crystal Sphere any longer.

"Where's Liori?" I asked.

"How do you know her?"

"We met in the Azure Mountains. Your pet lynx scared the hell out of me. Remember now?"

"What was the lynx's name?"

"Sarah. A mountain lynx. She lives with us now, in case you're interested."

"Sarah? She lives with you? She's alive?"

"Of course she is! She waits by the portal every day hoping you'll come and get her."

"Wait. I know you," she stepped closer. "Kyle, put your sword down. He *is* a friend."

"There're no friends here," the lad grumbled. "He's lying."

"Mind putting your fire away?" the sprite creaked.

What a funny trio. Still, we had no time to dwell on it.

"Can you hear the fighting? We did it deliberately, to come here and rescue you. Let's port to the castle and then we can talk."

Kimberly paused, then gave a resolute nod.

"Okay. Thanks."

Reluctantly Kyle lowered his weird microchipped sword.

It was the third time I'd seen one of those. The first time had been on Agrion market square. The second, during the Battle of Warblerford.

The lad's name tag was gray too: just a murky frame which hovered over his head. No name, no character class, no level.

I switched to the chat. "White, how's it going?"

"Three Harvesters down," his voice rang with the excitement of combat. "Still we'd better move it. They'll be bringing in reinforcements in a minute!"

"We're finished here. Let's port back!"

"Excellent," his voice was drowned out by more clanging of steel.

* * *

The portals awaited us. Ashes swirled over the glowing symbols of the Founders' language. This was another sign of the new era: wherever the Reapers arrived, earth soon turned into a crumbling mixture of ash and dust.

"So what happened to you and Liori?" I asked as we waited for White and his swordsmen to arrive.

"It's a long story. Liori is in Phantom Server

now. I've been stuck in the Corporate testing grounds all this time."

"That's several years!"

"I suppose so."

"Are you a Neuro?"

"No. It's more complicated than you think."

"Never mind. We'll talk about it in the castle."

By then, White's men had already entered the portal. It was our turn.

The Reapers' marquee was still smoldering. A stack of wooden crates next to it was ablaze. Scared horses ran amok. Our little sortie was definitely a success. We hadn't lost a single clan member.

"Get in," I said.

Kyle nudged the resisting Forrest toward the portal. For some reason, the sprite was too scared of entering it. Losing his balance, Forrest stepped inside and disappeared in a flurry of golden sparks.

Kyle unhesitantly followed him.

Five more warriors waited for us to walk in. The Reapers had already recovered from the surprise attack and were now hurrying toward the portal.

"Kimberly, don't stall!"

Warily she stepped into the golden circle, then disappeared in a cascade of special effects.

"Enea?" I contacted the castle. "Have they arrived?"

"Kimberly's here. It's okay."

I motioned the warriors in. We entered the portal simultaneously.

The portal zone closed, raising a disappointed howl from the arriving Reapers.

* * *

The portal was still flashing but Sarah the Mountain Lynx was already bounding toward her mistress. She leapt onto the girl, very nearly knocking her off her feet.

"Sarah baby!" Kimberly threw her arms around the lynx's neck and buried her face in the animal's thick fur.

For a brief moment, her eyes glinted with a long forgotten expression of happiness. Suppressing tears, she turned to us.

"Thanks," she said softly.

I turned away, giving the two some privacy. "Take Forrest to the Khmor alley. Kyle, we need to talk."

"Sure. Bet you have questions for me."

"Depend upon it. I want answers, too. Lots of them. Like where did you get the microchipped sword from?"

"Zander took it from some Reapers, already a long time ago. He got lots of other weapons from them, too. Jurgen tweaked it a little. He turned it into a Sword of a Neuro!" his voice filled with pride.

"Wait a sec," I said. I definitely heard the names before. And I knew that no one could adopt another person's name in the Crystal Sphere. "You mean Zander, the Paladin? And by Jurgen do you mean Master Jurg, the blacksmith?"

"Zander is in Phantom Server now," the lad replied. "There're no Paladins there. And Jurgen isn't a blacksmith, no. He's a Technologist."

Oh, great. What kind of riddle was this?

Kimberly turned back to me. "Alex, we really need to talk. You guys don't seem to know much, do you?"

"Whatever. We can talk here," I opened a portal to the Conference Hall.

We moved over there. I asked Lethmiel to serve a late dinner. Both Kyle and Kimberly must have been starving. Still, we had no time for the usual hospitality. They'd have to combine business with pleasure.

"Now," I said.

Seeing as not everyone knew of my earlier adventures, I decided to start from the beginning. "A few years ago in the Azure Mountains, as I was on my way to see Master Jurg, I met two Drow ladies. They were Liori and Kimberly. I never saw them again. When a few days later I wanted to revisit Master Jurg, he was already gone. Kimberly, where's Liori?"

"I thought I told you. She's in Phantom Server."

"Could you expand on that for us, please? What is Phantom Server?"

She stared at us in disbelief. "You don't mean it! What *do* you know?"

"Well, one thing we know is that we have a war with the Reapers going on. We also know that the Corporation used us to test neural implants," I purposefully omitted a few things I wasn't yet sure of. "What else did I miss?"

"Eh," her gaze shifted between us. "You might not believe what I'm going to tell you. It sounds weird. You'll just have to take my word for it."

"Come on, out with it."

"Okay. Kyle, would you please show them-"

"Not a problem," the lad activated a nanocomp bracelet on his wrist. The fact that this was supposed to be a Dark Ages sword-and-sorcery setting didn't seem to baffle him in the slightest.

A hologram expanded over the table. It looked like a video of planet Earth from outer space, taken from an approaching spaceship.

"This is footage from the Military Space Forces archive," Kyle explained. "They used me as an advanced neural computer in order to decipher the Founders' technical codes. This absolutely authentic information. Took me ages to piece it together."

"Wait a sec," Christa butted in. "The Founders are a myth! They're part of the Crystal Sphere's story!"

"Oh no. The Founders are real. It was them who created neuroimplants."

Noticing the suspicion on our faces, he shrugged. "Okay. Let's start from the beginning. I'm gonna give you a brief run-down. Details don't really matter. Eleven years ago, the military discovered an alien spaceship on one of Jupiter's moons. They found the bodies of three humanoid creatures on board. All of them had neural implants installed."

A shiver ran down my spine. I was right, then. It was an alien technology, after all.

In the meantime, Kyle spoke in a calm, impassive voice. He must have overcome the initial shock a long time ago.

"The military studied the implants. They proved compatible with organic neural networks. So the military decided to experiment. They hoped to find out more about the alien technologies which the implants might contain. All they needed to find out was how to decode the information."

'How about the human brain's ability for abstract thinking?" White offered. "That way they could at least get some visuals."

Kyle nodded. "Exactly. Still, it wasn't as easy

as they thought. They enrolled a few volunteers and fitted them out with the implants. Well, guess what? Their minds were immediately transported to another reality. It took the army scientists years to finally copy the technology and work out its purpose. Apparently, there is some sort of interstellar information network which the aliens used to travel through space. They simply beamed their identity matrices from one star system to another."

White raised a quizzical eyebrow. "And?"

"And that was the extent of it. The volunteers' minds didn't survive the actual travel. The intensity of their experiences was such that they all died. Which was why the military created the Crystal Sphere. They apparently discovered that gamers tend to possess exceptional mental resilience. Which is logical, really. We — gamers, I mean — take nothing too seriously. We've turned the suspension of disbelief into an art form. We can adapt to any kind of shit the devs throw at us, no matter how improbable. So the military wanted to mass-market neural implants and select potential candidates for further experiments from the numbers of the Crystal Sphere users."

"Okay. Let's presume we believe you," Allan joined in the conversation. "But what did they want to achieve?"

"There're other space stations built by the

Founders all over the universe. We could restore and use them. The military introduced all the codes they'd managed to decipher into the Crystal Sphere, disguising them as magic and special abilities. They created certain quests and development branches that would allow players to decode the Founders' command sequences while thinking they were learning uncategorized magic. The military began building proper spaceships which were to become the Earth's first colonial fleet. If some player showed a high adaptivity rate, they moved his in-mode capsule on board of one of the ships. The fleet was supposed to leave Earth once most of the codes had been deciphered."

"Why would anyone want to leave Earth?" Allan interrupted him.

Kyle paused. "It's complicated. I'll try to explain. The Founders traveled by porting their identity matrices across the Universe, right? But those digital matrices still needed to interact with the physical world. What they did, they built gazillions of tiny nanites which could cluster together and form physical bodies for their hosts. Logically thinking, in order for this to work, those nanites had to be already present at their destination point. So the Founders built special AI-controlled fleets whose job it was to deliver nanites to star systems everywhere throughout the universe."

White frowned. "So first they locked everyone up in in-mode capsules, and now they're moving them over to those spaceships? Why? What's the catch?"

Kyle frowned. "I can only tell you what I know. Apparently, while messing with all those codes and shit, the military mistakenly activated a beacon which sent an emergency signal into open space. Having received the signal, the nanites started storing up all the energy available in order to feed their universal network. And what better source of energy than the Sun? So they're now busy syphoning the Sun's energy, building a sphere around it which wouldn't let a single atom of solar energy out."

Christa snickered. "This does sound like a space game. Or a sci fi movie."

"I know. At first I couldn't believe it myself. But it's true, unfortunately. We were supposed to leave Earth, all of us, and start a new life on some planet far far away. Unfortunately, it's not an option anymore."

"Why not?" Enea asked.

"Because of the Reapers," Kimberly replied. "Their arrival put a lid on the project. All the information was stored in the Corporation's testing grounds. All the major experiments were held there. All their staff had neural implants and worked in VR. They became the Reapers' first victims. I was there when that happened. I saw everything. The Corporation has ceased to exist. The Phantom Server project has lost its technical support. All those people whose identities have been ported to the Founders' space stations in other star systems... I don't think they'll survive."

"What happened to all the others?"

"Most of the planet's population was transferred to communal in-mode centers. There, they could continue playing the game while their bodies were being transported and stored on the cryogenic platforms of Earth's colonial fleet."

"And what happened to the fleet?" White asked.

"It's drifting through space," Kimberly replied. "Their only chance of survival is if some of the Phantom Server project participants survive and find a planet suitable for human habitation. Then they might have a chance. But at the moment, the fleet has nowhere to go."

"How about us? Will we die too?" Christa struggled to sound calm.

"I don't think so," a hollow voice said behind our backs.

We swung round.

A shriveled old wizard stood in the doorway, leaning heavily on his staff.

It was one of Borisov's avatars.

"Bors? Is that you?"

"I suppose so," he shuffled his feet toward a chair. "Whatever's left of me," a smirk curved his pallid lips. "No idea how long I'm gonna last. What Kyle's just told you is absolutely true. Still, there is a chance of survival for all of us. Provided we defeat the Reapers and preserve the Crystal Sphere."

"How?!" White spat. "Didn't you see what the defense mechanisms do?"

"I did," Borisov exploded in a fit of wheezy coughing. He seemed to have spent his last strength on breaching the magic shields on his way to this room.

White turned pale. I could see he was struggling to suppress his unquenchable hatred of corporate workers.

Christa sprang from her seat and walked over to him. She put her arms around him and whispered something in his ear.

It was the first time that she'd showed her feelings for him so explicitly. She cast an anxious look around her, ready to confront anyone who'd dare challenge their budding love.

Still, you can't hide that sort of thing from friends. We'd known about their feelings for quite a while so now we silently rejoiced, seeing them happy.

"Do you know something that could help us fight the Reapers?" White asked, suppressing his anger.

"Unfortunately, not. I'm not the person I used to be. Dietrich's henchmen must have done something to my head. One thing I definitely remember from my Corporation days is that the Crystal Sphere is the only chance for humans to survive on planet Earth."

"Oh, great," Archie said, frowning. "Now I really don't know if it's worth fighting. Did any of you ask yourselves how long your in-mode capsules would last?"

"That doesn't matter," Kimberly spoke.

"Why not?"

"Because," she said in a low voice, "I died in Phantom Server several years ago. And then I came round and found myself here in the testing grounds-"

"You mean you don't have a physical body anymore?" Raoul interrupted her.

"No. I'm an identity matrix. And so is Kyle."

"Bors?" White swung round. "How the hell did you do that?"

Borisov didn't reply. He'd already zoned out, once again inert and irresponsive.

"They never completed their research of neural implants," Kyle explained. "It's true what Kim's just said. She and I, we're identity matrices. But we can live normal lives and experience the whole range of feelings. We still possess our freedom of will, at least as long as this Founders-

---

based virtual reality exists," he added defiantly.

Christa' gaze glinted with hope.

How I understood her!

"I think that our identity matrices are stabilized by some mechanisms located on the testing grounds," Kimberly added. "We need to survive the siege, defeat the Reapers and go back there to see if we can work it out."

"Kyle, what about your sword?" Enea wisely changed the subject, trying to relax the atmosphere. "Does it really work against Reapers?"

"Oh yes!" he exclaimed. "I'm actually a decent technologist. I could try and make a few more, I suppose. Provided I have the necessary equipment..."

"You can become a blacksmith," Enea interrupted him gently. "Things are different here from what they are at the testing grounds. But we have an excellent workshop and lots of Founders' books, don't we, Alex?"

＊ ＊ ＊

"Alarm! Man the walls!"

Our impromptu meeting was interrupted by the shouting of the sentries who'd sighted the Reapers' advance.

The donjon's elevated position offered a dramatically contrasting view. The many glitches in the game engine had created vast areas of wasteland while Rion Castle still stood amid an ocean of greenery.

The surrounding moors had almost dried out, the waterways between them small and shallow. The quagmires had turned into flat ditches, their beds filled with blackened driftwood. These days, you could easily walk right across them.

"So they finally decided to storm the castle?" White asked, peering into the distance.

"I don't think so," I activated my abilities and streamed the resulting picture to the others.

A nearby isle seethed with fighting just next to the ruins of the ancient camp. The black stumps of the siege towers rose in the gray of the dawn.

"What the hell's going on there?" Archie exclaimed.

That's Yorm, our scouts reported.

He must have been thoroughly fed up with lugging around stones in the dungeon so he'd decided to stretch his old bones.

"He doesn't have the protection veil on!" Christa exclaimed in anger. "The sun will rise any minute!"

"We need to help him," Enea agreed.

Lethmiel had already sent a Magic Eye to the site, allowing us to see the scene in every detail.

Armed with his club, the giant was scattering

the Reapers who'd attempted to take apart the old siege towers, apparently planning to clear some space to set up their catapults.

Jesus. The old troll had underestimated his opponents really badly. New Reapers kept flooding in. They'd already surrounded Yorm while staying out of our archers' range. And we couldn't even use the trebuchets because they weren't accurate enough. They would fire every which way, which made Yorm their main target.

"We can't send a sortie out," White said, taking stock of the situation. "Too risky."

"Then we need to port him out and chew his ears!" Enea offered indignantly.

"Very well. Let's do it," I channeled some of the castle's energy to create a cargo portal.

It didn't work.

Instead of the familiar flashes of light announcing a successful teleportation, we saw a weak glow at a distance. That was the extent of it.

"Wretched Dietrich again!" White clenched his fists. "He thinks he's at home already! Very soon he'll be roaming all around the castle!"

Lethmiel was the first to work it out. "I don't think they're preparing a space for catapults," he said. "They've probably used the island to install a fragment of the Veil of Silence," he added with superstitious fear.

"Which is what?" Archie demanded.

"The Veil of Silence is a powerful magic damper. It was invented by a dwarf called Mad Ghym. A very famous character."

"How does it work?" White asked skeptically.

"It's a charmed piece of very special rock," Lethmiel explained. "You can only find it in the Mountains Beyond the Clouds. When the dwarves and the Dark Elves went to war with each other, Mad Ghym and his kin faced extinction. That's when he made the Veil of Silence. He charmed the cliffs that formed the canyon leading to the Underground City. The Elves couldn't use their magic and had to retreat."

"Are those cliffs still there?" Kimberly asked. "Does the spell still work?"

"It does," Lethmiel said. "Not a single wizard has been able to reach the dwarven city. The place has been long abandoned but the Veil of Silence still guards it against any potential looters."

"A wizard, you said. Can't a common warrior get there?" I asked.

"In order to cross the mountains, you need magic," Lethmiel explained. "You can't travel there otherwise. The mountains are unscalable. Reaching the city requires a monumental effort.

"Well, the Founders apparently did it!" White said. "They must have farmed enough of it so they're now busy placing it all around the castle!"

Lethmiel nodded. "I'm afraid so. It definitely

looks that way."

"Is it strong enough to hinder the castle's elemental protection?" Enea asked anxiously.

Lethmiel shrugged. "I really can't tell. One thing's for sure: it can considerably weaken our defenses. The closer they manage to bring the rock fragments to the castle walls, the weaker our magic will be. Which means it'll require much more energy."

I didn't like it at all. "Platinus, bring the Disintegration Potions here *now*!"

White swung toward me. "What're you up to?"

"I'm gonna give Yorm a hand and get us a few samples of that rock. Togien! I need you here! Bring your pick with you. I've got a job right up your alley."

"I don't think you can break the rock with a pick," Lethmiel sounded doubtful. "Or even with Disintegration Potion. Magic dampers are indestructible."

"Are they really? In that case, how did the Reapers managed to get them?"

"I've no idea," Lethmiel admitted. "One thing's for sure: they appear to be working."

"How do you know?" Christa asked.

"The portal didn't work, did it? The Magic Eye didn't work at first, either. I had to launch another one and keep it at a safe distance. Alex, this is a trap! You can't go out! All your magic abilities will be blocked!"

"In that case, the magic damper should affect the Reapers too, shouldn't it?" I pointed out. "Which means they won't be able to use magic, either!"

"I'm not sure," he said.

I'd never seen Lethmiel so anxious before.

* * *

Act in haste, repent at leisure, as the old adage goes.

I couldn't agree more — still, recently we'd had to throw caution to the wind.

"Full combat alert for the clan! Archie, get everyone, no exceptions! I'll let you know if we need help. Just keep your eyes peeled, okay? I've no idea how these rocks work. They might disrupt our communications in which case you'll be the one making the decisions."

"Got it," he didn't sound too thrilled.

Still, we had no choice. We couldn't leave Yorm, no way. That was something we just couldn't do.

Platinus arrived, accompanied by Togien and Gwain.

"*You* are not going anywhere," I said to Gwain. "Your job is here, guarding the walls."

Gwain heaved a sigh. "Yeah."

"What's up?" Togien asked, still clueless about the reason for our emergency sortie.

"Yorm is in trouble, I'm afraid. If we don't help him now, he'll get himself killed."

"Sure! Let's go and do it! What do you need the pick for?"

"Ever heard of the Veil of Silence?"

"Are you joking? Every dwarf knows about it."

"The Reapers somehow managed to get to the Mountains Beyond the Clouds, broke up the charmed cliffs and brought a shitload of their fragments here."

"To dampen our magic?"

"They're trying to. The portal we set up for Yorm didn't work. Neither did the Magic Eye we sent there."

"Too bad. Actually, from what I head, the Veil of Silence was made using the magic of Earth.

That was useful. My Elemental Control ability just might help us solve this problem. Which meant we still needed a sample to experiment with.

"The thing is, I don't think we can carry an entire fragment," I said. "It's probably very big. That's why I want you to chip a piece off it."

"No way. A pick won't do that."

"And if we first treat it with Disintegration Potion?"

Togien shrugged. "We could try, I suppose. Plats, what do you think?"

"I've got some Disintegration Potion concentrate," the alchemist said, "plus a couple of new things I've been working on. It should work. If all else fails, at least we'll destroy the fragment. That's not so bad, is it?"

"I'd rather you brought back a sample so that we could study it."

As I clued them in, the others were preparing for the sortie.

Kyle walked over to me and handed me his microchipped sword. "Take it. I'm sure you'll need it."

I slapped his shoulder. "Thanks, man. It's all right. We won't be long."

I was a bit worried about Enea's light gear. She had no protection at all.

"I'd like you to wear your scaly armor set," I said. "Just in case we really can't use magic."

"Don't worry. I believe in the power of Nature."

"Enea, please."

"Alex, I know what I'm doing. Trust me. All the vegetation near the magic damper is still nice and green. It hasn't wilted. Which means that the aura of the Shrine of Nature still works there."

"Very well. But please keep your armor at hand."

"Actually, Yorm is doing a good job," White said as he watched the unfolding scene.

"Guys, this is a trap," Christa said, visibly nervous.

"I don't think so. How could the Reapers have known what Yorm was going to do? They couldn't have anticipated his attack. It all happened unexpectedly for them."

"I'm not sure. Yorm is quite smart in his own way. He always knows when the sun is about to rise so he can take cover. And now all of a sudden he decided to go and take on a few Reapers?"

"Do you think they lured him there?"

"I'm sure of it. Also, how did he port there if they have those magic dampers installed? A teleport error should have pulverized him! This is a trap, I tell you."

"Okay. So what if you're right? What other options do we have? Should we just leave Yorm over there to turn into stone?"

"He'll come back to life when the sun goes down again!"

"And how about those magic dampers which the Reapers are trying to install all around the castle? Should we ignore them too?"

"I agree with her," White said. "They're either trying to lure us out of the castle or it's a diversion for something else."

"So what do you suggest?"

He shrugged. "I just think we're being too rash."

"Maybe. Still, it's the best we can do. Once Yorm turns into stone, they'll take him away. The Cargonite Golem will be their next target — and he does rely on the castle's energy source. Once that's out of the way, the elemental sequences will give up the ghost. Don't argue with me. We need to destroy the magic stones and bring back a sample."

Still, White was especially prudent today. "And what if the Reapers are drawing their main forces up and creeping around the castle even as we speak?"

I turned to Enea. "You think you could check that?"

"In a moment. Give me some time."

She closed her eyes. A greenish glow formed around her in twilight, thin beams of light reaching out toward the growth of vegetation surrounding our island.

"There's no ambush there," she finally uttered. "There were thirty crossbowmen hiding in the vines. I've immobilized them."

I nodded. "The sun is about to rise. Let's go!"

* * *

We used a Mass Teleportation spell to move to the other bank of the large stream surrounding the castle.

"The area is clean," Stephen's voice encouraged us. "Potential enemy: fifty warriors who are fighting Yorm at the moment."

The troll's fierce roar was tearing through the morning twilight. The Reapers were killing him slowly but surely.

In the presence of the Veil of Silence, the icons of the magic abilities in my interface dimmed.

"Our connection with Nature is still strong," Enea said, disproving my initial suspicion.

A rustling noise followed the sound of her voice as a multitude of creeping plants slithered toward the scene. They trailed along the ground, enveloping the rocks in their way.

And there he was, our Yorm, on a small island overgrown with greenery. We reached it safely and lunged at the Reapers.

They crumbled under pressure. Our levels were way out of their league.

"Yorm, you old sonovabitch! What possessed you to leave the castle?"

"The rock called me! Yorm can feel it! The power of the Earth!" the troll swung his club, pointing it toward a heap of large boulders lying on top of makeshift log rollers. Those of the Reapers who'd been busy shifting them had already scattered to safety.

"I want you to go back to the castle now!" I

said. "The sun is about to rise!"

The exhausted wounded giant didn't dare disobey me. He turned round and trudged back to the castle. The water in the stream had got so low it barely reached his waist.

"Alex, the enemy's on the move," Stephen's voice resounded in the chat. "About two hundred riders coming your way from the direction of the wastelands. High-level Reapers. Range, fifteen hundred feet."

"You break the magic dampers," Enea exclaimed. "I'm gonna distract them!"

The powers of Nature obeyed her call. The wall of greenery stirred. The lithe vines reached out for each other, intertwining, until they formed a barrier impenetrable to the horses.

"The riders are dismounting," Stephen reported. "They're trying to hack their way through the plants but so far, without much success."

Okay. What really worried me was the slow expiration of my magic abilities.

"Togien, Platinus, move it!" I ordered, then switched to the clan chat, "Arwan, you think your archers can cover us at this range?"

"We can try."

A few arrows whistled overhead and stuck into the ground a bit further on.

"The flight is almost spent. I'm now gonna bring up all the archers who have unique bows."

"Stand by and be ready. We might need your support any moment now. Poison all the arrows so that even the slightest graze can deal some damage. Trebuchet teams, zero in! Aim for the dry tree," I added, setting up a marker.

Boulders shook the air overhead, hitting the water's edge to the right of the island.

The trebuchets' next volley proved more successful though, breaking a dry tree branch nearby.

"That's good! Enough!"

Now even if the Reapers hacked their way through the green wall, they'd be showered with boulders and poisoned arrows.

"Archie, keep an eye for any other potential source of attack. This might well be only a diversion. Iskandar, tell your wizards to be on full alert. The moment we destroy the dampers, they can join in!"

It was getting hot here.

Togien's pick hit the chunks of charmed cliffs in vain. All it did was strike off sparks. Platinus' potions made the rocks emit a weak trail of fumes but that was the extent of it.

How on earth had the Reapers managed to farm them at all?

* * *

"The rocks are making a humming noise," Platinus said. "They're getting hot," he snatched his hand away.

"I'm not surprised," with a gentle sweep of her hand, Enea sent a weightless cascade of green sparks flying through the air. Almost immediately, the sparks expired.

"The magic dampers absorb the castle's energy but they can't handle such huge amounts of mana," Enea explained. "They won't last very long here."

"In that case, why did they have to lug them all the way here?" Christa asked, casting watchful glances around. "Or was it supposed to be some kind of experiment?"

"They're about to storm the castle," White said confidently. "Even a small area free of magic might give them a decent fighting chance, allowing them to breach the walls and pour in."

"That was made too easy for them," Togien grumbled, working hard with his pick. "It won't do anything!" he finally concluded.

"The riders are still trying to hack their way through," Rodrigo reported, listening intently to the sounds coming from the thickets. "I don't like it."

He was visibly nervous — which was perfectly normal for a wizard suddenly stripped of all of the advantages of his class.

"Let's just break these wretched rocks and get back quickly," White agreed.

I glimpsed a vague outline which slid past at the far end of the clearing, disturbing the unhurried flow of the early morning mist.

Was it a ghost? Or just my nerves playing up?

"Give me a couple of minutes," Enea walked confidently toward one of the humming, shuddering rocks. She crouched and touched the ground next to it.

"What's that you've got, seeds?" Christa asked in surprise.

Enea flashed her an enigmatic smile. "Not exactly. These aren't just any old seeds."

"I don't like this silence, it's not normal," Rodrigo looked around anxiously. "Have you ever experienced a silence this deep?"

He was right. All sounds seem to wither the moment they were born. The noise of the Reapers hacking through the thickets had died away. Even the birds had stopped singing. The only thing which sounded even clearer than before was the humming of the charmed rocks.

The rustling of the foliage stopped. The air hung motionless, pregnant with menace.

The blinding flash of an opening portal made us jump. A rider barged out of it. Still, White's lightning reaction times didn't even allow the

Reaper to fully materialize. Lunging with his two-handed sword, White pierced the glowing image, disembodying the attacker.

A sad groan spread in the chilling air.

Portals began flashing non-stop.

None of us lost our cool. Rodrigo promptly disembodied another attacker with the tip of his staff. With a sweeping circular blow, Christa expired two more portals. Platinus hurled a few vials of Disintegration Potion at the Reapers who howled in agony when the acid burned through their armor.

Togien, however, was a bit too late. His pick pierced another Reaper's helmet just as the enemy's sword sliced through his own shoulder. The deep wound filled with the bluish haze of escaping neurograms.

The portals shut down. The earth hissed and bubbled where the drops of Disintegration Potion had touched it. The Reapers were gone like a sick illusion. Togien alone winced, pressing his hand to the wound.

"Help him!"

When we'd analyzed the logs after the Battle of Warblerford, we'd managed to work out that the first thing you needed to do when wounded by a microchipped sword was to promptly bring your health up to at least 80%. That alone would cause the wound to heal straight away. But it had to be done immediately. After just one minute, identity disintegration became irreversible.

"Alex, where are you going?"

"Dietrich must be here somewhere," I said. "His retinue are the only ones who have microchipped swords. I order you to go back to the castle. White, make sure no one follows me."

"Alex, please don't!" Enea protested.

Too late. They'd been right all along. This *was* a trap.

A silent, intangible cocoon formed around me, enshrouding me and cutting me off from my friends.

* * *

I'd explored dozens of game worlds. I'd fought hundreds of PvPs ranging from the tragic to the ridiculous. Still, I couldn't quite work out the nature of Dietrich, the First Reaper and the only human who'd thought of harvesting other people's neurograms to build his own hybrid identity. He was rather a composite character who'd absorbed the features of many.

Once again the faint ghostly outline flashed past me. He definitely didn't look as if he'd opted for humanity's nobler traits.

"Come out!" I shouted.

The disturbed fallen leaves rose swirling in

the air, then dropped again.

"What's up, are you scared?" I continued. "Are you hiding from me? Are you so useless?"

My mockery achieved its goal. The surrounding darkness welled up, sucking the hazy outline into its spiraling vortex.

A figure rose before me, clad in dark runic armor streaming with magic auras.

The magic dampers didn't seem to affect him. Most of my own abilities were still blocked — while Dietrich seemed to be able to use his just fine.

The First Reaper stood before me fully materialized, holding a heavy rectangular shield in one hand and a microchipped sword in the other. The visor of his helmet was closed.

Still, I could sense his unkind, fiery gaze focused upon me.

The air thickened around us, forming an impenetrable barrier. No one could come to my rescue now.

The fragments of his new hybrid identity seemed to have never properly alloyed together. His outline rippled with occasional surges of interference.

"I knew you wouldn't abandon that filthy troll thing," his hoarse laughter was laced with hatred — a sound which betrayed an undertone of fear.

"I don't have the time to besiege your castle," he continued. "Without you, it'll fall within days. So let's finish this thing here and now."

"Very well. Let's do it. Why did you have to make it so complicated? Couldn't you just challenge me? Or you knew you couldn't win without better odds?"

"All means are good if they lead to victory. You easily fell for my trap."

"Are you sure I fell for it? How about I walked into it consciously?"

He didn't like that idea at all. His confidence seemed to have taken a serious blow: the seed of self-doubt which had fallen on fertile ground. I'd managed to upset his mental equilibrium.

He attacked.

This was a lethal combo of a lunging blow followed by a circular slicing hit.

The microchipped blade struck sparks off my shield. I dodged the lunge, then somersaulted backwards as Dietrich's sword whooshed through thin air.

My counterattack failed. Exiting the combo, Dietrich attacked me with clots of dark energy which I chose to just block seeing as my shield could absorb magic so well.

"You think you could do this without cheating?" I wheezed.

"All I did I tweaked the program code a little," his armor plates rose and fell in unison with his hastened breathing. "There'll be no respawn for you this time, Alex. You can forget it."

"I know. Same goes for you too."

He laughed. In his opinion, with my magic abilities blocked I was only a warrior prone to physical exhaustion.

"You don't know what you're talking about," he said, then went for me again.

He showered me with blows, forcing me to spend my physical energy blocking them. His own strength and stamina were literally off the scale.

Finally, I caught him off-guard and gave him a brief illustration of my point. The Sword of a Neuro sliced through Dietrich's bracer, extracting a faint bluish cloud of neurograms from the shallow wound.

That wouldn't kill him but it'd teach him a lesson.

Dietrich recoiled, covering himself with his massive shield and giving me a chance to restore. His shock and disbelief were genuine. Even though the surrounding darkness had already healed his wound, he now knew that there was no escape for him. He could still activate the portal and flee, promising himself never to get anywhere near Rion again.

Now he'd have to give all Neuros a wide berth. We had a weapon capable of destabilizing and ripping apart his hybrid identity!

Charges of lightning clung to his sword,

elongating it. He lowered it in a wide sweeping motion, hitting the nearby trees, lopping off several branches and showering the ground with trembling leaves.

The blow grazed me, stripping me of 15% life. Even my shield hadn't helped much. It now sported a deep fire-swept scar which had dropped my gear's durability 30%.

By now, Dietrich had gone completely berserk. There was no stopping him. His lightning sword drew another semicircle through the air, followed by a series of blows which forced me to constantly somersault from one spot to another.

I was so happy for my Cargonite Golem and our sparring practice! It had proved truly priceless.

"I like your agility-" Dietrich cut himself short, sensing danger. He swung round, blocked my blow, then launched into a response combo, throwing in a fire attack for good measure.

A wall of flames reared up before me. Dietrich's sword came down on me as he performed a leaping blow, pointing his weapon diagonally down.

My shield split in two. My left arm turned numb.

Immediately, a flash of green light erased the pain, momentarily blinding Dietrich, as the Charm of Nature that Enea had given me crumbled to dust, absorbing all incoming damage.

An uneasy balance hung in the air. Both of us gasped, trying to restore. An impregnable thick wall of ashes encircled the scene of combat. The earth underfoot was blackened by fire. Tree branches smoldered. The humming of magic dampers reverberated through the air.

Noticing my life bar filling all the way back to 100%, Dietrich cussed unintelligibly. He put his shield back into his inventory and exchanged his weapon for a double sword: two long massive blades attached to both ends of a thick wooden haft.

A fetid haze of poison enveloped the blades. I could make out the Founders' symbols on the microchipped steel.

Dietrich clenched his teeth and came after me.

The tree next to me shuddered, sliced vertically in two. Whiffs of the poison spiraled through the air.

Dietrich stood in disbelief. I couldn't have microported out of his sword's path, surely? Procuring the magic dampers was supposed to have secured his advantage.

He was right. One thing he hadn't considered was that I still had my Neuro combat abilities. My maxed-out Reflex Optimization had allowed me to dodge his lethal attack.

I performed a series of response blows,

leaving deep dents in Dietrich's armor. Some of his fresh wounds started to seep neurogram haze.

Losing parts of his identity, Dietrich microported out of reach of my coup de grace and swung round.

A thick gray mist formed around him, building three warriors out of the ashes. They were armed with Spears of Gloom.

Four on one? This ratio left me no chance. There was no way I could successfully use Exorcism now. All I had left available was Centurion.

I activated it, summoning Helmud the Knight.

A flash of light sliced through the darkness. Helmud the Knight raised his shield, parrying the darkness' attacks. A golden aura surrounded his outline.

Two more enemy warriors stepped out of the cloud of gloom. There were five of them now!

I hurled a Disintegration Potion at the curtain of darkness which now concealed the First Reaper. I switched the grip on my sword, grabbing it with both hands and boring through my enemies in a long spiraling pirouette. That was something White had taught me.

Two of the warriors crumbled into a flurry of ash flakes, immediately replaced by even more menacing figures.

Acid hissed. It sounded like my Disintegration Potion had hit its target!

Helmud was fighting with a recklessness born of desperation. He realized the situation perfectly well. He knew he'd been summoned back from oblivion for a couple of minutes at most. So he gave it his all.

If only he were more prudent! I'd leveled up a lot since our last meeting — and the duration of this summoning had grown accordingly too.

Ignoring all incoming damage, Helmud hacked his way through the enemy ranks. Then he entered the swirling gray cloud.

The darkness fell apart, separating into layers of mist. Just as his brief existence expired, Helmud sliced through Dietrich's shield. With his gauntleted hand he ripped an amulet off Dietrich's neck — an exact copy of my own Charm of the Sovereign.

Beams of light shredded the darkness, scorching it and critting the dark warriors.

With a bitter heart I realized what had just happened. I'd never be able to summon Helmud again. He'd just sacrificed himself in order to release a little transcendental energy into this world.

The safe cocoon of Dietrich's passive shields and protection auras burned out almost instantly. His oxidized armor darkened. His runes faded.

The magic dampers reverberated, emitting an intense low humming noise. The impervious wall of gray haze around the scene solidified, its swirls freezing in blocks of gray stone. No one could penetrate it now until the fate of this world was decided.

Dietrich resembled an ancient tank wreck.

The dents in his armor oozed with the bluish haze of neurograms escaping his wounds.

He attacked me again, furiously but illogically, using an erratic choice of physical and magic abilities.

Could these be his death throes?

I struggled to parry his blows. I had to survive this final attack without letting him crit me.

The Shield of Reason icon began to flash as Dietrich desperately tried to use fire, lightning and darkness all at once to destroy me.

He'd almost succeeded. Even though his name tag didn't show his level, the sheer power of his attacks spoke for itself.

Then his movements slowed down. The neurogram discharges became more intense. Had he run out of steam?

Oh no, he hadn't. He'd simply changed weapons. A poleaxe wrapped in a shroud of darkness appeared in his hands.

My sword was damaged, I could see that. Thin discharges of blue light crackled between the ancient microchipped symbols.

I couldn't use it to block his blows anymore. I'd just have to dodge them. Still, by now my stamina was almost at zero, its green bar barely glowing, as some of the debuffs had affected me after all.

Suddenly, a fine web of cracks covered the magic damper rocks. The gentle new shoots of mountain vines peeked out of them: amazing plants capable of penetrating rock. So those were the seeds Enea had used!

Dietrich attacked me with renewed vigor. The powerful swings of his monstrous poleaxe left me no chance of dodging them. And I only had one ability left, the one I'd received just recently.

You've activated Steel Mist!

My split cargonite shield — which by now was utterly useless — disappeared in a silent flash. A faint cloud of tiny metallic particles enveloped me. They responded to the threat like living beings, accumulating in the area of the approaching blow.

With a metallic clang, the blade of Dietrich's poleaxe shattered, leaving only the wooden shaft in his hands.

He staggered. His strength wasn't infinite, either. I'd survived his attacks; the magic dampers had been destroyed while his own hybrid identity was rapidly disintegrating.

The unquenchable hatred in his glare burned a hole in me.

"You'll never win!" he gasped. "Ever! You can't!"

I invested all my remaining strength into a final lunge, burying my sword deep into his chest.

Neurograms gushed out of the wound.

The First Reaper dropped his broken poleaxe. Mechanically he grabbed at my sword's blade trying to pull it out of the wound but couldn't.

"You can't win," he croaked. "I'll have the last word. You'll die slowly... while watching the love of your life..."

His avatar rippled with surges of interference and began to crumble to ashes.

A flurry of strange-looking codes flashed before my eyes, followed by absolute darkness.

CHAPTER NINE

IN LIMBO

A DULL LIGHT assaulted my eyes.

I struggled to breathe. The air was cold and smelled of medication.

A pump heaved rhythmically next to my bed's headrest. My throat was rasping. My stomach was in stiches. Gradually, the pain began to subside.

Was this the real world?!

I was shuddering uncontrollably. The contract I'd signed with Infosystems had no provision for logging out.

Did that mean that Dietrich, in the last moments of his existence, had somehow managed to send my identity back into my mangled physical body which I'd been forced to give up after the car crash?

So what? Big deal, I could always log back in again. What had he been trying to achieve?

I struggled to make out my surroundings through the layer of brown dust covering the capsule's transparent lid. I could barely move. My normal physical perception hadn't come back to me quite yet. Virtually all of my nerve endings echoed with pain.

An alarm beeped. My mind cleared. System messages flashed through the inside of the capsule's lid,

Metabolic correction completed

Please wait while we're uploading new plugins to your neural interface

Your avatar has been temporarily disabled

Warning! Your neural implant is about to be restarted. This can cause temporary perception failures.

The messages disappeared. The stench of medications was gone. I could breathe freely now. The air was fresh and cold.

Success! Your neural implant has been restarted.

Please don't try to get up or open the in-mode

capsule. Environment scanning in progress.

> _Environment scanner report:_
> **_Radiation levels: lethal_**
> **_Air toxicity levels: lethal_**
> _Please wait while we're searching for the nearest evacuation module_

Ignoring the system warnings, the capsule's pneumatic drives hissed. The lid rose and slid backwards, letting the outside air in.

Mechanically I held my breath. Too late.

All the sensors began beeping. My mind blurred.

* * *

When I came round, I felt weak and unwell. New messages from the reinitialized neural implant appeared on the inside of my eyelids,

> _Your body's cybernetic components are being reactivated. Please don't try to stand up._

The servodrives squeaked.

My right arm and both my legs moved against my will.

I'd never bothered to wonder about all the consequences of that fateful car crash on my physical body. Once I'd signed the waiver agreeing to have the trial version of the implant installed, my life had been confined to virtual reality. I'd never taken Borisov's promises too seriously. At the time, all his assurances that my physical body would receive cutting-edge medical treatment, including all the latest breakthroughs in both servomechanics and neural cybernetics, had sounded pretty fantastical. In any case, I hadn't believed any of them.

> *Testing completed*
> *System report:*
> *Your body's organic content: 40%*
> *Condition: Poor*
> *Your body's cybernetic content: 60%*
> *Condition: Fully operational*
> *Motor skills synchronization in process...*
> *Data exchange test in process...*
> *Reflex check in process...*

Congratulations! All your virtual reflexes and skills have been saved. You can now use them in the real world.

Warning! The micro nuclear batteries feeding your cybernetic prosthetics are running low. Please replace the batteries.

Current charge available: 12.5% of the batteries' full capacity.

The squeaking of the servodrives faded to a faint rubbing.

Overcoming instinctive (and perfectly natural) fear, I opened my eyes.

Dozens of wires and tubes disengaged themselves from my body and hung in thick bundles, then got sucked out of my field of sight.

My vision filled with the icons of my game interface which hovered in front of my eyes, overlapping reality.

The interface was slightly different this time. Everything pertaining to magic was now gone, replaced by new foldable windows reporting the data from my cyber prosthetics.

I was a cyborg.

The thought didn't even hurt that much. For a brief second, it grated on my heart, then disappeared.

I glanced over the interface, swiping the windows open with my eye movements.

Infrared Vision
Environment Scanner
Life Form Detector
Energy Matrix Detector
Optical Multiplier

That much was pretty clear. Basically, they'd activated some additional sensory perceptions. I could use them, that's for sure.

* * *

My first attempt to climb out of the capsule wasn't very successful. Despite the recent synchronization, my cyber prosthetics responded much faster than my weak radiation-damaged muscles. Confused and disoriented, I lost my balance and struggled to control my awkward, jerky movements.

After several failed attempts, I finally climbed over the low side of the capsule and dropped to the floor.

Dietrich's cold impassive words still hovered in my mind.

You'll die slowly... while watching the love of your life-

I grabbed at a curved steel pipe running along the wall and pulled myself to my feet. I needed to take a look around.

The room must have suffered a lot in some technogenic catastrophe. The thick ceiling had caved in, a large gaping hole in it offering a peek of a gloomy sky.

Everything around me was covered in a thick layer of concrete dust. None of the computer terminals worked. Everywhere I looked, I saw signs of spontaneous combustion.

I took a tentative step. It seemed all right. I was adapting to my new state rather quickly. The cyber prosthetics automatically adjusted themselves to my reaction times and muscle tone.

The capsule next to mine was Enea's.

I touched it, brushing off the thin layer of brownish dust, and stared at her face.

My throat tensed. My heart began to race.

I had to get a grip.

This must have been Dietrich's plan from the start. He knew the exact location of our in-modes. So he'd set me up for this outcome regardless of whichever one of us won our duel.

He wanted me to die in the deserted bunker from the lethal dose of toxins and radiation while watching Enea in her safely pressurized capsule.

Bastard!

Well, he'd outsmarted himself this time, hadn't he?

Borisov had kept his word. The Corporation had had my mangled body completely healed and restored. Sixty percent of it was now cyborgized but that didn't make it any easier.

I looked at Enea's biochemical monitoring panel. Without bothering you with the details, I could see that her body was functioning just fine. Most of the indicators glowed a healthy emerald green. Her main vital signs were within the norms. If you considered the fact that individual in-mode capsules had been designed for use in deep space, then Enea was perfectly safe from both radiation and toxic environment.

And what about that yellow light?

Life support cartridge
Charge: 20%

I crouched next to the capsule and opened the protective lid at its base.

Not good. The cartridge clip was empty. This was the last one.

The moment I focused on it, a prompt came into my view,

The remaining cartridge charge is enough to maintain life in the subject for eight more days.

Oh no. This wasn't going to happen.

I moved around the destroyed lab, searching it. Logically, life support cartridges had to be fed into capsules automatically. And although now this system didn't seem to work, they must have had an emergency supply stashed here somewhere.

I tried to force a few wall panels aside.

Yes!

Behind them, the walls were lined with niches. In one of them, I discovered a large stack of plastic containers with familiar markings. Inside were several cartridge clips. I hurried to insert them into Enea's in-mode.

Life support cartridges successfully loaded.
Data update in progress...
The remaining cartridge charge is enough to maintain life in the subject for four more months.

That was a bit better. I was pretty sure that if I searched all the adjacent rooms I might find more of them.

You might not have it your way, Dietrich, I spoke to him mentally just to keep my emotions in check.

What now? I was getting worse, I could feel that. I wasn't going to survive these radiation levels for much longer. The cyber prosthetics could help me move around, but they weren't going to replace my dying brain.

I couldn't forbid myself to think about my approaching demise. I had to do something.

Should I try and contact the Crystal Sphere?

I checked the data saved in my mind expander. My friend list helpfully opened before me. I could contact anyone but what was I supposed to tell them?

How about White?

He was the only person who could probably

understand me without freaking out. I didn't want to lie to Enea or tell her it was all going to work out fine.

I clicked on White's icon.

After a few seconds' delay, I received a new message,

Connection established.
Would you like to connect your optic nerve to the data exchange channel?

No, I sent a mental reply.

"Alex?!" White's anxious voice echoed through my mind. "Where the hell are you?"

I gave him a quick rundown of the situation. "Don't tell anything to Enea, please. I'm not sure I can make it."

"Go and find a functioning in-mode. Do it now!"

Just as I expected, White hadn't fallen apart with the news. On the contrary: he'd mustered up all his willpower and spoke clearly and to the point.

"Okay. I'll see what I can do," I replied. "Do you know if I managed to kill Dietrich?"

"Absolutely. You finished him off, then you just disappeared. Vanished into thin air."

"Could you really see us fight?"

"We could see both of you perfectly well. The barrier was transparent. We even filmed it. Which makes me think that Dietrich was pretty sure he was going to win."

"How about the rest of the Reapers army?"

"It's falling apart like a rotten rag. The game's defense mechanisms just won't leave them alone. The world is losing the last of its vegetation but Enea's adamant she can restore it. Alex, please get out of there alive!"

"I'll do what I can. The place is pretty much dead. It looks like we've had a technogenic disaster of some kind which must have culminated in a nuclear reactor meltdown. I'll try to move Enea's in-mode to a safe place. Then I'll contact you again. Don't tell her anything, will you?"

"Alex, she loves you."

"I love her too."

I was about to disconnect when he interrupted me,

"No, wait! Just tell me. If indeed the Corporation's labs are destroyed, how long do you think Enea's in-mode will last?"

"It has enough life support cartridges for four more months. But I'm going to find more, I promise!"

"How about power?"

"Don't know. I haven't checked yet. It looks like the lab is self-contained. It must be powered by micro nuclear batteries."

"Okay, keep your hair on. Did you tell me

that the system had attempted to summon an evacuation module when you were coming round?"

"I did. It never arrived."

"Very well. I want you to listen to me very carefully. When I was looking for Enea, I seriously considered hacking into the testing grounds."

"It didn't work, did it?"

"I didn't get the chance to try. I took a different approach. But I still have a few emergency system command codes which I intended to use at the time. I'm sending them to you now."

"I got them. Did you memorize them?"

White chuckled. "I'm never without them. Seriously, before I left the real world for good, I uploaded all the important data to my mind expander just in case. You never know when something might come in handy."

"What good can emergency access codes be to me? Everything's dead here."

"Evacuation modules are complex robotic systems developed by the Military Space Forces. They're powered by their own reactors which makes them perfectly autonomous. The reason I know this is because my old company, TransEnergy, used to supply emergency power units for those and similar devices. For your information, the first in-mode capsules were based on the rescue capsule used on spaceships. Are you with me?"

"Do you mean that I might be able to move

Enea's capsule myself if I find a working evacuation module?"

"Exactly."

"But where do you want me to evacuate it to? Everything's really badly damaged. I don't think any of the cities have survived."

"Evacuation modules are extremely secure and have a ten year autonomy. I suggest you find a working in-mode for yourself, then have yourself and Enea evacuated. When you enter your destination, make sure it's as far from the cities as possible. Then just log back in. Once you're back, we'll think of what to do next."

"Okay. I got it. I'll see if I can do it. I'll contact you when I have something positive."

* * *

If the truth were known, his idea of finding a working in-mode for myself wasn't going to help me much. I'd received too much radiation to come out of this alive.

I tried not to think about it. White had been right: I had to act fast. But how did he want me to connect Enea to the emergency power supply if all of the lab's terminals were dead? Should I go and look for something that might still work?

Wait a sec. I thought these people used cutting-edge technologies here. Wouldn't that include a neural interface? I'd just received some messages via my mind expander, hadn't I?

I picked up an upended chair from the floor and slumped into it, then focused on my own interface icons which hovered in my mental view.

Despite all the changes caused by my return to the real world, my interface remained highly intuitive and efficient.

I clicked the Emergencies tab, then glanced over the Life Hazard button, activating it.

Please choose the action required

"Staff Evacuation."

Please provide the sector number

I looked around. The walls were marked with signs which said A3. I couldn't see any other information.

Next, the emergency system asked me to enter a code. This was a classified facility, after all. Not like in a city where any such system responded to all and sundry.

I entered the code White had given me.

After a few tense seconds, a new message came up,

Please wait

Soon the floor began to vibrate. The walls caved in. Pieces of broken panels started falling.

A huge shadow eclipsed the gaping hole in the sunken ceiling.

The evacuation module.

A bundle of long, snaking manipulators reached into the lab through the hole in the ceiling. Supplied with toolkits and covered in emergency power sockets, they unhesitantly reached for Enea's in-mode. It took them only a few minutes to detach it from its mountings and lift it effortlessly into the air, about to haul it up.

My heart clenched. Would they return for me too?

Please remain calm
Prepare for evacuation

A hatch opened. A steel ladder slid down. I hurried to climb in.

I was standing in a small cabin with bare walls and an anti-G seat mounted at the center.

Please buckle up and prepare for takeoff

I did as they told me. My mind was racing. My lips were chapped. I kept zoning out but my anxicty was stronger than my growing malaise. Where would the module take us?

In any case, Dietrich had lost. Yes, bastard, you heard me right. I might be dying but Enea was going to live!

New messages flashed through my foggy mindview,

Searching for available landing sites...
Search failed

Searching for available shelters owned by Infosystems Corporation...
Search failed

Searching for available communal in-mode centers...
Search failed

I was feeling increasingly worse. I had to do something, otherwise the module might simply return to its hangar nearby and stay there.

Struggling to remain focused, I mustered my last strength to issue a mental order,

Manual coordinates entry

Where could I possibly go, might you ask?

I still had the scroll Borisov had given me. This was my last resort. He must have had a good reason to enter real-world coordinates into it.

Authorization required

I tried entering White's codes again. They didn't work.

There was just one remaining option. I used my mind expander to access the number that Borisov had scribbled on the scroll just under the coordinates.

Command sequence identified
Execution protocol activated

The messages swam before my eyes. The cabin began to vibrate. The module must have taken off and activated its cruise engines. Not that I cared anymore.

The last message faded in my mental view,

Critical failure warning! Your organic components have shut down.

* * *

No idea how long I'd been unconscious. When I finally came round, the module was still in flight, judging by the faint vibration of its engines.

How come I wasn't dead? *Your organic components have shut down* — that sounded pretty self-explanatory.

That wasn't the last message, though. I must have fainted before I got the chance to read the rest.

Your neural implant has been successfully reloaded.
Please wait while we stabilize your identity matrix.
Your identity matrix has been successfully stabilized.

Kimberly had been wrong all along. The testing grounds had nothing to do with stabilizing our identity matrices. This was a built-in option in all of our implants. Logical, really. How else would the Founders have traveled between stars?

I didn't attempt to get up.

I didn't want to ruin the moment with the sight of my half-dead, half-robotic body.

Not that it mattered, really. I'd crossed the line between life and death — but I'd preserved my identity.

I still had all my feelings about me. None of them had faded, even though I could see a lot of things differently now. The wealth of data I'd uploaded in the Founders' library back at the Temple of Oblivion was stirring in the depths of my mind.

I could read it now! I could understand

every symbol!

For a brief moment, the entire Universe opened up before me.

I saw the map of our Galaxy threaded with the fine web of the ancient hyperspace network. Some of its routes were broken.

The star system closest to Earth was Darg. I'd never heard the name before. Still, it looked like the Space Forces had already set up a secure wormhole which opened into it.

My heart clenched, bringing back the smarting pain of my loss.

I didn't care about space travel. I wasn't interested in other star systems. All I wanted was to see Enea again, knowing she was going to be fine.

The moment I thought about it, I clearly saw her in-mode capsule safely secured in the cargo hold and illuminated by the flashing red emergency lights.

Congratulations! You've activated a new option of your neural implant.

You've received a new ability: Piercing Vision.

For Your Information: none of the abilities acquired in the physical world can be automatically transferred to digital reality unless it was previously integrated into it.

Oh wow. The opportunities it opened up!

Should I try it again?

I willed my vision to penetrate the flying module's hull.

The megalopolis lay below. I could see spots of raging fires — a sign of the failing technology in a world deserted by people. I could see dead maintenance robots frozen in the power saving mode.

The wind howled below. Windows were dark. A snowstorm thrashed among the precipitous canyons of streets, piling up banks of snow against abandoned cars.

Soon we left the city behind us. The tiered blocks of its outskirts descended towards the ocean.

The module banked into a smooth turn and began to land.

A snowed-in wasteland opened out before me.

The ground shuddered, revealing a giant camouflaged hatch below. It rose and slid sideways. A deep shaft gaped beneath into which the module dropped.

The electronic landing mechanisms clamped on to it and set it gently to the ground.

The module's hatches swung open. Maintenance robots began fussing about, unloading Enea's in-mode.

It looked like I could get out too. But should I? Where the hell was I, really?

I had no idea what this place was. What kind of "execution protocol" had Borisov's command sequence activated?

Reacting to my thoughts, a glowing 3D holographic image formed at the center of the dark cabin.

"Hi, Alex."

"Bors?! What are you doing here? What is this place? You sent me the coordinates but you didn't explain-"

"I'm not Borisov. Also, if you managed to activate the command sequence, it can only mean one thing. Borisov is in trouble."

"Who the hell are you?"

"I'm this facility's AI. Borisov is my prototype. He built me using his identity matrix."

"Where are we?"

"This is Infosystems' backup control bunker. It's been sealed and put on standby to ensure that nothing could damage the data and equipment stored here."

"You don't mean I activated it, do you?"

"Oh yes, you did. You entered a remote command known only to my prototype. This facility was built on his direct orders as an emergency measure. Borisov never trusted the military. He didn't think we could entrust our lives to some

---

alien space station many light years away."

"Sorry, I don't understand. What future are you talking about? The Crystal Sphere is dying. The Corporation's defense mechanisms have basically flattened it!"

"I know. Still, you can change that. Borisov did warn me about you. He said I should be expecting you if something happened to him. So now it's up to you to make the right decisions."

"Please explain."

A 3D map of the Crystal Sphere unfolded in front of me.

It was a miserable sight, I tell you. In their pursuit of the Reapers, the defense mechanisms had completely defaced it. Virtually all wildlife was gone, replaced by dead wastelands as the game engine tried desperately to fill in the blanks.

Protocol activation: Revival
The selected digital world is ready to be restored from backup.
Please introduce all necessary modifications, then re-enter the confirmation code.
For your information:
You're about to decide the fate of an immense world which has become the last refuge for everyone still left on planet Earth.
Please select the regions that can be closed or do not require reloading.

"Go ahead," the AI gave me a friendly look. "It's up to you. I'll take care of the rest. Don't drag it out. It's getting a bit urgent."

My vision clouded. A long list of locations unfolded in my mental view.

Corporation Testing Grounds, Untick.

Rion Castle, Add to exceptions. Enable overload protection.

Restore the Crystal Sphere from backup?

Confirm.

I re-entered the code and froze, awaiting our new future.

EPILOGUE

AGRION MARKET SQUARE was uncrowded. Not many players online today. Only the NPCs continued living their own computer-generated lives.

For them it was business as usual: merchants praising their wares, a crooked old lady shuffling her feet past the swordsmiths' row. She leaned heavily on her staff and mumbled something to herself as she cast watchful glances around in search for any newbs whom she might reward with a social quest for their penny's worth of alms.

Nothing had changed.

The sun shone brightly in the clear sky.

I used my key to unlock Dimian's old

---

shop, walked out into the back yard and activated a teleport scroll with the coordinates of Hinterwood already entered.

* * *

A sad girl stood by the pond. A giant Black Mantis hovered protectively next to her, casting watchful glances around.

"Enea!"

She swung round. Her eyes glinted with recognition. She ran toward me. "Alex!"

Love had returned to our world.

From now on, your dreams will come true, my sweet love. We'll have it all. We'll embark on new adventures and discoveries. Love will be for real. Death will be for fun. For ever and ever.

One day we might want to expand our horizons and sample the boundless star paths of the Founders.

But that will be a totally different story.

END OF BOOK THREE

The Neuro Development Branch:

Secret Knowledge:
Observational Skills, 4
Spell Interception, 3
Unity of Schools, 3
Acquisition of Blows and Combos, 5
Reflex Optimization, 10
Unity of Origin, 5
Legacy, 3
Artifact Building, 5
The Founders' Successor, 5

Evolution:
Intense Training, 3
Pain Threshold, 5
Synergy, 5
Crit, 7
Shield of Reason, 10
Spell Building, 10

Power of Reason:
Insight, 5
Self-Control, 4
Enhanced Perception, 5
Energy Transfer, 3
Elemental Control, 5
Steel Mist, 5

Secret Knowledge:

Eons ago, the Ancient Gods (sometimes also called the Founder Gods) tampered with our ancestors' evolution, endowing them with a number of abilities which are now almost completely extinct. Only occasionally do they resurface in certain individuals known as Neuros.

You're one of them. Both your body and mind harbor a potential yet unlocked.

+1 to Strength

+1 to Intellect

+1% to XP per each invested Ability pt.

Observational Skills:

You're highly perceptive. Whether reading ancient manuscripts or watching other people, you pay attention to every detail, immediately grasping the technique of a combat blow or a spell incantation. You can then enter the knowledge you thus receive into special books or dedicated parchment scrolls for further study.

Warning! The level of the blow or spell you intend to study cannot exceed that of your character.

Each Ability point invested gives +2% to your chances of studying the blow or the spell (regardless of whether the object of your study is an NPC or another player).

Spell Interception:

The fact that all spells are recited in the Founders' language combined with your ability to lip read allows you to learn any spell.

Warning! In order to successfully intercept a spell, the caster (observation target) should be located within your direct line of vision. At level 1, your lip-reading range is set at 30 feet.

Each Ability point invested adds 2 ft. to your lip-reading range.

Spell Interception does not preclude other possible ways of spell studying.

Acquisition of Blows and Combos:

You effortlessly memorize new movements while watching combat practice or live combat. Later, this allows you to make a drawing of the blow or even combo technique from memory, recreating both attack and defense maneuvers.

Requires Observational Skills and Intense Training.

Each Ability point invested adds +2% to your chances of studying a blow or a combo.

Unity of Origin:

According to legend, all living beings in the Universe used to have a single ancestor. Some might snicker saying that an orc and a human being can't possibly share ancestry. Still, every legend harbors a grain of truth.

Each Ability point invested adds +2% to your chances of intercepting a spell or learning a new blow typical of other races, regardless of their affiliation (Light vs. Dark).

Unity of Schools:

Some time ago, you chanced upon an ancient book. As you struggled through it, trying to make sense of the faded writings on its crumbling pages, you were surprised to discover the writer's heretic ideas. According to the book's author, all types of magic and sorcery, including elemental and mind control, are firmly rooted in the long-forgotten school of Chaos.

Later, as you watched the effects produced by various schools of magic, your conclusions confirmed the ancient author's ideas. The powers of Chaos had been the foundation of all modern schools and practices.

Each Ability point invested adds +2% to the Range, Strength and Duration of every spell you study, as well as removes all bans and penalties for combining various kinds of magic and sorcery.

Reflex Optimization:

As you watch wildlife species (whose survival depends on their highest levels of ergonomics), you can learn and adopt their energy preservation skills. Your movements become more precise and calculated.

Each Ability point invested gives -2% to your mental and physical energy expenditures in combat.

Evolution:

The activation of this particular characteristic allows you to receive a small but continuous boost to your main stats, depending on the type of your daily activities. These changes will be visible as special boost bars situated opposite their respective characteristics in your character panel. For instance, if you read a lot you might notice the increase of your Intellect boost bar. Once the bar is full, you will receive +1 pt. to its respective characteristic.

The above boost does not cancel traditional characteristic leveling. Neither does it affect your items' bonuses.

Intense Training:

Each spell or blow you study requires constant perfecting. In order to improve your attack and defense skills, you need to practice a lot, creating your own combinations and turning new moves into reflexes.

Ability bonus: your damage, defense, mob control and aura range will improve. This only

---

applies to the physical and magic skills you use on a regular basis, without affecting those you've learned but failed to apply.

Each Ability point invested adds +5% to attack strength.

Pain Threshold:

You learn to control pain. You might have already discovered, by extreme trial and error, that you don't experience pain as long as your Health is above 80%. As your HP dwindle, you start experiencing an increasing pain.

Each Ability point invested raises your pain threshold 3%. The maximum pain threshold allowed is 50% HP.

Synergy:

Everything in our world is interconnected. You can use various sources of energy, including elements, ancient artifacts and places of power marked by megalithic monuments. As you study them and listen intently to the world around you, you begin to tune in into various energy currents, allowing you to locate their sources and use them to restore your powers and even life.

Starting at level 20, you'll be able to trap and store any excess physical or mental energy within energy crystals.

+5% to your physical and mental energy

regeneration speed.

Power of Reason:

A Neuro's intellect affects everything he or she does.

Every 30 pt. Intellect add +3% to both attack and defense and +5% to the XP received for successfully using the blows or spells you've learned from other characters. All such blows or spells will add +3% to your chances of dealing critical damage or, when used in defense, to your chances of reusing the blow or spell with decreased cooldown times and -50% of required energy expenditure.

+10% to your mental energy regeneration speed.

Insight:

You're constantly busy studying everything around you, analyzing the nature of all events and perfecting your abilities and skills. Your goal is to get to the bottom of everything trying to work out how things work instead of mindlessly using them, be it a spell, a blow or a professional skill.

Each Ability point invested gives -3% to cooldown times and energy expenditure required for all types of physical and mental attack, defense and impact.

+2% to profession leveling speed for all

farming and manufacturing professions.

Self-Control:

You have a natural 25% resistance to all kinds of magic and mind control. You can successfully resist mental attacks, preserving clarity of mind.

Each Ability point invested adds +2% to your chances of repelling a negative effect or boosting a positive one, be it a spell or your opponent's ability. +2% to your chances of successfully casting a spell when attacked. +3% to mental energy regeneration speed.

On reaching level 5, this ability will allow you to consciously control your mental energy distribution between several recipients — for instance, a magic artifact or an item of gear.

Enhanced Perception:

You learn with remarkable ease. Your outlook isn't limited by racial or class prejudices. You're free from all phobias and superstitions.

As a result, you see and notice a lot compared to others. Your night vision and reduced visibility navigation skills are considerably superior to theirs. At level 20, you will receive a new primary skill, Twilight Vision, which you can consequently level up and improve.

Enhanced Perception allows you to detect

danger before others can. It also adds +20% to your chances of seeing a stealthed-up enemy stalking you. Each Ability point invested adds +1 to your Field of Vision Range.

Legacy:

From now on, you can control the ancient blood magic which exists in synergy with nature. The Founders' artifacts will reveal their secret properties to you alone.

Any acquired spells will be available 3 levels earlier than required.

-5% to Mental Energy required to cast a spell.

Crit:

+10% to your chances of dealing a critical hit. +5% to your chances of dealing damage with the Element of Chaos in a successful (i.e., not blocked by the enemy) attack. Every new level of the ability adds +3% to your chances of dealing elemental damage.

Energy Transfer:

You've learned to accumulate the surrounding Elements' energy in order to transfer it to stones or charge up magic scrolls. Every new level of the ability adds +5% to both energy accumulation and energy transfer rates.

Elemental Control:

Activated ahead of schedule

+20 to Resistance to the Elements

Currently, in order to interact with the elements, you're required to use one of the Founders' artifacts built for that purpose. Direct interaction is available from level 10.

Requirements:

Intellect, 25

Willpower, 25

Artifact Building

You've acquired Secret Knowledge, mastered Elemental Control, grasped Synergy and found the long-lost Object Replication spell. From now on, you can replicate artifacts. Replication type: simple (halves the artifact's properties). Each XP point invested into the ability will improve the replicated object's properties by 10%. That is to say, once you reach level 5 of the ability, the replicated artifacts won't suffer any loss in their properties. Further leveling can even improve their properties but no more than +130% of the original object's bonuses.

Restriction: The only items you can copy for the time being are those built by the ancient masters. You cannot create your own artifacts yet.

Shield of Reason

By having mastered Evolution, Power of Reason and Secret Knowledge, you've come to realize that each of us grows to become a unique universe best described as Ego.

The death of a human body isn't fatal. The disintegration of one's identity is.

You've spent a lot of time studying ancient scrolls which describe various methods of mind protection from any destructive external influences.

By repeatedly experimenting with the Elements within your control, you've managed to retrieve an ancient protection spell which prevents the enemy from controlling your mind. The protection spell has become your unique ability granting +70% to your immunity to all kinds of mind control. Each XP point invested into the ability adds +3% to the said immunity.

Once you reach level 10 of the ability, you'll be able to cast the spell on any one chosen item of your gear.

The Founders' Successor

You've perfected the control of your mind to the point where you've successfully managed to keep it together, saving your identity from disintegration.

This ability will allow you to train others in the basics of the Neuro development branch. It will also enable you to stabilize your allies' identity matrices in case of emergency. Cooldown: 1 hr.

Every new ability level you receive will shorten the cooldown time by 5 minutes. Once you reach level 5, you'll be able to create a Shield of Reason spell and copy it to a scroll.

Spell Building

You've used your Spell Interception ability to study various schools of magic and their practices. Your knowledge of Synergy as well as your mastery of Elemental Control will now allow you to combine the elements of various spells in order to build your own. You can, for instance, create an illusion capable of dealing Elemental damage.

Every new ability level you receive will increase both the duration and the effects of the spells you build.

Steel Mist

You've mastered the long-lost magic practice of substance manipulation.

Whenever mortal danger threatens you, select a gear item of your choice which will disintegrate, its particles forming a damage-absorbing spherical shield around you.

Cooldown: 1 hr.

Every new ability level you receive will improve the damage-absorbing properties of the Steel Mist while also increasing its duration.

ALSO BY ANDREI LIVADNY

The Edge of Reality (Phantom Server Book #1)

He is a cyber dweller. A gamer who's grown up in the web of virtual illusion woven from hundreds of phantom worlds. His biggest dream is to dump the real world for good.

His desperate hunger of new experiences forces him to take a risk and become one of the first proud owners of a neuronet implant. The new gadget becomes part of him — but soon it's not enough. If only he could finally burn all his bridges and make a step beyond the real world!

He soon gets this opportunity. A new universe, overflowing with mystery and unimaginable, mind-blowing authenticity, opens up before him.

This is Phantom Server. The game of the future where your pursuit of an adrenaline rush soon turns into a battle for survival. But the most terrifying mystery lies ahead when you gradually start to realize: this is a road of no return. Your every decision may become your last. Your every step leads you further along the abyss between life and death.

The Outlaw (Phantom Server Book #2)

The Eurasia fleet has entered the Darg star system. The unsuspecting players look forward to the adventure of their lifetimes. Zander alone is now facing a harsh and unpredictable "alternative storyline".

The girl he loved is gone. His nervous system is impregnated with artificial neurons that contain fragments of ancient AIs and their identities. Zander's body is implanted with alien artifacts that allow him to survive in the deadly cyberspace of Phantom Server. But his unique development branch pushes him toward the edge of the precipice where his every step may become his last; where future itself is vague and uncertain.

Black Sun (Phantom Server Book #3)

Zander and his gamer friends used to face danger without fear, finding strength in the promise of a safe respawn. Nothing could harm or destroy them. This was only a game... or was it?

A game, played in an ancient hyperspace network. A game involving dozens of real-life alien civilizations. Earth is deserted. The fate of humanity is unknown.

The few human survivors are now stuck in the Darg star system. All they can do is fight to the last. They must find the Phantom Server — the nucleus of the interstellar network created by the ancient civilization of the Founders. In order to live, they must solve its mystery or die trying.

The Crystal Sphere (The Neuro Book #1)

Alex is one of us. An office rat during daytime, he spends sleepless nights playing his favorite MMO game: a familiar, predictable world which is about to collapse. A new virtual universe arrives to replace it, aggressively devouring all others: the Crystal Sphere.

Alex gets involved in testing new technologies which promise to revolutionize gaming. Fitted out with a neuroimplant which provides a 100% authenticity of experience, he has to survive in the Crystal Sphere against all odds. What is he turning into? Will he become yet another expendable test subject — or the first player to transcend reality?

Humans have to deal with the treacherous nature of cyberspace in this powerful prequel to *Phantom Server*.

The Curse of Rion Castle (The Neuro Book #2)

Rion Castle! Alex and Enea are facing a serious test of courage if they want to keep this unique citadel built by the lost civilization of the Founder Gods. Abounding with mystery and powerful artifacts, its dungeons are a complex maze of tunnels swarming with creatures of Inferno. What's even worse, Alex's "impulse buy" risks to trigger the first clan war in the Crystal Sphere. And they don't yet know that the donjon's dark bowels harbor a nightmare about to become the new curse of Rion Castle.

In the meantime, Infosystems Corporation begins an aggressive marketing campaign pushing its state-of-the-art neuroimplants onto unsuspecting gamers. A new era of reckless destruction is looming over the real world...

Blind Punch (Expansion: The History of the Galaxy Book #1)

Year 2197.

Earth is suffering from the consequences of an environmental catastrophe. Cities the size of continents are drowning in a toxic industrial fog.

Max Bourne is a typical teenager. Like billions of other people, he is forced to live in the protective shell of the individual life support module. His habitat is the virtual Layer. But one day, circumstances force the young man to leave the in-mode. He has no idea that fate will lead him through unimaginable hardships, bring him face to face with military AIs, and teach him to survive in the distant Outlands. He will come to understand that the sum of all technologies, possessed by the four leading corporations of Earth, can either open the way to the stars or destroy human civilization.

The Shadow of Earth (Expansion: The History of the Galaxy, Book #2

The time of the Great Exodus is over. Centuries have passed. Earth is overpopulated and the fate of the colonists who traveled to the stars is unknown. An attempt to start the second wave of expansion has led to a shocking discovery: all accessible planets located within one hyperjump from the Solar System have been settled during the Great Exodus. The colonists have created unique and distinctive civilizations — but none of that matters when the survival of billions of Terrans is at stake.

ABOUT THE AUTHOR

Andrei Livadny is a popular Russian science fiction author. Born on May 27 1969 in the city of Pskov, he was an avid reader from an early age. But it was the Russian translation of Robert A. Heinlein's *The Orphans of the Sky* that decided his choice of future occupation. The story has become a pivotal moment in the boy's life, leaving a lasting impression on him.

Andrei wrote his first book at the age of eight. Since then, he's never stopped working on new books. His passion for science fiction has gradually become his career.

In 1998, Andrei debuted in Russia's leading publishing house EKSMO with his novella *The Island of Hope*. Since then, he has penned over 90 books that have enjoyed a total of 153 editions.

Andrei has created several unique worlds, each unlike the previous. He wrote *A History of Our Galaxy* with humanity itself as a protagonist. This sixty-book series creates a history of our future civilization and its contacts with alien races, forming a convincing and logical picture of humanity's development for two millennia from now.

Besides hard science fiction, Andrei Livadny also works in cyberpunk genres which allow him to focus on human relationships and raise questions about artificial intelligence and identity uploading, describing cyberspace as humanity's future environment.

The English translation of *A History of Our Galaxy* will be available shortly.

Want to be the first to know about our latest LitRPG, sci fi and fantasy titles from your favorite authors?

Subscribe to our **NEW RELEASES** newsletter:
http://eepurl.com/b7niIL

Thank you for reading *The Reapers!*
If you like what you've read, check out other sci fi, fantasy
and LitRPG novels published by Magic Dome Books!

Dark Paladin LitRPG series by Vasily Mahanenko:
The Beginning
The Quest

**The Dark Herbalist LitRPG series
by Michael Atamanov:**
Video Game Plotline Tester
Stay on the Wing
A Trap for the Potentate

The Neuro LitRPG series by Andrei Livadny:
The Crystal Sphere
The Curse of Rion Castle
The Reapers

**The Way of the Shaman LitRPG series
by Vasily Mahanenko:**
Survival Quest
The Kartoss Gambit
The Secret of the Dark Forest
The Phantom Castle
The Karmadont Chess Set
Shaman's Revenge
The Hour of Pain (a bonus short story)

Galactogon LitRPG series by Vasily Mahanenko:
Start the Game!

Phantom Server LitRPG series by Andrei Livadny:
Edge of Reality
The Outlaw
Black Sun

Perimeter Defense LitRPG series by Michael Atamanov:
Sector Eight
Beyond Death
New Contract
A Game with No Rules

In order to have new books of the series translated faster, we need your help and support! Please consider leaving a review or spread the word by recommending *The Reapers* to your friends and posting the link on social media. The more people buy the book, the sooner we'll be able to make new translations available.

Thank you!

Till next time!

www.ingramcontent.com/pod-product-compliance
Lightning Source LLC
Chambersburg PA
CBHW051521050726
47503CB00014B/329